WHEN THE RAIN FALLS

BLACK SKIES: BOOK ONE

Sasha A. Linderson

First published in 2021 by Linderson Creations Limited

Paperback ISBN: 978-0-473-60340-3
Epub ISBN: 978-0-473-60341-0
Kindle ISBN: 978-0-473-60342-7
iBook ISBN: 978-0-473-60343-4

Linderson Creations Limited
Auckland, New Zealand

www.lindersoncreations.com

To Dad, for encouraging my wayward dreams, and to Mum, for
keeping me grounded enough to make sense of them.
~ Sarah

To Grandma, I hope this book is better than the first time
you read it.
~ Ashley

CHAPTER ONE

LEVI

NEW ZEALAND USED TO be a place people wanted to live. If you looked hard enough, you could imagine why. Beneath the weed choked lawns, pot-holed roads, and houses crumbling from disrepair lay a country that could have been rebuilt if it was given the chance. But we were left to rot—shunned by the rest of the world.

The gate creaked as I pushed it open and walked down the cracked garden path. Dylan's place was pretty flash, but you wouldn't guess it from the curbside. That's how it was everywhere these days—ever since the contagion destroyed our country. Worn-out houses lined tired streets that were in desperate need of repair.

I moved to knock on the door but it opened before I could make contact, and Traci, Dylan's mom, bowled into me. I stumbled backward off the porch but managed to keep my balance.

"Levi!" she exclaimed. "I'm so, so sorry."

I stooped to grab the keys that she had dropped. "Don't worry about it."

"I didn't know you were coming over," she said, flustered. "I would have made you boys something to eat."

"You don't need to worry about me, Mrs. Saville," I said as I handed her keys back.

"Dylan, Levi's here," Traci called out, before turning her attention to me. She smiled softly and studied me with a motherly gaze. "Have you grown? It feels like years since I've seen you."

"It probably has been," I said. Dylan and I had been friends since birth but didn't hang out as much as we used to since he moved up to Auckland for university.

"What are you doing these days?" she asked me.

I was about to answer but Dylan cut me off.

"Stop pestering him about his future, Mom," Dylan said as he sauntered down the hall. His blond hair was gelled into spikes, and a friendly smile spread over his face. A plain black t-shirt hugged his muscular frame. Dylan had got jacked. He crossed his arms and leaned against the doorframe.

"I wasn't pestering," Traci said and pursed her lips.

"I thought you were leaving, Mom," Dylan hinted. "You said it yourself, the polling booths are only open for a couple hours this year."

Traci checked her watch. "I've still got a few minutes. And I haven't seen Levi since you two were in high school. You've grown into a fine young man." She smiled at me the way mothers do.

Dylan sighed and rolled his eyes.

I shrugged and ran my fingers through my scruffy hair, embarrassed. "Thanks, Mrs. Saville."

"Mom, you're so embarrassing," Dylan said under his breath.

"Fine, fine, fine," Traci said as she adjusted her glasses. "I'll go. There might be a lineup at the voting station anyway."

"Who do you think will win the election?" I asked. It wasn't really a question—everyone with half a brain knew the Prime Minister had rigged it. That's why I wasn't upset about not being able to vote this year. What was the point when the whole thing was a sham? Bloody waste of time, if you asked me. "Prime Minister Marion seems pretty confident about re-election."

Dylan scowled. "He's a fascist pig."

"That's harsh, Dylan," Traci said with a frown.

"What? It's true," Dylan muttered. "He increased the voting age this year so us young liberals can't sway the vote."

"You young liberals are the reason behind all those riots," Traci replied.

"They say twenty people were killed by riot police up in Auckland yesterday," I said, recalling the news on the radio from the drive over.

"Exactly," Traci said. "Like Marion said when he changed the age to twenty, voting is a privilege."

Dylan's cheeks flushed. This was something he was clearly passionate about. "You sound just like him."

Traci tutted. "You're being dramatic, Dylan. You'll get to vote next time. Besides, you can hardly decide what to have for dinner. How do you expect to make a responsible voting decision?"

"Don't you have a vote to cast?" Dylan said pointedly.

Traci shook her head, and walked toward the gate. She turned around and asked, "What are you two planning on doing today, anyway?"

"We're going hunting," Dylan replied.

Traci's scowl was immediately replaced with a look of concern. "You're not supposed to leave the city. You know this, Dylan. Marion's troops are out there keeping the peace."

"Honestly, has he brainwashed you, Mom?"

"You know the risks of being out past curfew. I don't want to have to bail the two of you out of jail," Traci said, evidently worried.

"Don't worry, Mrs. Saville. You don't have to bail me out of jail," I said to Traci with a grin. "Dad would probably let me rot in there, but I'm sure Mom would want me back."

She gave me a reproachful look. "I'm serious, boys. Marion isn't messing around. The military is enforcing it. Mrs. Greenwood said she heard they arrested some people who tried to escape the city last night."

"Can't you admit we're grown up enough to make our decisions now?" Dylan asked.

Traci studied both of us, concerned. "You think it's a joke, don't you, how I get wound up so much all the time? I can't help worrying that someday, something will happen."

"Nothing's going to happen," Dylan insisted, crossing his arms.

"Well… just don't go getting yourselves shot," Traci eventually said, relenting.

"We'll try not to," I said.

She sighed and walked to the car. "Oh, Dylan, I almost forgot. Your dad called earlier. He's working late again tonight."

Dylan shrugged. "Must be a busy time at the Port right now."

"Yes, but they're short on staff after all the redundancies. I think more long nights are on the calendar," Traci said.

"Maybe you'll have to bail him out of jail for being out after curfew," Dylan commented dryly.

Traci didn't laugh. "The curfew's serious, Dylan. Please be careful."

"We will. I promise," Dylan said, sincerely this time.

Traci shut the door of the car, and we watched her drive off.

"Sorry about that, mate," Dylan said with a broad grin once his mom's car was out of sight. "Mom's been difficult since I've been back."

I shrugged and walked up the step to the house. "I don't mind."

"How've you been?" he said, greeting me with a customary

slap on the back.

"Don't get me started," I said as I followed Dylan inside.

"That bad, huh?"

The stark white hallway walls were hung with pictures of Dylan and his little sister. I stopped in front of one taken at our school ball over a year ago. So much had happened since then. The world had changed. Those were the carefree days before the virus hit. I thought back to that night, where we partied like there was no tomorrow. For some people, there wasn't one. The virus was probably already circulating then. We just didn't know it.

"You were so wasted that night," Dylan commented, reminiscing.

"So were you," I replied. In the picture, Dylan looked like he was swimming in his poorly fitted suit, with an uncomfortable look plastered over his face and his blond hair gelled back. I was standing awkwardly next to him, trying to act sober, my dark hair a mess.

"Why did your mom pick that picture? You can tell I'm hammered."

"Apparently, it's the only one where my eyes are open," Dylan explained as he continued down the hall to the kitchen. I laughed and followed him. The guns and cleaning kits were already out on the table.

"I thought we could give them a quick clean before we head out," Dylan said.

I picked up one of the rifles—a Winchester model 70 bolt-action. "Sounds good."

I grabbed the cleaning rod while Dylan sat down beside me and started cleaning the other gun. I gave the bolt a quick once-over and applied some wood cleaner to the stock. There was something comforting about the greasy smell of gun oil. I went through the motions mechanically, barely even thinking about it as I reassembled the gun and lay it on the table. I grabbed the old rag that lay over the back of one of the wooden chairs to wipe my hands.

"You're quiet," Dylan commented eventually, glancing across at me as he started oiling his gun.

I didn't respond. Dylan knew my home life was pretty shit. I hated my dad, and Mom was on my case all the time. She meant well, but…

"What's your dad done this time?" Dylan said, knowingly.

I tossed the rag onto the table. "He's trying to force me to join the army," I muttered. It was my dad's way of trying to make me less of a disappointment. In his eyes, I was never good enough. And never would be unless I followed in his footsteps.

But I never would. My childhood was full of missed birthdays and lonely Christmases as Dad committed to the army way of life. When he was home, it wasn't much better. My parents fought hard. Yelling and screaming. Smashing plates. Dad was distant and angry, pacing the house like a prison cell. Mom said the army changed him, and eventually, she couldn't take it anymore. So, they got a divorce. Dad was addicted to the life of a soldier, and I was hell-bent on never becoming one.

"If you're not keen, don't do it," Dylan said.

I shuffled uncomfortably in my seat. "You know him. Going against his will is playing with fire."

Dylan placed his gun down on the table, and looked up at me with concern. "Did he hit you?" Dylan was my only friend who knew about Dad's temper—he'd witnessed it firsthand.

"Nah. He got close though," I admitted.

"Shit," Dylan said as he put his gun away into its case. "Does your mom know about this?"

"No way. She'd freak out," I said.

"I don't know what to tell you," Dylan said with a grimace.

"It's OK. I'm not looking for pity."

"But… I do know a bit of possum hunting will make you feel better." Dylan held up his rifle and grinned boyishly. "And I have beer." He strode into the kitchen and pulled a six-pack of cheap stuff from the fridge. "Only the best for you, Levi."

I couldn't help but laugh. I grabbed my coat and slung my rifle over my shoulder. "You know me too well."

"I'll drive. We'll go in my car," Dylan said. He handed me the beers and swiped the ammunition off the mantelpiece in the lounge. We trudged out the door to Dylan's beat-up hatchback. Red faded paint, chipped in places with rust. I dumped the guns and beer in the back and slid into the passenger seat after pushing some empty energy drink bottles to the floor.

"Which road should we take?" Dylan asked as he coaxed his car to life.

"Take one of the back roads. We don't want to get stuck at a checkpoint," I said. The checkpoints were a stubborn remnant from the pandemic. Marion kept them up long after the virus was under control. The public was mad about it, but Marion insisted it was to protect us from a resurgence of cases. But there were ways around them. Backroads, dirt tracks, farm trails. If you knew your way around, you could get out of town unseen.

Dylan put the car into gear and we sped toward Dylan's block of land that backed onto Crown forest. As I watched the familiar streets pass by, an uneasy feeling began to inch its way up my spine. The city streets felt oddly deserted as we barreled along as fast as Dylan dared to go. No cars. No people. Just us.

"Where the hell is everyone?" I muttered.

"Voting probably," Dylan replied as we rolled up to a red-light, the only car in either direction.

"It feels quiet."

"Too quiet," Dylan said, grinning. He noticed my concerned look. "Also, it's about to piss down with rain. No one wants to go out in weather like that."

"You're probably right," I muttered, looking out at the storm on the horizon that had taken permanent residence over the mountain ranges and was rolling rapidly toward us, growling with thunder.

ONCE WE REACHED THE outskirts of the city, Dylan turned off the main road and took a maze of backroads until we had escaped the big smoke entirely. As we cruised along the open country highway, it started to rain. The odd droplet here and there. And it was quiet out here too. More so than usual. I thought back, I hadn't seen a single car since leaving town. Strange. I peered over my shoulder again, still no one. The last rays of sun were peeking over the horizon to the west, but there were no lights on in any of the houses and nobody finishing up their last farm chores.

"Maybe we should turn back?" Dylan suggested as he watched the black clouds loom closer.

"We've come this far," I said. "If the weather's too bad, we can park up and have our beers in the car. Like the old days."

For a second it looked like Dylan wanted to go back as he looked anxiously in the rearview mirror. But then, "Hell. Screw it. I'm keen. I'll be going back to uni soon so we might not get another chance."

"My thoughts exactly," I agreed.

A couple moments of silence passed before Dylan spoke. "You should come with me."

"What?" I asked as it began to rain harder. Within seconds rain whipped against the windows. Dylan turned the wipers to high and sat forward on his seat, trying to see better. He already had his lights on full beam as it was getting dark.

"Come to uni. We'd have a riot at the clubs in town," Dylan said.

"Uni's not my thing."

The rain was coming down in buckets now. And Dylan slowed the car down as the road started flooding with surface water.

Dylan laughed. "But what? Working at that burger joint is?"

"You sound like my mom," I grumbled as I wiped the window to defog it.

Dylan smirked. "Maybe if you had your life sorted, she wouldn't be on you so much."

"You can't talk, all you do is party...I've seen the photos," I said, a smile pulling at my lips.

"Mom doesn't know that," Dylan said, laughing. "As far as she's concerned, I'm studying law, and my life is on track. You should come to university next year, though. We'd be —"

A dog ran out onto the road in front of the car.

"Watch out!" I yelled.

Dylan swerved and braked hard, the tires sliding on the slick tarmac. We came to a stop, the rain pinging ominously on the roof. My heart thudded in my chest.

Dylan was breathing heavily. "Shit. Did I hit it?"

I looked over my shoulder out the back window but couldn't see anything through the teeming rain. "I can't tell."

"Don't just sit there. Go check. It looked like someone's pet," Dylan said.

"It's pouring out there," I complained. "You do it."

"A little rain never hurt anyone," Dylan said. "Wuss."

"Fine." I thrust open the car door and stepped out into the rain. Within seconds I was soaked to the skin.

"Do you see it?" Dylan called from the car, sticking his head out of the window.

"No," I said, wiping the water from my face. I scanned the road behind us but couldn't see anything. Just as I was about to give up, something on the side of the road caught my eye. "Wait."

Through the storm I could make out a small shape in the ditch. I ran over, and breathed a sigh of relief. A small, but sodden, Bichon Frise cowered in a puddle.

"Come here, little guy," I encouraged it. "Come on."

It stared at me, gave an indignant bark, and bounded across the road, disappearing into a farm paddock.

"Come back," I called after it, but it was no use. The dog had run off. I ran across the road and looked hopelessly out over the paddock through the fading light. But I couldn't see anything except a few sheep.

"So?" Dylan called.

"You didn't hit it. But it ran away," I replied as I walked back to the car.

"We should probably let the owner know," Dylan said as I clambered back into the car, shivering.

"We have no idea who it belongs to," I said, my teeth chattering. I reached in the back to get my coat.

"Probably that house," Dylan said, pointing to an unremarkable farmhouse about fifty meters up the road. He was already driving slowly toward it. "See, the gate's been left open. That's probably how the dog escaped."

We pulled into the drive, and both of us got out of the car. Our shoes crunched on the gravel as we jogged to the front door through the rain.

Dylan reached the front door first.

I came up behind him, and immediately felt like something was wrong. The night was still, except for the rain pounding on the verandah. But an undercurrent of unease made the hairs on my arms stand up in alarm. To top it off, the front door swung on its hinges with the wind, banging rhythmically against the doorframe.

"What the hell?" Dylan said as we both stared at it.

"I don't like this," I said. All my instincts told me to run.

"Is anyone home?" Dylan called out. "Is everyone OK?"

No answer.

"Hello?" Dylan said, louder this time.

Nothing.

"It looks like the place has been broken into. Should we go

in?" I asked. "Or maybe we should just call the police."

"It does. Someone might be hurt, though," Dylan said. "We should check just in case."

I ignored the feeling in my gut that told me to get the hell out of there, and stepped forward. I pushed the door open, revealing a long, dark hallway. I glanced back at Dylan, who encouraged me forward with a small nod. With an air of false confidence, I stepped into the dark house. My sodden shoes squelched along the wood floor, and water dripped from my soaked clothes. I crept down the hallway with Dylan at my back.

"Over there," Dylan whispered.

We went through the first doorway on my right. At first, all I saw were the signs of a struggle. A smashed lamp. The recliner chair tipped over backward. Cushions strewn across the floor. But my breath caught in my throat when I noticed a dark red stain on the carpet. I looked into the gloom of the living room and stumbled back in shock. A young man was lying face down, a gunshot wound blown into his back.

"Oh sh-sh-shit," Dylan stuttered as he came up behind me.

"What… do we do?" I managed to say, my voice shaking.

I forced myself to look past the body, and saw a woman sprawled out on the couch with two bullets in her chest. Another body, an older man, was in a seated position against the far wall. Headshot this time. Everything about this told me to run. Call for help. Get as far away from this place as possible. But I couldn't move. I was frozen in place. And, I couldn't look away either. The horror in front of me kept me transfixed.

Dylan broke my trance. "Do you think they're dead?" His face was white, and his eyes wide with fear.

"I don't really want to…" I trailed off. The thought of touching one of the bodies made my stomach churn. "They look dead."

"We should call the police," Dylan said. At least one of us was thinking clearly.

With a trembling hand I reached into my pocket to grab my phone. I had left it in the car.

"I don't have mine either," Dylan said in a weak voice.

"Maybe they have a landline?" I said as my mind started working again. Help. That's what we needed. I turned away from the scene in front of me, trying to regain some composure. I closed my fists, trying to stop my hands shaking.

A desperate scream pierced through the night.

Dylan and I looked at each other, scared. I ran to the kitchen and threw open the curtains. I could just make out the neighbor's house a hundred meters away. An army truck was parked in the driveway, and a woman was being dragged from the house, kicking and screaming by two men in army uniforms.

"Holy shit," Dylan said from beside me, I could feel him trembling.

"What the hell," I heard myself say.

We watched in horror as the men wrestled her into the back of the truck and unceremoniously slammed the door shut. Two other soldiers came out of the house dragging a man. He struggled against his captors and managed to break free, sprinting across their driveway. But the men in uniform didn't hesitate. They raised their assault rifles and shot the man in the back as he made his escape. The man dropped to the ground, unmoving.

Dylan and I watched on in shocked silence—we had just seen a man killed in front of us. And we were standing in a house filled with more victims. The soldiers, or whoever they were, returned to their vehicle, driving off into the night. Probably to the next house, I thought, grimly.

"We need to get the hell out of here," Dylan said.

I didn't need telling twice.

We backed away from the window, afraid that whoever those soldiers were might see us. And we might face the same fate as the people in this house. Or the man next door. Dylan and I ran from the kitchen, blew past the living room and out the front door, leaving the house of horrors behind.

Dylan fumbled with the keys and tried to open the car door. It was dark now, and the rain showed no sign of relenting.

"We should ditch the car," I said, looking around in case more soldiers showed up.

"Are you crazy, Levi? Why would we ditch the car? It's the only thing we have. We're out in the middle of nowhere, with soldiers or God knows what..." Dylan said, finally getting the door open. Thunder grumbled and lightning flashed across the sky.

"We'll stand out cruising round in a car," I said as my mind raced, trying to figure out the next logical move. I opened the backdoor and reached into the back as Dylan got into the driver's seat. I pulled out the rifles and slung them both over my shoulder.

"Get in the car, Levi," Dylan said as he buckled himself in.

"No way," I said. "It's safer on foot." I grabbed the ammo too and started tucking it into my pockets. There was no way I was going anywhere in that car.

"What the hell are you doing?" Dylan said, exasperated. "What do we need the guns for?"

Dad trained me to be prepared for everything. I wasn't leaving our only chance at self-defense behind. "I'm getting a bad feeling about everything. Something's wrong," I said, walking to the passenger seat and hunting for my phone. "Something's been wrong ever since we left your place." My phone had slipped down the side of the seat. I grabbed it and shoved it in the back pocket of my jeans.

"No shit, we just saw a man get shot," Dylan said, getting out of the car.

"Think about it, Dylan. We don't know why those people were taken or shot."

"It was probably the virus again. That's all," Dylan said as I slammed the car door shut.

"They never shot people before," I said, trudging away from the car.

"Levi! Where are you going?"

"I'm getting out of here, and finding help," I said as I left Dylan standing in the downpour.

"But the car," Dylan said as he ran after me, his boots splashing in the puddles.

"We'll get it tomorrow if it turns out this is nothing," I said. "But let's get off the road in case those soldiers come back."

"I think you're overreacting," Dylan said as we jumped a wire fence and took cover in a patch of trees. The trees offered a bit of shelter from the rain. I pulled my phone out and the screen blinked on, a beacon in the dark. 18:45.

"There's no service," Dylan muttered. I knew I usually had service out here, I had phoned Mom a bunch of times after a successful hunt. But my phone also had no reception. Panic was beginning to take over.

"Me neither."

"What now?" Dylan said. "We can't hide here all night with all those…"

"Soldiers," I said. "They were soldiers."

"With all those killers on the loose," Dylan said, pacing.

"We find somewhere, or someone that has a phone. A landline," I said. "And call for help."

"Where?" Dylan asked. "Where the hell do we go?"

A few more gunshots rang out through the night. They came from farther away this time.

I handed Dylan his rifle and a handful of ammunition.

"I think we should run," I said, my heart pounding in my chest.

"Where?" Dylan asked me, his knuckles white as he gripped his gun.

"Anywhere but here."

CHAPTER TWO

LIZZIE

LOOMING PURPLE CLOUDS BLOTTED out the evening sun, and in a hurry, the rain came. Living rurally, I was well used to the sudden nature of it, especially now, in springtime. Before long, the paddocks were swamped with deep puddles, and the sheep huddled under a dripping tree, staring bleakly back at the house and cursing us for their freshly shorn coats.

Not that I felt sorry for them. I was still bruised black and blue from helping Dad wrangle them for the shearer, who hadn't been impressed at our amateurish methods, and our kitset yarding system. It was clear we were new to sheep farming. Cattle had been much easier, but no one in New Zealand ran cattle anymore.

There was a rustle of movement as Grace pulled a barstool from under the kitchen counter and perched next to me. I flashed her a smile as I cupped my hands around a warm mug of hot chocolate. Grace's chestnut brown hair fell flowing down her back and her familiar round brown eyes looked at me sympathetically. I admit, I had always been a little jealous of her.

She was pretty and wore her sun-kissed face make-up free. She always wore simple jeans and a t-shirt that hid her petite, athletic figure. Because of all this, she was fairly popular at school, but in actuality, she was alone.

"You look like you're thinking about Ryan," she said. A compassionate smile pulled at her rosy lips.

I sighed. "Actually, I was trying not to."

Grace was a good friend, always there when I needed her, and she knew me well. I knew her inside out, too. On the outside, she was happy. But on the inside, she was depressed. It was unsurprising after all the trauma she had been through, but it was also incredibly sad. She had pushed everyone away except me. Her boyfriend had been the first. She distanced herself from him, and eventually, he couldn't take it anymore. Instead, she busied herself in trying to make my life better. And at the moment, Ryan was a large problem.

The beginning of our relationship had been perfect. He was sweet, lovable, and we got on well together. Lucky for me, he was also dreamy: the epitome of tall, dark and handsome, with roguish brown hair and brown eyes so deep they were nearly black. But now, a few months in, everything seemed to be falling apart. It felt like he didn't care about anyone or anything, and frankly, I was sick of it.

"I'm sure he still loves you," Grace said as she threw a marshmallow into my mug and popped one into her mouth.

"I'm not sure anymore," I said as I watched large droplets of water drip from the eaves.

"What did he do this time?" she asked as she got more comfortable.

I looked away from the picturesque countryside out the window. "Nothing. Absolutely nothing."

"And you're complaining about that?" Grace asked as she offered me another marshmallow.

"Yes. He doesn't want to do anything with me, or without me, for that matter… he doesn't care about what happens between us," I said with a hint of annoyance seeping into my voice.

Grace listened patiently.

"I mean, I called him yesterday and asked if he wanted to do something today. Do you know what his answer was?" I asked, fuming.

Grace didn't reply, she just stared at me with those searching brown eyes.

"He said he didn't care! Can you believe it?" I said and grunted in frustration.

There was movement coming down the stairs, and I watched my brother as he rounded the corner into the kitchen. He gave me a pathetic look as he scratched at his newly grown beard. I didn't think it suited him, but he insisted it looked cool.

"Is she having boy trouble again, Grace?" Jaden asked with a small laugh. "Seems typical of her these days."

I fumed silently in my seat. My brother drove me crazy.

"Yeah, it's about Ryan."

I shot Grace an evil look that she simply ignored.

"For the record, I told you I didn't like him, Lizzie. Why don't you ever listen to your big brother?" Jaden said with a shake of his cropped brown hair.

"Stay out of my business," I said. "I don't care what you think."

Jaden laughed at me, came over, and tousled my hair. "You're so cute sometimes," he cooed.

"Why are you bugging us anyway? Didn't you have some stupid gaming tournament?"

"The internet's been a bit spotty. It won't connect for some reason," Jaden said with a shrug.

"Well I hope you don't think you're hanging out with us. We're having a girls' night," I said to Jaden, hinting heavily.

Jaden ignored me and flopped down onto the sofa. "Have you heard from Mom and Dad?" he asked. "They said they'd be back by now. It's nearly half six… at this rate they'll miss curfew."

"No, they haven't texted. I'm sure they're fine, I bet they just got held up. There's probably a huge line up at the voting booths this year," I said.

Jaden caught my eye. Our family wasn't heavily into politics, but it was all over the news when the new voting bill had been pushed through. If it hadn't been for the new age restrictions, Jaden would have gone with our parents. He was a couple years older than me and was looking forward to being able to vote for the first time. Especially since it was such a contentious year.

"I hope so," Jaden said, looking out the window for any sign of our parents. But it was peaceful outside. Quiet, except for the pattering rain.

"Jay, they'll be fine," I said again, more firmly. "Come on, maybe we should watch a movie or something."

"Oh, that's a good idea," Grace said, brightening. "Do you have popcorn?"

"In the pantry," Jaden directed.

I walked through the open-plan living and, grabbing the remote from the coffee table, I flicked on the TV. "Argh, I forgot. No internet connection. I guess Netflix isn't a goer."

Jaden got up and wandered over to the TV cabinet. "Doesn't matter. We can watch a DVD."

"But I've seen those a million times before," I complained.

"Suck it up. It's all we've got," Jaden said as he pulled a DVD from the drawer.

"What one is it?" Grace called. She leaned out of the walk-in pantry, a packet of popcorn in her hand.

Jaden held up the DVD for us to see. "Terror in Townsville."

"Oh no, I am not watching that," Grace said flatly.

"Jaden! You know horrors scare the shit out of Grace," I said, snatching it from him.

"It's just a movie. Nothing will hurt you. Plus, you've got me here to protect you," Jaden said with a sly wink to Grace. Ugh.

Jaden had a bit of a thing for Grace, but it couldn't be more one-sided. I knew for a fact that Grace had her eye on the cute guy working at the burger takeout not far from her house.

I rolled my eyes at Jaden. "You're disgusting."

I rifled through our meagre stash of DVDs, before facing Grace. "Actually, I hate to admit it but Jay's probably right. It's this or some random exercise video. We really don't have a good selection."

"What's wrong with exercise?" Grace said as she put the popcorn in the microwave.

I raised my eyebrow and stared at her. "Grace, please. Can we just watch the movie? We can always turn it off if it gets too scary for you."

Grace thought about it for a moment. "Fine. But I know I'm going to hate it."

"I know I'm going to love it," Jaden said with a grin. But his shoulders were tensed, and he looked down at his watch again.

"You're still worried about Mom and Dad, aren't you," I said, pulling him aside as Grace busied herself grabbing a bowl for the popcorn.

"Lizzie, they were supposed to be home half an hour ago," Jaden muttered, anxiety swimming in his royal blue eyes.

"Just try to relax," I said and punched his shoulder lightly.

"I just can't shake the feeling something's wrong. If they get pulled over after curfew—"

"That's not going to happen. You know the military presence isn't as intense out here. So long as they got out of the city, they'll be OK."

"But what if—"

I pushed the DVD back into his hand and stared long and hard at him. "Jaden. It's OK. Trust me. Just put the movie on, why don't you?"

Jaden obediently traipsed back to the TV set and inserted the DVD into the player. Grace brought over the bowl of popcorn and we all sat lazily around the TV, Grace with a blanket draped over her, oblivious to Jaden sneaking looks at her as the movie began. I grabbed another blanket from the arm of the sofa and threw it over myself. But before I could get truly comfortable, the phone rang.

"Oh my god, that gave me a fright," Grace said.

"The movie hasn't even started yet, Grace," I said, my voice laden with sarcasm as the phone continued to chirp in the background.

Jaden hit pause. "Can you get that Lizzie?"

"It'll be telemarketers, Jay. No one ever calls the landline."

"Lizzie, please. It could be Mom and Dad."

"OK, OK." I threw my blanket off my legs and padded over to the phone, picking it up on the sixth ring, just before the answer phone kicked in. "Hello?"

There was some heavy breathing, and for a moment I felt sure it was a prank.

"Beth?" My dad was the only one who ever called me that. The only one who I ever let call me that; I hated my name, and how many derivatives could be made from it.

"Yeah, Dad what is it? Are you guys OK? Jaden's been so—"

"Beth, just listen." My dad was speaking really quietly, so quietly I had to turn the volume up on the phone. Then I heard Mom in the background.

"Did you get hold of them? Did you reach them?" Her voice sounded panicky and high-pitched.

Jaden looked over to me. "Is it Mom and Dad?"

I nodded back and motioned for him to be quiet. Jaden came up to me, anxious and impatient.

"Put it on speaker," Jaden whispered. I shook my head at him and kept listening.

"You need to get out," Dad said. "There's something happening here, Beth. When we got here, they led us through to what we thought was the voting booths, but..." I pressed the phone even closer to my ear.

"Give it here, let me talk, Lizzie," Jaden said.

"No Jaden, don't," I said, and pulled the phone away as he tried to grab it from me. "This is important."

"Then put it on speaker," Jaden said again.

"Fine." I hit the speaker button.

"…soldiers everywhere. They won't let us leave," Dad was saying. "I think they're going to come after you next. You need to get out now. Are you listening, Beth?"

"We both are, Dad," Jaden said into the speaker.

Snakes of dread were beginning to writhe in my stomach.

"Are you sure you're OK, Dad? This isn't a joke, is it?" I asked him.

"No. Your mom and I—"

Suddenly, there was a cry of alarm in the background and some muffled noises. The voice that spoke next was not my dad.

"This is Lieutenant Williams, can I ask who I'm speaking to?" a calm and professional voice came on the line.

Grace stood up from the sofa, the blanket still wrapped tight around her small shoulders. We all swapped fearful looks with one another.

"Don't say a word," Jaden mouthed.

"It's the military. We don't have a choice," I mouthed back.

Finally, out loud I said, "I'm Lizzie Watson."

Jaden flashed me an angry look.

"Right, Lizzie. I need to know exactly where you are. We've had a few riots in the city tonight, and—"

"Can you put my dad back on? Are he and my mom OK?" I cut the lieutenant off.

"They're fine. Everyone is OK, but we're going to have to keep everyone here for the time being. And we're a little concerned about young people like you being left to fend for yourselves."

"We're fine here," Jaden said harshly. "There's no need, thank you, sir."

"No, I must insist that you stay where you are, and wait for one of our trucks to pick you up. No harm will come to you or your parents if you follow our instructions."

No harm? What did he mean by that?

"Are you there?" Lieutenant Williams said. "Your address, please."

I clamped a hand over the speaker and looked over at my brother.

Jaden paced the floor, but when he saw me looking at him, he stopped and stared at me, fire in his blue eyes. He was as stubborn as I was; a family trait we inherited from my mom. "I don't think you should tell them. Dad wanted us to get out of here."

"They're the military. We can't refuse them, Jaden," I said. "Besides, where would we go?"

He shrugged.

"My mom wouldn't want me disobeying the military," Grace said, as she hugged the blanket tightly around her body.

I took my hand off the speaker. "Sorry, sir," I said. "We're rural, quite a way out of the city."

"That's no problem. In fact, we already have some of our men stationed out there tonight," the lieutenant told me in a calm and reassuring tone. "Let me know your address, and I'll send them on their way."

"109 Crown Forest Road," I said.

"Great. Thank you, Lizzie. It won't be too long, you can expect my men there shortly."

There was a click, and then the dial tone. I hung the phone back in its cradle.

For a minute, none of us said anything. We stood in silence.

"Do you think my mom's OK?" Grace said in a small voice.

"I don't know Grace," I said.

Grace walked over and fished in her handbag for her cellphone. "No service," she said. I watched her try to dial on the home phone but after a minute she hung it up again. "I keep getting her answer-phone."

Then Jaden gave me a slight shove. "You shouldn't have done that, Lizzie," he said, anger trailing into his voice. "After what Dad said, you have no idea who you've invited into our home. And if things are really that bad in town…"

"The lieutenant said, nothing will happen to us if we follow instructions, Jaden. What do you want to do about it?" I argued.

"I don't know, but Dad told us to get out. I'd rather trust him than God knows who, Lizzie!"

"It was the military," I said, crossing my arms.

"Whose military? Did it ever cross your mind that it might not be ours?"

"That's stupid," I said. "And if you're so worried, you go, and Grace and I will stay here." I stomped back over to the couch and pulled my blanket back over myself, determinedly ignoring Jaden. Grace wandered unsurely back over to the sofa and sat beside me. I flicked the TV back on.

"You always have to have it your way, Lizzie," Jaden said, fuming. But he relented and eventually came back to the sofa and slouched next to Grace, staring broodily at the TV.

"Maybe we shouldn't watch a horror. I'm kind of freaked out after that," Grace said, looking sideways at me. "Besides, those people will be coming soon. Can we just talk?"

Looking at Grace, I felt sympathy well in my chest. She'd never really gotten over the death of her dad and her siblings in a car-crash only a year ago. Now, anything out of the ordinary made her anxious, and I was worried she'd break again. Like last time.

"Yeah, we can talk," I said, and offered her a small smile.

Grace looked over to Jaden.

"Don't look at me. Apparently, anything I have to say doesn't matter," Jaden muttered.

"Just ignore him. He's sulking because he didn't get his way.

Now… why don't you tell me about that guy from the burger joint?" I said, turning my back to Jaden.

"Uh…" Grace flicked her gaze over to Jaden, but he didn't seem to care. Instead, Jaden was immersed in eating all the popcorn.

"Are you going to ask him out?" I prompted.

"No way," Grace said. She pulled her dark eyes away from mine, blushing fiercely. So, it was like that, I thought. Grace was clearly into this guy, whatever his name was.

I laughed. "So, you're just going to continue stalking him then."

"I'm not stalking him."

"Yeah, whatever," Jaden said with a snort. "Because Little Miss Health-Freak really likes fast-food."

Grace looked over at Jaden, flabbergasted.

"Shut-up Jaden. You're just jealous," I said, smirking.

Jaden was saved from replying when the power cut out. I looked up at the lights, the faint glow from the power-saving lightbulb eventually dying and leaving us alone in the black.

"This is too weird," Jaden said as he stood up.

I crossed over to the light and flicked the switch a couple of times, to no avail.

"What do we do?" Grace whispered.

"We need to go. We should have left before," Jaden said.

I wasn't sure what we should do, but there was something wrong about this. I felt it, deep down. Maybe Jaden had been right all along.

A loud and sudden banging on the front door mimicked my heartbeat, and I said, "I think we're too late for that."

CHAPTER THREE

GRACE

"Don't you dare open that door, Lizzie," Jaden threatened, standing protectively between Lizzie and the doorway.

Lizzie looked unsure about what to do next. Her gray eyes darted between the door and her brother. "If it's the military… we don't want to get in trouble."

The furious knocking on the door resumed, and I instinctively backed away. My heart threatening to beat out of my chest.

"Always the goody-good. You don't see it, do you?" Jaden said, desperate and refusing to move. "This whole thing's wrong. We should be running like Dad said."

I was starting to regret telling that soldier where we were too. My mind raced through the events of the evening, trying to piece together everything that had happened. Lizzie's parents were late, the phone call, the soldier on the other end, the power outage… I didn't know what it all meant, and I didn't want to wait around to find out.

"I'm sure there's a reasonable explanation for all of this," Lizzie said. "You're acting like there's a serial killer out there."

She let out a weak laugh and tucked a stray wisp of blond hair behind her ear. But I could hear doubt creeping into her voice.

"We don't know what the hell is out there," Jaden said in a low voice, pointing at the door.

I didn't know about Lizzie, but the feeling of impending danger was building—fear tightened its grip over me as the seconds ticked by.

"Maybe Jaden's right, Lizzie," I said. "We can't just believe some random man on the phone. He could have been lying that he was a soldier."

"Is anyone there? Open the bloody door!" a guy's voice yelled over the knocking.

We all exchanged worried looks. Jaden shook his head, warning Lizzie not to do something rash.

"Maybe we should run," I said, voicing my instinct to flee.

Lizzie gave her brother a defiant look and called out, "Who is it?"

"What'd you do that for?" Jaden said under his breath.

"Thank God, someone's alive," a different guy said. "Let us in, please." There was panic in his voice. He didn't sound like a soldier. I began to relax.

Lizzie pushed past her brother and opened the door, letting the sound of the storm in along with two teenage guys, who barged through the door and slammed it shut behind them. Their silhouettes stood still for a moment on Lizzie's doormat, dripping wet, with rifles slung over their shoulders, breathing heavily.

Thunder growled through the dark, lightning blinked across the sky, and Lizzie finally spoke, her hands on her hips, "See, not soldiers."

"Soldiers are definitely coming," the taller boy said, as he tried to catch his breath.

"We know that," Lizzie said, crossing her arms. "They told us to stay put, and they'd—"

"Then we don't have much time," the taller one said as he started fiddling with his rifle. Was he loading it?

"We need to use your phone," the other stockier one said as he rushed into the living room, trailing mud and water over the carpet.

"Hang on," Jaden said, cutting the guy off. "What the hell is going on?"

"There's no time," the taller one said, frantic. "We should get out of here."

"Who the hell are you?" Jaden demanded, preventing them from reaching the phone. "And why are you running around with guns?"

"Maybe we should wait for the soldiers to arrive... they can explain everything," Lizzie muttered.

"Only if you fancy getting shot like your neighbors down the road," the stockier one said.

"Wait, what? Who got shot?" I asked. "Are they OK? Did you call the police?"

"There's no cell service, Grace," Lizzie reminded me.

"Some folks down the road. And no, they're not OK, they're dead," the tall one said.

"Dead?" I said, my voice weak. I hated hearing that word. It always brought back memories that I wished I could keep buried.

"Was it Mary and Terry?" Lizzie asked.

"I don't know. We need to call for help and get out of here," the stockier one said.

"Whoever those soldiers are, they aren't friendly," the taller one said. "I don't want to be around when they get here."

"Please, let us use your phone," the other guy said.

"You're not using the phone until you tell us what the hell is going on!" Jaden shouted, putting his hand firmly over the phone receiver.

"I don't think you all realize the shitstorm we're in," the tall one muttered.

"Tell them, Levi," the other guy finally said.

"They're not going to believe us, Dylan," Levi said.

"We have to try," Dylan said.

Levi shuffled anxiously. "Fine."

As Levi quickly recapped what happened, the knot of fear in my stomach tightened. Soldiers taking people captive? Killing people? It sounded ridiculous. Crazy. That would never happen here; New Zealand was safe. Surely, they misinterpreted what they saw.

But I could hear it in Levi and Dylan's voices—genuine fear. Whatever they saw out there scared them enough to flee with guns in hand. And I couldn't ignore the mounting feeling of dread threatening to take over. If what they said was true, there was more than a storm raging outside. It sounded like all hell was about to break loose.

"So, can we use the damn phone?" Dylan finished.

Jaden didn't respond, but Dylan pushed past him anyway, picking the phone up. He held it to his ear and then slammed the phone back down. "Seriously?"

"What?" Levi asked, rushing forward.

"It's been cut off," Dylan said, running his hands through his hair.

"What? That's impossible. It was working a minute ago," Lizzie said, running over and picking it up. "My parents called, and…" She held it to her ear and then put it down limply. "It's not working," she admitted.

"Can this night get any worse?" Levi said as he hit the benchtop in frustration.

Jaden walked over to Lizzie and put his hand on her shoulder. "Lizzie, I think we should—"

The sound of truck tires crunching on gravel silenced us.

I rushed to the window and cracked the blinds. Two army trucks crawled up the drive, their headlights beaming harshly.

"Soldiers are here," I whispered as I backed away.

"That's our cue to run," Levi said, his voice low as he ran to the backdoor. "Come on!" Dylan was right on his heels.

"Go, Lizzie," Jaden said as he dashed into the kitchen and pulled a butcher's knife from the drawer.

Lizzie followed Jaden into the kitchen. "But, Jaden—"

"Go!" Jaden ordered, giving Lizzie a little push.

I gabbed Lizzie's wrist. "Come on, Lizzie," I said, as we stumbled together to the backdoor where Levi was frantically trying to open the ranch slider.

Heavy boots pounded up the wet path to the front of the house.

Levi jiggled the key in the lock, frustrated. "Damn it. It's stuck."

"It does that sometimes," Lizzie said, pushing her way to the front and taking over. "Let me do it."

"Elizabeth Watson. Open up. This is an order!" a man yelled as he bashed his fist against the front door.

My heart pounded against my ribcage as the furious knocking continued.

"Hurry the hell up," Dylan said.

"Elizabeth Watson. Open the door. This is your final warning!"

"I got it," Lizzie said, sliding open the door and revealing the storm raging outside. Levi and Dylan sprinted out into the night. But it was too late for us.

With a thunderous crash, the door was kicked down, splintering off its hinges and smashing into the floor. I screamed as two shadowy figures stormed forward, their guns aimed.

Jaden faced them head-on, his knife raised. "Don't come any closer."

"Drop the weapon and put your hands where I can see them!" a soldier yelled.

Jaden didn't flinch.

"I said, drop it!" the soldier yelled.

I raised my hands shakily, but Jaden refused to budge. He held the knife steady, ready to use it.

"What are you still doing here? Run!" Jaden screamed over his shoulder at Lizzie and me. But I couldn't move my legs. Lizzie swayed on the spot, unsure what to do. I knew she'd never leave without him. A scream caught in my throat as a gunshot cracked through the night. I watched, numb, as Jaden collapsed in a heap on the floor, a dark patch spreading from his chest. Blood.

Lizzie let out a desperate scream and raced toward her brother.

I tried to grab her as she lunged forward. "Lizzie, no!"

"Jaden!" Lizzie cried, pushing me aside and kneeling next to her brother's body. "What have you done to him?" she screamed at the soldiers as she tried to stem the bleeding, tears streaming down her face.

I ran to her and frantically tried to pull her off him. "Lizzie! Leave him!"

A boot connected with my ribs and sent me sprawling to the ground. I clutched at my side, yelling in pain, and tried to get up. But the soldier was faster. He grabbed my ponytail, yanking me to my feet.

"Get in the truck, girl," he spat at me and shoved me forward.

I stumbled and fell to my knees, tears falling down my face.

"I said, get in the truck," he growled and struck me in the back with the butt of his gun. My face smashed into the floor, and quickly, the metallic taste of blood flooded my mouth.

I spat blood to the floor and struggled to my knees. "Why are you doing this?" I cried, wiping the blood from my cut lip.

The soldier never got the chance to answer.

Two gunshots rang through the night, and the soldier fell next to me, dead. I looked over my shoulder and saw Levi and Dylan standing there, their rifles still raised. The other soldier lay by Lizzie with a bullet in his back, unmoving. Levi ran forward and helped me to my feet before taking the soldier's gun.

"Come on!" he yelled, grabbing my wrist and dragging me to the backdoor. "We have to run!"

"But, Lizzie!" I said, struggling against him. I couldn't leave her behind. I couldn't let the soldiers get her.

Lizzie knelt at Jaden's side, clutching his body. "I can't leave him," she cried, resting her forehead against Jaden. "I can't leave him!"

"He's gone, Lizzie. There's nothing you can do. We have to run!" Dylan said as he gently tried to pry Lizzie away from her brother.

Shouting, and the sound of a truck door slamming came from the front of the house.

"Come on, Dylan," Levi said as he pulled me outside into the rain. "We're going to have to leave her." For a moment, Dylan looked like he was about to abandon Lizzie. But at the last second, he turned around and grabbed her, hauling Lizzie away from Jaden with brute force.

"Get the fuck off me!" Lizzie shrieked at him. She kicked and punched, but Dylan refused to let go. He dragged Lizzie from her house and into the night. Levi pulled me along behind him as we followed them into the storm and into the darkness.

Large droplets of rain splashed on my face and drenched my t-shirt. I knew I should feel cold, but I couldn't feel anything except the primal instinct to run—to save my life. Somewhere ahead of me in the dark, I could hear Lizzie's tearful breathing as we ran farther from the house. Levi and I sprinted, together, across the open paddocks, tripping and stumbling over the ruts, and scrambling over the wire farm fences. My bare feet were frozen and cut-up, my clothes soaked to the skin.

I looked back over my shoulder at Lizzie's house. Torch beams scanned the paddocks we had just run through, and the bright lights from army trucks glared at Lizzie's house. Fear overtook me, and I stopped running, too afraid to move.

"We have to keep going," Levi grunted as he pulled me onward.

"Where do we go?" Dylan called from somewhere ahead.

Lizzie spoke through her tears, "The forest."

I stifled a scream as the popping of automatic gunfire cut through the night. Again, fear paralyzed me, and I froze, an open target in the field. But Levi was having none of it. He pulled me forcefully forward as the forest loomed in front of us. We darted into the trees as the soldiers continued to shoot. Bullets slammed through the trees on either side of us and tore up the ground all around. We stumbled blindly over fallen logs and stray branches as the gunshots sliced through the brush. Levi still had a firm grip on my wrist, and he dragged me farther into the dark bush.

As we ran deeper into the forest, the crack of gunfire faded into the distance, and I could breathe again. The forest floor was damp and springy beneath my freezing bare feet. Rain dripped from the canopy above, splashing onto the soggy ground. Off in the distance, thunder cracked across the sky.

I looked around, disorientated and confused. The dark shadows of trees and ferns pressed in from all sides, indistinguishable. I had no idea where we were or where we were going. And now that the danger felt farther away, I was beginning to feel the cold. First, a shiver down my spine. Then gooseflesh rising on my skin. And finally, my teeth chattering as a gust of wind blew through the trees, chilling my bare arms.

"How far do we go?" I asked shakily, finally getting the courage to speak aloud.

At first, no one answered me. Only the crunching of their footsteps through the underbrush and the splashing of rain on the canopy above broke the quiet of the night.

"Until we can't run any farther," Levi said to me eventually, his hand still gripping my wrist tightly. Like he was afraid if he let go, I might disappear. And he'd be left alone. I didn't blame him. The thought of being out here by myself with soldiers terrified me too.

"I'm Levi, by the way," he said to me.

"I figured that out," I replied as I gently touch my cut lip. The bleeding had stopped, and it didn't feel that bad.

"And?" Levi asked.

"Sorry. I'm Grace," I said.

"And you're Dylan, right?" Lizzie said from somewhere to my right, her voice quiet.

"Yup," Dylan said. "I'm guessing you're Lizzie."

"You can let go of my arm now," Lizzie said moodily. "I'm not going to run off." Dylan released her. She started wiping her hands on her skin-tight jeans.

Levi realized he was still grasping my wrist and let go quickly. "Let's keep moving," Levi said as he shoved his hands into his jacket pockets. "We need to put as much distance between those soldiers and us as we can." Levi turned and charged into the bush, leading the way. But there was a yell as he disappeared from view.

"Levi?" I asked, running forward.

Dylan pushed past me. "You all right, mate?"

I could hear Levi swearing from somewhere up ahead before he finally reassured us. "I'm fine."

"He's always been clumsy," Dylan said as he helped Levi up a small bank that Levi had evidently slid down.

"Be careful, it's slippery," Levi muttered as he emerged, with a streak of mud down one side of him. But there wasn't any time to waste. As soon as Levi was back on his feet, we were running again. The ever-present threat of those soldiers catching us, and killing us like… like Jaden kept me going. Every time I felt I couldn't take another step, my mind flashed to the gunshot, and it forced me to keep running. But the farther we got away from Lizzie's house, the thicker the bush became.

We fought our way through tangled vines and dense undergrowth. Bush-bashing through waist-high ferns and shrubs, sinking into muddy hollows and scrambling over fallen logs. With no trail to follow and no idea where we were going, I was soon exhausted.

Eventually, I lost sight of Levi as he took a particularly tricky path through the trees and disappeared from view. I stopped to catch my breath.

"Levi," I called out.

"You've got to stay close," Levi said to me, appearing through the mist. "Or you'll get lost out here." The rain had briefly stopped, and faint light from the moon shone through the trees, illuminating Levi's face. A mix of sweat, rain, and dirt covered his handsome face, glistening in the moonlight. His strong facial features were softened with cute almond eyes. He pulled at his soaked t-shirt that clung fittingly to his lean body under his open coat and ran a hand through his brown hair that was messed at all angles making him look boyish. He looked familiar to me, and I couldn't quite put my finger on it.

Then I realized Levi was the burger guy.

I felt like an idiot for not realizing it sooner. But it had been dark, and Levi only a murky silhouette. He looked different from how I remembered. Something in his face had changed, too, just like Lizzie's. I wondered briefly if I had changed during our escape. I didn't think I had—I still felt the same.

"Stay behind me," Levi said, as he started to push his way through a stubborn web of supplejack.

"I'll try," I replied, as I readjusted my ponytail and plodded on behind Levi in a trance, sopping wet from the rain and sweating from the exertion of our escape. Stumbling along behind Levi, my mind wandered. I hadn't had any time to process what had just happened. But as the adrenaline slowly ebbed away, my thoughts became clearer, and soon my mind was churning with questions. How much farther would we run? What was happening? Why were the soldiers taking people? Was Lizzie going to be OK? Was Mom all right? The uncertainty was dizzying, and I had to stop again. I grabbed onto a thin sapling to support myself.

"I need a minute," I said as Levi turned around to see where I had gone. I staggered to a sturdier tree and leaned my back against it, taking deep breaths. It was all too overwhelming.

Lizzie and Dylan came up next to me. I closed my eyes, breathing deeply to calm my panic.

"OK, one minute," Levi said impatiently, standing tall and slender, silhouetted in the moonlight.

"Why did you come back?" Lizzie finally said, breaking the silence. "I saw you run out into the dark. You could have got away. But you came back."

"We couldn't let the soldiers kill you," Dylan said. "We couldn't stand there and do nothing."

"I'd never be able to live with myself," Levi muttered. "Knowing we could have helped but didn't."

"Thank you," Lizzie said, her voice flat as she looked down at the forest floor. Her white t-shirt clung tightly to her slim frame but was streaked with dark stains—Jaden's blood.

"Don't mention it," Dylan said, wrapping his jacket around him tight to shut out the cold.

Lizzie was silent as she retied her long sopping hair into a bun to keep it out the way. "We should keep moving."

I shivered uncontrollably as we walked through the night, tears flowing down my cheeks. In a heartbeat, the rest of my world had crumbled around me. Mom was the only family I had left, and now she was probably gone. I clenched my hands into fists to try and stop them shaking, but it was pointless.

It felt like death was following me, hanging overhead like a storm. Luckily, I hadn't seen the car-crash that killed Dad and my siblings, but I did see the gun that killed Jaden. It was staring at me, slung across Levi's back. I tried to push the image of Jaden's limp body from my mind, but it was no use. I focused instead on following Levi's back through the woods. But the gun glared right back, the gun that changed everything.

Chapter Four

Dylan

Cold rain dripped through the dark woods, splashing on the sodden leaves, while the earthy smell of the forest hung heavy in the wet night air. The shadows of trees loomed endlessly in all directions, closing in on us, and we had no choice but to keep trudging forward.

"Where are we going?" I asked Levi quietly, afraid to make too loud a noise.

"No idea," Levi said from somewhere in front of me. "But right now, I don't care. I want to get as far away as possible."

So, we ran, looking back every so often to see if we were being followed. The rain had been falling relentlessly, and I was soaked to the skin. I felt sorry for Grace and Lizzie, who wore nothing but t-shirts and jeans, and neither of them had shoes. They looked soggy and frozen but somehow had the strength to keep going. A branch snapped close by, and I flinched instinctively, paralyzed by fear.

Lizzie gripped my arm, her fingers ice cold. "What was that?" she whispered. We listened in silence for a few moments. There was nothing but the soft dripping of rain through the ferns and the murmur of wind through the trees.

"Must have been a possum," I said, trying to push the fear back. I had never felt this afraid before. It was instinctual, pervasive, and I hated it.

"Let's hope so," Lizzie said.

Hope was pretty thin on the ground right now. I started thinking about my parents. I assumed Mom would have gotten stuck at the voting booths. If I hadn't hurried her out the door so fast there might have been a chance—she might have got away. Who knew what had happened to Dad. Most of all, I was worried for Rosie. As much as the little ratbag drove me mad, she was my sister. With any luck, she and her friend had followed orders, and gone quietly. I hoped like hell that was the case. After the incident at Lizzie's, we now knew disobedience was a death sentence.

The brief thought of Lizzie's place summoned waves of nausea. Maybe it was fear, but more likely, it was guilt. I thought about letting it take its course, purge myself of the sin. It would be futile, though. I could feel the darkness in me now, and there was no ridding myself of it.

Instead, I tried to clear my mind and calm myself down, but the sickening feeling refused to leave. The old Dylan was gone with one pull of the trigger. I was guilty, and I didn't need a law degree to tell me that. Legally and logically, I could argue self-defense or temporary insanity, but I couldn't convince my internal jury I was innocent. The sickening guilt returned, and I concluded there was no justification for murder. I struggled to force it to the back of my mind and focus on the good: We saved people. Glancing ahead of me, I watched Lizzie and Grace as they stumbled through the undergrowth. They were alive because of us.

Grace tripped on a root and grabbed at a tree to stop her fall. "I need to stop, I can't take another step," Grace said. I couldn't blame her. She looked exhausted and defeated as she stared down at her battered feet. "If we keep going, we'll end up on the other side of the forest, right?" she said, trying to convince us to stay where we were. "There hasn't been a gunshot for hours," she pointed out.

"I don't see what good running farther away would do," I said.

"I guess here's as good a spot as any," Levi said, hunching over to catch his breath.

"Thank God," Grace muttered.

Lizzie had barely spoken since we dragged her away, and it didn't appear she was going to open up anytime soon. She stared into nowhere with dry eyes and a blank face. Her dirty blond hair was fastened in an unraveling bun, while her fair skin seemed soft and ghostly by the light of the moon.

Grace looked over at her, sympathy spreading across her face. She took Lizzie's hand and led her over to a fallen log. "Are you OK, Lizzie?"

It was like Grace's words broke her out of a trance. For a moment, Lizzie seemed to lose her composure, her face trembling and working. Then she bit her lip and closed her eyes, like she was focusing very hard on something. "I... I don't want to talk about it now," she whispered slowly.

Grace placed her arms around Lizzie in a hug. "It's OK, we don't have to talk. I understand."

I looked at Levi who had sunk to the ground on the leaves, just sitting. He shrugged at me. There was nothing we could do. He pulled his sopping jacket tighter around himself and leaned back comfortably against a tree. His ash-brown hair was matted to his head, but he ruffled it casually and crossed his arms. Typical Levi, the world around us was unraveling yet he was relaxed.

"If you two want to sleep, we can keep watch for a bit," Levi said, trying to shake more water from his hair.

Grace let out a half-hearted laugh. "Have you seen the state of me?" she said, shivering.

"I don't think anything is more impossible," Lizzie said. "I'm not sure I'll ever be able to sleep again." She folded her arms and looked up at the treetops, and I could tell she was trying hard not to cry.

I wanted to somehow make it better, but I knew nothing about her. I needed to start a conversation, about anything to try and distract her, but I couldn't think of what to say. Where do you start in a situation like this?

"Those soldiers went way off script," Grace said finally.

"You're telling me," Lizzie said.

"Jaden was innocent. Why kill him? It's not like he was ever any real threat," Levi said, frowning. "Dylan and I were the ones with the guns."

"He was trying to defend me," Lizzie said, and bit down on her wobbling lip. Grace put a comforting hand on Lizzie's back, which Lizzie quickly shrugged off.

"And that's not to mention those people we found at that house," I added.

"My house, the other houses... they were rounding people up," Lizzie muttered.

"You think it's another pandemic?" Grace asked.

"No, that's not what I mean," Lizzie said impatiently. "Come on, isn't it obvious?"

Nothing looked obvious about it to me.

Lizzie took our silence as an invitation to continue. "There's something Jaden said, before you guys came," she said, looking at Levi and me. "He mentioned the possibility of it being another country's army."

The idea sounded ridiculous. Another country invading? In our small corner of the world, we were the last place anyone would bother going to the trouble of invading. Hell, half of the world left us off the map entirely.

"But why? Our economy has gone to crap. There's nothing here," Grace said.

"Exactly. We're at our weakest right now. What better time to attack us?" Lizzie said.

"I don't know," Grace said, unconvinced. "That man on the phone spoke English."

"Newsflash, Grace. Everyone in the world speaks English these days," Lizzie said.

"Did he have an accent?" I asked.

Lizzie shrugged. "Maybe. It was hard to tell through the phone."

"I think Lizzie's right." Levi said. "The timing is too perfect. My dad always said, the best time to start a war is when you can easily contain any resistance. Adults all over New Zealand would be gathering at the voting booths."

"Well, at the very least... our military will put up a good fight. They were out in force today," I said. I locked eyes with Levi. He'd put up with his dad's shit all his life, but deep down, I knew he still cared about him. And maybe his dad was out there on the frontline somewhere, fighting for us.

Silently, we each thought of our own families, stuck in town while a fierce battle raged around them. The thought made my stomach turn. It couldn't be true.

"We still don't know it's a war," I said. "We need more than a hunch. We need proof."

"My brother was killed tonight," Lizzie said, rounding on me, "we don't need any more proof than that! If I'd just listened to him and Dad..." Her shoulders shook, but her eyes remained dry. It was painful to watch, her grief so unbearable that she couldn't let it out of her body. She held his memory trapped inside; the last remnants of our rapidly dissolving pasts.

"Maybe we should stop talking about this for now... get some rest," I said quietly.

"No. For the last time, I don't want to sleep," Lizzie snapped.

"Now, did anyone else notice anything? Anything at all?"

"I did," Levi said. We all turned to him. "Those soldiers… they weren't wearing our flag."

"Then whose flag was it?" I demanded.

"No one's. They weren't wearing any."

That killed the conversation. If it was our military, they would wear a flag. They always identified themselves. I didn't know what military wouldn't.

After a long pause, Grace shook her head in disbelief. "We're being stupid, right? This isn't happening."

"Well, I don't know about you, but for something that never happened, I'm beat. We basically ran a marathon tonight. Last time I ran that hard was for those stupid beep tests back in school," Levi said in a joking tone. For Levi, that joke was poor quality. But Grace burst into laughter, verging on hysterical.

"Must make a change from handing out burgers," Grace commented once she got a hold of herself.

"Wait, you know where I work?" Levi asked, smiling a little.

Grace shrank back out of Levi's view. What was going on?

Lizzie caught Grace's eye. "She's been practically stalking you for weeks," Lizzie said to Levi, forcing a stiff smile to her face.

"Lizzie!" Grace said.

"What? It's true."

"No, wait, I remember you!" Levi said. "You're the cheeseburger fan, right?"

"You're totally busted," Lizzie said, giving Grace a nudge in the ribs with her elbow.

"So why do you work there? Are you having a gap year?" Grace asked him as she tried in vain to wipe the rain from her face.

"Something like that. This topic is getting worn out, eh Dylan?" Levi said, looking at me.

"We talked about it all afternoon," I said. "Trouble is Levi has no ambition, so he doesn't know what he wants to do."

"Shut up. I have ambition. But having a good time is more important," Levi said, grinning.

Yep, he definitely wanted to impress Grace.

"Forget about me. What about you two? Are you still in school?" he asked them.

Lizzie nodded. "Our final exams are soon, though."

"Looks like you won't have to worry about them anymore," Levi said.

He was right. I guess I didn't have to worry about my law exams either.

"That means you're both eighteen, right?" I asked. Talking about our normal lives was a welcome relief.

"Grace is. I'm a year ahead, so still seventeen," Lizzie said.

"What about you guys?" Grace asked.

"Looks like we're the same age, Grace," Levi said, getting up and joining them on the log. "Apparently, Dylan's the grandpa here. He turns nineteen in a couple months."

Lizzie rested her head on Grace's shoulder. "God, I've got a massive headache. I'd kill for some ibuprofen right now."

Then, there was silence before Lizzie let out a wild and hysterical noise that sounded closer to tears than laughter. Those sayings we would utter without even thinking about them had so much more meaning now. I was scared that maybe she was right. Would we have to kill for something as simple as ibuprofen? My stomach squirmed at the thought.

"You all right, Dylan? You look like shit," Levi said, looking at me with genuine concern.

"I feel like it too," I said. The image of the soldier I killed reared up, and I resisted the urge to vomit. "What are we going to do?" I asked.

It was time we thought of a plan. We couldn't sit here in the bush in our state. Lizzie and Grace would freeze to death, and we would starve.

"Even if it's not war, clearly, something has happened," Lizzie said. "We should stay down here in the bush. Our parents would want us to take care of ourselves. Though, we would have to go and get supplies."

"Shoes would be pretty useful right now," Grace said.

"We should go tomorrow," Lizzie said.

"Shouldn't we wait a bit longer? Until we're sure the soldiers are gone," Grace said.

"We can't put it off too long. We're all soaked, you look frozen, and I don't know about you guys, but Dylan and I haven't eaten since lunch," Levi said.

"They should be finished by tomorrow, right? If this was a planned attack, they would clear people out fast," Lizzie said, rubbing her temples.

"That does make sense. But why here? Why now?" I asked.

"Our port. It's the biggest, and the easiest to access. Their army would depend on it," Levi said.

"How do you know that?" Lizzie asked.

"The History Channel," Levi said with a laugh. "And Dad's in the army."

"If we travel back the way we came, we should be safe... at least... safer than when we were before, right?" I said, looking around the group.

"Who knows? But it wouldn't hurt to scope it out," Levi said.

Lizzie still had her eyes closed and her head in her hands as she tried to ignore her headache.

Grace looked at her worriedly. "You sure you're OK, Lizzie?" Grace asked, carefully trying to read the emotions buried deep within her.

"How many guns do we have?" Levi said in a quiet aside to me.

"Enough, including the two we picked up from those soldiers," I said, my stomach churning. I didn't want to remember those soldiers. "Do you know how to work them?" I added needlessly. Levi's Dad had always trained him in little pieces of knowledge like this. He knew how to operate almost every type of gun, be it automatic, semi or bolt action.

"What kind of question's that, Dylan?"

"Sorry."

"We should make sure Lizzie and Grace know how to use them before we go out tomorrow," Levi muttered to me.

"You're talking about the guns, aren't you?" Lizzie said as she opened her eyes. "You need to teach us."

"I don't think—" I began uncomfortably. I didn't want Lizzie and Grace to feel like I did right now.

"Dylan, they need to know," Levi cut me off. "There's no debating it."

"If we get caught with guns, we're dead. Maybe they won't kill them if they're unarmed," I said. I looked up to see Lizzie and Grace glaring at me with a fire that hadn't been there before.

"Dylan, shut up," Lizzie said. She stood up from the log and stared at me with her hands curled into fists. "You're being sexist. It didn't stop them from killing my brother, and they won't hesitate to kill us too. This isn't about you. If you won't teach me, it seems like Levi will."

Levi smirked at me. "Lost for words, Dylan?"

"Screw you, Levi."

"Do you actually think we shouldn't shoot because we're girls? Get a life. We have a right to take revenge if we want," Lizzie said, bringing herself up to her full height. She barely came up to my chin.

"I never said that," I argued back.

"You were going to," Lizzie snapped.

"Fine. You have the right to do whatever you want. I'm not going to stop you. But, have you thought this through? Do you want to kill? Because Levi and I have, and it's pretty shit."

"Let us make our own decisions," Lizzie snapped back.

"It won't make you feel any better, Lizzie. I feel like shit. I feel like I don't deserve my life. I'm a murderer now… trust me, you don't want that." I folded my arms to stop them shaking.

"I might not feel better, but at least I'll be alive." Lizzie challenged me with her fiery gaze.

"Lizzie, Dylan, be quiet," Grace said, sternly yet calmly. "Whether it's for protection or revenge, it doesn't matter, we have to learn. Because, if we're right about this... we need to be able to look after ourselves. The best way to do that is to equip ourselves with the same knowledge they have, and that means learning how to fight, even if we don't want to."

Levi nodded silently in agreement, and Lizzie turned away, her delicate features relaxing as she realized Grace had won the argument.

"I'll go along with whatever you want to do. But I meant what I said..."

With that, we dropped into silence. Grace wandered into the forest, looking for ferns, trying to keep herself busy as the night dragged on. Levi worked with her, cutting the leafy branches loose with his pocketknife, which they then used to make a buffer from the sodden ground. It wasn't dry, but it offered a bit of protection. Grace shivered, drawing her knees up to her chest.

"Here, take my coat," Levi said, offering her his thick woolen jacket.

"No, no, I'm fine," Grace said through chattering teeth.

Levi touched her arm briefly. "Bloody hell, you're frozen, Grace! Take it," he insisted as he tossed it into her lap. She looked unsure whether to accept it, but Levi took matters into his own hands and wrapped it around her shoulders.

"Thanks," she said, pulling it tighter around her.

Lizzie had reclaimed her seat on the log, deep in thought. I kept my distance, leaning against a tree trunk and watching her from the corner of my eye. Through the gaps in the trees, I could see the gray clouds that still hung, oppressive, in the sky. We had been spared the worst of the rain when we made our way into the bush, but we were still soaked through. Now that the adrenaline had worn off, the cold bite of the night air cut through me. I folded my arms to try and keep the warm in. Maybe I should give my coat to Lizzie as a peace offering? After all, I had been a jerk. Lizzie whispered something to Grace, stood up, and walked over to me. We stood in silence for a bit, staring into the greenery that surrounded us.

"Sorry," Lizzie said quietly, still looking away from me.

"For what? I'm the one who should apologize."

"For going off at you. It's just… I'm like that sometimes. I've always been like that," she said, turning to face me.

"Forget it. You didn't do anything."

"No, I take things to heart and then defend my beliefs. Sometimes I lose myself a bit and don't think about the other person. Usually, they have a reason, like you, and I don't give them a chance."

"Like how I was only trying to protect you."

"I can protect myself."

"I know that now," I muttered. "I don't want you feeling like I do after killing that man."

"He was a soldier," she said.

"He was a man, too."

I looked at her and realized this was the first time I had actually seen her face properly. She was pretty. And fierce. There were lavender shadows around her gray eyes that were puffy from tears.

"But he killed my brother. Doesn't that make it OK? He would have killed me too."

"Maybe. I don't know. I feel like… it's not our place to decide who lives or dies, to murder simply for revenge."

"It's not murder when it's war," she said. I wasn't so sure she was right. A big gust of wind surged through the forest, blowing the clouds away and allowing the moon to bathe us in its light.

"Looks like we're in the eye of the storm," Lizzie murmured, staring up at the moon.

"Something like that," I agreed. With the clear sky above, I noticed the small tendrils of dawn's light beginning to break through the dark.

"You know, every time I close my eyes, I see him die," Lizzie said, her voice shaking.

I didn't know what to say, so I dug my hands into the pockets of my jacket and looked at her with sympathy.

"Do you think it will go away?" she asked, trembling.

I glanced downward as the face of the soldier I'd killed reared up. "No," I said honestly. "But, after a while, it might lose some of its sting, and some of its power to hurt you," I said with a hopeful smile. I prayed the same would be true for me.

"Are you usually this sensitive?" she asked.

I laughed. "Yeah, people have mentioned it before."

"I think it's refreshing. My boyfriend's nothing like you," she said distantly.

"You have a boyfriend?" I said, my heart sinking a little. I was disappointed at the mention of a boyfriend. Although, it was unsurprising someone like her was already taken.

"Supposedly. To be honest, I'm not entirely sure where we stand at the moment. Ryan... he's been absent lately," she muttered. "So, let's change the subject. Have you got a girl somewhere?"

"Not anymore," I said. "We broke up a little while back. I've been up in Auckland for university and came back here for a break before exams."

"What are you studying?" she asked. Did the outbreak of war mean I was still studying?

"Law."

"Law... that sounds hard," Lizzie said, grimacing.

"It's not so bad," I said. "Have you thought about what you want to do after school?"

It was an idiotic thing to ask. We were in a suspected war zone, what was the point? If it really was war, things that used to worry me were meaningless now. Was there any point thinking about the future anymore? After all, we could be dead tomorrow.

"I think nursing would suit me. I like the idea of saving people," she said thoughtfully.

"So, you're like a saint or something?" I asked, forcing a grin to my face.

"Not exactly," she said with a reproachful look. "I feel like it's my calling, you know… helping people."

"Fair enough," I said.

By now the sun was truly up, and the birds were making themselves known to us, oblivious to what had happened the night before. They were awake and chattering excitedly to each other. It comforted me, as if our voices could just blend into the forest surroundings. Somehow the dark world seemed less scary in the light of day.

Grace had fallen asleep sitting upright against the log. "I feel worse than I did before," she complained as she woke up, stretching. I caught a glimpse of her lean stomach as her shirt lifted above the waist of her jeans.

"Sleeping on the ground isn't so bad," Levi said from where he was lying, staring at the canopy several feet away. "It's like a camping trip," he said with a weak laugh.

"More like exile," Grace said sourly.

Occasionally, way back before the military curfew had been established, Levi and I would sleep out in the bush if we were hunting too far from the farm. Usually, we'd bring a tent, but sometimes if it was nice enough, we wouldn't bother setting it up, and sleep under the stars. At first, it seemed uncomfortable, but Levi was right—you got used to it.

"So, when does the teaching start?" Grace asked.

"Right after the gourmet breakfast," Levi joked as he stood up. Grace didn't laugh.

I walked stiffly over to the guns. My thighs cramped from the physical exertion of our escape the night before. I handed the

Winchesters to Lizzie and Grace, after checking the chambers were empty.

"Do you know anything about guns?" I asked Lizzie.

Meanwhile, Levi walked over to Grace and started teaching her about the different parts.

"Dad kept a .22 at home, but I've never used it." She held it in both hands, turning it over to examine it. "It's pretty heavy," she said. "They look lighter on TV."

"First, open the bolt." I pointed at it. She looked at it critically for a moment before pulling the bolt back.

"Is that right?" she asked.

"That's good. Check it's empty."

She obeyed and looked at me for more instructions. I quickly went through how to load the gun. She seemed to grasp it easily enough.

"OK, good. Now, if you wanted to shoot something, do you know how to hold it?"

"Um," Lizzie said uncomfortably, "against the shoulder, right?"

"Here," I said, standing behind her and adjusting it in her grip. I caught a whiff of the remnants of her sweet floral perfume. "Then flick the safety off, and you're ready to shoot. This one has a scope, but if it didn't, line up through the front sight."

"Right, I think I've got it."

I stood over her shoulder, studying her closely. She was trying to stay composed and was purposefully putting all her energy into mastering the gun. Her small frame looked comical supporting the gun, but it suited her. She broke away from the scope and looked back at me.

"I want to learn the automatic one now."

"Are you sure?" I asked.

"Anything for my brother," she said, her face full of vengeance.

CHAPTER FIVE

LEVI

WE WERE IN A war now. That much was clear. I didn't care what the others thought. It was the truth, and I knew it. Ironically, becoming a soldier was the one thing I had been fighting against my whole life. I wrecked my relationship with Dad over it. Now, whether I liked it or not, I was about to become one. I stood in the dripping forest, watching Grace struggle with the hunting rifle. My hands were shoved deep in my pockets as I leaned against a tree. It's like Dad knew this was coming. Did he? I hated to think it.

"I can't keep going… I'm exhausted," Grace said as she hung the gun down to the ground in one hand. Her tanned face was streaked with mud, and her sparkling brown eyes were still puffy with tears from the night before. Her long chestnut brown hair was pulled back in a messy ponytail. She sat down heavily on a nearby log, leaning the rifle carefully against a tree. "I can't get my head around being in a war," Grace said as she rested her head in her hands and sighed. "It's like I am moving through a dream… a nightmare I can't wake up from."

"Yeah, me too," I agreed, sitting down next to her. She was pretty, I thought. At least I got to be stuck with her in this war. Jackpot.

"We're actually learning to use these guns to shoot people, that's not normal. None of this is normal."

"Yeah," I said, thinking back to the soldier I had killed hours before. Nausea swirled in my stomach, and I took a deep breath to steady myself. The whole event had been a blur. One moment Dylan and I were charging back into the house. Then, there was a haze of gunfire. After, the soldiers' bodies were lying on the floor with Lizzie and Grace staring up at us, shocked. It took me a second to connect the dots. We had killed them.

"Did your Dad really teach you all this gun stuff?" Grace asked.

"That's what an army father does," I replied as my stomach grumbled uncomfortably. "Or at least my father," I added.

"Do you think he's OK?" she said, sounding worried for me.

I leaned forward to catch a glimpse of her face. Tears were streaming down her cheeks again. Her lips were full and rosy pink. She licked a tear from them, before screwing up her face and crying into her hands. I made a move to put my arm around her, but I restrained myself at the last second. I barely knew her. Grace looked up at me, she had noticed but chose to ignore it.

"I don't know," I said.

If Dad knew about this, why didn't he warn me? A few days ago, Dad and I had argued, again. He yelled that the army was my future. "The army rears strong men who fight for their country. They have honor," he had said to me furiously. "It's an embarrassment to have you as a son." That cut deep. He always made me feel like I wasn't good enough. He raged about my indecisiveness in life. But I didn't care. His fits of anger didn't work on me anymore. Then he left to go back to the base without a goodbye. Mom was always upset with how he treated us. I didn't want to become like that.

"Maybe he will come and save us," Grace said hopefully.

"Doubt it."

"Oh," Grace said, sounding surprised at my directness. "Sorry, I didn't mean to offend you."

"Dad isn't like that. He does his own thing and doesn't give a shit about Mom and me," I said angrily. "What about yours? Would he come?"

Grace sat silent beside me. I looked over at her. Her face had fallen, etched in pain.

"Actually," she said quietly, "my dad's dead."

"Oh," I said, feeling guilty. "I'm sorry."

She looked down at the ground. "He died a little while ago," she continued. Before I realized what I was doing, my arm was around her shoulder. She felt so small and vulnerable.

"Sorry, I had no idea," I said softly.

"It's fine. There's no way you could have known," she said, shaking her head. "Do you think the soldiers took everyone?" she said, quickly changing the subject.

I pulled my arm away from her shoulder and placed it awkwardly in my lap. "I think so. It seemed well planned."

"So… they probably took Mom?" She sniffled, and unglamorously wiped her nose on her sleeve. I didn't reply, and I knew she didn't really want an answer.

"Do you think we'll run into any soldiers when we go back tonight?" she asked.

"I hope not, especially with you holding the gun," I joked.

She punched me playfully in the shoulder. "Now, that was mean," she said, smiling. "I'm not that bad… I'm just not used to it."

I laughed.

"Where'd Lizzie and Dylan go?" she asked, looking around for them.

"Maybe making out somewhere," I said. I wouldn't put it past Dylan.

"I doubt that. Lizzie has a boyfriend… or had a boyfriend…" she said, clearly trying to decide whether the war meant they were still together.

"And you don't?" I asked, trying to carry on the conversation. She shook her head.

"My last one was a jerk, so I've put off dating for a bit," she said.

"What did he do? If he cheated on you, I'll kick his ass," I said, laughing. But I wasn't joking.

Grace gave me a half-hearted smile. After an uncomfortable silence, she looked up at the trees above and sighed. "Things weren't the same between us after Dad died."

"Sounds like a shit time," I muttered, running a hand through my hair to cover the awkwardness that had settled between us.

She laughed weakly. "You could say that. He gave up on me when I needed him the most."

"He really is a jerk," I commented.

I could hear chatting coming from the distance, and Lizzie and Dylan appeared from the depths of the forest carrying armfuls of wood.

"Firewood," Dylan said as he dumped it on the ground. There was a huge smile over his face. He ran his fingers gruffly through his blond hair as he stared at us with his blue eyes. Girls loved his eyes. He rubbed his nose in annoyance at the mud that had managed to accumulate over all of us.

"Good thinking."

"It wasn't my idea," Dylan said as he nodded at Lizzie who seemed overly enthusiastic for someone who had been through so much. That was the keyword: Overly. It was obvious she was trying to cover up how she felt. Instead, she was throwing herself headfirst into our new life. Lizzie added to his pile of firewood, and they busied themselves, stacking it near where we decided a shelter would go.

The noon sun was shining brilliantly through the trees. Now

all that was left to do was wait till darkness fell. Grace and I worked together to clear a spot in preparation for the shelter. We planned to get supplies later tonight.

"I can't believe we have to live out here in the woods," she said.

"You don't like the outdoors?" I asked as we dragged a log out of the way.

"I actually love the outdoors. Dad and I went tramping all the time," she said. "But this is so sudden. Yesterday, I had a house, and now I'm hiding out in the bush, fearing for my life. I watched my best friend's brother get murdered for Christ's sake," she continued, distressed.

"It's going to be OK," I said, trying to comfort her.

"Is it really?" she asked, turning to face me with her hands on her hips. "Let's at least be honest with ourselves. We're screwed. Was fleeing the best thing to do?"

"Of course, it was," I said. "We still have our freedom, and now we can fight back."

"So, you're going to turn me into one of those killing machines?" she said with tears springing to her eyes. I had always been bad with words.

"I mean, what use would we be locked up? At least now, if we ever wanted to, we could get revenge. But until then, we'll stay alive and hope like hell everyone's OK," I explained as we crawled around on the ground, removing any roots and rocks.

Lizzie and Dylan had taken off with renewed vigor to explore our new home. Lizzie thought there might be a stream nearby, and they had gone on a quest to find it.

Grace turned and looked up at me for a moment.

"What?" I asked.

"I know I just met you… but you're a good guy," she said with frank honesty.

"What do you mean?" I asked, feeling a little self-conscious. How did she have this effect on me? "You've been stalking me at work for weeks," I added, trying to cover up my embarrassment. Grace chose to ignore my comment.

"First, you risked your life to save me. Second, I feel like I'm dying inside, but somehow you make me feel better. It's strange," she said awkwardly.

"Honestly, I'm scared shitless, but being afraid isn't going to help."

"I can't believe how calm you are about this," she said, shaking her head.

"Calm, cool and collected," I said with a wink.

Grace gave me a strange look before laughing unsurely at me.

"Some people think I'm funny," I added as an afterthought.

"Oh, you were trying to be funny," Grace said as the afternoon sun caught the natural highlights in her hair. She smiled, and I was entranced. Damn it. I had only just met this girl, and I was falling for her. There was a connection with her I'd never felt before. Maybe it was because I'd saved her life. But, I could feel it, and I knew she could feel it too. There was also something about Grace that intrigued me. One moment she seemed put together, but at the same time, she was spiraling out of control. And, I couldn't help feeling like she needed me.

Lizzie on the other hand was easier to read. And that wasn't a bad thing. Grace was obviously lost in her life. But Lizzie was strong. That much was clear from the moment I met her. Lizzie knew what she wanted, and nothing would deter her. She was a one-woman band, and I knew she would fight, even if no one would fight with her.

"What are you staring at?" Grace said, breaking my reverie.

"Nothing, I'm shattered. I keep zoning out," I said with a nervous laugh, running my fingers through my hair.

"Me too, I feel like I could fall asleep on my feet. But, when I close my eyes, I'm wide awake," Grace said.

Lizzie's voice interrupted our moment, as she and Dylan returned to the campsite. "We found the stream," she said. "I know roughly where we are now."

"Do you think there're any houses nearby?" I asked.

"This stream comes out near some farms by Pyes Pa," she said. "I've hiked along it before."

"I'm sure we can find supplies there," Dylan said.

"And food," I added. "I'm starving." My stomach felt like it was eating itself.

"Me too," Grace said.

As DUSK FELL, WE began a trek out of the forest. Lizzie was familiar with the area, and now that the stream had been found, she thought we were only a couple hours walk from a small patch of houses. We each slung a gun over our shoulder. Lizzie and Grace walked side by side.

"I'm terrified," Grace whispered to Lizzie.

"Me too," Lizzie whispered back.

Obviously, they didn't want us to hear. But I was feeling the same way. If I had a choice, I would stay in the forest. Unfortunately, we needed food and supplies to build a shelter. There was no choice but to suck it up and get over it.

"What if more soldiers come?" Grace asked as she clambered over a large log.

"There is nothing we can do about it. We'll have to fight back," Lizzie said determinedly.

Grace didn't respond, and frowned deeply.

Lizzie looked up at her. "I am going to get them back for killing my brother," she said, her voice shaking with anger.

"Are you sure you really want to do that?" Grace asked her.

"Why wouldn't I?" Lizzie said as she thrashed her way through the bush.

"You would be killing someone."

"It would be revenge," Lizzie corrected her.

"It's still murder," Grace said.

Lizzie glared at her. "Do you have any idea how I'm feeling?"

Lizzie shouted, facing Grace with rage. We all stopped in our tracks.

"Yes," Grace said calmly. Lizzie looked at Grace as if she was going to hit her. Grace stood there, composed.

"And you didn't want revenge for your family?" Lizzie asked.

Tears sprang to Grace's eyes, but she didn't shout back. "Of course I did. But eventually, I realized revenge isn't the way. I could never forgive myself."

"Grace's family is dead?" Dylan whispered in my ear.

"Well, I knew her Dad was…"

Dylan glanced at her sympathetically.

"I'm not like you, Grace. I'm stronger," Lizzie said.

"I know. But I don't want you making a mistake you'll have to live with forever. If you do this, you can't take it back," Grace said through tears.

"I don't care what you think," Lizzie said with a careless shrug of her shoulders.

"OK," Grace said. "You don't have to. I was only trying to help."

"Well, you didn't," Lizzie said as she stalked off.

Dylan and I made to follow Lizzie. I glanced back and saw Grace hadn't moved.

"You go ahead," I said to Dylan before I returned to Grace. I walked slowly over to her. "Are you OK?" I asked.

She blinked her tears away. The moonlight revealed the glistening snail-like tracks down her cheeks. "No, I'm not OK."

"She doesn't hate you," I said, trying to be comforting.

"I know. But that doesn't change what she said, and it doesn't change the fact that she might kill someone."

"She might not."

"I know we all will. Eventually. You already have," Grace said.

She was right. I had killed someone, and I had been trying to forget about it all day. It was impossible. The thought tormented me. My mind kept snapping back to that gunshot, reminding me of the unbelievable situation we were in now. I tried to justify the killing in my head. If I hadn't done it Grace would be dead. But did that really justify murder?

"Come on," I said and gently pulled her hand.

"I don't know if I want to," Grace muttered.

I turned and looked her in the eyes. "You don't really have a choice… but I'll watch out for you," I said.

"Thanks," she said, as she wiped her tears away. "I don't think I can see someone else die. I've been through enough of it in my life already."

"No one's going to die."

"I hope you're right," she said. After composing herself, she walked purposefully in the direction of Lizzie and Dylan.

I hesitated a moment and looked up at the starry sky. What were we getting ourselves into? This was stupid. I saw Grace's small form disappear from sight and I followed. I could make out Lizzie walking determinedly in the distance and ran to catch up with her.

"She was worried about you," I said to her quietly.

Lizzie looked up at me with a slight frown on her delicate face. "I know," she whispered back, "I'm the worst friend. I really upset her."

"She knows you're not yourself at the moment." I pulled back a stubborn branch so Lizzie could pass through.

"If Grace was yelling at me like that, I would have hit her," Lizzie said, shaking her head. "She just stood there."

"She knew you needed to vent. Plus, Grace doesn't seem very violent," I added.

Lizzie smiled. "I'm not sure she could kill anything."

I glanced behind me at Grace. She walked awkwardly with the gun over her shoulder, her eyes cast down, watching her footing.

Lizzie brought her finger to her lips. "We're close," she whispered. "Levi, you and I will go ahead to the edge of the forest to check it's quiet."

Dylan looked disappointed that he wasn't going but didn't say a word. Lizzie and I crept from the edge of the forest into an open field. This farmhouse was like Lizzie's and backed onto the forest.

The picturesque cottage sat exposed on a hilltop up ahead. We would have to make a run for it. Out in the open. Uncomfortable waves of vulnerability washed through me. We were exposed and unprotected. I pushed the lump of fear in my stomach away and tried to ignore the feeling I was being watched.

Lizzie and I sprinted through the field, flicking water up my legs as I ran. My only focus was to make it to the house without getting killed. As Lizzie and I approached the house, we hid in its shadow. With our guns held steady, we stalked the perimeter, checking for any sign of movement.

"Looks clear," Lizzie said in a hardly audible whisper. She moved in plain sight of Grace and Dylan and waved. A few moments later, they were crouched with us in the shadows.

"Dylan and I will go first and check the house is empty," I said.

Lizzie made to argue back but relented. Dylan and I moved silently forward. The door's glass panels lay in shards on the weather-beaten verandah. Dylan had my back as I slowly turned the antique door handle and pushed the skeleton of the door open. The house was dark and quiet. I took a hesitant step into the entrance. The glass cracked underfoot as we tried to move soundlessly into the house. Dylan was quickly beside me, and we walked down the hallway. I pointed my gun into the living room. There was no sign of movement. I spotted the kitchen up ahead and started toward it. A sudden scuffling noise behind me made me turn around. I stared at the barrel of a gun shoved in my face. Shit.

"Move to the wall," a girl said.

I raised my hands and moved slowly back, pressing my back hard against the wall. Dylan was soon beside me, fear bright in his eyes. Moonlight shining through the window illuminated the faces of two teenage girls holding guns firmly in their hands.

"Who are you?" the blonde demanded.

"We're just like you," I said, feeling nervousness creep up within me. Would these girls actually shoot?

"You lie!" she shouted at me and pushed the gun against my

face. I shut up.

"Keep it down, would you?" Dylan begged them. "They might hear us."

"Who? Your soldier friends?" the dark-haired one asked.

"We're not soldiers."

"Why should we believe you?" the blonde said. I heard the conviction waver in her voice. I didn't think she would shoot. But it wasn't worth the risk.

"Look, we're not wearing any uniforms," Dylan said.

"Where are your fellow soldiers?" the blonde insisted as she shoved the gun harder against my face.

"Right here," someone said from behind them. I looked past them to see Lizzie and Grace with their guns aiming to shoot.

"Put the guns down," Lizzie said calmly. Her finger was on the trigger.

"I knew you were soldiers," the blonde said as she threatened to shoot.

"No one is a soldier," Grace said angrily. "We're free like you. So put the gun down," Grace said forcefully as she took a step forward.

The blonde flinched but didn't make any move to surrender the gun.

Lizzie and Grace had had enough. They marched forward and put their guns against our attackers' backs. "Drop the gun," Lizzie demanded. "Or I will shoot you."

Fear spiked in the blonde's face, and slowly, she put the gun on the ground.

"That's better."

Grace held her gun steady against the dark-haired one as she too lowered her weapon. Then Lizzie and Grace promptly kicked the discarded weapons out of the way.

I looked carefully at the blonde girl standing next to me. She was shaking with fear.

"I think you can lower your gun now, Lizzie," I muttered.

Dylan peeked out the window into the dark, checking for any signs of movement.

"We aren't going to kill you," Grace soothed.

The dark-haired one managed to collect herself. With a clearer look at her face in the moonlight, she looked young. Maybe fifteen? But I couldn't be sure. Her hair fell around her baby face in messy waves.

"My name's Jess," she said as she extended her shaking hand. Grace took it.

"Grace," she answered.

"We shouldn't hang around for long," Dylan said nervously. "Let's gather the stuff and get the hell out of here."

"I'm not letting you ransack my house," the blonde said.

"You have no choice. We risked our lives coming here, so we're taking supplies and leaving. You can come if you want, but it's up to you," I said. We were in a hurry. I didn't want to stand around arguing and waiting for the soldiers to come.

The blonde studied me critically. "I'm Leah," she said finally, as she straightened her back and flicked her waist-long hair over her shoulder.

"Levi," I said offhandedly as I moved off to a bedroom. She followed me in like a lost puppy. "Do you have a brother?" I asked.

"Yeah, but he's not here," she replied, sounding confused.

"How old is he?"

"Twenty, why?" she asked, bouncing at my shoulder.

"I need his clothes. Where is his room?" She pointed down the hall. "You should go and pack if you're coming."

"Where will we go?" she asked, wide-eyed.

"Forest," I said. There was no time for her dumb questions. She trotted off to her room. I walked briskly to where she had directed me. I pushed the bedroom door open, found a large duffel bag and stuffed it full with dark clothes. I held a t-shirt up to me. It should fit, I thought. Not that I really had a choice. The jeans I grabbed looked a bit short for me, but would easily fit Dylan. I took a moment to take in Leah's brother's room. He obviously liked guitar, from the electric and acoustic guitars propped up against the wall. Posters of bands were plastered all over the room and his bed was a mess. Normal, I thought, and wondered where he was now.

I slung the bag over my shoulder and returned to the living room, where I tossed it to the floor and went to help Grace gather food from the kitchen. Lizzie had packed a bag of clothes for her and Grace, while Dylan had searched the attached garage. He managed to find a few tarps and some rope. Grace tucked a few blankets into the food bag. Jess returned with some tramping packs that we loaded with as many sleeping bags as we could find and then packed in whatever small pots and pans we could fit. Minutes later, all of us, except Leah, were ready.

"Where's your friend?" Dylan asked impatiently.

Jess shrugged. "She always takes a while to pack," Jess said with a nervous smile.

"Now's not the time to worry about what to pack," I said sourly.

"It's how she is," Jess said in her defense.

Lizzie stood impatiently with crossed arms. Eventually, Leah appeared with a neatly packed bag.

"Finally," Dylan commented.

Leah threw him a dirty look but maintained her aloof appearance. I wasn't sure I wanted them to come with us.

"Come on," Lizzie said irritably as she and Dylan stalked out the door lugging their heavy bags behind them. Grace and I followed in moody silence.

Leah decided she had to talk. "It's cold," she said loudly.

"Shut up," I snapped. "Don't talk."

Leah gave me a snobby look.

I grabbed her roughly by the arm. "Our lives are at risk," I whispered furiously in her ear. "Get that through your head. Act like people are looking to shoot you."

"You don't have to be mean about it," she said.

"Yes, I do. You could get us all killed. This is no joke. Shut up and follow us," I muttered angrily as I walked ahead through the open field.

My nervousness was back. The thought that the soldiers could be around any corner was nauseating. If there were any of them about, they definitely would have heard Leah's outburst. The shelter of the forest brought some comfort, but not enough to ease my mind. Even after the hard slog back to camp, lugging our heavy bags of supplies, the nervousness wouldn't go away.

Dylan and I built a shelter from the tarpaulins while the girls made a small meal. We all sat together in the shelter and ate some baked beans on bread. I'd never eaten anything that tasted so good. Grace had even packed a tin of hot chocolate. When she passed me a steaming mug of it, I was so happy I could have kissed her.

We sat around the small fire in companionable silence. The camp wasn't perfect, and we had forgotten some important things. But for now, we were dry and warm.

"Thanks," Jess said, finally cutting the silence. Her wild wavy hair was tamed back in a ponytail. By the light of the fire, I could tell her hair was a deep copper color that looked almost red with the flickering of the flame.

"For what?" Lizzie asked as she wrapped a blanket around her and Grace's shoulders.

"For letting us come with you. And sorry for holding you at gunpoint," she added, looking at Dylan and me.

"It's OK," Dylan said, shrugging it off. "We would have done the same thing." His new t-shirt was a bit small for his shoulders, and he looked hulky with the shirt pulled so tight across his chest. Lizzie seemed to be eyeing him up. If I were a girl, I'd be staring too.

"So, are we going to stay here?" Leah asked quietly.

Grace nodded.

"For how long?"

"Until we have to move," I said.

"Cheer up," Grace said, looking at Leah's furrowed face. "It won't be so bad here."

"Whatever you say," Leah said moodily, crossing her arms. She was sapping the energy from our group. Grace shuffled back a bit. She was done listening to Leah.

"Maybe we should go to bed," I said awkwardly, deciding I didn't really want to make small talk anymore either.

"Yeah," Lizzie said sleepily as she rubbed her eyes. Grace nodded in agreement. The girls wrapped themselves in hoodies and blankets. I lay down next to Grace and stared up at the blue tarpaulin above my head.

The events of the past two days whizzed through my mind like a movie on fast-forward. I closed my eyes to try and make it stop, but it looped on repeat. I just wanted to open my eyes and have everything back to the way it was. But that was wishful thinking. When I opened my eyes, the same bleak forest would be waiting. All that was left to do was fight through till the end… to stay alive.

I glanced over at Grace trying to sleep next to me. At least I had her. Was it fate that we met? Probably not. But it didn't stop me wondering why we chose that night to go hunting. Or, why was it that road we chose to escape down, and Lizzie's door that we knocked on? Maybe something good would come from this, after all. Perhaps, despite all the bad, if we could make it through whatever the hell was going on, there would be something worthwhile farther on down the road.

CHAPTER SIX

JESS

I SLEPT UNTIL TWILIGHT. After setting up camp a few days ago, we were all so exhausted and overwhelmed, we spent the next few days lazing around, trying to process our new normal. Our internal body clocks were confused, and the need for sleep battled against constant anxiety. The birds were singing their final song before they settled in their nests. I listened, half-awake, to a native Tui and rubbed my eyes. As I crawled out of the shelter, I saw Leah sitting across the stream by herself, looking lonely and out of place. I shook the sleep from my limbs and ambled over to the stream, skipping across some rocks to reach her.

Leah sighed as she dangled her long, pale legs into the water. She had a perfect slim body, porcelain skin, and her bleached blond hair was paired with misty blue eyes veiled by long lashes. When I first met Leah, I had secretly been surprised that a girl like her would want to be friends with me. She often claimed to be jealous of me, but I didn't understand why. She had everything she could ever want, until now.

"So, what do you think of the others?" Leah asked, breaking the silence. Across the stream, it was quieter, and we were sufficiently out of earshot of the others. I could see the light of the few lanterns they had lit flickering between the trees. They claimed they didn't know each other before the war. It was hard to believe, watching them. Maybe this was what happened when you lost everything? You grab onto whoever you can find, and try to remember what was. Already, I felt comfortable around them. But not all of us were getting along so well. Leah and the guys constantly argued. I couldn't work it out. Boys had been a huge part of Leah's life since we were twelve or thirteen. She was always with one guy or another, and she was constantly breaking their hearts or complaining about how all they saw when they looked at her was someone to show off. But despite that, Leah had a lot of male friends, so it was funny to see guys who obviously didn't find her as enchanting as everyone else.

"Jess, did you hear me?" Leah asked, splashing me with water and giggling at my expression as I was shocked back into reality.

"Of course, I heard you. I was thinking. I don't know. They're really nice, I guess," I said with a shrug.

"Hmm. I can't decide what I think of them," Leah said absently. "Levi and Dylan are pretty hot, don't you think?"

"I thought you didn't like them."

"Don't get me wrong, I don't very much. But I can still admire their looks, can't I?" she asked, raising one demure eyebrow.

"I can't believe we're in the middle of a war, and you're still thinking about boys, Leah," I said, shaking my head. "There really is no hope for you."

Leah laughed as she played with the glittering diamond cross at her neck. "Old habits die hard I guess," she admitted. "I don't see the point in getting down and sad," she said after a moment. "Why should I change who I am because of this? Why does everyone expect us to be depressed?"

"People have died, Leah," I said, "maybe not people you

know, but the others out there… not everyone was as lucky as we were."

"Don't be stupid, Jess. I have feelings, but I can't truly feel anything for people I don't know."

"Don't you feel worried at all? What about your parents and everyone else?"

"A little. But I'm lucky. My parents will be working at the hospital. They'll never be out in the thick of it. Plus, I don't see collapsing into tears being very helpful either. We have to be brave for everyone out there and for ourselves. Our loved ones wouldn't want us crying over them, would they?" she asked.

"Maybe you're right," I said slowly, "but it doesn't change the way I'm feeling. You're lucky, Leah. Last I knew, my parents went to vote… I don't know what's happened to them now. And I pity Lizzie. She acts so strong, but she is obviously upset."

Leah didn't reply. She lay back against the bank and stared up at the moon that was peeking through the trees. "Let's stop talking about war," she muttered, "I'm sick of hearing about war."

I lay down beside her and stared up. For a moment, I was shocked by the beauty of the night and could barely conceal my amazement at the stars. We didn't get to see them in the city. The streetlights blotted them out. I glanced at Leah. She was still staring up toward the trees, her eyes fixed on the moon.

To be honest, I didn't want to talk about the war either. But it didn't matter whether we wanted to or not—this was the world we lived in now. How could we not talk about it? And even if we didn't speak of it, there was nothing that could stop us from thinking about it. Leah's blasé act didn't fool me. I could see the effort it took her to appear light, chirrupy, and happy. I was the only one who knew her well enough to realize she was burying her emotions deep inside so she wouldn't freak out over all the things that had happened in the last few days.

"Leah, Jess, do you want something to eat?" Levi called out

across the stream to us in the black of the night. I sat up and picked a few of the leaves from out of my wavy copper hair.

"Sure," I called back as I stood up.

"Coming Leah?" I asked her.

"Yeah, OK," she said, sitting up and smiling at me.

We made our way carefully over the slippery rocks of the creek and scrambled up the bank, strolling over to the tarpaulin shelter we had set up. We'd argued about whether we should have a lantern lit or not, but eventually, Lizzie put her foot down and said she'd rather have light and kill whatever soldiers approached than go without. We kept it mainly under the shelter though, scared that maybe an over-passing helicopter or plane might see it. I was on Lizzie's side and didn't believe the soldiers would be able to see our few measly lights under the thick canopy of trees. Even helicopters wouldn't be able to spot us in the dense bush. Only in the places where the trees thinned out, like by the stream, did we really have to be careful. Our shelter was built in a dense patch, on the edge of a clearing. We covered the tarp in leaves and ferns to try and make it look less conspicuous.

"Here," Lizzie said, handing me a plate of spaghetti and sausages cooked on the embers of a fire someone had dared to light.

"Thanks," I said as I took it from her.

"Maybe we should be thinking a little about self-sufficiency," Dylan said as we ate. "We would be able to minimize risks by making fewer trips to houses for food if we could grow stuff down here."

I agreed, "That's not a bad idea. I was thinking yesterday, maybe we should be keeping a record of our time here and what we do." I thought of it as we were setting up our campsite but wondered how they would react to it… would they turn it down immediately or think of it as something we could be remembered by?

"What were you thinking exactly?" Grace asked, interested. "Like a diary?"

"Yeah, maybe. I thought if everyone did their own part, it would be good to look back on later," I said, feeling self-conscious.

"Why would we want something to remember this time by?" Lizzie asked, considering me with her fiery gaze.

"Not something for us to remember, but something for others to remember us by, if anything happens," I said quietly.

"If something happens? Nothing is going to happen to us, so there's no point," Leah said.

"Don't write anything if you don't want to," Levi muttered, annoyed. "Nobody's forcing you to do anything. It's just an idea."

"We can't guarantee anything, Leah," Dylan said seriously.

"Even if something does happen, I don't want my family to remember me by experiences I've had in war. I want them to remember me exactly as I used to be, before all this." Leah put down her plate, staring around us all. "So, you guys are seriously considering this?" she said after a moment. "What if soldiers find it?"

"Do you really think soldiers will care about a teenager's diary?" Levi mused.

"They won't find it," Lizzie assured us, "and even if they did we'd be just as screwed with it as we would be without it."

Leah didn't reply. It was obvious she had been outvoted, and it was decided. We would each write what we wanted, about anything we wanted. Lizzie and Grace confessed to being avid writers and both got rather excited about the whole thing, spending the rest of the meal talking about it and trying in vain to find pens and paper. I wasn't a writer, but I liked it because it gave me some space for my thoughts. Maybe once they were out on paper, there would be more room for the rest of my brain to cope. It relaxed me to write and talk about the simple little things that happened in camp. Plus, it had the added effect of making things seem less real, less close.

All of us had our own reasons for wanting to write, except Leah, who adamantly refused to be any part of it. We didn't have many writing materials to start with. Grace and Lizzie were keen on getting some pens and paper the next time we went to get food.

After the meal, I piled the plates and went to wash them in the stream. I'd barely started when Grace came to join me. "Would you like some help?" she asked, kneeling down.

"Um, yeah, that would be great," I said. We set to work, not saying much.

"Is Leah always like that?" Grace asked me after an awkward minute of silence.

"Like what?" I asked carefully and a little defensively. At times I got annoyed with Leah, but she was still my friend and had been for the longest time.

"Like... she's either running someone down or she's the opposite—really cheerful. She swings from one to the other so often it's hard to know how to react."

"I know what you mean," I said. "She's a bit like that. With the war and everything, she is trying so hard to be cheerful it's almost tiring to watch, and it makes her seem shallow."

"I see," Grace said, tossing her chestnut hair over one shoulder. "And I also see you're the complete opposite, Jess. It's the same with Lizzie and me, too. We couldn't be more different, but you still have to love them for being that way, right?" she asked with a little smile. Her brown eyes seemed warm and kind, but sad. I wondered what had happened to make her that way.

"You're completely right," I said, "Leah's been my friend for so long I wouldn't be the same person without her."

We finished washing the plates and stacked them. I picked them up and carried them back over to the shelter, Grace trailing along behind me. We sat down on the soft sleeping bags. They were cozy to sit on, and I collapsed backward, for a moment closing my eyes in bliss as I felt the poufy sleeping bag close around me.

"Dylan said you were staying at Lizzie's when it started?" I asked Grace.

"Yeah," she said. She looked like she was about to say something else but instead looked skyward. Obviously, she didn't want to talk about it.

"Leah and I were at her place when we saw them coming."

"Were her parents at the voting too?" Grace asked.

I shook my head. "They were at the hospital. Both of her parents are doctors."

"I guess not everyone was out voting, anyway," Grace said.

That was true, I thought. Not everyone. Not Leah's neighbors, who we had watched being dragged away, screaming, into an awaiting truck. Leah and I hadn't known what was going on, but we didn't wait to find out. We ran to hide.

"How did you stay hidden?" Grace asked, as if reading my mind.

"Leah's house has a safe room that her parents installed when they built it."

"A safe room? That's a bit over the top, isn't it?"

I grinned. "I know, right? You wouldn't know it, but we are both from America. We lost our accents years ago," I added, seeing a look of confusion pass over her face. "Leah's parents were paranoid. In America, robberies were more common, and Leah's parents were wealthy. They got worried about their stuff... Leah and I used to joke it was because her parents were wanted criminals. We never guessed one day we'd lock ourselves in it for real."

"A lot of unexpected things have happened," Grace said with a sigh.

"Who knew something like this could happen here," I said.

Leah's parents had first come to New Zealand on a vacation and, shortly after, decided to immigrate. My mom and dad followed them a year later because of job opportunities and the supposedly safe environment. I still remembered the excitement of the move. My uncle Ross had waved a tearful goodbye to us and hugged Mom. Then we boarded the plane, and I watched America shrink and disappear as the plane soared into the sky toward New Zealand. I was only five years old.

Thinking of my mom and dad brought tears to my eyes.

"Do you wonder how your parents are?" I asked, "It seems like forever since I saw mine, and I didn't even say goodbye properly. I thought I'd see them the next day, and now I don't know if… if they're still OK or if…" I found I couldn't finish the sentence. My throat had closed up painfully, like I was trying to breathe past a large lump that clogged my windpipe.

"Jess, I'm sure they will be OK," Grace soothed, looking at me with sympathy. "I wonder how my mom is all the time. I don't know how she'll cope without me," Grace mumbled, not meeting my eye. She went quiet and gazed off into space.

It took me a moment to work out what sounded so different about her sentence. It sounded like Grace's mom relied on her, and not vice versa as you'd expect in any other family.

"What about your dad?" I asked.

"My dad and siblings died."

"I'm sorry," I said gently. I wanted to ask how they died, but it seemed insensitive.

She got to her feet. "I'm um… I'm going to go talk to the others," she said. "Do you want to come?"

I nodded in response, crawling out of the shelter after her.

They weren't far off, gathered near a large kauri tree that seemed to command the clearing. It towered majestically over all the others. Levi and Dylan were leaning against the thick trunk with Lizzie and Leah sitting cross-legged opposite them. They were laughing and talking about something we had missed. I watched as Grace went and joined them, sitting down between Levi and Lizzie, her face brightening as she caught onto the conversation.

Our lives were divided into 'before' and 'after.' Two pieces of us that crossed all the time but never seemed compatible with the other. The 'before' side of ourselves made us who we were today, but it was the carefree side, the side that was tame, obedient, and innocent. The side of ourselves we knew, the side we were comfortable with.

The 'after' side of us was different. We were still us, but something had changed. I couldn't have guessed I would be able to survive in the bush with only these five people and the birds for company. I couldn't have guessed I could hold a person at gunpoint with a bullet ready in the chamber and demand to know who they were. I hadn't killed anyone, but the people I stayed with... they were only a few years older than me, and they had killed. Was it only a matter of time before I was forced to do the same? The 'after' side was very different. It was wild, it was primal, it was instinctive, but more than that, it was strong.

CHAPTER SEVEN

LIZZIE

DYLAN WAS SITTING AGAINST the kauri tree, his eyes closed as he rested his head back against the trunk, deep in thought. He could have been asleep, but I knew better. None of us were sleeping much since all of this started. There was a slight furrow between his eyebrows. I walked over and sat down beside him. Dylan didn't move or open his eyes.

"You know, if I stay like this with my eyes closed, I can almost imagine I'm at home, sitting in front of the TV with Mom in the kitchen," he said to me, finally opening his eyes and looking at me. "But then a breeze comes along and rustles the leaves, or I hear something that brings me back to reality, and I know I'm here."

"Sorry, I didn't mean to disturb you," I said.

He smiled half-heartedly. "Don't apologize, Lizzie, it's not like any of this is your fault."

"Then I'm not sorry," I said, smiling a little as well. I glanced up at the swaying leaves and took a twig in my hands, crumbling it piece by piece onto the grass in front of me. It seemed so wrong to me to be here, safe. Why had fate picked us out of everyone to be down here in this bush away from it all? It didn't make any sense to me. Were we just lucky, was it coincidence, or was there some greater force at work? I believed in God, but I had to say lately, I didn't believe in him the same way I used to. God was an asshole. Why did he choose me to survive and Jaden to die? Why was there a war in the first place? I had so many questions for him, and he wasn't answering anything at the moment.

And as for Dylan… Grace had asked me whether I liked him or not only this morning. I wasn't really sure. There was something about Dylan that made it impossible not to notice him. Despite this, I still thought that deep down, I loved Ryan. Ryan hadn't treated me the best in the past, but he was still my boyfriend. He was still the dreamy guy who had bought me roses and taken me to dinner when we were first dating. I wondered how he was doing and if he was all right. If he hadn't been so annoying and actually decided to stay over, we might have been together now. Things would have been a lot different if it had been Ryan and not Grace with me that night. I wasn't totally sure whether I would have wanted things to be different or not.

"Do you think we should be doing something?" I asked Dylan.

"What do you mean?" Dylan raised an eyebrow. It looked like he knew what I was getting at.

"Like… you know… wage our own war against the soldiers. Guerrilla activity." For some reason, it felt dangerous saying it aloud.

"I don't know, Lizzie," Dylan said, looking at me intently. "Maybe we are expected to, but then… we're not heroes. If we went out there to purposefully do damage, we'd probably end up getting ourselves killed."

"I know. I don't mean huge things," I said. "Maybe we can

start small and work out what's going on out there. It must have crossed your mind… we can't stay hidden down here forever."

"This is a revenge thing, isn't it, Lizzie?" Dylan asked quietly. Immediately, my cheeks heated in anger, but I kept quiet, not answering him, daring him to continue. "It's perfectly understandable you want to get back at the soldiers for screwing around with your life and taking your brother from you."

"Why does everyone think I should be crumpled in a depressed heap on the floor, or wanting revenge? I thought you understood, Dylan."

"Lizzie, I—"

"My brother is dead. Of course, I hate them. But right now, I'm thinking logically, Dylan. Logic. That's all it is. We can't bury our heads in the sand, we have to do something. Anything."

I stormed off, ignoring him pleading for me to come back. I sat down by the stream and tried not to cry. The thing was, if I was honest, I was angry because deep down, he was right. I wanted revenge. I wanted to tear the soldiers limb from limb for what they'd done to my brother. And I hated the fact that all we were doing was sitting meekly in the bush and hoping they weren't going to discover us and kill us off. Everyone assumed we were doing the only thing we could to stay alive.

But how could we not fight? It might sound heroic and stupid when you say it out loud, but it was the truth. How could we not do something? Everything we had ever known collapsed around us, and the only thing left to do was to fight. We could hide, but was hiding going to fix our problem?

"Lizzie," Dylan said as he followed me to the stream's edge and sat down beside me on a flat rock. "I didn't mean it like that. I'm sorry. Maybe I don't want to admit it, but I'm worried you might be right about this. That's all. And if you are…" he trailed off, staring into the distance.

"If I am right, then some or all of us might die," I finished the sentence for him. I knew it, he knew it, we all knew. "I… I know it's our lives we're risking, and I know this isn't a game," I said, looking up at him. I was close to tears but didn't want to cry. Not again.

His face softened with understanding. "You're right, it's not a game. This is real."

"Even if we stay hidden, there's every chance we'll be hunted down anyway. We're already running out of food… and we have no clue why this is happening to us," I said, and looked out over the gurgling stream. Dylan edged a little closer to me. My heart skipped.

"There's a difference between gathering information and waging war," Dylan said wisely.

"I know." I wanted to convince everyone to do something… anything. Perhaps a reconnaissance mission wasn't such a terrible idea. "We have no idea who is involved, or what's going on. Maybe if we got some information, we could prepare ourselves for what we might be in for."

"That might be an idea," Dylan agreed hesitantly. He was listening, and I felt like I was turning him to my side.

"How long do you think this war might last? A few months? A few years? We have no idea what scale this war is on. I think we might need to consider how to survive long term, and look at the bigger picture," I said more passionately this time.

"I get it. I do, and I think… maybe you're right," he said. He looked over at me, his blue eyes sympathetic.

"Just maybe?" I asked, stirring. "I know I'm right." I glanced up at him.

"We still have to talk to the others about it. Maybe next time we go to get food and supplies, we could have a decent look and see if we can work out exactly what has happened. My guess so far is this is a war over land. Maybe someone decided it was time for us to share."

"Maybe. War can start for a lot of reasons," I said.

"Lizzie! Oh my gosh, Lizzie!" I heard Grace calling excitedly and glanced up to see her bounding our way, her chestnut brown hair bouncing over her shoulders and an excited gleam in her brown eyes.

"What?" I asked, laughing as she lost her balance on the edge of the bank and almost catapulted herself onto the grassy patch where Dylan and I were sitting.

"Whoops," she said breathlessly. "There's… something… you… need to see," she puffed as she caught her breath.

"What's so important?" I asked her. I glanced at Dylan, and he shrugged.

"Come on, I'll show you," she said, standing up, more carefully this time and pulling me to my feet. She started to lead me back to the campsite.

"So, this thing I need to see is in the shelter?"

"Not exactly," Grace said as she reached the shelter and began combing through some clothes that lay in a messy pile at the foot of her sleeping bag. "Here, you might need these." She chucked me some skimpy shorts and a t-shirt.

"So, you're going to leave me guessing?"

"Jess, Leah, and I were exploring, and we found something," Grace said as she pulled me by the hand out of the shelter, a huge smile on her face. "Levi, Dylan, you guys should come too," she called to them as Levi had taken a seat near Dylan on the grassy bank. "Come up the stream this way, and you'll find us pretty easily."

I followed Grace upstream along the bank and finally saw why she had been so excited. Near our campsite was a deep water hole. A pretty waterfall cascaded down into its depths. Bright green ferns and shrubs surrounded a massive flat rock that jutted out to the water. Grace had always been a swimmer. She swam competitively, but after the tragedy, the pressure of five a.m. trainings became too much. It didn't mean she liked swimming any less though. She lived near the Mount, minutes away from the beach where we'd surf, swim, and fish all summer long. Often, Jaden would come with us, and on occasion, even Ryan came to help out with the boat. I ducked behind a tree and changed. Leah and Jess were already swimming, treading water below us. Grace wore a tight muscle-back tank and some running shorts that showed off her lean swimmer's body and toned legs. I looked over my shoulder to see Levi eyeing her up. Typical, I thought.

"It's quite a drop," I said, grinning at Grace. "Also, Levi's staring at you," I added in a whisper. She blushed but didn't offer any reply.

"How deep is it?" Grace called to Jess and Leah.

"Really deep. You don't need to worry about hitting the bottom," Leah called back.

"You know what this reminds me of?" Grace asked. "Remember that time we jumped off the bridge into the river, at camp?" I flashed her a grin in remembrance. Those times seemed so far away, though I could still picture it clearly in my mind. There we were, standing on the edge of the bridge with the water flowing smoothly below us. For a moment, I thought I would never have the courage to jump, and then, we both leaped off the edge, screaming and kicking our legs as we hurtled through the air into the water below.

"Ready?" Grace asked.

"More than ready."

"Together," she said, and I nodded. Grace and I ran up to the edge of the rock, leaping into the water with a shriek.

It was icy as I plunged underneath, my hair flowing in a wave of gold above my head as I sank down into the water. I came up gasping for air and feeling refreshed with Grace right beside me, her brown hair slick and dark.

"It seems like ages since I last swam," she said, treading water effortlessly before drifting onto her back. "It feels amazing to be back in the water again."

"It feels cold." That was Leah.

"It's not that bad, Leah," I said, "it's rejuvenating, don't you think?"

"Rejuvenating my ass," Leah replied, but even Leah looked mildly happy swimming. I dived down into the water and swam for a way underneath, enjoying the feeling of the water rushing past me, coming up near the waterfall. I watched as Dylan came running up the big rock.

"Make way!" he yelled as he bombed into the water. Leah, Jess, and Grace barely had time to part before he made his entrance.

"Levi, you coming in?" Grace called to him as he sat on the edge of the rock.

"Nah, I don't really feel like swimming," he said.

"Oh, come on, everyone's down here," Jess called.

Levi shrugged. "I'm all right. It's fine up here."

"What he means is he's a terrible swimmer," Dylan said bluntly.

"Great mate you are," Levi said.

"You can't be serious?" Grace said.

"I can swim, sort of," Levi grumbled, embarrassed.

"He flounders," Dylan said helpfully.

"Shut up, Dylan!" Levi said angrily from the bank. I saw Dylan hiding a smile. Grace saw it too.

"You know, it's kind of horrible to laugh about it," she scolded Dylan. She swam over to the edge and pulled herself out of the water, sitting on the edge with Levi.

It was so nice in the water that it was hours before we finally retired to the flat rock with Grace and Levi, who were bathing in warm sunshine.

Leah stretched out on her back with her hands behind her head. "Looks like spring is finally here."

"At last. I thought the rain would never stop," Grace said. I agreed absentmindedly with Grace but couldn't relax like the others as they soaked up rays of sunshine with contented smiles on their faces. I was far from relaxed; too distracted thinking about the conversation Dylan and I had earlier, trying to get the nerve to bring it up. I knew not everyone would agree with it, but I was done pretending the war didn't exist. I wanted to do something about it, and I needed to see who was going to be on my side.

"There's been something I've been meaning to talk to you guys about," I said with a quick glance at Dylan. He nodded for me to continue. "Dylan and I were talking and—"

"And you'd like to announce your love for each other," Leah said, giggling stupidly.

"Of course. We are gathered here today to tell you all we are engaged," I said, rolling my eyes as Dylan completed the look by putting an arm across my shoulders. "No. We thought we should try and work out what exactly this war is all about and… what we can do to stop it," I said, laying it all out in one sentence. Silence hung heavy in the air. Grace sat upright, pulling her tanned legs to her chest. Levi avoided eye contact and looked out over the water hole. Jess and Leah looked uneasily at each other.

"Someone… say something," I urged.

"What we can do to stop it? What does that even mean?" Jess said eventually, her copper hair sparkling in the afternoon sun. "We can't do anything to stop it. We're only teenagers. I mean, I know you guys are a bit older, but no one out there would expect us to participate. We can't give up our lives or put ourselves in that kind of danger."

"All the people out there gave up their freedom. We still have ours, so what are we going to do with it?" I argued. "I'm sick of moping around and making out like we're having a nice little camping trip while our parents, and everyone we know, are in danger."

Grace was looking at me carefully, scrutinizing every aspect of me. "I don't know what to think, Lizzie," she said quietly. "My mom would want me to keep out of this if I could, and so would yours—especially if she knew what had happened to Jaden when he tried to stand up to the soldiers."

"Does anyone here actually agree with me?" I asked, almost desperately.

"You know that I do, Lizzie," Dylan said.

"I think you're right, too," Levi said, as he reclined back. He had taken off his shirt, and his olive skin stretched tight across his lean torso. "I mean, hell yeah."

"You guys are talking about war like it's nothing," Jess said, "like it's some kind of sport," she said looking disgustedly at us.

"I'm not saying that," I said hotly, "I know it's not all black and white Jess. But still… we can't sit here doing nothing. It's not right!" I said, raising my voice.

"What do you think is right, Jess?" Levi asked her.

"How are we supposed to know? And why should we have to deal with it?" Leah immediately responded, defending Jess.

"Because we all know people out there who have probably died. What, are you going to wait until one of your parents gets killed before you step up to the plate, Leah?" Levi said angrily.

Grace put a hand on his shoulder to calm him down. "That was uncalled for, Levi," Grace said quietly.

Leah bit her lip to hold back tears, got up and left, with Jess shadowing after her.

"Levi, look what you've done," Grace said, running a hand through her damp hair, glaring at him in irritation.

"What I've done? Don't you mean what Lizzie's done? You're the one who started this, Lizzie," Levi said, turning to me. "You should at least be thanking me that you have Dylan's and my support."

"I am grateful, but you could have been less confrontational about it," I snapped back angrily.

"Why doesn't everyone shut up?" Grace said angrily. "I don't know who is right, Lizzie, but sometimes you need to shut up and take notice of the people around you. You're not the only one entitled to an opinion, you know." She got to her feet and stormed off in the same direction as Jess and Leah.

"Oh great. So now I've made my best friend angry too," I muttered. I suddenly realized Dylan still had his arm around my shoulders. I quickly squirmed away and went to the edge of the rock, and stood there for a moment before I dove back into the water hole, letting the water engulf me once again before I rose slowly to the surface and began to swim lengths, lashing my arms against the water. I knew I was right. I knew it. And even though I had gone off at Levi, he was right too. How differently they would all feel if it had been their brother, or their mother, father or sister that had been killed in front of their eyes. My mind replayed the moment Jaden had been standing there, pathetically holding the knife. Trying to protect me.

I swam even harder, pounding at the water like it was the enemy. But it didn't seem to ease the pain in my heart. If anything, I felt worse. There was so much pent up anger inside of me and I didn't know what to do with it all. I was angry; at the soldiers, for doing what they did. At Jaden, for trying to protect me. And at myself, because Jaden had been right. I never listened to him and Dad, and now, he had paid the price for my stupidity.

My arms cut the water, stroke after stroke. But after a little while longer, I ran out of energy, and I was flailing. Still trying to chop at the water, but getting no where. Exhausted, I pulled myself over to the bank and dragged myself up on shaky limbs. I lay back, breathing hard. It was useless.

I was useless.

I had been helpless against the soldiers invading our home. I should have done something, but now it was too late. I swore to myself I would do everything in my power to stop the soldiers from taking anything from me again. All I had left was the will to fight back, to survive. I had to, because Jaden couldn't.

Chapter Eight

Grace

I left Lizzie, Dylan, and Levi on the rock overlooking the swimming hole. I couldn't understand Lizzie sometimes. I knew deep down she cared, but her beliefs were so strong she was blind to others' feelings. I walked briskly past the camp and toward the stream where earlier I had found a patch of water where I felt at peace. I was still in my wet clothes, and I waded into the calm pool and floated on my back. The water had always been home to me. It was somewhere I could let my thoughts drift and body relax. I lay there on my back, letting the light current gently push me along. I closed my eyes and let the water drown out the outside world.

The water cocoon had the desired effect. My breathing calmed, and eventually the anger passed. Lizzie didn't mean any harm. She was determined to make a difference, and that was something I could easily understand.

What would my dad want me to do in a situation like this? Mom would tell me to stay safe and stay hidden. Wait it out. Dad had always been the opposite. He was a risk-taker, and an adventurer. If he was still alive, he would have told me to do what I thought was right. The Grace from a few days ago would have said staying safe was the only option. Now, there was a small voice in my head telling me to make a difference. And to the new Grace, that meant fighting back. Tears pricked the back of my eyes. The thought of my dad always had this effect on me. I had made peace with the fact he was gone… that they were all gone, but sometimes stray thoughts would wander into my mind and remind me it was permanent. I stood up. Levi was sitting on the bank watching me.

"What are you doing here? Spying on me?" I asked, wringing the frigid water from my hair.

"I was worried. You were gone for ages," he said with a casual shrug.

"Well, you found me," I said, feeling self-conscious standing alone in the stream. I made for the bank and rubbed my hands against my arms in a futile effort to stop the chill.

"Are you all good?" he asked, looking up at me sheepishly with his warm brown eyes.

"Yeah. The water helps me think," I said, wading toward him and climbing out of the stream. He offered his hand and helped me up onto the bank. I sat next to him, pulling my knees up and shivering. The sun had ducked behind the trees and was casting long shadows onto the forest floor. I pulled my hair into a bun, then looked directly at him. His face was boyish and kind, with dark stubble starting to show on his chin. His brown hair was messed at all angles. A casual smile sat across his light pink lips as he looked over at me.

"What were you thinking about? Me, I hope," he said, sticking out his tongue. I humored him with a weak laugh and wiped my tears away. I hoped he hadn't seen me crying, again. I was doing that far too often these days. It was probably my coping mechanism, I thought. Lizzie's was anger, mine was tears.

"No, Lizzie, actually," I said. "I think she might be right."

"I wasn't sure you were going to come around to the idea," he said, sounding a little surprised.

"I needed time to think it over myself. You can't spring decisions like that on people."

"You're full of surprises," he said, giving me a playful shove.

"What do you mean?"

"I mean, you seem like someone who would play it safe. I'm seeing another side of you," he said.

"I think it's the right thing to do. Dad would agree, I think." The thought of Dad brought fresh tears. I thought I was past this. Maybe the war was bringing my old wounds to the surface. I hoped not. I didn't want to sink into the depression again. It was a dark and painful place that took a lot of strength to climb out of. I wasn't sure if I had the energy to do it again.

"Hey, it's all right, Grace," Levi said, putting a comforting arm around my shoulder. "I'm not going to force you to fight if you don't want to."

"It's not that," I said. "I want to fight."

We sat in silence for a bit, watching the sun sink farther below the trees, plunging us into shadow.

"For what it's worth, I think your dad would be proud of whatever you choose to do," Levi said, and gave me a supportive smile.

"Th-th-th-thanks," I said through chattering teeth.

"You should get warmed up." He helped me up, and we made our way back to camp.

Lizzie and Dylan were busy preparing dinner, while Jess and Leah sulked in the shelter. I gratefully changed into warm, dry clothes and joined Lizzie outside.

"I'm sorry," Lizzie said immediately. "You know I can get ahead of myself. But that's no excuse," she said, looking up at me over her pot of baked beans. I hated baked beans.

"It's fine."

"So, you're not mad?" she asked, testing.

"No," I said. "I've had a chance to think."

"I'd still be pissed," Dylan interjected, as he took the pot from Lizzie and held it over the fire. Lizzie grabbed some plates.

"Grace is obviously a better person than you'll ever be," Levi joked.

"I actually think you're right, Lizzie," I said.

"Really?" Lizzie asked, her face brightening.

"I told you she'd come around," Levi said.

"Yes, really. We need to make a difference. And from where we are, the only way to do that is to fight back."

"We should start planning," Lizzie said, getting overly excited at the whole idea.

"We need to take it slow, Lizzie," Dylan said steadily.

"Dad says the most important weapon a soldier has is information," Levi said, as he casually leaned against a log and stretched his legs out.

"OK…" Lizzie started, "what are you saying?"

"I'm saying, apart from making a quick trip to get food, we have no idea what we're up against," Levi said. "The first logical step would be gathering intelligence."

"And how do you propose we do that?" Lizzie asked.

"Go for a walk out there," Levi said as if it was obvious. He laced his fingers behind his head, leaned back and closed his eyes.

"We could start in your little town," Dylan said to Lizzie. "See how many soldiers are about and check if any other civilians are still around."

"That seems logical," I said.

"I'm on board," Lizzie said. "It doesn't seem too dangerous."

"There's nothing stopping us going tonight, right?" Dylan asked.

"No, we could leave after dinner," Lizzie said, almost bouncing with anticipation.

"I am not coming," Leah yelled from the shelter. "You can go on your suicidal scouting mission without me."

"Me neither," Jess called. "It seems like a terrible idea."

"I guess it's us four. It's probably better that way," Levi said in a low voice so they couldn't hear.

WE LEFT JESS AND Leah unceremoniously with the dinner dishes, while we changed into our black clothes we took from Leah's house when we rescued them. I couldn't help but feel nervous. The other three were unnaturally calm about going out there again. Lizzie was actually excited, and Levi was joking around as usual. It was almost as if none of this was happening. Were we all losing our minds? That was fairly likely, I thought. Dylan was the only one who appeared moderately sane under the circumstances. I couldn't tell whether his aloofness was put on to cover up the fear he was feeling, or if he was crazy like the other two.

"Are you nervous?" I whispered to Dylan.

"Hell yes," he said. "Don't tell Lizzie, though," he added with a forced smile.

"Me too," I said.

"I think it's normal, right?" he asked, fidgeting.

"Definitely."

Levi shoved a rifle into my hands. "I hope your aim's improved," he said with a wink.

"Me too," I muttered under my breath.

"Hopefully, we won't need to use them," Dylan said to me. At least someone was still sane.

"See you guys later," Lizzie said to Jess and Leah.

"Good luck," Jess said. Leah cleared away the dishes moodily, refusing to speak to us as we headed out into the bush. It was a hard slog through the dark back toward Lizzie's place. At least we had a torch this time, and shoes.

Several hours passed, and eventually, we came to the edge of the forest by Lizzie's farm paddock.

"Where to?" Levi whispered.

"We should head down the road toward the other houses," Dylan said.

"Lizzie? What do you think?" Levi asked.

She was silent, staring ahead at her house sitting up on the hill across the paddock.

"Lizzie?" Dylan said, moving close to her. "We shouldn't go in there," he said, reading her mind.

"There's nothing for you there anymore," I said. "Trust me, I know."

"We could go get Jaden," she said.

"It's not Jaden anymore. He's gone. It will only make the pain worse," I said, remembering back to the day I had to identify my dad, little sister and brother's bodies in the morgue. Mom was too upset and had collapsed from the grief. I offered to do it, foolishly thinking it might give me some closure. It didn't. They lay on the steel morgue tables, their bodies cold, dead and mangled while I succumbed to grief. I managed to identify them before the mortician had to help me from the room. Nothing good would come of us going back into Lizzie's house.

"Grace is right," Dylan said. "We have to move on." He pulled gently at her arm, and we walked along the fence line to the neighboring house and made our way to the road.

As we expected, the houses were still empty and the streets still dark. We had only been walking a few minutes when the sound of rhythmic marching echoed down the roadway.

"Come on," Levi said, pulling us inside a nearby house. He eased the door open, and we slipped inside. Immediately, we were greeted with the stench of rotting flesh. I dry heaved and put my hand over my mouth.

"Dear God, that's rank," Levi said. We ducked below the window ledge and out of sight of the passing soldiers.

Dylan peeked over and peered into the dark. "They're checking the houses, one by one," he whispered fearfully. "We need to hide." We crept low through the house, skirting a dead body in the living room. Lizzie and Dylan peeled off into the bedrooms, tucking themselves away in the closets. It was a small two-bedroom house, and Levi and I frantically searched for somewhere to hide. I refused to hide in the living room, the smell was too horrific. There was nowhere else.

"In here," Levi said and pulled me into the bathroom. We stepped into the bathtub and pulled the shower curtain across.

"This is an awful hiding place," I whispered. We heard the door to the house open. We had no choice now.

"God that smells foul," a soldier said.

"Poor bastard," another said. We heard them move through the living room and down the hallway.

"Bedrooms look clear," one said. I held my breath as their footsteps neared the bathroom. I grabbed Levi's hand and squeezed tight. Footsteps echoed on the bathroom tiles and came toward the tub. Levi and I were both trembling. We were done for. In one swift motion, the soldier pulled back the curtain. A soldier, tall and of Polynesian descent, stared back at us. A look of surprise came over his bearded face. He can't have expected to find anyone here. Levi and I were too petrified to move.

"Have you found something Colonel Scott?" the other soldier said. A look of indecision passed through Scott's dark eyes. Levi's hand slowly inched toward his rifle. The Colonel shook his head in warning: move and I shoot. Levi showed his hands in submission.

"No… no, there's nothing here, soldier," he said confidently, staring directly at me.

I stared back. "Thank you," I mouthed.

His face was impassive. He pulled the curtain shut and marched from the room. I sunk to my knees in tears as we listened to the soldiers leave the house and move on to the next.

"I think we need to get out of here," Levi said, his voice shaking. He helped me up, and we quietly stepped from the tub.

We ran into Lizzie and Dylan in the hall. "Let's grab anything useful and head back," Levi said.

"We only just got here," Lizzie complained.

Dylan noticed the shocked look over our faces.

"What happened?" he asked.

"A soldier found us," Levi said. "And for some reason, he let us live."

"Oh," Dylan said.

"I think he fancied Grace," Levi said in a weak attempt at humor.

"If he changes his mind, they might come back," I said.

"You're right. We need to get far away from here," Dylan said. Lizzie grudgingly agreed. We moved through the house, grabbing whatever was useful. I found some pens and paper on a desk, which would be perfect for keeping our war journal. I stuffed them in the small backpack I was wearing. I tossed a few books and a pack of cards in too. There were a few cans of food in the cupboard and a couple bottles of fizzy drink, which I grabbed. I left the moldy loaf of bread and rotting fruit on the bench. A couple minutes later, we were gone. We headed directly back into the forest.

When we were a good distance into the bush, I finally felt safe enough to talk. "He let us live, Levi."

"I know," Levi said. "I feel like we cheated death."

"Me too. Why would he do that?"

"No idea," Levi said. "Maybe some of the soldiers have a conscience."

"I guess not all of them are monsters," Lizzie said.

Something had been bothering me since our encounter in the house. It was nagging at me, but I couldn't place it. Was it something the colonel had said? Suddenly it hit me. "Did anyone else notice… that they sounded just like us?"

"What?" Levi asked.

"I swear they had a kiwi accent," I said.

"I didn't notice," Dylan said.

"They might have," Levi said. "But I can't be sure."

"I don't know, Grace," Lizzie said.

"What would it mean if they did?" Dylan asked.

"I don't know," I said. There were a lot of unknowns in this war. Why had it started? Who had started it? What the hell was going on? There were so many questions that we wanted answers to, but no one was here to answer them. One thing I knew now was that everyone has a conscience. Even the soldiers. They were human too. I imagined them as stone-cold killers patrolling our streets. Some of them were heartless, but it seemed others were like us. It was clear there would be a lot of pain in this war. I just hoped humanity would shine through.

Chapter Nine

Levi

THE RAIN HAD FINALLY eased, but the sky was still a steely gray and threatened to soak us. Grace and I seized the chance for a walk. It had been pouring relentlessly for a week since our failed scouting mission, and we spent the long hours sitting cramped in our makeshift tent, trying to stay remotely dry. Lizzie wanted to head back out, but truthfully, I was a little shaken after encountering the soldier. We planned to do something once the rain had stopped.

"Why did you come?" Grace asked me.

"Why did I come where?" I asked, confused. Grace wrapped her arms around herself, trying to get warm. For a moment, I thought about being a gentleman and giving her my jersey, but I was freezing. I wasn't going to give it to Grace… no matter what I thought about her.

"Why did you come on this walk with me?" she asked with a cheeky smile on her face. Grace grabbed my elbow as I slipped in the mud, about to fall. "Watch yourself," she said.

I pulled my elbow away, embarrassed.

"You haven't answered my question," she said, feigning annoyance and placing her hands moodily on her waist.

"I wanted a walk," I said, casually shrugging. I wanted a walk with Grace.

"In the freezing rain?" she said disbelievingly.

"Yep," I said simply, but not totally convincingly.

"You're lying," she said back as she flicked her hair behind her ears. Of course, I was lying. I wasn't going to tell her my feelings. Not yet anyway.

"I wanted to get away from Leah," I covered.

She laughed loudly. "Do you really hate her that much?"

"Yeah. She looks at me weird, like I'm a piece of meat. And she acts like a bitch," I said.

"I'm glad you don't like her either. She's one of those girls who thinks she can have whatever guy she wants because of her looks," she said. "It really bugs me."

"And you don't think you can have whatever guy you want?" I asked, trying to be casual.

She shook her head vigorously. "Are you kidding me?" Grace smiled as she pushed her way through a particularly stubborn part of the forest. "I'm not that vain, or that pretty," she commented.

"You shouldn't talk yourself down."

She looked at me questioningly with her probing brown eyes but didn't say a word. She knew I liked her, right?

"You must be happy it was Lizzie's door you knocked on?" she asked.

"Of course," I said truthfully. "It would have turned out differently if it was a family," I added.

Grace laughed. "Yes, it would. You know," she said, perching on a damp log, "I'm glad we met."

"Me too," I said with a smile, but refusing to sit on the wet log. "I feel like I've known you my whole life," I added. Was she going to find this too much?

"I know what you mean. It's really strange. I feel like we were supposed to meet," she said, shaking her head. She felt the connection too. "Is that too cheesy?" She glanced up at me.

"A little," I said, trying to seem nonchalant. She grimaced with embarrassment.

"I really want Dylan and Lizzie to get together," she said, changing the subject.

"I'm not getting involved," I said instantly. Dylan hated it when I interfered with his game.

"You don't find it intriguing that Lizzie has a boyfriend, but she seems close to Dylan? It would have scandal written all over it if there wasn't a war going on."

"I suppose. Dylan usually gets what he wants."

"So does Lizzie," Grace said.

Maybe they would be perfect for each other, I thought.

"What about you?" she asked, prying.

"I don't have much luck," I said, laughing nervously.

"Really?" Grace asked, sounding surprised.

"I'm pretty clumsy."

"I think your clumsiness is cute."

"Cute isn't what I'm going for."

"What are you going for?" she asked. She squeezed the water from her hair as the thunder rumbled threateningly.

"Girls love a bad boy," I said with a smirk.

"Seriously? Maybe you should try a new angle, or just be yourself," Grace offered with a friendly smile.

"And, maybe we should head back before it rains again and we get soaked," I added.

"That's probably a good idea."

I pulled her off the log to her feet. The rain fell, starting as a drip, and then as we entered the shelter, it began to pour.

"Just in time," Dylan said, gesturing to the downpour.

"Yeah," Grace replied as she tied her soaking hair up in a bun and sat down wearily next to Lizzie.

"We're running really low on food," Lizzie said, a worried tone creeping into her voice.

"I thought we only went a week ago." Grace sounded nervous.

"We can go get some from one of the farmhouses," Leah said with her fake smile.

"We need clothes too," Lizzie said. "Grace and I basically don't have any."

I looked over at Grace who wore one of my hoodies over a pair of jeans she had belted with some rope. It was cute, in a homeless sort of way. Lizzie liked tighter fitting clothing, and Grace had let her wear the better things they had taken. Consequently, Lizzie wore some hip hugger jeans with a loose-fitting t-shirt.

"Maybe we should go into town," Dylan suggested tentatively.

"Definitely not," Leah said with outright refusal. "That's the stupidest idea I've ever heard."

"What about the mall?" I said.

"That's still in town, and still a dumb idea," Leah said defiantly. She pulled the blanket around herself for warmth.

"Maybe it's not so bad," Jess said, a thoughtful look on her face. "The mall would have everything, and we would only have to make one trip."

"You can't possibly be siding with them," Leah said to Jess.

"We have to leave this camp at some point," Grace said, "maybe the mall won't be such a bad place to start. It will probably be deserted so we can get in and get out."

"Are you all going mental?" Leah said, anger creeping into her voice. "This idea is crazy, not to mention dangerous. Is there no talking sense into any of you?"

"We can't go for long on the food we have, and I need to get out of this shelter or I'm going to go mad. We also need information... and at least see what's happening," Lizzie said.

"But we could get killed." Leah was adamant, with her arms crossed and stubbornly refusing to cooperate.

I decided to say something. "As Grace said, we can't stay here forever. Eventually, we will have to leave the bush. I think the sooner we know what's going on the better."

"I think we should wait as long as possible. If we don't need to put ourselves in danger, why should we?" Leah huffed.

"I'm going to go to the mall whether you want to come or not," Lizzie said hotly. Lizzie glared at Leah while the rest of us shrank back from the fight.

"Fine… fine," Leah said, staring fiercely back. We sat in tense silence, not sure whether Leah was going to stand up and storm off into the forest or if the tension was going to evaporate. "All right," Leah said as she visibly calmed down and took a deep breath. "I'll come but only because I don't want to stay here alone. I don't think I could handle that either."

Dylan and I glanced at each other. I wasn't sure whether any of us knew what we were getting ourselves into, but we were finally plucking up some courage to stop hiding, again.

"I think we should go tonight," Dylan said.

"That might not be such a bad idea," Jess said. "There will be no moon, so it'll be extra dark." At least Leah's friend was tolerable. Even though the age gap between us was only three years, they were immature. I couldn't help wondering what would have happened if we had chosen a different house with less irritating occupants. Regardless, I had to deal with it now.

"And maybe there won't be as many soldiers around… because of the rain," Grace said hopefully as she dried her face on a towel.

"I doubt a little water will put the soldiers off," Dylan answered with a smile.

I peeked out of the shelter at the rain that was now coming down in buckets. There was a small waterfall of rain pouring off the roof. I sure as hell didn't want to go out in that weather. But it seemed I was going to have to go out there anyway. At least there were some benefits—the prospect of leaving the camp was a relief. The forest was huge but not big enough to hide from Leah. She was always there, and she was always on my nerves.

"We'll leave as soon as the sun has set," Lizzie said resolutely.

"We won't be able to see the sun," Dylan said, tongue in cheek, as he pointed to the grumbling gray clouds that obscured the sun completely.

"You know what I mean," she said in an exasperated voice. "You enjoy mocking me, don't you," Lizzie accused with a sharp look at Dylan, who smiled cheekily.

Grace caught my eye. "See," she mouthed.

"There's not much else to do around here," Dylan sniggered. "Plus, it's endless entertainment."

"You're unbelievable," Lizzie said, shaking her head.

Grace chuckled to herself, watching them with thoughtful eyes, trying to deduce the point in their relationship.

"I know, I'm an amazing guy, aren't I?" Dylan said.

"Ugh! Just go away," Lizzie muttered. It was all an act. Grace was right.

"I can't really do that… you're stuck with me," Dylan smirked. Lizzie rolled over dramatically on her camp bed in feigned annoyance.

"We have enough hot chocolate left for one more mug each," Leah interrupted. "Should we make some?"

"Good idea," I said. I was still frozen from my walk with Grace.

"I'll take that as an offer to get some water from the stream," Leah hinted. It really bothered me. I looked out at the storm raging, and sighed.

"All right, Dylan and I will go," I muttered.

"Woah, I never agreed to that," Dylan exclaimed.

"Oh Dylan, I would love it so much if you went," Lizzie said with a comic grin on her face.

"Yeah Dylan, she would love you so much," I teased. He flashed me a warning look. I smiled innocently back.

"Fine, Levi, let's go," Dylan said as he stood up and strode out of the shelter. I grabbed a pot and followed him, jogging to catch up. I shivered as the wind whipped the rain against me, soaking me through.

"Why did we agree to this?" Dylan demanded.

"I don't know why you agreed to it," I said with a shrug. "Damn it." My foot sunk deep into the mud. Dylan laughed and carried on.

"It wasn't raining this hard a minute ago," Dylan said.

"Stop complaining,' I said as I clambered along the slippery rocks to the fresh flowing water and filled the pot. "This hot chocolate better be worth it," I muttered to myself.

I didn't hear Dylan creep up behind me and shove me hard. I tumbled into the frigid stream with a shout of surprise. "The hell was that for?" I yelled as I clawed my way out of the rushing water and felt my teeth chattering uncontrollably.

Dylan shrugged before laughing. "Don't interfere with Lizzie and me." His tone was playful, but I knew he was serious. Sometimes he needed to relax.

"You ne-ne-need to chill, mate," I said. Dylan laughed harder. "It's not funny," I said as I swiped my hair off my face and gathered the discarded pot that had wedged itself between two rocks. I filled it again and stormed off to the shelter.

"You fell in the river, didn't you?" Grace said, laughing as she caught a glimpse of me.

"Not this time," I muttered as Dylan came in behind me, still laughing.

"Sure, sure. Don't lie, Levi," Lizzie said with a mocking smile on her face.

"Really, Dylan pushed me," I said grumpily.

"I'm sure he did," Jess retorted. I looked at Dylan for support.

"He fell in," Dylan said. "It was hilarious. He slipped. You should have been there."

I shot him a furious look and handed the pot to Leah, who lit the small gas burner under the awning and began heating the water. I got out of my sopping clothes and into my last set of dry ones and snuggled into my sleeping bag, trying to warm up.

Grace looked at me sympathetically. "The water must have been freezing," she said.

"Bloody freezing," I said as yet another bout of shivers rattled my teeth. She handed me a steaming mug of hot chocolate, which I gratefully accepted. I felt its warmth spread through me as I took a lengthy sip.

Lizzie glanced eagerly at her watch. "We should leave in three hours."

The others agreed anxiously before we drifted into silence. I rolled over, staring at the wall of our shelter. I still couldn't believe this was happening. War was here, and we were about to venture into the fire. Again. I was terrified, but we needed to know what was going on. For all we knew, the war had ended, and we were hiding for no reason. Maybe Mom was out there searching for me. I knew it was unlikely, but why couldn't it be true? The moment I thought this, I knew. Deep in my gut, I could feel this wasn't over. We had a long way to go in this war yet. Dad always used to say soldiers could feel war. Was this what he meant?

I remembered back to when I was nine, and Dad took me out to Dylan's block of land for the first time. "Son," he said to me. He always called me that. Why couldn't he just call me Levi? "Today, you are going to learn to shoot, to defend yourself." I remember staring at him and thinking he was insane. "It's the first step to becoming a soldier. Soldiers have honor. Soldiers save the world. One day you will be one, like me."

"Yes sir," I said, saluting him.

"That's the spirit little general," he said, smiling at me.

Dad had army blood running through his veins. He was

determined I was going to defend my country when the time came. Every weekend he was home, he'd set up targets in the field, and we spent the afternoons shooting and running practice drills. He never gave up the idea that I was going to be like him. I was nothing like him. But now, I was about to fight for my freedom. I couldn't sit around cruising through life anymore. Too much was at stake. Now was the time to grow up and become a man. The kind of man my father had never been: decent.

Tonight, I wasn't taking any chances. I was bringing a gun and I would shoot if I had to. Dad taught me to be prepared for everything. There was every chance things would go wrong. No matter what, I was going to be ready. I hoped it would go smoothly. It was only the mall, what could possibly happen?

"IT'S TIME," DYLAN WHISPERED in my ear. Darkness was creeping into the world around us, and it was going to be our best friend. I pulled on my damp black t-shirt and grabbed a gun and ammo from the pile in the corner. Grace reluctantly gave up my black hoodie she was wearing. She changed into the only clothes she had that fit—a tight pair of black jeans and a long-sleeved black polyprop. She kept them dry and refused to wear them except when going on missions. Lizzie woke Jess up gently while Leah and Grace silently got ready.

We walked out into the freezing rain and made our way purposefully toward town. Dylan and I led the way, with a torch in his hand and a knife in mine. I felt strangely calm as we headed away from camp. Leah and Jess looked uncertain as they trailed at the back of the group. This was their first time leaving camp. Lizzie, on the other hand, had a look of determination set on her face. Her gray eyes were steeled and focused. We hacked our way through the stubborn branches and undergrowth. The rain eventually eased, and an eerie mist hung above the ground.

"Are we getting close?" Grace whispered. She sounded

nervous, but her eyes were alert and ready.

"We're almost out of here," Dylan said, "I can see the road." The road glowed ghostly gray ahead.

Suddenly, I wasn't so confident. We were about to enter the war zone. There was no turning back now. This was real. Dylan turned the torch off before we reached the road, and we stopped to let our eyes adjust to the dark. We walked inside the bush line along the road in case the road was patrolled. My finger wavered over the safety of my rifle. Should I turn it off? The forest started to thin, coming to an end a few hundred meters from the edge of the city. Downtown loomed dauntingly in the distance. All the lights were still out, and a blanket of darkness covered the land.

"So, we have to get over there without being seen," Leah said nervously. "It seems impossible."

"Of course it's not. We have to be positive," Lizzie said.

Leah scowled at Lizzie. "Whatever you say."

"She can't be this negative," Lizzie whispered to me before moving off to talk to Dylan.

"Let's creep along the buildings," Dylan suggested, pointing to a row of stores barely visible through the dark. We had to cross a couple open fields to reach the safety of the buildings.

"OK. You go first," Lizzie said.

"Cover me."

I nodded as Dylan took off across the two hundred-meter stretch of open space to the cover of the buildings on the other side. I vaguely saw him wave to signal the next person. I sent Lizzie and Jess across next, followed by Grace and Leah. When I was sure they were safe, I went, dashing across the fields and crossing the road, listening for any sound out of place. I found them crouched in the entrance of a thrift shop.

"So, we've made it this far," Grace said. The open sprint across the fields had given her confidence.

"Yeah," Leah muttered.

Lizzie was about to say something angrily, but Dylan placed a hand on her shoulder, stopping her. She sat tight-lipped, and a look of annoyance slipped across her face.

Dylan led the way, with me bringing up the rear. We crept down the road, hugging close to each building. As we approached a side road, the scuffing of boots and the muffled whispering of soldiers broke the stillness of the night. I tapped Grace urgently and pulled her into a shop through a smashed door. She was about to say something, but I put my hand over her mouth and motioned for her to be quiet. I hoped the others, who had already crossed the street, had heard the soldiers too. I should have warned them. The soldiers came closer, and their voices echoed along the streets. Grace and I slipped farther into the depths of the shop and out of sight. "There's never anyone around," a soldier muttered in annoyance. "What's the point of all this patrolling?"

"We caught a group of rebels the other day," another soldier said.

"What were they doing?"

"Planning an attack," he said offhandedly.

"What happened to them, sir?" the soldier asked.

"They fired at the battalion. Three of them are dead. The other two... Colonel Scott hasn't decided what to do with them," the other man explained. "They should be executed if you ask me. Disturbing the peace and killing my men."

"Serves them right."

"It does," the soldier said, as their voices faded.

I glanced at Grace. Her face was white and fearful. "You can breathe now," I whispered.

"I guess the others are OK," she said, her voice shaking.

"I hope so." I stood up to leave.

"Don't you think we should wait a moment... make sure they're gone," Grace whispered.

"If it makes you feel better," I said and sat back down. Grace sat next to me, shaking with fear. She looked so vulnerable.

Then, a feeling came over me. I wasn't sure why. But it compelled me to grab her hand, freezing cold and trembling. She looked up at me but said nothing. We waited like that for a few minutes until Grace finally calmed down. We stood up together before I dropped her hand awkwardly.

"Thanks," she whispered, with a sheepish smile.

I made my way to the door and looked out. The streets were deserted again. I motioned Grace to follow me, and we quietly walked down the road, looking into each shop for the others. I caught a flurry of movement out the corner of my eye, but before I could react, I was pinned to the ground with a gun at my chest. I looked up into the face of my attacker. It was Dylan.

"It's me," I wheezed, his foot crushing my chest.

He breathed a sigh of relief, let the gun fall to his side and helped me up. "Sorry."

"Let's just go."

We jogged our way through town. The number of soldiers we spotted made me uneasy. We had to sneak past numerous groups of them patrolling every street and neighborhood. Luckily, we had seen them all from a distance and managed to hide before they saw us. My unease was magnified once we reached the mall. It was a huge two-story building, constantly patrolled by soldiers.

"We need to get closer,' Dylan said.

We stood stock-still against a row of houses across the street, watching the soldiers pace around the outside. Dylan and I carefully watched their patrol.

"There's about a thirty second gap between each one. That should give us plenty of time to get closer."

"OK, when the next guard passes, Lizzie and I will run and hide in that garden over there," Dylan coordinated. "You follow after the next guard goes past."

"All right."

Grace, Jess, and Leah merely nodded. Dylan and Lizzie took

off across the road and dove into the garden.

"Should we go?" Leah asked.

"No, better wait until the next guard comes past."

Leah shrugged. She was fidgety and nervous. We all were.

After the guard wandered past, I sent Jess and Leah across. Grace and I figured there was enough time, and we followed immediately after. I tried my best to get comfortable in a huge flax bush.

"Now," Leah said, "how the heck are we going to get in?"

"We could use the door," Jess said.

"No, there're guards." Lizzie pointed to one we could just make out through the rain. I realized how lucky we had been to not get seen.

"What about that loading dock over there," Grace suggested. It seemed like a logical option. The huge number of guards here was suspicious, and I couldn't settle my nerves. We were in too deep now, and there was nothing I could do about it.

"Levi and I will go first," Dylan said, "and if the coast's clear, we'll wave you over." Dylan and I crawled out of the bushes and sprinted across the asphalt to the loading dock. There was a huge metal roller door that blocked our entrance. Otherwise, the coast was clear. Dylan and I pulled the door up as much as we could. It was just enough for him to squeeze underneath and survey the inside.

"It looks clear."

I waved the girls over. They came running and clambered through the opening of the roller door. I crawled in after them, and we closed the door. We were plunged into complete darkness and felt our way along until Lizzie triumphantly found a door. We had made it this far. That was a feat in itself. Things were looking up. Perhaps this mission was going to be just fine.

"Come on, Levi," Grace said, "let's go get some food."

I smiled and followed her through the door into the mall.

Chapter Ten

Dylan

"This way," I whispered and ducked around a corner. I peered into the blackness engulfing the mall as we made hesitant progress into the unknown. The heavy damp smell of stale air overwhelmed us. It was too risky to use a torch, so we moved slowly through the darkness, trying to be silent.

The clacking of soldiers' heavy boots on crisp tiles came from somewhere up ahead. I stiffened and put my hand up to warn the others. After a few frantic moments, we all managed to crouch behind a couple oversized pot plants and a bench. I hoped like hell we were well hidden. Lizzie was right next to me, breathing rapidly but softly by my ear.

Clack-clack, clack-clack. The soldiers marched closer, and I risked peeking over the rim of the planter. Their bright torch beams scanned the inside of the empty stores with eerie manikins still modeling the latest fashion, as they walked toward us. I quickly ducked back down and closed my eyes, hoping to meld into the dark.

"There's nothing out of the ordinary here," one said to the

other, standing only a few meters from my head. They did a rapid sweep over our hiding spot with their flashlights. My heart leaped to my throat. This was it.

"There never is," the other eventually replied. They turned briskly around and walked back the way they had come. I breathed a sigh of relief and watched them disappear into the darkness.

"Let's go," Lizzie said.

I got up quickly and moved stealthily toward an open shop where clothing racks hung dead in the darkness. It looked completely deserted. I took a few covert steps and stooped around the entrance before ushering the others in after me. Levi was trailing at the end, making sure we hadn't been seen. Suddenly the sound of rapid footsteps returned, echoing through the shadows. Levi froze, before diving behind an oversized pot plant. The rest of us crouched on the ground, peeking through the display window.

"I swear I heard something," a soldier said. We should have known better, I thought.

"It's always a false alarm," the other said in an exasperated voice but flicked on his torch all the same.

"No, there definitely was a noise from over there," the first soldier said with conviction, pointing vaguely in Levi's direction.

"Shit," I whispered under my breath, Lizzie's hand gripped my arm vice-like as we waited fearfully. Why did we decide to come here? This was a mistake.

"Fine, go over there. Check it out," the second one muttered, shining his torch on Levi's pot plant.

"No, don't go over there," I muttered to myself. "Don't do it." They walked over to where Levi had been, and stood in front of the planter he was hiding behind. "No, no, no, no, walk away," I begged.

"See, there's nothing, it's a stupid tree," the second soldier said as he harshly shook the tree.

Grace let out a barely audible squeak of fear from somewhere to my right.

There was a moment of silence as the first soldier listened to see if the noise came back. "All right... let's move on," he said eventually. The soldiers walked lazily back the way they had come, sweeping the torch in front of them. I let out a breath. Lizzie's grip on my arm loosened. Luck was on our side so far.

Levi joined us a few moments later. "That was close," he said shakily as he ducked into the shop entrance.

"Too close," Grace agreed. I noticed her hands were shaking uncontrollably. They locked eyes, and Levi gave her a comforting look.

"Maybe we should leave," Leah said nervously, "it's too dangerous."

"We've come this far. I'm not backing out now," Levi said resolutely as he ran his hand through his scruffy hair.

"You could have been killed back there," Leah whispered. Levi ignored her.

"Shut up, you two, you're going to get us caught," Lizzie said as she put her finger to her lips.

"It won't help anyone if you're dead," Leah retorted, turning her back to Lizzie.

"No one is forcing you to stay. If you don't want to be here, leave and find your own way back," Levi said nastily.

"Cut it out, Levi," Jess finally snapped. Levi threw his hands in the air and walked over to Grace. I knew how he felt, Leah irritated everyone.

Jess locked eyes with Leah. "Look, Leah, we've come this far, and we need food and clothes. We have no choice," Jess said. "Go back if you want, but Levi's right. You would have to go on your own because we're going to see this through."

"Fine," Leah said with a hint of malice in her voice. The hairs on the back of my neck pricked up as I heard a faint rustle of noise behind me.

"There's somebody behind us," I whispered urgently in Grace's ear, trying not to move. I felt her tense in fear and then stealthily pass the message to Levi. I readied the gun and tried to steady my shaking hands. Grace caught my eye and nodded. All at once, Grace, Levi, and I spun around and aimed at the two shadows standing a few meters behind us.

"Drop your weapons," I said, attempting to sound intimidating.

"Please… don't shoot," one of the shadows whimpered.

"I swear we're not soldiers," the other one said.

"Who the hell are you, and what are you doing here?" Levi demanded as he walked closer to them, following him with my rifle raised and ready to shoot if necessary.

"Please be quiet," one of them pleaded, "the soldiers might hear us."

"Tell me who you are, and why you're here," Levi said in a low growl. Lizzie, Jess, and Leah were now standing behind Grace, watching. The shadows were silent. If they weren't soldiers, who were they? "Tell me!" Levi hissed.

"Wait," Lizzie said, walking forward.

"Lizzie, stay behind me," I said urgently. She ignored me completely. I should've known better than to try and tell her what to do.

"Are you free like us?" Lizzie asked, moving hesitantly forward.

"Not quite," one of the shadows piped up.

"Jennifer!" Jess whispered in excitement and ran forward, giving her a crushing hug. "What are you doing here?"

"Shhh! It's too dangerous standing here. Come with me." We followed Jennifer into the back of the shop, to the changing rooms.

"Evee!" Jess said when we finally caught a glimpse of the other shadow.

"Jess, is that you?" Evee asked disbelievingly.

Oh no, there were more of them.

"What are you doing here?" Grace asked again, sounding irritated. Levi and I stood guard at the door, peering into the darkness.

"We're… prisoners," the girl called Jennifer whispered, sounding terrified.

"What?" Lizzie said. Impossible.

"So, this is a prison camp?" Levi asked for confirmation.

"Yes."

Just our luck, I thought.

"We're screwed," Levi whispered in my ear. He was right—we were in a whole lot of hell right now. We were going to have to get out of here. Fast.

"We should leave… now," I said to Levi. We had walked right into danger. Levi shuffled nervously.

"How did you get in?" Evee asked.

"Through the loading dock," I answered. "Wait, where is everyone else?" I asked, worried we were standing in a cell.

"Some of the bigger shops are guarded cells," Jennifer explained with a look of concern passing over her face.

"Then, why are you here?" Levi asked.

"They were going to transfer Evee to another prison… so we're hiding," Jennifer said.

A hopeful look came to Jess' face and she said, "Our parents must be here."

Grace walked over to me and Levi, pacing nervously. "I want to get out of here."

"Guys, we should go," I said. They barely spared a look in our direction.

"I assume they must be," Jennifer said to Jess, continuing their conversation, "but I've only seen Leah's parents." Jennifer turned to Leah and smiled. "They are perfectly fine—they've been helping people who got wounded on the way here—but they're worried sick about you."

"Let's get a move on," Levi warned as he readjusted his grip on the gun.

"We should go and rescue them," Leah said determinedly, ignoring Levi.

My palms were starting to sweat, and my breathing quickening as panic set in. An overwhelming desire to flee came over me. But not all of us were so worried about getting caught. Lizzie moved toward the newcomers. She was still torn up about her brother's death and the possibility of reuniting with her parents had sparked her interest. I just hoped that it wasn't going to make her do something stupid.

"No, that's stupid. You'll get killed..." Evee said. "There's too much security, you'll never get close. I can't believe you managed to get in here!"

But Lizzie wasn't so quick to dismiss Leah's idea. "Maybe we could do it."

"Seriously, let's get the hell out of here," Levi said. He looked anxiously out toward the shop's entrance. Grace stood between Levi and me, on edge, her hands gripping the rifle she held.

"Hang on, Levi," Lizzie said. "Give us a minute."

"No, you can't break them out," Jennifer said, "they'll catch you."

Lizzie glanced at me, hoping for my support.

"Jennifer's right. It would be suicide to even try."

Lizzie shot me a look of annoyance but didn't push the matter.

"Why don't you come with us," Levi suggested. Anything to hurry this along, I thought.

Evee looked hesitantly at Jennifer before meeting Levi's gaze. "I'm not up for anything like that."

"So, you're going to stay here till they find you and kill you on the spot," I said, trying to convince them.

"I'm not letting you stay here." Lizzie's voice was just above a whisper. "If I can't rescue my family, I'm going to do everything

I can to rescue you."

Jennifer bit at her lower lip. "You seem nice, but I can't let you risk your life. You're free, and you deserve to stay that way."

"You deserve your freedom back, and you can't do anything about me risking my life for yours. I can do whatever I want. You're coming with us, and that's final."

"...OK." Jennifer still looked uncertain, but at Lizzie's insistence she stepped forward.

Evee looked around nervously. "I'm ready to get out of here."

"Let's leave." I didn't want to waste any more time.

"This is a bad idea," Grace whispered in my ear. "We don't know what we're doing... someone's going to get killed."

I looked at her worriedly. "We can't leave them here."

"I know."

"I'm sure it will be fine," I said, but for some reason, I had the feeling getting out was going to be a lot harder than getting in.

"I hope you're right," Grace replied.

We crept out of the changing rooms and walked quickly through the shop.

"Dylan, you go first, and I'll bring up the rear," Levi said.

I glanced over to him. "OK. Ready?"

Levi nodded at me, and I sprinted a hundred meters to the cover of a hallway, gripping my automatic rifle tightly. I ducked around the corner and peered into the darkness. Footsteps were approaching, and I saw the slender form of Jess materialize through the blackness and hide around the corner with me. She had a knife at her side. I gave her an encouraging smile. Next came Lizzie, who ran almost silently across the floor and knelt beside me with a look of intense concentration set on her face, her rifle held confidently in front of her. Then came more footsteps. At first, I thought they were Jennifer's, but I quickly recognized them as the sound of military boots. I froze.

The crack of a gunshot cut through the blackness, lighting up the mall with a sharp orange glow. An excruciating scream echoed through the darkness, and a ball of fear tightened in my stomach. I resisted the urge to shoot back, empty my magazine and kill every one of the soldiers, but it was too dangerous—I couldn't see them in the dark. Another shot blasted through the air and smashed into the wall above my head. Then, all at once, the mall echoed deafeningly with the rapid-fire of machine-guns.

The discharge of gunfire lit up the mall like a firework gone wrong, and finally, I could see. Instinctively, I lifted the gun and held the trigger down, aiming at the soldier spraying bullets in our direction. The gun pummeled my shoulder as it spat bullets at the soldier. Jess let out a piercing scream as she saw the body of Evee lying dead on the floor, her blood slithering into a large puddle on the cold tiles. Lizzie stood up to run to her. I grabbed her arm and pulled her back.

"You're going to get killed," I yelled over the gunfire. "You don't even know her!"

Lizzie struggled against me, her tears slipping uncontrollably down her cheeks.

A fresh barrage of bullets crashed into the wall above us, forcing us to dive to the ground and showering us with plaster and dust. I managed to get back up to my knees and fired back at the soldiers, their figures appearing and disappearing with every burst of fire. Anger boiled in my chest, and it fueled me to keep shooting. Another shot slammed into the floor at my feet, and I launched a fresh onslaught of bullets at one of the soldiers who finally dropped to the floor.

When the last soldier collapsed to the ground, I heard Levi yell at Leah to run to safety. She was almost halfway to us when a sharp gunshot sliced through the eerie silence, and Leah screamed as she fell to her knees. She tried to crawl toward us, one hand gripping her abdomen, trying to staunch the flow of blood that was beginning to drip steadily onto the polished tiles. Her eyes met mine with a pleading stare, and her face strained with a grimace of pain. She couldn't move anymore, and her head slumped forward as she tried to summon the strength to keep going. Jess cried out and ran out to help Leah, but before she could reach her, the wounded man shot Leah one more time. Leah sagged on her side and closed her eyes. Her chest stilled, and she was gone. Lizzie had sunken to her knees beside me.

"Jess! Come back!" I yelled at her, but it was futile. There was a hideous moan from the soldier as Jess stabbed him. Levi, Grace, and Jennifer ran from the cover of the shop and dragged Jess back to where we were hiding.

"Leah!" Jess cried as she fought to run back. Levi and Grace restrained her.

"We have to go!" Levi yelled at her. "We can't stay… there are more soldiers coming… we have to go now!"

"No! I can't leave her!" Jess screamed with tears streaming down her cheeks.

"Come on!" Grace said as she and Levi pulled her down the corridor back to the loading dock from where we had come in. The pounding of heavy army boots reverberated behind us.

"Run!" Levi shouted as he ducked from a fresh assault of bullets. He lifted his gun up and shot blindly behind him while Jennifer and Grace continued pulling Jess away. Lizzie and I led the pack, racing to the roller door. We skidded to a halt at the door, hauled it open and fled into the night. Looking over my shoulder, the dark silhouettes of a squad of soldiers gave chase. Lizzie ran confidently beside me. How could she be so calm in this situation? The fire of machine-guns cut through the otherwise still night, while soldiers' shouts echoed through the deserted streets. But we kept running.

Grace caught up to me and Lizzie. "This way," she said. We turned down an alleyway. I followed Grace and hoped the others would do the same.

"Where are we going?" I asked Lizzie as we followed in Grace's steady footsteps.

"Beats me," Lizzie puffed, "but Grace used to live around

here."

Grace led us on a tiki tour of the neighborhood, twisting and turning down side-streets and through small alleys. The pursuing soldiers lagged farther behind, and their gunfire became more sporadic. Finally, after turning down a small hidden walkway between two houses, the soldiers were gone. But Grace kept running, taking more shortcuts to throw them off our trail. Eventually, she led us the back way to a school where we were finally able to rest, hidden behind the caretaker's shed. I leaned against the structure to catch my breath.

"If we can make it across the field… and jump the fence…" Grace wheezed, "…it's a clear path back to the forest."

"I can't take another step," Jennifer cried.

"You have no choice," Lizzie said, hunched over gasping in the cold night air.

"Think of it like cross-country at school," Levi said between deep breaths.

"That's not funny," Jennifer said. Levi shrugged and rubbed his calves. Mine were seizing up too.

"OK, let's go," I said. "The sun will be up in a couple hours."

Grace led again, sprinting across the open sports field with the rest of us close behind. Levi gave her a boost over the concrete wall, while I helped Lizzie. Once they had a knee over, we helped Jess and Jennifer. Finally, I gave Levi a boost. He straddled the fence and helped pull me up. We landed heavily on the ground on the other side. The street was quiet. After listening for a few seconds and looking for any sign of movement, we decided the soldiers were gone, so we ran.

Along the way, Levi had the presence of mind to stop by a house and grab enough food to last a few days. As the sun was rising, the forest came into view.

"Over here," Levi yelled as he ducked into the cover of trees. Finally, we were safe. We made it a few hundred meters into the bush before Jess collapsed to her knees and wept. I watched her with a strange sense of guilt and sadness swelling through me. Grace was sitting on a log, her gun discarded in the mud, crying into her hands. Levi sat next to her, whispering softly in her ear with an uncharacteristic look of sorrow on his face. Jennifer stood alone, staring into the depths of the forest with tears streaming down her cheeks. Looking around at the painfully sorrowed faces of my new friends, the reality of the war came crashing down. Freedom was a price we would have to pay with our lives.

"It's so unfair," Lizzie said, her head resting against my shoulder. "Why did it have to happen to her... she was so young!" I refrained from saying we were all too young to bear such a heavy load. Instead, I put my arm around her and tried to tell her it would be OK. I had never told a bigger lie.

Chapter Eleven

Lizzie

Numbness. I lay in our shelter. I was alone, emotionless, and in a state of shock. We had arrived back at camp in the late morning. Not only was our mission a failure, but we had also lost a friend in the process. She may not have been the easiest person to be around, but we weren't heartless. She had been a part of our group—a friend. In the safety of the bush, I had lulled myself into a false cushion of confidence that had come crashing down horrifically last night. We weren't invincible, and let's face it: we were amateurs. The weight of Leah's death burdened me the entire way back. I couldn't help but feel some responsibility. In my desperate need to make a difference, I had carelessly put my friends' lives in peril. Leah had paid the price. The body count was three now. Evee, Leah, and Jaden. How many more would suffer before this war was said and done?

"Lizzie?" Grace whispered, interrupting my quiet.

"Yeah," I heard myself say.

She crawled in. Her face was a mask of sorrow, but her eyes were dry. She flopped prone onto her sleeping bag, with her head buried in her makeshift pillow. "What were we thinking?" she asked in a muffled voice.

"I was wondering the same thing."

"Was it our fault?" Grace asked me, rolling over onto her back.

I didn't answer her. We both knew the answer anyway. "This war is real, isn't it," I said eventually.

"Sure is," Dylan said as he entered the shelter too. His blond hair was a sweaty mess, and his eyes were puffy. Had he been crying? He rolled onto his bed and stared blankly at the ceiling, looking worn out.

"It was a mistake," I said to no one in particular.

"It was stupid," Grace said.

There was a rustle at the entrance to the shelter. Jennifer stood there, tear-streaked and trembling. Her shoulder-length brown hair hung dead straight, and her porcelain skin was flushed with red. "I wish I never came with you. Evee is dead because of you," she said to me, her voice quaking. Tears streamed down her face.

"You didn't have a choice," Dylan said defensively. "You were as good as dead once the soldiers found you hiding."

"You don't know that." Jennifer's lip quivered. "We might have been fine."

"And you might have been fine with us. You both chose to come. We didn't force you," I said to her.

"We feel terrible," Grace said with guilt in her eyes. "Maybe some tea will help?" she offered. Grace was of the opinion a cup of tea could ward off anything. I wasn't convinced it was strong enough for this. She dragged herself from the shelter to fetch water from the stream.

I took a deep breath to stop the tears from falling. "I'm sorry, Jennifer. We didn't mean for any of this to happen."

"It's Evee you should be saying sorry to," Jennifer spat, before dashing from the shelter in a fresh wave of grief.

"God damn it, we only wanted to help," I said, finally letting the tears flow.

"It's not our fault," Dylan said.

"Try telling that to my conscience."

Dylan rolled over and looked at me, his blue eyes fierce. "It's not our fault," he repeated.

"Are you saying that to make me feel better, or to make yourself feel better?" I asked him as I wiped the tears from my cheeks.

"Both. But it's also the truth."

I managed to drag myself up into a seated position. "We forced them to come along."

"Everyone made their own choice," Dylan said. "It could have been any of us that were killed."

"But we weren't. It was Leah and Evee. They didn't want to come," I said.

"We didn't pull the trigger," he said. "It's tragic... it sucks. But we can't blame ourselves."

Grace had returned, I could hear her preparing tea by the fire.

"I'm sure this isn't going to be the last time we'll have to deal with something like this," Dylan said.

It sounded like foreboding in his voice, and it sent waves of dread through me. They crashed against my heart, who was going to be next? What if it was Grace... or Dylan... or me? My mind began to swirl with thoughts about what could happen. They were nauseating, and I lay back down. Dylan was right, I thought. I had to mourn them both, and Jaden too, and then let it go. Dwelling on this would consume me.

"Come on," Dylan said, standing stooped under the low shelter, and holding out his hand to me. "Let's go help Grace with the tea."

I took his hand and stood beside him with renewed strength. We would get through this together. Dylan grabbed a bottle of whiskey he had taken from a house we ransacked and tucked it into the pocket of his hoodie. I gave him a questioning look.

"Something tells me tea won't be strong enough today."

Grace had a row of mugs out and was carefully dishing everyone a portion. Dylan walked over and started topping them up with a generous pour of whiskey.

"Dylan," Grace said, "what are you doing?"

"It's not too much. Just something to take the edge off," Dylan replied.

"Fine. Just don't put any in mine," she said.

Dylan shrugged. "OK then. How about you, Lizzie?"

I looked carefully at Grace and wondered if I should tell Dylan what had happened in her past. But, for now, her eyes were dry as she collected several mugs to take to the others.

"Sure," I said cautiously. Dylan passed a steaming mug into my hands.

"Jennifer, have some tea," Grace said. Jennifer was sitting outside the campfire circle, with her back turned.

She looked over her shoulder at us. "I'm fine," she said.

I grabbed a mug and marched it over to her. "Drink," I urged her.

She obligingly took the mug and drank deeply. "Ugh, what's in this?"

"Dylan fortified it with a bit of whiskey. It will help."

She looked at me suspiciously but continued drinking it.

"Where's Jess?" Grace asked me.

"I haven't seen her." I scanned the clearing near our campsite. Levi was seated at the foot of the kauri tree, deep in thought. But there was no sign of Jess. "Maybe I should go find her," I said. Grace nodded, a look of concern passing over her tear-streaked face. I got up, grabbed a mug of tea and wandered toward the stream, following our roughly hewn path. As I neared the gurgling stream, I saw Jess sitting with her back hunched through the scrubby bush.

"Can I sit?" I asked her. She didn't look over, so I sat anyway. "Here," I said, pushing the steaming cup of tea into her hands. She accepted it in silence but didn't drink it. "Do you want to talk?" She didn't reply and just kept watching the stream bubble along. "…I'll just sit here then."

"I'd rather you didn't," Jess said. I looked over at her. Her face was blotchy with emotion, and the rims of her green eyes were puffy with tears. I was shocked to see the soldier's blood had caked onto her hands in a grotesque glove. Her shirt, too, was stained dark with blood. I held back my tears again. It reminded me the shirt I had worn that first night, stained with Jaden's blood, which was now balled at the bottom of my pile of belongings. I hadn't been able to bring myself to wear the shirt since that night, but I couldn't get rid of it either.

"I only want to help," I said to Jess.

"I don't want your help. You've done enough."

"Jess… talk to me."

"No. I don't want to talk to you. Or any of you." Tears fell silently down her cheeks.

"Please, just let—"

"Get out."

"It might be helpful to talk."

"Get. Out," she seethed. I got up resignedly. Looking over my shoulder as I left, I watched Jess throw the tea out into the bushes in anger and then collapse into tears, hugging her arms around her body. She didn't want to let me in. I trudged back to the fire.

"Did you find her?" Grace asked.

"Yeah, she's pretty upset."

"I'm not surprised," Grace said. "She's lost her best friend. I'd be pretty torn up if I lost you."

"Me too." My face broke out into a weak smile. Sometimes I forgot how lucky I was. Even though we were stranded in this hellish war, I had my best friend. I could have been alone or with complete strangers. Instead, Grace was here by my side. At first, part of me had wanted Ryan here. But now I knew, I wouldn't have it any other way.

Chapter Twelve

Jess

THE DULL RAYS OF first light poked through our shelter. I hadn't slept at all. The grief of it was too crushing. All night, flashes of Leah's final moments forced me to relive the pain over and over. Bang. I watched her crumple, struck with a bullet. Bang. Dead. Collapsing forward, blood pooling. I couldn't get to her in time. Like I was running, but my legs wouldn't move fast enough. Then, the cold-blooded murder. I didn't remember clutching the knife. My body took over, and all I could remember next was the sickly warm blood from the soldier spilling over my hands, and the feeling of his life draining away. I thought I might feel bad about it, but I didn't care. He deserved it. Leah was dead because of him. There it was again. Those three words. Leah was dead. Fresh tears came to my eyes, and I curled into a ball, sobbing.

"Jess," Grace said softly, kneeling next to me and placing a hand lightly on my shoulder.

"Go away."

"I think it might be helpful to talk," she persisted gently. I ignored her, but she stayed next to me. After a couple minutes, I realized she wasn't going to leave. Rolling over, I forced myself to look up at her. Her eyes were puffy from crying too, and her face streaked with tears . Her long chestnut hair was roughly pulled into a ponytail.

"Talking really helps… well, it did for me," she pressed.

"I don't feel like it," I sobbed. It was too raw and too soon. She nodded in understanding.

"If you need to, I am here," she offered. "I know what you're going through… trust me. I can sit with you if you want," she said, crossing her legs and making herself comfortable.

"No. I want to be alone."

She looked a little hurt that I didn't want her there, but she obliged and left the shelter. I chanced a quick look around and was relieved to see no one else was there. Lying on my back, staring up at the blue tarpaulin, tears spilled down my face. It was all my fault. That was the thing I couldn't forgive myself for. Leah didn't want to come. She had been perfectly content to stay put, but I had convinced her… no… guilted her into coming. And now she was gone. Some friend I was. We had always promised to be there for each other no matter what. But when she needed me most, I failed. I cried again, uncontrollably this time.

At some point, despite the tears, I managed to drift into an unsettled sleep but muffled chatting from the others along with the smell of breakfast cooking wafted into the bivouac and woke me up. Baked beans again. My stomach grumbled uncomfortably. It had been over a day since I last ate. I tried to ignore the hunger, but eventually, I couldn't stand it anymore. I extracted myself from the tangle of blankets and shuffled outside. Grace and Levi looked up at me with sympathy.

"Tea?" Lizzie asked brightly, holding up the pot, smiling. Anger rose in me as I looked over at her. She looked perfectly fine: not a tear shed.

"How can you sit there like that?" I spat at her.

"Like what?" she asked calmly.

"You look like nothing has happened. At least Grace and Levi have the decency to look sad."

"Jess, I am sad. I feel terrible…"

"You don't look it, you never cared about her. I saw the way you looked at her. You hated her."

"I never hated her," Lizzie said. "Of course, I cared about her… how couldn't I? We were all in this together."

"This is so typical of you, Lizzie. You only care about your problems and don't have the heart to care about anyone else," I garbled the words before I burst into tears again.

"Get over yourself Jess, I am dealing with her death the only way I can," Lizzie snapped, before standing up. "I held my dying brother. Don't tell me how to feel," she said, storming off. Grace and Levi watched her back as she disappeared into the forest.

"Jess," Grace soothed, turning her attention toward me, "Lizzie has always been like that. She always tries to hide her emotions… and sometimes it comes off…"

"Bitchy," Levi said, completing Grace's sentence.

"I was going to say insensitive." Grace glared at him and then turned back to me. "We all felt like Leah was family."

"Don't say that. You didn't know her like I did," I cried.

"No… you're right. We didn't, and we aren't going to pretend like we did," she said softly, her eyes welling with tears again. "But that doesn't mean we aren't upset by what happened. She was part of our little family… and it hurts." Levi put a hand on her shoulder.

Grace shrugged it off and came to sit next to me instead. "I know you are blaming yourself," she whispered so Levi couldn't hear. I nodded shakily. "Don't do that to yourself. It is no one's fault. You might feel that she only went because of you… but she made her own choice."

I sobbed harder.

Grace embraced me in a tight hug. "Shhhhh," she cooed into my ear. "This is something we all have to come to terms with. None of us caused this… it was a disgusting choice by a soldier. And he paid for it. You made sure of that."

All I could do was cry. I was listening to what she was saying, and I wanted to believe her. But deep down, the tendrils of guilt were still snaking into my heart.

Grace and Levi sat with me for a while. Dylan was off walking to clear his head, and Jennifer had gone to sit by the stream. I had no idea where Lizzie had got to, and frankly, I didn't care. As I looked around the place we were supposed to call home, I couldn't stop myself wanting to give up.

It was bleak.

Our shelter was a poorly erected tarpaulin that barely kept out the rain. We shared clothes, ate whatever canned food we could find and huddled around a pathetic excuse for a fire so the soldiers wouldn't find us. Everything in our life had been taken; our homes, friends, and family. Our whole way of living was snatched from us with no warning. And the first chance we had to take some control back killed my best friend.

This was no way to live out the rest of my life, hiding in fear, barely surviving. Leah was gone, and there was nothing I could do to change that. Who knew where my parents were? Dead, most likely. My new 'friends' weren't real friends. I hardly knew anything about them. We pretended to get along, but the reality was that it was all forced. I didn't really care about them, and I was damn sure they didn't actually care about me. Grace put on a convincing charade, but Lizzie didn't even bother to try. Levi and Dylan were too smitten with Grace and Lizzie to have any capacity to think about another person, especially an outsider like me. They probably wouldn't even notice if I left.

"I'm going for a walk," I muttered. I was done with all of it.

"Do you want company?" Grace asked me.

"No. I think I need to be alone for a bit." I ducked into the shelter to grab a jumper before walking off into the bush without a backward glance.

At first, I thought of leaving. I could walk out of the campsite and into the bush. It would be a couple hours before they noticed I was gone, and by then, I would be far away. But then what? I would still be in this godforsaken country with no escape, waiting for the soldiers to find me. And I would be alone. The only thing worse than being in this war, was doing it alone.

As I walked, I pulled out the hunting rifle I had taken from the shelter. Initially, I had brought it for protection in case I decided to leave. They would understand. But now I wasn't so sure. Everything that had ever mattered to me was gone. What was the point of continuing on? There was nothing left to fight for. No one left to fight for.

After walking a fair distance through the trees, I slumped down under a big tōtara tree, propping the gun up next to me. The sun was sitting bright and high in the sky now, but a southerly breeze kept the forest cool. I hugged my knees tight to my chest.

I could use it, I thought.

If I used it on myself, the pain would be gone. The guilt would be gone, and I wouldn't have to live in this war. Would they miss me? Initially, it would be traumatic for them, I thought. But they were strong. They would get over it quickly, and I would be just a memory. I shook this idea from my head. I couldn't do it. If my parents were alive and found out, they would be devastated. As it was, they were probably dead anyway.

I glanced over at the gun. The long black barrel of the rifle pointed up the tree, and the dark wooden stock rested sturdily on the ground. It would be difficult to shoot, I thought. An awkward angle.

But not impossible.

Again, I tried to push the thoughts from my mind. It was only because of Leah's death that I was thinking this way. Until a few days ago, this war felt like one big adventure. Best friends taking on the foes of the world. We felt invincible—like we were chosen and had a purpose. But we weren't special. We were just lucky… or unlucky.

Maybe it would have been better to be captured. We could have gone quietly with the soldiers and be tucked up in one of those prison cells now. Leah would be alive, and we would be happy… well happier than I was now.

I noticed I was subconsciously playing with the cross around my neck. Leah had given it to me, right before we left. *I want you to have it,* she said. *In case anything happens.* I told her she was being dramatic. But I allowed her to put the delicate chain around my neck, and I gave her my charm bracelet in return.

I took the cross from around my neck and held it in my palm, watching the sun sparkle off the little diamonds set into the cross. I hadn't forgotten my faith, but I felt it wavering. I always thought times of struggle would strengthen it, but all it did was make me question. Where was He now? Leah and I had prayed together often at our campsite, asking for guidance and thanking Him for saving us. Now I was wondering if it had actually been a curse. I was angry. Why take Leah? She hadn't deserved it. None of us did. We were all good people. I tucked the necklace into my back pocket. It was a reminder of everything I had lost, and it would go with me to the grave.

Chapter Thirteen

Grace

Dew dusted the grassy clearing by the stream, the tiny droplets clinging onto each blade of grass. Jennifer sat in a small dry patch. She was pretty in her own way, not stunning nor gorgeous, but innocently beautiful. Her plain brown hair was tied back in a ponytail, framing a babyish face that hadn't quite lost its roundness. Her green eyes were bloodshot from tears, and her pale skin bright red from crying. But for now, she seemed to have her emotions under control.

I smiled and walked over to her, my feet flicking the dew in all directions. I knelt beside her on the soggy grass, the damp quickly soaking through my pants, but I didn't mind. It seemed I was always soaked these days, and I supposed a little water never hurt anyone.

Looking at Jennifer, she reminded me of a younger version of myself. She was sixteen and innocent. My mind drifted to when I was sixteen. Back then, everything was carefree, and I was a tad rebellious, but then life happened. My dad and siblings died, there was the break-up, and school started to become important.

So then, I was forced to grow up. That was where I was now. My innocence was gone, and acting grown-up was the only way to survive. I wished there was an adult here to tell us what to do. The decisions we were being forced to make were too important to be entrusted to us. Looking at Jennifer, I could see the same change growing in her eyes that had grown in mine.

"How did you know?" she asked finally.

"Know what?" I asked, as I delicately pulled at the grass beneath me.

"How did you know war was coming? How did you escape before they found you?"

"We didn't. I was staying with Lizzie. Levi and Dylan came to her house looking for help," I said shakily, reflecting back on the vivid scene for the thousandth time. It still felt just as terrifying. "But before we could get away the soldiers found us, and killed Lizzie's brother. If it hadn't been for Levi and Dylan, they would have killed us too," I finished with as much composure as I could muster. Reliving the memory was more difficult than I thought.

"It must have been hard for Lizzie to leave her brother," Jennifer said.

"You could say that," I said as I remembered Lizzie screaming at us, determined not to leave Jaden behind. Thinking about that night still brought panic. My stomach fluttered nervously, and my pulse quickened. I forced myself to remain calm. It was over, in the past. But, would I have to face something like that again?

"How about you?" I asked, turning the spotlight off myself.

"My little brother and I were playing a game on the computer when the power went off. We thought it was fun, you know, being in a power cut, so we started playing in the dark, just being stupid kids, trying to scare each other. That's when they came. We couldn't do anything. They aimed their rifles at us and motioned for us to get into the truck outside. We ended up at the mall with a bunch of others," she said. "That's how I ran into

Evee, we were in the same section. You know the rest."

Like me, her story was short and concise, a story too painful to tell in any other way.

"You um, you didn't run into a woman called Sophie by any chance, did you?" I asked desperately.

"Is that someone in your family?" Jennifer asked me.

"My mom," I managed to say. Jennifer shook her head in response to my question. I felt my eyes well with tears, and I blinked a few times, trying to regain some sort of control.

"Hey Grace, are you OK?" Jennifer asked me as she watched my face transform with grief. I realized I was crying again and tried to wipe the large wet tears dripping down my face.

"I'm OK," I said with a watery smile, "I guess I was really hoping you had some news." I stifled a noise that was somewhere near a sob. "I'm sorry, Jennifer, you must be feeling so much worse, I mean, we've been free all this time, while you've been torn from your only friend in that place," I said. "It should be me comforting you."

I was doing a terrible job trying to be there for Jess and Jennifer, I thought. Jess had walked off into the forest after I tried talking to her, and now I was breaking down in front of Jennifer.

"We've all lost people," she replied, sighing, clearly thinking about Evee. She was right. "How's Jess? She seemed really upset when I saw her last night," she added with a frown.

"She walked off a while ago to clear her head. I wish there was something I could do, some way to make everything right again, but I can't," I said bitterly. "I feel like I have to be your older sister and protect you," I said with a warming smile. "My life was ruined just like yours, and I wish I had someone to protect me." For me, the one person I always counted on was Mom. We got through what we thought were the hardest days of our lives, and we were sure we would be together through everything else. Now, I didn't even know if she was alive. There was no one here for me now, save Levi who tried his best, but it wasn't the same. If I had no one to protect me, at least I could try and protect someone else.

"Maybe one of us should talk to Jess," Jennifer suggested, "and check she's all right."

"None of us are all right," I said with a sigh. "How can we be? We're emotional wrecks. I tried talking to her, but I don't think it helped."

Jennifer shrugged. "It helped me," she said, her eyes clear and green. There were no tears for the moment, only the faint hint of the memories that had been. To be honest, I felt better too.

"I'll try again," I decided with a small smile and walked off to the shelter to find Levi alone in it, lying on his back, staring at the ceiling. I had the urge to lie down beside him and spill all my emotions onto him; let him hold all the pain I held in me. I knew he would do it for me, but he had his own troubles. His heart was already heavy. "Levi, have you seen Jess?" I asked instead.

"I haven't seen her since she left us this morning," he replied absently. Deciding that Levi wasn't going to make any further comment, I ducked out of the shelter and looked around. Lizzie and Dylan were seated at the foot of everyone's favorite tree, talking. Jennifer was still where I left her by the stream. Jess, on the other hand, was nowhere in sight.

"Lizzie, Dylan, have you seen Jess anywhere?" I called across the clearing.

"No, not since this morning." Lizzie looked at me sheepishly. We hadn't spoken since her outburst at Jess earlier.

"I might have," Dylan said.

"Where?"

"Oh no, sorry, that was yesterday," he said, frowning. "I don't think I have either."

Where had she got to? I huffed, and stomped off in search of Jess, taking the usual track to the toilet. I didn't want to disturb her, but if no one knew where she was... well, it was better to be safe than sorry. The toilet was undisturbed, the thin layer of leaves and debris scattered across the wooden board that covered the long drop. I glanced around. If Jess wasn't back at the campsite and wasn't here, then where could she have gone? Uneasiness began to creep into the pit of my stomach. Where was she? I was about to turn back when I caught sight of a footprint in the dirt not far from the toilet, leading away from the track. I stepped toward it, my heart racing. Why would she have gone off the track? I followed the direction the footprint was headed in, feeling wary as I continued to travel deeper into the forest.

"Jess, where are you?" I asked aloud, frustrated. It would have been nice if she had told us where she was going. I brushed my way past several more shrubs and trees, heading away from the steady gushing of the stream and farther into the bush. After fifteen minutes of following scattered footsteps and broken twigs, I started to get worried. Had she left? Did she walk from our campsite and keep going? She had been gone for hours... she could be miles away now. Should I turn back and get the others? Just as I decided that I had gone too far, I spotted movement by one of the trees up ahead. I dodged around a tree, trying to get a better view.

"Jess?"

She turned as I came out from beside the tree and stared at me, the gun in her grip glinting in the sunlight. It looked too real and too heavy in her small pale hands. She couldn't tell me she had taken the gun from our camp for protection—why had she walked so far alone? We both knew why she was there. I felt panic beginning to rise in my throat, but I forced it back down. I was going to help her.

"Jess, what are you doing?" I said very calmly, almost casual. The hairs on my body were rising with a chilled fear as I stared at Jess. Her face was streaked and blotchy with tears, eyes sunken and dark from lack of sleep.

"Grace, don't come any nearer, or I will shoot, I swear it," Jess said, staring at me desperately, warning me to stay away. I took a small step forward. She had the gun pointed at me with shaking hands. I took another step forward, and she turned the gun on herself. "I swear I'll do it," she threatened coldly.

"Jess, you can't possibly expect me to leave you," I said weakly, my voice coming out in a frightened squeak. I gave her a smile, trying to be light and cheery despite my urge to cry. I doubted I would be able to move if I had wanted to. Shock had rendered my legs useless, paralyzed with dread. I didn't want to lose someone else. I couldn't.

"I don't want to do it in front of you. Please go away, Grace."

"Jess, you know I can't leave," I said shakily. I knew I had to sound confident so I tried again. "I can't walk away and let you die too, Jess," I said with slightly more surety. "I can't let you do it."

The wind brushed past her tangled wavy hair, sweeping it across her face. "You'd rather watch me die?" Jess asked, her finger tightening threateningly on the gun trigger.

"No, Jess, don't. I'd rather watch you live," I said, pleading with her. I couldn't stop the tears from flowing now. They spilled out and ran in smooth, warm lines down my cheeks. "Jess, this isn't the only way. I promise it will get better."

"It won't." She shook her head. "I know you think time can make everything all right, Grace, but there are facts in this world that will never change. Leah was my friend," Jess said fiercely. The haunting in her eyes was replaced by blazing anger.

"Leah was my friend, too. But you are distancing yourself from her with your grief. What she shared with you will never change and will always be with you. If you give up on your life, then you're giving up on Leah completely. She will always be remembered, so long as there are people left to remember her," I said, the words flowing from me like an elixir.

Jess' blaze of fierce determination was faltering.

"Don't do it, Jess, I don't want to lose you too." I wiped at my tears with one hand and hesitantly took a step forward. "I can't lose you. I've lost everyone I've ever cared about: my father, my brother, my sister, and now my friend," I said teary-eyed. "I can't lose anyone else. You don't think I know how you feel?" I said, almost accusing her, the tears streaming thickly down my face.

Jess looked at me with confusion swirling in her eyes. She was questioning.

"I know exactly how you feel. I've been there more than once, and I'm still standing here."

"You don't know how I feel," she said feebly.

"You feel guilty, and think there was something more you could've done, you think there was something you shouldn't have said." I knew I was on the right track because I had been there.

Jess continued staring at me.

I took a deep breath and continued. "You think life has lost its point. All the dreams you had are now gone because what you loved is gone. You think if you join them, they can forgive you, and you can see them one more time."

I cried as those all too familiar feelings flooded through me. I remembered the funeral; three coffins lying still at the front of the church. The guilt sat heavy in my stomach as I had wondered why they had died. If I had gone instead of my sister, she would have been here today. I remembered the overpowering grief of my mom. I recalled the lack of the will to live, the inability to feel, and the overwhelming desire to join them because life didn't seem worth the fight anymore.

"Jess, give me the gun," I urged. I had come back from the brink. She could too.

"No Grace I can't… don't you see? It would be so much easier," Jess begged with me.

"Only for you," I whispered. "What about your parents? What about us? What about the life you will miss out on?"

"But don't you see, Grace? If I stay, I'm never going to be me anymore. There is no life to miss out on. I don't want to be in this war zone. My parents are probably dead, and how can any of us be the same now Leah's gone? If my parents are alive, they would prefer to remember me happy… not depressed, not like this," Jess sobbed. "Who wants to see anyone like this?"

"This war isn't going to last forever, there is going to be light at the end of this, and I'd rather see you like this than dead," I said, anger clear in my voice as I furiously wiped the tears from my cheeks.

"You don't need me, and I don't deserve you." Jess was trembling with emotion.

"It hurts to even think we're not good enough for you. You don't think we can help, but you haven't given us the chance. How do you think we can cope with you gone as well? Do you want us to go through that pain?" I asked, willing her to understand.

"But Grace, please… I can't live like this," Jess said, tears streaming down her cheeks.

"Please Jess, hear me out… it gets better," I begged, reaching forward to take the gun off her.

She froze, frightened and unsure what to do.

"Jess, losing Leah is not the end. It may feel like it sometimes, but one day you'll wake up and everything will seem a bit better," I said, the words coming from deep within my heart.

Jess stared into my eyes, and I knew all that was there was true. Jess closed her eyes, thinking.

I took another step forward, with my hand outstretched shakily. "Give me the gun Jess. I promise things will be better. I will help you. I promise." I was crying just as much as she was.

Jess finally took a reluctant step forward, the gun trembling in her hands. With effort that appeared to take all of her strength, she dropped the gun to the ground. It landed with a dull thud that seemed to echo around the forest. Then Jess collapsed to her knees in grief. I kicked the gun to the side and crouched next to her, putting my arms around her in a hug.

"I'm sure you must hate me right now, but trust me, I have been where you are. It's dark and lonely, but there is a way out, you just have to find the thing that will pull you out," I said softly to her as I put my arm around her shoulder.

"I don't think anything is ever going to be the same," Jess cried.

"Honestly, you're right. Nothing will ever be the same… for any of us," I added. This was not only about Leah dying, this was bigger. "As long as we keep going through each day, eventually things will work themselves out," I said, trying to convince myself as well.

Jess looked up at me, teary.

"It's not going to be easy," I said with flashes of my own struggle coming back to me. I forced them back down and let a weak smile form over my face. "But it will get better."

Jess nodded. I crouched there with her for a moment before standing up and getting the gun, removing the ammo and pocketing it.

"I hate guns," I muttered under my breath.

Jess let out a sad smile that quickly disappeared. "I didn't know that stuff about you, Grace. I'm sorry," Jess said quietly.

"You can't try something like this again," I said, changing the subject. I didn't want to think about Dad right now. "Whether we like it or not, we're a mismatched family now," I said with a smile. "When my family died, it was like trying to function without a limb. The limb never grows back, but you can get used to it if you give yourself time."

"How do you get used to something like that?" she asked. "It seems impossible."

"At the start, it feels like it is impossible. But each day, it gets a little easier."

We walked in silence together for a few minutes back toward the campsite.

"Promise me you won't try that again," I said with a steely glance.

Jess let a small sigh escape and pushed her unruly wavy hair behind her ear. She wiped at her eyes and looked across at me. "I promise."

That was all I wanted to hear, but I wasn't sure if she was telling the truth.

"I mean it," she added with sincerity in her voice.

Warm relief spread through me, and I resisted the urge to hug her again.

"Grace, please don't tell the others about this," Jess said after a moment as we continued trudging through the bush.

"I think I should," I said slowly. "They should know, so everyone makes an effort."

"There isn't any real need," Jess said, shaking her head as she brushed her hand past a fir tree. "I don't want them to worry about me. Everyone has enough to think about without me adding to the pile."

"We care about you, and they will want to help," I said. "Trust me."

Jess looked embarrassed.

"No one will think of you any different if they find out. Inside we all feel like you," I explained honestly.

We broke through the trees into the clearing, and I paused as Lizzie came bounding up to us, leaving Dylan sitting by the tree. Lizzie noticed the tear streaks on my cheeks and gave me a small questioning look. I was sure she would ask me later.

"There you guys are, I've been wondering where you got to. I was going to make some lunch, but it would be good to have some help and Dylan isn't much use," Lizzie said and grinned.

"I heard that," Dylan called from the kauri tree, "I could cook better than you any day Lizzie."

Lizzie rolled her eyes as Jess and I sat down by the fire and began pulling out some pots and food from the shelter.

"Ungrateful sod," Lizzie muttered under her breath. Then, in a louder voice, "Spaghetti today."

The majority of us groaned, except for Dylan, who actually liked spaghetti, no matter how many times we had it. I kept one worried eye on Jess as we began cooking. Although she outwardly appeared happy, I wasn't fooled. It would take her months to feel any sort of normality to her life, but I hoped talking it over had helped.

"Hey Jess, can you go get some water from the stream for boiling? Then we can at least have some hot drinks," Lizzie said as she busied herself over the saucepan.

"Sure," Jess replied as she got to her feet, grabbing another saucepan. I watched her go, still concerned. Lizzie intercepted my look.

"What's the matter, Grace?" Lizzie asked. "What happened?"

"It's nothing, Lizzie," I said quickly, shaking my head and smiling faintly.

"Sure, nothing has you looking so flustered and bothered," Levi said as he came out of the shelter. He studied my face. Levi could read my expressions like a book.

"It's not my place to say," I said, suddenly realizing how difficult it was going to be.

"Don't be so touchy, we were worried is all. You keep looking at Jess like she's a twig about to snap," Lizzie said.

"Stop being such a bitch, Lizzie," Levi muttered.

"I'm not," Lizzie said hotly, looking at Dylan for support.

"Sometimes… what you say comes off a bit harsh," Dylan said delicately. Lizzie's face contorted into rage. I couldn't deal with another fight today.

"Well?" Lizzie turned to me, hands on her hips expectantly. "What's going on?"

I didn't reply. I couldn't keep this secret from the rest of them. It was too much for me to handle. Perhaps sharing the load would make everything more bearable.

"Can't you tell she's upset with whatever happened?" Levi said, trying to defend me.

"She can speak for herself, Levi," Lizzie argued.

Levi looked like he was about to say something nasty back, but I interrupted. "I found Jess with a gun," I said as I held up the rifle I had put behind the log. I handed it to Levi. That shut them up. They looked at me dumbly. "She was going to kill herself," I said with fresh tears beginning to fall. I wanted to melt into Levi just to feel some sort of comfort. The others sat in shocked silence. Levi put a hand on my shoulder.

"God," Levi uttered at last.

"Well… shit," Dylan said.

"I can't believe it," Lizzie said, shaking her head.

Jennifer sat silently next to Levi, too stunned to speak.

"I can," I said through tears. "Sometimes you want everything to stop." Levi stroked my back gently. I turned and sobbed into his shoulder.

After finally regaining composure, I turned to them again. "She didn't want you guys to know… but you needed to. I couldn't deal with it on my own. She can't live with it on her own," I said, trying to make excuses for my telling them.

"You did the right thing," Levi said.

Lizzie nodded, speechless.

"You have to act normal," I pleaded with them. "Please."

We all dropped into silence as Jess returned. Despite my pleading, they stared at her like she was a bomb about to explode.

"Lunch is ready," Lizzie said finally with an over-enthusiastic smile on her face. As if she had broken some spell, Jennifer pulled out plates, and everybody gushed into meaningless chatter.

Jess stopped the chatter immediately. "You told them, didn't you, Grace. It's been what… two minutes and you've already blabbed."

"I told you this was something everyone needs to deal with. It affects us all, and trust me, you will be grateful," I explained to her.

"We noticed something was wrong, and we were worried," Lizzie said. "Jess… we don't know how to react."

"I'm fine," Jess said, embarrassed. "Here's the water."

Lizzie took it and put it on to boil before grabbing the plate Jennifer handed her.

"'Fine' doesn't really match up with what Grace told us," Levi said sincerely. "Jess, you should have talked to us… we could have helped."

"Grace has already talked to me. And the only way you can help is by acting normal, please."

Levi relented and went back to his meal.

"I'll talk to you guys from now on," Jess said honestly.

Jennifer let out a muffled sob. "Please don't ever do it, Jess," Jennifer said as she threw her arms around Jess.

Jess' eyes moistened with fresh tears. "Don't worry Jennifer, I promised I won't," Jess replied as she hugged Jennifer back tightly.

OUR PLATES WERE EMPTY, and most of us had retired to bed, the day's events weighing heavily in our minds. The lights were out, and the forest was black. I sat outside in the cold on my own, a blanket pulled around my shoulders to keep out the chill. The stars sparkled through the trees above me. I remembered stargazing with my dad when we went camping. We would lie out in the night, and he would point out the different constellations. I felt tears stinging my eyes as I thought about him.

"That one's Orion," Levi said, coming up beside me and pointing to the sky. I smiled and brushed a tear from my cheek. He sat down next to me, at ease. I didn't say a word.

"Are you OK?" he asked softly, barely above a whisper.

I looked over at him. "Yeah... it's just a lot," I said and sighed.

"We're all here for you," he said with a look of concern blossoming over his face.

"Do you think he's up there?" I asked. I glanced upward again, trying to find comfort in the stars.

"Who?" Levi asked gently.

"My dad," I replied as more tears fell.

"I'm sure he's there," Levi said, trying to be comforting. He wrapped an arm around me, and we sat in silence for a while. Somehow Levi was able to calm me down and make me feel safe.

"I feel like death follows me, like I'm cursed," I said. I had often wondered this... why me? My family's deaths had hurt and left a gaping hole. Every death of someone I loved made the hurt heavier. There was something I hadn't admitted it to Jess. I was selfish in saving her. Saving her was another way to try and save me.

"You're not cursed. Bad things happen, and we have to figure out how to carry on," Levi said with so much logic it surprised me. "You're one of the strongest people I know."

"Lizzie's stronger," I replied instantly. "Her brother died in her arms." A purpling cloud floated past the moon, briefly darkening the night.

"Lizzie has no idea what you've been through," Levi continued. I didn't really believe what he said, but it did something to brighten my spirits. I was still moving forward, trying not to sink back into the depression I knew too well.

"Losing her brother is tragic, but losing your entire family is more than that. I can't believe you haven't crumbled into nothing during this war. Your mom is everything to you, and you don't know if she's alive."

I had never thought of myself as strong and still couldn't really see it. In my mind, Lizzie was the strong one, and I was the one who was barely holding it all together. I was coming apart at the seams but somehow stitching myself back up at the same time.

"You're going to get through this war, I can feel it," Levi said. I hoped he was right.

CHAPTER FOURTEEN

LIZZIE

I FELT GUILTY. IT was a bright late spring day, and light flitted happily through the trees onto the grassy hillock I was sitting on. The tense atmosphere after yesterday's events prompted my escape to a secluded patch of forest. That was the hardest part about living down here; despite the vastness of the bush, everything felt confined. A small disagreement would morph into a massive argument that inevitably ended in someone storming off. Admittedly, that's what I had done.

Firstly, I had snapped at Jess even though she was having difficulty after Leah's death. It was insensitive, but I was too stubborn to apologize. I thought she would get over it. Then I had upset Grace. It was easy to forget everything she had been through, and she was only trying to help. We had been friends for years, and she would forgive me. Despite knowing that, I still felt bad. Maybe Leah's death was affecting me more than I realized.

A long sigh escaped my lips as I leaned back into the grass, savoring the silence of self-reflection. I opened my eyes, rolled over onto my stomach and propped myself up on my elbows. Grace's laugh echoed through the bush. Levi's chuckle followed as I heard a splash of water and a shriek from Grace.

"Hey, stop it! You're not allowed to splash me," she said feigning annoyance, but her tone was playful. No matter how far away I tried to walk, it was never far enough. Quietly, I walked in the direction of Grace's laughter. From behind a tree, I could see them below me on the riverbank. I felt a bit bad for spying on them.

"I'm sorry, I didn't realize there were rules to sitting by the river," Levi said, grinning, and splashed Grace again.

"Well, there are… I just invented them," Grace said matter–of–factly.

"Please share these rules with me." Levi smirked at Grace, one eyebrow raised as he leaned back on his elbows, relaxed. His foot trailed in the water, ready to give Grace another lashing at not a moment's notice.

"The first rule is… you're not allowed to splash me. The second one is… I'm allowed to… splash you as much as I like." Grace laughed and kicked a torrent of water onto his face. Levi responded by playfully pushing her into the water. She plunged into the stream with a squeal.

"Hey, that's not fair," Grace said, standing up, annoyed.

"You only said that I couldn't splash you, you never said anything about pushing," Levi said. Grace sighed and began to climb the slippery bank. Levi obligingly helped her out. Upon reaching the top, Grace turned around and shoved Levi into the stream. Levi let out a surprised yell. Grace walked away triumphantly, ignoring Levi's shouts that followed her.

I laughed to myself seeing Levi standing sopping in the stream, watching Grace walk away. He clambered onto the bank and sat there. I couldn't quite understand their relationship. On the one hand, I was damn sure Grace liked him, but on the other, she seemed to be holding him at a distance. Levi had absolutely fallen for her. I hoped Grace would let him get close to her. He was a genuinely good guy, despite the persona he sometimes put on. She needed someone like him. Someone who was caring, down–to–earth, and protective. I saw the way he looked at her. At the moment, she was his world. If only she could see it, I thought.

Closing my eyes, I tried to regain a sense of self-awareness. It was something I hadn't been able to accomplish since this war started. I had no illusions as to why this was. I was far from being at peace with myself and even farther from being at peace with my surroundings.

My thoughts drifted to Dylan. What was I supposed to do? He was cute and sensitive, the total opposite of Ryan. Was I still with Ryan? No one knew the answer to this. I was so confused, and worried that the only reason I was attracted to Dylan was because he saved my life. But I did feel there was a connection between us, something instinctive. There was a sudden noise beside me, and hands grabbed tightly at my shoulders as I lay against the tree. Fear rose within, and I struggled blindly against my attacker, rolling madly in the grass, not wanting to open my eyes and see my own death staring me in the face.

"Lizzie," Dylan said and laughed as he rolled over with me and finally managed to pin me to the ground. "It's me, Lizzie." I opened my eyes to see Dylan grinning at me, and I felt anger boil up within me.

"Don't ever do that again!" I yelled at him, shoving him off me. Maybe he wasn't so sensitive after all.

"It was a joke," he said with a shrug.

"A pretty stupid one if you ask me." I turned to walk away.

"Wait," he said, grabbing my wrist, "...I'm really sorry."

"You better be," I said, trying to walk away.

He pulled me back.

"What?" I folded my arms, annoyed.

"I just want to talk."

"So talk to Levi."

"But I like talking to you." The wind blew his blond hair into his face. With a flick of his head, he moved it away. The light dazzled his face making his handsome blue eyes glimmer.

"Guys never want to talk," I said.

"Well… maybe I'm different."

Dylan was different. There was more to him than met the eye. He thought so deeply about things that somehow, I didn't mind talking to him.

"You're easy to talk to," I agreed, looking at him. "Ryan was terrible at talking and trying to work things out… it was frustrating."

Dylan briefly frowned at the mention of Ryan.

"To be honest, I was pretty bad before. The war—it's making us change. Leah made me realize how fast things can change. I guess I finally noticed that I had to treasure what I had left. Make the most of it. All I have left is you guys. Nothing else," he said, looking upward at the trees as if in a trance. He then brought his eyes down, staring into mine. In his eyes, I found a glimpse of the peace I had been searching for. My heart was pounding in my chest.

"I have five things. That's hardly anything, yet it is everything. For all I know, you could be gone tomorrow. What then? I would have wanted to spend more time with you, know you better," he said, looking directly at me. I couldn't come up with the words to respond. This guy was confusing my emotions with every word he uttered.

"You people here in the bush… you're all I have left to hold onto. It's you guys that will get me through the war. Not the guns, not brute strength, not bravery," he continued.

"I know what you mean," I said, finally managing to form a complete sentence. He continued as if he never heard me.

"If I had nothing to fight for, all the tanks and bombs in the world would do me no good. But, I have so much to fight for. I'd die to save you, Lizzie. I would die to save any one of the people here at the camp. If me dying meant they would live, I would do it in a heartbeat. I wouldn't even think twice," Dylan said. He looked on the verge of tears with the weight of the war on his shoulders. I completely understood where he was coming from. It wasn't the first time I had seen this side of Dylan. He had a deeper side to him no one else seemed to notice. "Don't you see? We are each other's reasons for staying and fighting. If we were here by ourselves, I can guarantee we wouldn't stand a chance," he said.

"What about hope? What about our families?" I asked him. He sat down against the tree.

"What about them?" he said with a shrug. "We only have five things. No matter what happens today, tomorrow, or the day after that, we have to treasure them. We can't see hope, we can't even see our family. Let's face it, Lizzie, we don't know if they are alive or dead. How can you fight with all your heart for something you can't touch or even truly believe is alive? We have no rules, no police, and no law. We have no photos for memories," Dylan said, his face charged with intensity. Everything he said rang true. There was nothing to hold onto except our ever-present dream of peace that hung from a single silk thread of hope and bound the six of us together for eternity. We were joined in a never-ending circle of fate. What happened to one of us, affected us all. Our lives were balanced precariously, dictated by the coming and going of soldiers, and by our own determination.

"Don't you see Lizzie, talking is good," he said and laughed.

"You're right," I said with a smile.

"This has to be a first. You finally admitted I was right. You never say that," Dylan said, his face relaxing.

"I guess all of us are changing," I said. Dylan laughed again and shook his head.

I sat down beside him. "I'm really sorry, I should have let you talk, I was rude and… and… inconsiderate."

"Hey, don't worry about it," Dylan said. "I shouldn't have scared you. It was uncalled for."

"It was a joke," I said, defending him. "I should have let it slide and laughed."

"No, it was my fault. We are at war. It was stupid. There was no need for me to creep up and scare you. I should have known better," he said quickly.

"It's fine."

"Wait, why is Levi sitting there all by himself?" Dylan asked curiously, "I thought he didn't like swimming," he said, noticing Levi's sopping clothes.

I laughed. "Levi was… being Levi."

"So, he fell in?" Dylan asked.

"Surprisingly, no," I said with another laugh, "Grace pushed him."

Dylan grinned. "I'm sure he deserved it."

"He sure did. They should get together already."

"I am not getting involved with this. It's their business," he said, raising his hands and backing away. "I don't mess with him, and in return, he doesn't bother me. We've had this pact for years, and I'm not breaking it now. Even for Grace."

"Oh, come on," I said playfully. Dylan shook his head and wandered back to camp. I was left alone again, watching his back melt into the bush.

The sky was darkening with the sun dipping behind the trees. Summer was getting closer. It was hot during the day, but still cool in the evening. As soon as the night's hand came over us, she blew a chilling wind. I pulled my jersey around me tightly and walked over to our makeshift tent. Jennifer was busy making a fire. She spat out orders for Levi and Dylan to find some firewood. Jess and Grace were carefully making dinner.

"We're going to try to make bread today," Jess said brightly.

"Oh," Levi said as he came through the bush carrying an armful of branches.

"Don't sound so skeptical," Jess said.

"I'm not touching it if Grace has any hand in making it," he said lightly.

Grace shot Levi an angry look. "I guess you won't be eating then."

"That's a relief," Levi commented, "I was worried I might end up dead from your cooking."

I watched in mild amusement. Grace gave an exasperated sigh and ignored him. There was a yell of triumph as Jennifer successfully lit the fire. It crackled into life.

"See, I can be useful," Jennifer said to Dylan.

"I never said you wouldn't be able to light the fire," he said in defense.

"You implied it, I saw the way you were looking at me," Jennifer accused him.

Grace opened a couple of cans of spaghetti, and she tipped them sloppily into a pot. I took it off her and put it on the fire to heat it up. Then she set to work making bread with Jess. I watched them work quickly but messily. Grace had flour all over the front of her clothes while Jess had wiped her flour-covered hands through her hair, leaving a hardening white smear.

"How are you going to cook it?" Dylan asked.

"Um… maybe I'll fry it," Grace said, flustered.

"When's the bread going to be done?" I asked as the spaghetti boiled furiously, tempting us to eat it.

"I'm not too sure," Jess said, "I didn't realize how difficult it is to make bread when you are roughing it."

"Maybe we should eat this first before it burns, and we can have your bread later," Jennifer suggested.

"That sounds like a good idea. That way at least something will be edible," Levi teased.

"All right," Jess said. Grace and Jess hurried to the stream to wash the dough off. I sat as close to the fire as I dared, trying to absorb every last ounce of heat from it. Dylan and Levi quickly found the plates and began to serve out our meal. I gratefully took a plate from Dylan and hungrily began to eat. Cozy warmth spread through me, dispelling the cold.

"You know," Jennifer said, "this is really nice."

"Yeah, the food today is really good," I replied.

"That's not what I mean. Today has been really nice. It seems like there is no war anymore. It feels like we are just camping, having fun."

"You're right," Jess and Grace said together as they took a place around the fire, shivering from the cold.

"How about you, Lizzie? You've been really quiet all day," Jennifer noted with concern.

"I've been doing a lot of thinking," I said. She nodded absent-mindedly. Too much thinking was something we were all used to lately. We sat in silence, finishing our meal. Soon Jess and Grace were back to making their bread, and an hour later, we all had a steaming slab of unleavened bread, that was only a little charred.

Levi looked at his, trying to decide whether it was fit to eat or not. "Is this safe?" he asked. Grace and Jess ignored him. I hesitantly took a bite. The scalding bread burned my tongue, but I was surprised to find that despite the saltiness and slightly burnt flavor, it was pretty delicious.

"What do you think?" Grace asked eagerly.

"It's not bad if we forget about the burnt taste," I said.

"See Levi, we can cook," Grace exclaimed. He shrugged.

After finishing our bread, we all sat back in comfortable silence, full bellies and sleepy from the food.

"We're going to bed," Grace and Jennifer announced as they stood up and walked away. Jess, Levi, and Dylan went off to the shelter a few moments later. I was left alone.

The fire had died to just a few embers. I found a thin branch and let it sit in the glowing embers. The tip quickly caught alight. I sat there, letting it burn. I lifted my twig from the fire. The flame slowly burned down the stick. Right before it reached my fingers, I blew it out. Poof, it was gone. The smoke trailed heavily from the tip, wafting higher and higher in delicate spirals, out of sight. The glowing tip became fainter before disappearing completely. I sat quietly by myself in the darkness before pouring a bucket of water onto the embers. With a quiet hiss, the fire was gone. A plume of smoke rose to the air and then all was quiet. So quiet.

Chapter Fifteen

Jennifer

I THOUGHT THE DARKNESS in the prison camp was bad. My new life in the forest made me realize the pitch black of the bush was worse. In prison, the presence of soldiers was a known fact, and as long as you obeyed, you were safe. Here, I felt they could be hiding behind any tree, or sneaking up on us unawares to shoot us in our sleep.

The nightmares weren't helping either. Multiple times a night, I would wake up, drenched in sweat having relived Evee's death again. This is what had just happened. The shelter was filled with the soft rhythmic breathing of the others, and Jess' quiet tears.

I sat up and listened to the pitter-pattering of rain on the roof. Rain again, I thought sadly. It seemed there was no end to it. I had always hated spring. Back before the war, spring meant unpredictable rainy weather and exams. Now, forever, it would mean war.

The rain soon turned into a heavy downpour, and I watched as the middle of the tarp shelter sagged with a puddle of water.

My eyes were still heavy, but once again, my mind was startlingly alert and conscious. I had barely slept in the few days since escaping. Frustrated, I got up and crawled outside. I needed to be alone. The rain was cold, but I ignored it. I picked up a spare cup and made my way over to the stream to get a drink of water. I looked up at the grumbling sky.

"They'll be all right. In heaven somewhere." I tried to reassure myself, but to me, it was a lie people used when they didn't want to face the truth—I was never going to see Leah or Evee again. Even now, when I wanted to believe in God for the sake of them, the logical side of my mind pointed out there was still no solid proof that he existed, and to believe, I needed facts. I dipped my cup into the stream and let the cool water run down my throat, and made my way back to the shelter. I found some spare dry clothes at the foot of my sleeping bag and quickly got changed. They smelt earthy, mixed with a slight flowery perfume. They were definitely Leah's clothes, I thought.

I snuggled back into my sleeping bag and took my place next to Jess, who was still curled up against the wall crying. Though she seemed much better, she still cried in the night, when she thought no one was looking. I didn't know whether she wanted to talk about it or be left alone. For now, I would leave her alone.

I desperately wanted to talk to her, though. We were probably the only two people in this group who really understood the pain each other was going through. I was closer than anyone to Evee, and she and Leah were childhood best friends. Of course, the people who we had just met had known Leah for a brief moment. But none of them knew Evee, and none of them knew Leah as she had been before the war began, so their deaths were merely a shock; an unpleasant experience in their lives they would soon be able to force from their minds. Fresh tears sprang up as memories of Evee flooded back. I closed my eyes and let the warm tears slip down my cheeks. The rain pattered soothingly on the tarpaulin and eventually lulled me to sleep.

I awoke in the morning to the happy chirruping of fantails. Apparently, the birds didn't give a toss about what we had been through. I looked over and saw that Jess' bed was empty. In fact, everyone was gone. Somehow, I had managed to sleep. I pulled a jumper over my head and crawled outside. The rain had cleared, and the early morning sun peeked through wispy clouds painted on the blue sky. I was relieved to see Jess sitting with the others, a mug of coffee in hand, sipping it with a tear-free face. She wasn't exactly smiling, but this was a start. I breathed in the damp morning air and felt invigorated. It was amazing what a few hours of nightmare free sleep could do. Already the thought of Evee had crossed my mind, but I let it pass without tearing up. Baby steps, I thought. Lizzie pushed a cup of coffee into my hands. I gratefully accepted it.

"Morning," she said.

"This one isn't spiked, is it?" I asked suspiciously.

She let out a brief laugh and shook her head, her blond hair twinkling in the morning sun. "It's much too early for that," she said.

Lizzie seemed nice but intense. I expected that losing her brother the way she had, had changed her. She was passionate and wore it on her sleeve. Already, I got the impression she wasn't going to sit idly and let this war pass her by. Dylan sat next to her. He was obviously into her. It was clear by the way he looked at her, and how he was always jostling to be by her side. I couldn't tell how Lizzie felt about him. She seemed wary and held him at a distance. I couldn't understand why. He seemed almost perfect to me—muscular and blond with a smile of perfect teeth. I could tell the kind of guy he was... or used to be: the center of attention. Who knows how the war had changed him?

My gaze moved onto Levi, who leaned back against a log, mug of coffee in hand, joking with Dylan. Levi was a bit of a goof, but a good-looking one. His brown hair was unkempt, which matched his easy-going attitude. He didn't seem too bothered by anything, except Grace. He had absolutely fallen for her. Their non-relationship was so intense it was even hard to handle as an outsider.

"Do you think you could eat something now?" Grace asked me, interrupting my thoughts and searching my eyes with her warm and pleasant brown ones. I shrugged helplessly and ate a few spoonfuls of the porridge they had concocted. Grace was the friendliest of them all. She had an earnest smile and tried to make me feel welcome. Despite her cheerful persona, I could see the darkness in her. Even in the short time I had been here, glimpses of her broken soul seeped through cracks in her bright exterior. Levi seemed perfect for her. He was a rock she could ground herself on. Something had happened in her past. Something that ran deeper than this war.

I was suffering too. This war had taken a toll, and there was no one to mend my cracks. But the morning sun brought hope, and so far, the darkness within had been warded away by food and tea. Breakfast wound to an end, and the others wandered away from the fire pit. I was left alone and found my thoughts wandering back to the prison camp.

The others hadn't asked me about it yet, but I assumed the questioning would start at some point. When the time came, there wouldn't be a lot to tell. No, I didn't know what was going on. Our guards were very tight-lipped about that. Unsurprisingly, the soldiers were bloodthirsty and ruthless. Disobedience was dealt with swiftly. A bullet to the back of the head took care of troublemakers.

At the start, there were a few groups dedicated to an uprising. They quietly spread orders through the hordes of us civilians packed into the small confines of the stores. The braver ones even managed to get the word out to other cells. How they managed it, I would never know. But soon, the soldiers became aware of the plot. They used fear to weed out the leaders of the uprising who were executed in front of the whole camp. This was the end of our resistance and the acceptance of submission.

After a few days, the camp was full to bursting. Families had been split up to help with our obedience. I shared my new cell, an old children's clothing store, with about eighty other people. There was hardly room to sit, let alone lie down to sleep. It was there that I found Evee.

We tempered our initial joy at meeting up again—we were afraid the soldiers would separate us. Our conversations were held in whispers when the guards weren't looking. Soon, word spread among the prisoners that our cell, and a few others, were going to be split, and we were to be moved to nearby camps to ease the load. I couldn't be alone again. Evee and I tried to plot a way to stay together. But we were too heavily guarded, and the whole mall was constantly patrolled.

That evening, a group of us were escorted to the bathrooms. On the way, a small band of resisters tried to attack our guards. A small fight broke out. The resisters were killed quickly, but it gave Evee and me enough time to slip away from the group. We found an empty janitor's closet that we hid in for the first couple of hours. It felt like we had been handed a miracle, a chance to stay together.

Once darkness fell, we crept from our hiding place, dodged the guards, and found a store that had recently been emptied. That was where we had been hiding when the others found us. When they showed up, heroic and free, it felt like God was intervening. He had sent them to help us escape.

As it turned out, none of it was divine. It was all coincidence, and I wasn't sure if I made the right choice. Yes, I was free. But at the moment, it wasn't worth it. All Evee and I wanted was to stay together. That dream was now in tatters, Evee was dead, and I was more alone than before.

The overwhelming grief at losing her came over me again. I

crept back into the shelter and lay back, exhausted. My body was tired, I needed sleep. But my mind wasn't finished working yet. It continued to try and comprehend the events recently passed, trying to force everything into a logical pattern.

"It wasn't my fault, it wasn't anyone's fault," I whispered to my mind stubbornly. I closed my eyes, and my mind drifted to the what-ifs. What if the war had never broken out over New Zealand? No doubt I would be staying up late at Evee's house watching a movie. It seemed impossible that those times could end. But already, they seemed like a lifetime ago. Evee's smiling face flashed in my mind, and then I saw her slumped form on the floor of the mall, her blood pooling on the cold tiles.

I couldn't breathe again.

Wrenching gasps made my whole body shudder. Then I heard whimpering and recognized it as my own voice. Finally, tears flowed silently and unabatedly down my face. She was gone.

Chapter Sixteen

Grace

STRESS AND HUNGER GNAWED at my stomach as I studied our ever-dwindling pile of food in the corner of our shelter. Only a scant amount remained, perhaps enough for one meal.

"Lizzie, can you come help me make some dinner?" I called. Lizzie, Dylan, and Levi were sitting in a circle around the campfire, perched on some small logs Dylan and Levi had hauled into a semi-circle only this morning.

"Sure, coming," Lizzie called back, standing up. Jennifer and Jess were playing a game of cards. I remembered impulsively grabbing them from the house we'd raided back before we lost Leah. Sadness creeped behind my eyes as I thought of the last time we played them together—the night Leah died.

"There's not much here, Grace," Lizzie said, sighing as she approached our stack of food.

"I know." It didn't seem to matter how much we rationed ourselves. It all disappeared so fast.

No one wanted to admit it, but since Leah and Evee died, we had been procrastinating about our next trip, not wanting to leave the safety of the bush.

"I was thinking we could cook up what's left of the rice with…"

"With what?" Lizzie commented dourly. "Spaghetti?"

"Yes. Spaghetti. There isn't anything else."

Lizzie sighed. "We need to go get more food."

"Maybe we could go tomorrow night," I said.

"I meant tonight, Grace. There is nothing left. What are we meant to eat tomorrow?"

I shrugged, pouring the rice into the pot of water I had already taken from the stream.

Lizzie opened the can of spaghetti and dumped the contents unceremoniously into another pot. "Come on, we'll take these over to the fire and cook them."

I followed her to the fire and put the pot over it, waiting for it to boil.

"Low on food?" Levi asked, glancing at the hodgepodge dinner.

"We're completely out," Lizzie informed him as she stirred the spaghetti. "We need to go get some more… tonight."

Dylan grunted while Levi didn't say anything.

"So, who's going?" I asked. Steam was slowly beginning to rise from the water, curling upward. No one was keen to volunteer.

Lizzie huffed to herself. "I will. I'm not going to starve tomorrow, even if everyone else seems to be fine with it."

"I'll join you, Lizzie," I said. The only thing sitting in my stomach at the moment was guilt, because Lizzie was right. We needed food, it was as simple as that. But seeing Leah die had awoken me to the fragility of our situation. The initial shock and disbelief were followed by a gaping hole that still hadn't healed. And I was reminded again that death can happen to anyone, at any time. Since the accident, I learned the only way to move on was to accept that life is dangerous. Things happen. We could stay here in the bush and hide, but eventually, we would have to leave, and chance it out there.

"Grace, your pot is nearly over-boiling," Levi said, pointing.

"Oh no!" I cried out as the boiling water surged over the edge and scalded my fingers where I was holding the pot. I withdrew them quickly, dropping the whole thing into the flames.

Levi caught the handle from me and lifted the pot from the fire. "You should pay attention, Grace," he said. "Otherwise, I'll lose my 'world's clumsiest' title."

"That's not fair, I'm trying my best," I said. Levi just kept grinning in his goofy way, and I finally cracked a smile. It was hard to stay angry with him. "Are you coming with Lizzie and me?"

"I think we should all go," Levi said, his eyes meeting the others'. "If we do it in two groups, we should be able to get enough food between us to last a while, and it won't take as long."

Lizzie nodded in agreement with him. "Good idea."

Jennifer and Jess packed up the cards in the shelter, and came and joined us. Jennifer looked anxious. I wondered what it must be like for her, going out into the open for the first time since escaping the prison camp. Jess looked calm, like she had found the same stage of acceptance I had—what would happen would happen.

Lizzie served up the spaghetti while I took the pot back from Levi and drained the rice using a sieve we had stolen.

"Dinner is served," I announced as I added the rice to the plates. It didn't look very appetizing. Maybe the small servings were a good thing, I thought. My stomach was somersaulting as it always did before going out, and I picked at my food. Silence hung over our group as we ate.

"We'll leave at ten," Lizzie said. She looked the most relaxed out of all of us, sitting casually cross-legged and leaning back against the log. Unlike me, she didn't have a problem wolfing down her meal. I didn't know where she got her confidence. I looked at my watch. There were still two hours before we could leave, but I stayed awake while the others tried to get some rest. I was too anxious to get any sleep. A light breeze ruffled the forest, and I savored the peace of the night. Even though we were in a war, down here in our little haven, I could still relax. It wasn't going to be the same out there. Ten minutes later, Levi emerged from the shelter. I glanced up at him.

"Can't sleep," he said, and smothered a yawn with his hand.

"I know what you mean." We sat next to each other in companionable silence.

"Are you nervous?" he asked.

"About going back topside? Yeah," I said with a sigh. "Sometimes I wish we could hide down here forever."

"But we can't."

"I know that."

"I think it will be good to get out of here for a bit. Maybe everyone will be less shitty," Levi said with a smirk. I caught his eye. There had been a lot of arguments recently, which made the forest seem cramped.

"Let's hope it all goes smoothly."

AT TEN P.M. WE assembled underneath the awning of the shelter.

"We need to split," Dylan said. Jennifer and Jess automatically moved toward each other. They were becoming increasingly good friends, and I knew we could rely on them as a team.

"I'll go with Grace and Lizzie," Levi said to Dylan.

Dylan made to argue but gave in and shrugged. Evidently, he was disappointed. His eyes lingered on Lizzie for a moment. "Then I guess I'm with Jess and Jennifer."

"OK then, it's sorted," Lizzie agreed, "Levi, Grace, and I will head up toward Pyes Pa, and you three can go up the track toward Omanawa." Lizzie seemed completely oblivious to the situation that had just unfolded. Levi caught my eye and winked. I shook my head and looked away. Somehow, he always managed to make light of these serious situations.

"What's the matter?" Lizzie asked Dylan, who was still sulking about the teams.

"Nothing," he muttered unconvincingly. Dylan hesitated and then decided to say something after all. "Well, it's just that—"

"Let's roll out then," Levi butted in before Dylan could say any more. I jabbed Levi with my elbow. "Ouch, Grace, watch it," Levi said with a chuckle.

Levi took off in the lead, a few yards ahead of Lizzie and me. By now, we were all familiar with both tracks that led out of our clearing, though the rest of the region still remained an unmapped mystery to me. It took us several hours to make it out of the bush and into the open space that was near Lizzie's old home.

"Where do we go this time?" Levi asked.

"Toward the gravel on Taumata Road," Lizzie directed. Levi obligingly set off, while Lizzie and I hung back and talked.

"Dylan's really into you," I whispered to her.

"No way," she said, shaking her head vigorously.

"Come on now, you must have noticed."

"Noticed what?"

"You're impossible."

"Look, I don't know what to think, OK?" she said.

"You should go for it," I said to her. That set her off.

She rounded on me. "I don't know how to feel about him, Grace," she said furiously. A look of confusion passed by her face, and I knew she was thinking of Ryan. As far as I was concerned, Ryan was a part of the past. Lizzie had to move on from him, and sometimes she needed a push.

"You're being stubborn, Lizzie. I can tell."

"This isn't being stubborn. It's being realistic, Grace. There's a difference," Lizzie replied. "You daydream too much."

I snorted and didn't reply. There was no point in talking about it anymore. Maybe she did need more time to see what was so obvious to me.

"But, you're right about one thing," Lizzie whispered after a moment's thoughtful silence. "Perhaps next time we split it should be in three groups. I feel like a third wheel. You should go talk to Levi," Lizzie urged me, giving me a small push forward.

"I don't need any encouragement," I snapped back.

Just then, Levi turned around. "Were you two talking about me?" he said with a grin.

"Oh, no, you misheard," I said, feigning confusion.

"Actually," Lizzie began with a mischievous gleam in her eye, "Grace was saying how impressed she was with you in this war." She smiled innocently.

"Oh," Levi said, a little awkwardly, but pleased all the same. "Thanks." Levi turned around and carried on, his chest puffed up with a little extra importance, staring suspiciously around. Alert.

"You didn't have to say that, Lizzie," I said. "His head is big enough already," I added under my breath.

Lizzie sniggered. "Come on, Grace, you like him, and you know he likes you too... did you see how proud he was when you complimented him?"

"You complimented him, not me."

"Whatever. You guys should get together already," Lizzie said, shrugging. Somehow it seemed she had successfully steered the conversation off herself and onto me. I was saved answering by our timely arrival at a house we hadn't yet raided. Levi called us to a stop, and Lizzie thankfully stopped talking.

"We'll check around the house, see if anyone's inside... the usual drill. Lizzie, you take that direction, Grace and I will go the other way. Check all the windows," he instructed.

Lizzie ducked off in the direction Levi had pointed and began checking windows on the side of the house. Levi peered through a dusty window next to us. "Stay behind me," he said, with military-like authority.

"Typical," I muttered quietly to myself. The compliment had gone straight to his head.

"Did you say something?" Levi asked.

"Nothing," I replied. He didn't look as if he believed me, and I decided to play on what Lizzie had started.

"I'm scared," I said, casting my eyes down. "What if someone's in there?"

"It will be fine, Grace," Levi said. "I promise." He touched my shoulder in a comforting way, and I felt guilty. Levi was genuinely concerned about me and wanted to help, while I watched him make a fool of himself. Clearly, I was the fool, not him.

"Thanks," I said, sincerely this time. We crept around the side of the house, and I stepped up onto a porch, quietly inching toward the window. I peeked in. There was nothing, and I breathed a sigh of relief. It seemed the house was completely empty. We were safe.

Lizzie joined us around the back of the house.

"Did you find anything?" Levi whispered.

Lizzie shook her head. "There's no one in there."

"Good. We make this quick, go in, get the food, and leave back toward the bush," Levi whispered. Lizzie and I nodded. The backdoor was unlocked, so Levi creaked it open, and we crept inside. I still couldn't shake the feeling that I was stealing. It felt wrong, going into other people's houses and taking their food.

"Do you think this is considered stealing?" I voiced my concerns.

"There's no other choice," Lizzie commented.

"I know,' I said with a sigh.

The crunching of tires on the gravel driveway cut through the night. A vehicle was approaching.

"Hide," Lizzie mouthed. Lizzie squirmed into the linen

cupboard in the hallway, and I jumped straight into the walk-in pantry, squeezing myself underneath the bottom shelf. I watched Levi's feet move unsurely in one direction, and then in another, trying to find a decent hiding place.

"In here," I whispered at him. He followed my voice, joining me and closing the door behind him. He squeezed under the shelf with me. The vehicle engine cut into silence. Maybe they'd stopped for a break and would continue on soon? We heard the slamming of doors, and my hopes were dashed as footsteps pounded on the front porch. My heart slammed against my ribcage as I tried to stay silent. Levi obviously felt my nervousness and put a calming hand over mine. It didn't make me feel any better, but I appreciated the gesture.

"Come on Grayson, you're being stupid. What the hell is all this about anyway?" I heard a man ask.

"Are they soldiers?" I mouthed at Levi. He shrugged.

"Carter, shut up," the other man said. "I want to be sure we are alone."

There was a snort of annoyance from Carter. "We haven't exactly been quiet. Anyone here would have been scared off already. The house is empty. Tell me what you want to say. I have to be somewhere in"—Carter paused—"exactly an hour or I get my ass kicked. And it takes bloody ages to drive back to headquarters from this far out."

"Fine. I'll be quick."

"Spit it out."

Grayson paused, like he was trying to find the right words. "When all this started, the orders from up top were confine, contain, control. It sounded… simple and harmless. But it's not like that. Not anymore. The guys at the top… they're not on the frontlines, they don't see what we see."

Carter shuffled on the spot. "And what's that, Grayson?"

"I hate what we've done to our country. To our own people. I hate myself, more than anything. But it's not our fault. We have to do what we're ordered, and it's all coming from the top. Marion called it a state of emergency. But that's only pretense. He's launched full-scale civil war."

"It's not a civil war, you know what it is. We had to restrain the public to prevent—"

"—a revolution from occurring. I know Carter. But isn't it strange that Marion would go to such extreme lengths just because of some riots?"

"You think anyone else could have done better? Marion did what he needed to maintain order. I hate to think of what would have happened if he didn't step in when he did."

"He didn't have to use violence to control the people," Grayson argued.

Carter laughed. "Next time an angry mob's charging you down, try talking to them. We'll see how far it gets you."

"So, you believe him, then? You think this is right?" Grayson said. He sounded close to defeat.

"And you don't?" Carter answered. I could hear him pacing now, a heavy noise as his boots hit the wood floor in the kitchen. Thud, thud, thud.

Confusion clouded my thoughts. I heard what the men were saying, but my mind didn't want to put the pieces together. It was easy to blame this war on some foreign power because it was what we wanted to hear. The alternative… no one wanted to think about it. Civil war wasn't something that happened these days. Not here. Civil war was for poor countries. Countries with civil unrest. Countries with hardship. Countries… like ours.

So, this was what it had come to. The pandemic ruined us. And Marion wanted to destroy what was left. Beside me, Levi had seemingly come to the same conclusion and was shaking with silent anger, a scowl on his face.

"I know there's good in you, Carter. When you saved—"

"That was a mistake. I know that now," Carter interrupted him.

"What they did to you—"

"They put me in my place. I was wrong, before," Carter said. But the confidence in his voice was waning.

"You weren't wrong, Carter," Grayson said, quietly. "Marion isn't the good guy he claims to be. He's turning us against each other."

"Don't make me do this, Grayson. We've been friends for too long." Carter pleaded, close to tears. "You don't understand. If they find out, you'll be OK. But I've already got a black strike against me. It'll be worse for me than you, and I can't go through that again."

"Marion's a traitor," Grayson said.

"That all depends on where you stand," Carter said. Thud, thud, silence. Then there was a clicking noise. I drew in my breath as I recognized what it was. It was the noise of death. The beginning of the end.

Two deafening cracks echoed through the house. The shots were followed by someone crying. I thought it was Grayson, but it was Carter's voice that came next, thick with tears. "I'm sorry," he said before he walked away. Thud, thud, thud. They weren't just any boots. They were army boots, worn by a soldier. And the soldiers weren't foreign, as we'd first supposed.

Once Carter's boots faded into silence, Levi burst from the pantry and ran up to Grayson, who was sitting clutching his abdomen and bleeding out onto the floor. If Grayson was surprised to see us, he didn't show it. Levi stood in front of him, unsure of what to do.

"You can't help me," Grayson said shakily. "Get out of here. He might come back."

I grabbed a dusty tea towel from the kitchen and tried to compress his wound, but it was useless. The blood quickly soaked through the towel and oozed between my fingers. Grayson's hardened face began to pale.

Lizzie came charging out from her hiding place and crouched

next to Grayson. "What's going on in this war?"

Grayson shook his head weakly.

"Please... tell us something. Where is everyone?" Lizzie urged.

Grayson stared up at us, his chest heaving, trying to get air. "There's a warehouse." I kept my hands pressed firmly over his wounds, in vain. "In the industrial sector." His failing body racked with effort. Blood trickled out the side of his mouth. "They have the records." His voice was faint, and his eyes began to droop shut, his head lolling forward. Levi helped ease him to the floor.

"Why is this happening?" Lizzie asked desperately.

But Grayson couldn't answer. His skin looked gray, and his breathing was coming in periodic gasps. When his moment came, it wasn't that he stopped breathing, but rather, he never started again.

I looked up at Levi and Lizzie. "I think he's dead," I said, letting the blood-soaked towel fall to the floor. Shock was beginning to set in, and all I felt was a peculiar numbness. I wiped my bloodied hands on my jeans and stood up shakily. Lizzie, Levi, and I looked around at each other, processing what we had learned. We'd been attacked by the man we'd elected to represent us. Our land, our blood, our war.

Chapter Seventeen

Dylan

I STOOD WAIST-DEEP in the cool flowing stream by our camp in my boxers, lathering shampoo through my hair. The mid-afternoon sun beamed down onto my exposed back, taking some of the chill away. The low whistle of a kōkako echoed through the trees as it bounced from branch to branch. It was peaceful down here.

A few days had passed since we had gone to get food, and my initial outrage at the Prime Minister had been fierce. But eventually, it subsided, and I shut myself away in silence. We all had. It was unnatural for us. Usually, the camp hummed with incessant chatter as we passed the time reading books and playing cards. Instead, everyone sulked and took time alone to process what we had learned.

The realization that no one was coming to help was crushing. I had been holding out hope someone would come and pull us out of this horror, but that dream was now dead. Our own army was on the wrong side, fighting against the citizens, not for them. How could they do this to us? It was traitorous and cowardly. After the pandemic, we trusted them implicitly. Now, they imprisoned and murdered their own people. Fresh anger boiled within me, and I punched the water with all the strength I could summon.

"We have to go back up to the camp soon. They'll be wondering where we are," Levi said, disrupting my thoughts. I had forgotten he was there.

"Mm," I grunted. I rinsed my hair and shook out some droplets that were running down my neck. Levi and I made our way to the stream bank and grabbed our towels, drying off the cool water. I pulled my t-shirt over my head and stepped into a pair of sweatpants. Then we wandered back up to the camp.

"Oh, there you are," Jess called to us. "How was the stream?" she asked when she noticed our wet hair.

"Freezing," Levi replied grumpily.

"You'd better come in. We've been waiting for you," Jess said, and we followed her into the shelter. The girls were sitting in a circle, chatting.

"You're back," Grace said, looking over her shoulder at me and Levi. I squeezed into the circle next to Lizzie.

"We need a plan," Lizzie said, getting right down to business. She was hot-headed and determined to fight. This wasn't the first time she'd brought up getting back at the soldiers. Lizzie looked around at everyone expectantly, waiting for an answer. None came.

"I'm thinking you already have one," Levi said.

"If no one else has thought of one… then, yes," she said. "I'm going to save my parents."

"We all know what happened when you tried to rescue me," Jennifer said pointedly.

Lizzie bit her lip to hold back her anger, and she seethed silently. It was a tense moment. No one spoke. Thoughts of Leah and Evee haunted all of us.

"I suppose you would rather do nothing," Lizzie said at last, unable to contain her frustration.

"Last time we went out there," Jennifer said, pointing dramatically toward the city, "people died!"

"Well, what would you prefer, Jennifer? To sit here while they kill our families and friends? You're unbelievable," Lizzie scoffed.

"We're no good to anyone dead, are we?" Jennifer said, folding her arms and surveying us like we were naughty children. The fact that she was the youngest of us almost made it comical. That was, if it hadn't felt so condescending. She had been out of the prison camp for all of five minutes and was already telling everyone what to do.

"We're no good to anyone if we sit here doing nothing like cowards either," I spat, glaring at her. That struck a nerve. Jennifer shut up and seemed to be on the verge of tears.

"Nice going," Jess said sarcastically.

Grace flashed me a harsh look as Jennifer stood up to leave.

"Wait!" I grabbed at her wrist. "That was uncalled for... I'm sorry."

She looked back at me, clearly hurt by what I had said. "When you guys decide what to do, come and get me." With that, she strode out of the shelter and disappeared. We could hear her walking through the bush before she was out of earshot.

"Dylan, Lizzie, what's wrong with you?" Grace scolded.

"I don't know. Why does she get special treatment? All of us are worried, but we know we can't stay here and do nothing. Does she even get it?" Lizzie asked.

"She hasn't been here very long. And she watched her best friend die. Have a little compassion," Grace said in her defense.

"Maybe you should stay behind with her," Lizzie said under her breath.

"Look, I know you want to help. We all do. But some of us take a little bit longer to come around to the idea," Grace said, ignoring Lizzie's nasty comment. I was about to jump to Lizzie's defense.

"Just leave it," Levi muttered aside to me. I sighed and grumbled under my breath. I knew he was right.

"I still think that despite the danger, we should do something. What was your plan, Lizzie?" I said.

"I agree we need to do something too," Grace said carefully, looking at Lizzie.

"All we need to do is break into the warehouse the soldier told us about, find their records, and figure out where everyone is," Lizzie said. "Then stage a breakout."

"One step at a time," Levi said.

"We need to find the warehouse first," Jess said. "The industrial section of town is huge."

"Let's scout it out. If we find it, and it looks easy enough to break into, we can make the decision then," Grace said. Her eyes went glassy with unshed tears. "I really want to know if Mom's alive. Actually, I'm pretty sure we all want to know about our families."

"Let's go tonight," Lizzie said.

A wave of emotion rose within me. I purposefully hadn't thought about my parents and Rosie for a while. Every time a memory of them crept into my mind, I pushed it away. It was too painful to think about. If all went to plan, we would know what happened to them tonight. Was I ready to know? Not knowing allowed me to believe they were still alive, and still OK.

"I'll go tell Jen," Jess said as she stood up and left the shelter.

Meanwhile, I ducked out to get some air. I sat down in the clearing near our campsite. A butterfly flittering along caught my eye. It bobbed up and down in the breeze. When a particularly strong gust surged through the bush, it was blown, tumbling back. For a moment, it was stuck in midair, flapping madly to try and move forward. But the wind was too strong and it was flung backward, swirling out of sight.

The butterfly was like us, I thought. We were living normal lives until the war broke out and sent our reality spinning into chaos. For a little while, we managed to get back some control, but now, we had been thrown a wild pitch.

I caught sight of the butterfly again. It fluttered past me, and into the safety of the trees. Was this a sign of hope? Perhaps it was telling me that no matter what, we had to take our lives back. It was a scary thought. It meant charging into certain danger. All we had to do was take a hesitant step into the unknown. Was that so hard? Sitting here in the safety of our camp, it didn't sound difficult. It was only a step forward, after all. I was beginning to realize there are moments when running and hiding is acceptable. But sometimes, to stand up for yourself, you have to fight. Now was one of those times.

"Dylan," Jess said from behind me, "Jennifer's going to come. Do you have a problem with that?"

"No, I don't have a problem with that. Why would you think that?"

"Judging by how you reacted, I got the feeling you didn't like her," Jess said.

"It's nothing like that."

"Well then, what is it?"

"She has to learn to pull her weight around here. We know she misses Leah and Evee. But missing them doesn't mean she should cower away. If Jennifer is going to stay with us, she has to be willing to put her life on the line. If not… she should leave," I said.

"That's a bit harsh, isn't it?"

"Our lives are at risk. We fight for each other. Either she pitches in, or she can get out."

Jess looked shocked at my blunt response. But it was the truth. I refused to support someone who didn't support us.

"We make decisions as a group and execute them as a group. We can't have a tag-along who only helps when it's convenient for her," I added.

"That makes sense, but you didn't have to be horrible about

it," Jess said.

"I'm not apologizing. It was her fault too."

IT WASN'T LONG BEFORE the sun started to dip below the horizon. We were all dressed in black and milling impatiently around the clearing.

"It's go time," Levi said, checking his watch. "SEAL team six, move out," he said with a cheeky smirk.

Lizzie sighed at him. "Stop goofing around, Levi. This is serious."

Levi ignored her and led the way with Grace following him close behind. We aimed to reach the edge of the forest by nightfall to give us the maximum amount of time snooping. I lagged behind a bit, reluctant to leave the safety of our camp. Although I never mentioned it to the others, the crushing weight of my anxiety was back. As our departure to the city loomed, the nausea returned. I wiped the sweat from my brow and unzipped my jumper. Despite the cool dusk air, I was suffocatingly hot.

Finally, I made to follow them, but Jess pulled me up, and we trailed the others at a small distance. I wanted to yell at her to leave me alone, but I managed to maintain control.

"You should apologize," Jess whispered. I wasn't in the mood for a lecture from her.

"Drop it, Jess," I said, giving her a warning look.

Jess looked indignantly at me before storming off. I watched her push her way to the front. Now, my eyes were fixed on Jennifer, who walked alone in front of me. I did feel sorry for her, I thought. After an hour of trudging through the bush behind her, I couldn't take it anymore. What if something went wrong? Now was not the time for fighting.

"Screw it," I said to myself. Despite how I felt about her, I should apologize.

"Jennifer." I jogged to catch up to her.

"What?" she huffed.

"I wanted to apologize," I said, trying to put as much emotion into my voice to sound genuine. I knew it was an empty apology, but it would make me feel better. Selfish prick, I thought.

"I'm not going to forgive you," she replied, averting her eyes from mine, and quickening her pace.

"At least try," I said, trying to mask my annoyance as I ran to keep up.

"Fine," she said, and looked at me expectantly.

"I understand why you want to avoid going out. It's dangerous and bloody terrifying. But the truth is, eventually, you will have to go. I want you to be prepared." Stony silence greeted me. I was terrible at apologies. "Regardless, I shouldn't have spoken to you like that, but... we are all stressed. Small things annoy us," I added.

Jennifer examined me critically. "...Thanks for trying to apologize. I appreciate it," she answered robotically before walking away. I hung back a bit to tail the group, and Levi dropped back to chat. I noted the rifle slung over his shoulder, the dark clothes and the brave face. How had our lives come to this?

"You look like you're going paintballing," I said.

Levi let out a weak laugh. "You're the funny guy now, eh?" Levi said with a playful elbow to my ribs.

"Apparently."

"How did your apology go?" he asked, smirking.

"Just fine."

"So, she's still pissed then?"

"Basically," I said and laughed.

Levi rolled his eyes. "I'm not surprised."

"The road must be close," I said.

Already, the dense bush was thinning, and I could just make out the clean lines of the road. We skirted it, sticking to the safety of the trees. Eventually, the dark silhouette of the city was visible.

"Here goes, guys," Jess whispered.

I took a deep breath and forced myself to walk forward. One step forward into the unknown. Lizzie caught my eye and flashed me a secret smile before I followed her stealthily into the bleak city ahead. No lights blinked from the windows, while the streets were dead and dark. A breeze whispered between the buildings, bringing with it a feeling of foreboding that I couldn't shake. I looked at my feet and saw a dark stain that hadn't been cleaned off the street. All around me, the road was a collage of crimson.

Lizzie came beside me. "What happened here?"

"I don't want to know," I whispered back.

Jennifer looked on with horror on her face.

"Let's keep moving," Grace said, tearing her eyes away from the grizzly scene.

Levi led the way, jogging slowly toward the industrial area of town. As the office blocks of downtown merged into run-down factory buildings, we knew we were close. The night was still with an eerie silence, only broken by our panted breathing and the patter of our footsteps. It seemed like our small noises echoed for blocks. We traveled cautiously toward a roundabout that sat in the shadowy distance. As we reached it, we slowed to a walk and passed under a dark bridge. Ahead of us, the once smoking chimneys of busy industries had slipped into a deep slumber. We stopped in front of a large concrete mechanics' workshop.

"Are those... lights?" Grace asked, pointing to a large warehouse building up ahead.

"I think so," Lizzie answered with traces of excitement trailing into her voice.

"Come on," Levi said.

Sticking to the shadows, we crept closer, and eventually, the humming of generators buzzed through the silent night. The warehouse had smooth concrete walls, with windows far above the ground, too high for any of us to see in. As we were deciding what to do, I caught sight of a tiny movement out the corner of my eye. I grabbed Lizzie and Grace, and dragged them out of sight, putting my finger to my lips in warning. Levi and the others were nowhere to be seen. I hoped they were well hidden.

We huddled in an inset doorway, trying to be as quiet as possible. Heavy, slow footsteps plodded forward, echoing down the dark street. My heart thundered in my chest. I felt light-headed, and all my attempts to take long, deep breaths were useless. Our mission felt more impossible by the moment. We pressed ourselves closer into the doorway, shrinking out of sight. A man's solid silhouette strode into view. He meandered past, seeming casual and unobservant. The machine-gun held tightly and rigidly in his hand said otherwise. We held our collective breath as he slowly passed us and rounded the corner of the building.

Once he was out of sight, Lizzie rested her forehead on my shoulder in relief. "Holy crap… that was close."

"We should wait to see if he comes around again," I said.

"OK. It's a miracle he didn't see us the first time," Grace said shakily.

We hid there for another couple of minutes until the guard came past again. There was definitely only one guard. After the man patrolled past a third time and rounded the corner out of sight, we acted. Lizzie and I ran forward and stopped against the wall of the building, breathing heavily.

"I'll keep watch," Grace whispered, turning away from us and readying her rifle.

The window was too high for either of us to see what was going on inside. "Lizzie," I said in a husked whisper, "you'll be able to see if you stand on my shoulders."

"Maybe," she whispered back. "I'll try."

I knelt down, placing my hand against the smooth wall for support. She stepped onto my shoulders. I stood up slowly, my thighs burning with effort. Lizzie steadied her hands on the wall to keep balanced as she was raised off the ground.

"Can you see anything?" She didn't answer. It ached where her boots dug into my shoulders. "Lizzie?" I whispered again.

"Hold on," she whispered back.

"Guys, hurry up," Grace said urgently. "Time's nearly up."

"Lizzie, I'm bringing you down," I said with finality.

"Just a second longer."

"There's no time," Grace said. "I can hear him."

"Now, Lizzie." I began to ease her down. Grace offered one of her hands to Lizzie to steady her, and she jumped the rest of the way to the ground. We took off again, running out of sight of the soldier. I stood hunched in the doorway, catching my breath as my legs cramped. Lizzie pulled me back into the shadows in anticipation. Right on cue, the soldier marched past. The moment he was gone, we ran from the building into an open shop with a smashed window. The crunch of broken glass deep within the shop made us bring our rifles up, ready. I made eye contact with Lizzie and Grace, directing them to follow me into the depths of the store.

A shadowy figure appeared from behind the shop counter. "It's me," the shadow said with his hands up.

"Levi?" Grace asked, clearly relieved. I let my gun fall to my side and sat down breathless on the cool floor.

"Did you manage to get a look?" Levi asked. I looked over at Lizzie, who nodded.

"What was it?" Jennifer asked nervously.

"Computers," Lizzie replied as she caught her breath. "Computers, soldiers and technicians, I think. It has to be the information hub the soldier was talking about." Lizzie was breathless but clearly excited. We had found it.

"Is there any way in?" I asked.

"The doors," she said obviously. "Or those air conditioning fans that lead to the roof."

"Is a break-in possible?" Levi asked.

Lizzie shook her head. "If the whole room cleared out, then maybe, otherwise probably not. There's nowhere to hide and too many people."

"It sounds impossible," I said, feeling a little disappointed.

Lizzie looked thoughtful. "I don't know. There has to be a way."

"We need a diversion to get everyone out of the building. If we can keep them out for long enough, maybe we can find some information," Grace said, thinking out loud.

"Maybe we could make an explosion nearby, and they'll come running out," Jennifer said.

"Won't work," Levi said instantly. "We can't be sure the whole building will clear out."

Jennifer wasn't bothered by the quick dismissal. She quickly came up with another idea. "We could poison them?"

Lizzie was quick to point out the flaws. "There's no way we'd ever pull that off. For starters, how could we be sure that they'd all taken the poison? And then… it would look pretty suspicious if everyone suddenly keeled over at their desks and didn't answer their comms. Plus, it would take months of planning."

"And I'm not so sure I can kill that many people in cold blood," Jess added, sounding uncomfortable.

"No, wait, Jennifer might be onto something," I said, undeterred as hope burgeoned. "What if we gas them out? Find a gas bad enough to make them evacuate."

"If we could get our hands on some sort of gas, how can we get in without breathing it in?" Jess pointed out.

"We could come in with scuba tanks… look at their computers and then get out of there," I suggested, now convinced my idea would work.

"It sounds a bit Hollywoodish, and there're two problems with it. First, how do we get our hands on this gas, and second, how do we set it off in the building?" Lizzie said.

"Well… the air conditioning vents in the roof are an obvious option. Someone can let the gas in the top while the rest of us go in and look on the computers," Levi said as he began to warm to my idea.

"Still, where will we get the gas from?" Lizzie asked.

Grace's face lit up. She pointed at a huge silent factory up on a hill in the distance.

"FertCo?" Levi asked. "But they make fertilizer."

"They also have ammonia. I had to research them for a chemistry project. Trust me, they'll know when it is in the building."

"Are you sure it's… strong enough?" Lizzie asked.

"Yes… from my chemistry project," Grace repeated.

"I don't know, Grace. What if you're wrong?"

"Trust me, Lizzie. I could recognize the smell of ammonia anywhere. One time in class, we used too high a concentration of ammonia, and it stunk out the whole room. We had to evacuate. Trust me, if we use ammonia, they will be out of that warehouse so fast."

"So, it's not toxic?" Jess asked.

"I don't know…" Grace said.

Jess bit down on her lip, a worried expression on her face, and her fingers toyed nervously with the cross at her neck.

"They probably won't die," Grace assured Jess.

"I think this idea can work," Levi said with a confident smile.

"How about Jess, Levi, and Grace go and get the gas. Dylan, Jennifer, and I will get the scuba tanks," Lizzie decided.

"Don't forget goggles," Grace piped up. "The ammonia will burn our eyes otherwise."

"How'd you know that?" Jess asked. "This doesn't sound very safe."

"Let me guess," Lizzie muttered, "chemistry class?"

"With goggles and a respirator we'll be fine," Grace said confidently.

"If you say so," Jess murmured.

"There's a scuba shop not too far from here," I added, gesturing in the general direction.

"All right," Levi said. "Let's meet back here in an hour." He helped Jess and Grace to their feet, and they slipped quietly into the dark without looking back. The moon was temporarily hidden behind a thick blanket of cloud, giving them a little extra cover in the night. I watched my best mate jog away from me, and after a couple seconds, the three of them disappeared into the darkness.

"Will they be OK?" Jennifer asked.

"Let's hope so," Lizzie managed to say.

"You didn't say goodbye to them," Jennifer said.

"It would only make the feeling worse," Lizzie replied blankly. Lizzie looked down at her watch.

"Try and forget about them," I said, pushing my feelings of anxiety down.

"We need to go. Looks like there's a way out the back." Lizzie pointed at the rear of the store.

Jennifer walked over and slowly opened the door, peeking outside. "It looks clear," she said, and began to walk out.

"Wait!" Lizzie grabbed Jennifer's wrist and dragged her back inside. The sharp crack of a gun tore through the air. Jennifer gasped but managed not to shout out. "Be careful," Lizzie warned, "the soldiers shoot at everything."

"We can't go that way," I said hurriedly. "We have to get out of here."

"The soldiers will be here any minute," Lizzie added.

We ran out the front door and sprinted along the street in the opposite direction to Levi.

Soon the dive shop came into view. It was empty like all the others, with smashed windows and glass strewn across the pavement. I stepped through the broken window, squinting to see through the heavy blackness. I couldn't make out anything.

"Can you see anything?" I asked.

Lizzie stepped inside, glass crunching beneath her feet. She walked forward, disappearing into the dark.

"Dylan, over here," Lizzie whispered. I stumbled through the dark, following the sound of her voice. I could just make out her petite frame in front of me.

"Here," she said, holding up a heavy black vest with a regulator dangling from the top. "I've got the goggles too."

"We need the tanks, as well," I said.

"These things?" Jennifer asked, somewhere to my left. I found my way toward her. She pointed to a row of cylinders against the wall.

"Yeah, those are them. Bring them over," I said, grabbing one and carrying it to Lizzie. I worked as quickly as I could in the dark, attaching the tank to the vest. "They're heavy," I warned as I helped Jennifer into her vest that she would carry back to the shop. Her knees buckled, but she managed to stay standing.

"They are heavy," she commented.

Lizzie struggled into hers. Unsurprisingly, she didn't complain about the weight.

I shoved my arms into the vest and lifted it onto my back.

"You make it look easy," Jennifer said.

"She's not wrong," Lizzie agreed, eyeing my muscular arms as she handed me a couple pairs of goggles.

I felt my cheeks redden under Lizzie's gaze, but all I said was, "Let's go."

We left the shop and returned to our hiding place near our target. We were relieved to put the tanks on the ground.

"We need four," Lizzie said.

"OK, I'll go back," I said.

"You can't go alone. That's stupid," Lizzie said, "I'll come with you."

A look of apprehension passed over Jennifer's face. "I don't want to be here by myself."

"Well, we can't all go. Someone has to stay to keep an eye on these, and wait for the others," Lizzie said, gesturing to the scuba gear. And then when she saw the look on Jennifer's face she relented. "Fine, you go with Dylan, and I'll stay here."

"But—" Jennifer began.

"But what?" I asked.

"Nothing." Jennifer stared down at the ground. She was still angry with me, that much was clear.

"Let's get a move on," I said. We took off into the night once more. And again, our journey to the shop was uneventful. We hurried into the shop. Immediately, Jennifer went to find another vest and regulator, while I made my way toward the tanks.

A faint scuffing noise made me freeze. But it was too late. A light blinked on and illuminated Jennifer. I shrank into the corner.

"Hands up where I can see them!" a soldier yelled. I was frozen with fear. We had no gun—I had forgotten it with Lizzie. "Is there anyone here with you?" he seethed, shoving his gun up against her forehead.

"N-No, I'm alone," she stammered.

I felt along the shelf behind me, searching for anything I could use for a weapon. My hands grasped a thin metal pole. It would have to do. I grabbed it, my eyes still fixed on Jennifer. He had let his gun drop while he unfastened some handcuffs. Jennifer whimpered, her eyes searching for me, but I was still hidden in the shadows. I glanced down at what was in my hand; a spear gun. I silently undid the safety and grasped my finger around the trigger. I calmed my breathing and carefully crept forward.

"Why are you here?" the soldier said as he brandished his gun at her.

"I wanted to go diving and get some fish. I'm starving," Jennifer replied. It was the most hopeless lie I had ever heard.

"That's ridiculous," he said with a snigger. For a split second, his gun dropped complacently to his side. I acted, sprinting forward with my speargun in my hand and pulling the trigger. There was a soft ting as the spear was released. The soldier heard the sound and spun to face me. With a sickening thud, the spear impaled his chest. He coughed, stumbled back, and reflexively clenched his fingers. His assault rifle sprayed a stream of wild bullets. I hit the floor and tried to roll toward some cover. Jennifer shrank down against the wall. After a few seconds of deafening shooting, the magazine was empty.

In the deadened silence that followed, I rushed forward and retrieved the soldier's weapon. I glanced at him as I tugged the rifle free from his grasp. A dark patch bloomed around the spear centered in his chest, oozing to the floor. He coughed violently, and blood foamed out the corner of his mouth. He looked up at me, pleading for help. He coughed again and then fell silent. I watched his eyes became glassy in the light of his torch. He was gone.

Jennifer ran to me, sobbing. "Thank you," she managed to say.

"Shhh, it's OK," I said, trying to comfort her. But I was also reeling, trying to swallow my nausea back down, my mouth dry.

"He was going to kill me."

"We have to get that tank and get out of here," I said, trying to get ahold of myself.

"I can't go back out there."

"You have to. Lizzie is there by herself. Levi, Grace, and Jess are relying on us. I'll leave you and take the tank if I have to," I said. She just didn't seem to get it.

Jennifer didn't answer me. It seemed her anger at me was renewed.

"What should I do?" she said finally.

"Bring the vest over here," I said softly.

She skirted the soldier and came over with the vest. I quickly fastened it to the tank. Then I walked over to the soldier and took the spare magazine off his belt. I reloaded the gun. Finally, I lifted the tank onto my back.

"Let's get the hell out of here," I muttered.

Jennifer and I crept from the shop and ran as fast as we could with the heavy tank.

"What took so long?" Lizzie asked. Neither of us answered, but Lizzie never missed a thing. Her eyes took in the blood splatter on Jennifer's shirt and the gun I held in my hand.

"We had a bit of trouble," was all I could say. Lizzie didn't question any further. Sometimes silence is as good as words.

CHAPTER EIGHTEEN

JESS

MOONLIGHT DANCED OFF THE concrete buildings, bathing the night in a pale blue glow. The hardened prying eyes of shadows and darkness followed us with ease. I felt like we were bright beacons running through the streets, chased by demons with nowhere to hide. I never dared to look behind me. It was better not knowing what was there. If soldiers were chasing me, I'd rather not know. I preferred death as a surprise, a shot in the darkness. Unanticipated.

Our thundering footsteps on the concrete played havoc with my mind, and suddenly I was transported to the night of Leah's death. The constant slap of boots on polished tiles as we fled from gunfire that left our ears ringing. Leah's curdling scream as she collapsed to her knees, her eyes emptying of all light and leaving her face frozen in a grimace of pain. I slowed, trying to shake the memory, my breath coming shallow and uneven.

"Just wait," I managed to gasp at Levi and Grace, bending over with my hands on my knees.

"Jess, we can't wait, we'll get caught," Levi said. I felt Levi grab my wrist and pull me around the corner of a rusted tin shed. "Keep focused," he warned. I nodded absently while trying to will my mind out of the dark. Grace stood beside me, panting heavily.

"What's going on?" I said quietly in Levi's ear.

"There was a loud bang in one of the buildings. It could be soldiers. We can't afford to take chances right now," Levi explained quickly.

Guilt washed over me as I came to the grim realization that Grace and Levi were actively watching out for me. Everyone knew I wasn't focused. Especially Dylan. His speech earlier about Jennifer was aimed indirectly at me—a warning I had to remain heartless when we went on these missions, or risk putting everyone in danger. Unfortunately, that was what I had just done. My lack of concentration had potentially compromised Levi and Grace. I took a slow deep breath to clear my thoughts.

Levi listened intently to the silence of the streets. "It must have been a cat," he said eventually. "Let's go."

We darted out onto the open street once more. The factory loomed dark and dead up ahead. Tall chimneys that once pumped acrid smoke into the air were still. The regular clanking of machinery and rumbling of trucks had been forced into silence. We ran the last few hundred meters to the factory. There we stood, in front of the large slate concrete wall. The coiled razor wire prevented any attempt to climb over it, and there was no gate on this side, so we began to follow the wall around the factory. As we came up to the first corner, I heard a noise. I stopped, silent. Grace stood impatiently behind me. Levi hadn't heard it. I sprinted forward, grabbing Levi's arm and dragging him back. He realized what was happening and mouthed a thank you. There it was again, the crunching of boots. We all stood still and listened intently, but the sound had disappeared.

"What do we do?" Grace whispered in my ear.

"I have no idea."

Levi quietly armed himself with the rifle he had slung across his shoulder, and then turned to me. "I want you to make a small noise to bring him around the corner. Then, drop to the ground. When he comes around… I'll do the rest."

I relayed the plan to Grace, who nodded uncomfortably in understanding and immediately shrank to the ground, lying flat on her stomach against the wall. I looked at Levi, fear fluttering in my belly. He gave me a determined nod and readied his gun, pointing it where the guard was sure to appear. I let out a subtle cough and dropped like a stone. My face was flush to the concrete, my eyes closed tight. A loud bang echoed through the still air, and a bullet whizzed above my head and buried itself in the wall. Then there was a quick retaliation of fire. I covered my ears, trying to shrink myself so that the soldier wouldn't see me. Then silence. A pair of strong hands helped me to my feet. It was Levi.

"Are you OK?" he asked.

"I'm fine," I said weakly.

"Are you sure?"

"Yes," I insisted, trying to seem strong. I could hear the fear in my own voice, but Levi didn't push it. He went past me and helped Grace to her feet.

"Thank God you're OK," she said, hugging him, "I thought you had been shot."

"I'm fine, I just didn't expect him to come around the corner so fast. He must have been closer than we thought." Levi looked worried, but he shook off the incident and turned back to the dead soldier, several meters away. He bent down to check the soldier's pulse.

"If you're sure you're OK…" Grace said, following Levi and giving him a concerned look.

"I'm sure." Levi took the soldier's standard-issue weapons. He slung the soldier's assault rifle over his shoulder before turning to me and handing me his own hunting rifle. "You might need this."

The gun was heavy as I held it in my shaky hands. I hadn't touched a rifle since the day I'd nearly taken my own life. Was I ready for this?

"To shoot just take off the safety." Levi showed me, pointing to the safety mechanism. "And then aim and fire."

Grace already held a semi-automatic rifle we'd had back at camp, but when Levi pushed the soldier's sidearm at her, she tucked it into her waistband without a word.

"Come on," Levi said, and we cautiously rounded the corner. Levi had his gun pointing ahead as we rounded each turn. Our firefight had been loud, and we were certain someone would've heard us. We stuck to the wall, trying to meld with the dark shadow it created in the moonlight.

"There," Grace said, pointing up ahead. An opening into the factory was just visible through the night.

Levi turned to me. "Stay here. Grace and I will go ahead and check. Come when we give the all-clear."

"Why can't I come?" I asked, annoyed they were leaving me behind.

"You're the backup."

I knew he was making an excuse because he was worried about me, but I didn't argue. There wasn't time for it, and I knew he was right. My head wasn't in the right state for this. I should have stayed behind.

"Fine," I grumbled.

Levi and Grace quickly walked to the gate with their guns drawn. In one fluid motion, they turned the corner into the factory enclosure, and then they were out of sight. There was silence. A few tense moments ticked by, but warm relief spread through me when Grace reappeared, signaling the all-clear. I hurriedly joined them. Emerging through the gate, there was a huge cobbled courtyard leading to a massive building. The whole facade had been glass, now in shards across the ground. Elegant halogen lights would have illuminated the entrance, with crisp sliding doors. I had envisioned a grungy, dirty brick front with working, oily machines through the door. But inside, there were the remnants of a sleek metal reception desk on a polished concrete floor. Large canvases of local artwork punctured with bullet holes decorated the walls with a shot-up watercooler tucked away in the corner.

"This way," Levi said as we made our way through the entrance. Glass and grit cracked beneath my feet. The inside was darker than the cruel night outside. We followed a gleaming white sign: Ammonia Plant. After passing through a few confusing corridors, we reached a glass door that stood atop a large set of rickety metal stairs. Beyond, the stairs descended to the factory floor. Machines were stopped in mid-motion, their joints oozing with oil. Unknown chemicals sat still in huge vats. Levi took the butt of his rifle and looked at us both. Grace and I nodded before Levi smashed his rifle against the glass pane. The door shattered and fell.

The pungent smell of chemicals wafted through the door and quickly became overpowering. Grace covered her mouth, wheezing, and looked around. She handed me a mask from a large bin behind her. "That would be the smell of ammonia," she coughed. I pulled the full-face respirator mask over my head.

"There," Levi said, pointing down. There was a conveyor belt with hundreds of gas canisters lined up. The stairs creaked and clanked with every step as we descended. We moved as quietly as we could toward the canisters.

Levi struggled to lift one down and grimaced. "They aren't too heavy."

He wasn't fooling me. They looked about twice the size of a scuba tank. Grace and I dragged one down together, and it hit the floor with a heavy thud.

"I won't be able to carry this all the way back," I said.

"Neither," Grace added as she looked around for something to help us, eventually wandering off into the dark.

"Grace, wait," Levi called, but there was silence.

A few moments later, she returned, pulling a red, two-wheeled trolley. "Will this work?"

"Yes, that's perfect," Levi said, "are there more of them?"

"I think so, "Grace replied.

"Jess, go and get two more while Grace and I get the canisters down," Levi ordered.

"OK," I said and ventured into the dark. I wandered aimlessly for a few moments before I made out the red glint of steel. I headed toward it, finding two trolleys standing idly against the wall.

I went to grab them but felt the hairs of my body stand on end as I heard footsteps right behind me. Fear rose, and I stood paralyzed as the ice-cold steel of a rifle pressed against my back.

"Don't move," the soldier warned me. Would this be my end? My hand was clutched tightly around the rifle at my side. With speed that surprised even me, I spun around, and in one quick movement, raised my rifle and fired two shots into his chest. His rifle let out a cracking shot, the bullet burying itself into the concrete at our feet. I stumbled back with the force of the recoil and watched, horrified, as the soldier's face went blank before collapsing to the ground. Blood pooled. I sank to the ground, shaking.

"Jess!" I heard Grace call and heard her footsteps racing toward me. She skidded to a stop as she approached the soldier dead on the ground, terror in her eyes. Levi appeared a few steps behind her, and a look of concern passed across his face. He held his finger to his lips and then departed, scouting the area for more soldiers.

Grace pulled me up and prepared for a fight. She directed me to the left of her. Picking up the rifle the soldier had dropped and slinging it over my other shoulder, I stood ready. Grace moved off in the opposite direction, disappearing out of sight. Then I was alone. Flashes of the night at the mall came to my mind again. This time, however, I drew strength.

I looked around, peering into the darkness for any sign of movement. I hesitantly rounded a huge vat, my gun pointed in front of me, ready.

A sudden burst of machine-gun fire sent me diving for shelter behind a stack of steel piping. The steady pinging of bullets against metal froze me in my hiding spot. I knew I had to move or shoot back. If I stayed here, they would eventually move forward and capture me… or kill me. With a deep breath, I popped my head over the pipe stack but saw nothing but blackness. Another quick burst of fire made me drop to the ground, but not before I saw the muzzle of the gun light up in the dark. Now I knew where he was. I crawled along, using the pipe for protection.

When the firing stopped, I jumped to my feet, aimed the gun at the faint outline of the soldier, and fired. A scream of pain and a thud on the ground told me I had hit my target. To my right, another spray of bullets sent me clambering for cover. The instant the firing ceased, I stood up and fired blindly in the direction the enemy bullets had come from. The soldier yelled, toppled forward, and lurched over the rail he had been standing behind, falling with a sickening crunch to the ground.

All at once, there was an onslaught of gunshots. I crouched behind the pipe, with my eyes closed, praying for them to stop. Stray bullets punctured the pipe, whistling past me, and burying themselves in the concrete wall behind. I pressed myself as hard as I could into the floor, and eventually, the shooting stopped. It was my chance. I slowly emerged and fired at the nearest noise. The soldier fell. I took aim again and fired. I missed. I fired again, but the gun clicked. Blank. I tried the other gun I had. Click. Empty.

"Shit," I said under my breath and began to crawl, leaving the safety of the pipe and moving along the ground toward one of the soldiers I had shot. Heavy fire blanketed me overhead as I forced myself to keep going. I finally reached the fallen man, grabbed his gun, and moved back to my place of cover. For a moment, my mind wandered. Grace and Levi were out there somewhere. Where they dead? Was I alone?

I froze.

The deafening blast of guns and the clamor of bullets ricocheting off the metal machinery faded into a blur of noise. I sank to the ground and hid, burying my head in my hands. I wanted to get out, leave, and never come back. I wanted it all to end. After what felt like hours, the firing finally stopped. I waited in tense silence for a few more minutes but heard nothing. Deciding the soldiers were gone, I got up and ran to where the canisters were.

"Grace? Levi? Are you OK? Where are you?" I called, crying.

"Jess, oh my God, you're OK," Grace echoed from somewhere in the vastness of the factory. She came running and hugged me. I crumbled into her embrace.

"Grace? Is that you?" I heard Levi shout.

"Levi!" Grace sobbed and fell into his arms. There was blood splattered all over their clothes, and their masks smeared with oil.

"It's all right," Levi said, trying to soothe her, but I noticed his hands shaking. He was as scared as us. I ran and got the two red trolleys to pull the canisters on. When I returned, Grace was still in Levi's arms.

"We should have been more careful," Grace said tearfully. "Next time, we will be."

"At least there is a next time," Levi said. They pulled away when they saw me and began to help me load up. Two canisters fit snugly on each trolley. Pushing a trolley each, we ran out the backdoor. Once outside, we tore off the masks we were wearing and sucked in breaths of clean air. Grace's face was streaked with tears, oil, and soldiers' blood, but Levi remained composed. We tore along the streets. The shop by the warehouse came into view, and we slowed to a walk. We carefully crept forward, looking out for the guard, and when he wasn't in sight, we slipped into the shop.

"There you guys are! We were getting worried…" Lizzie exclaimed. Her face lost color when she saw the state of us. "What happened?" she asked. Her eyes moved from the bloodstained clothes, to the machine-guns we all held in shaking hands, and our white faces.

"Soldiers found us," Levi answered.

"How many?" Dylan asked.

"Doesn't matter," Levi said, "I'll tell you later."

"What happened to you?" Grace asked Jennifer, noting her ghost-white complexion.

"A soldier found me, but Dylan killed him," she said, her voice shaky.

"Dylan? Really?" I interrupted.

"Yes."

"He shot him with a spear gun," Jennifer said tearfully.

"Did you get the air tanks?" I asked, trying to change the subject.

"Yes," Lizzie said, pointing to four tanks complete with vests and masks, propped against a wall.

"Who's going to let the gas in?" Levi said. "There are only four tanks."

"I will," Jennifer said. I felt compelled to join her but knew they wouldn't let me. No one volunteered.

"I'll go too," Dylan muttered eventually.

"But we need you," Lizzie pleaded with him.

"And I'll be helping," he said. "And you'll have Levi with you."

"Great, what more could I want," Lizzie said sarcastically under her breath. Levi scowled but didn't say anything.

"While you were gone, I scouted out the building," Dylan continued, leaving Lizzie to sulk. "There is a ladder on the right of the building. We can pass the canisters up to the roof. Then there's a backdoor barred shut from the outside. You can enter through there."

"OK," Levi said, taking in all the information. "I think Dylan and I should go and take these up to the roof," he said. Dylan nodded, and with that, they left. I sat down on the floor next to Jennifer.

"How many soldiers were there?" Lizzie asked Grace.

"Five to ten," she replied wearily. "It was horrible. We were in a factory, hiding behind machines in the dark. We couldn't see where the shots were coming from, and we were completely separated."

"Shit."

"I don't want to talk about it. Let's get this mission over with," Grace said with finality. We sat in silence. The minutes turned into an hour. There was no sound or sight of Dylan and Levi. I glanced at my watch. There were only three hours until the sun came up. Finally, Levi and Dylan came in the door.

"OK, it's done," Levi panted, drenched in sweat. Jennifer stood up to leave, joining Dylan, who was waiting by the door.

"You have… twenty minutes before we let the gas in," Dylan said, looking at his watch. "You have to be on your way to camp in an hour, so you'll have forty minutes in there. We'll meet you back at the campsite. It's too risky for us to stay around here and wait," Dylan said.

"Good luck," Lizzie said, giving him a hug. Levi shook his hand and clapped him on the back. There was no goodbye, nor any mention of never returning. Then Jennifer and Dylan were gone.

"Let's get suited up," Levi said. We all struggled into the heavy scuba tanks. I then checked the gauge and noted it was only half full. Hopefully, it would be enough. Lizzie checked her watch. "We have ten minutes," she muttered. I nodded. Grace sat calmly in the corner with her eyes closed, breathing softly. This was it. In a few moments, we would be inside that warehouse. Anything could happen. There could be another gunfight. With that thought, my hands began to tremble uncontrollably.

"It will be OK," Grace said, standing up and grasping my hand. I stared into her eyes. I wasn't so sure.

"Come on," Levi said, looking at his watch. "We want to be waiting at the backdoor before they all come running outside and see us here," he said.

I moved awkwardly out the door with the tank on my back and the goggles on top of my head. If their information fell into the wrong hands—ours—it could be damaging. I hoped it would be as damaging as possible. For all the grief they had caused us, for all the pain they had inflicted, we deserved every detail we could get our hands on. It was time to find our families.

Following Levi's lead, we slipped around the building to the back. I could see a steel bar jamming what looked like a worn metal door in place. This must be the door Dylan was talking about.

"Can anyone smell that?" I heard a female voice ask loudly, breaking the quiet of the night.

"No, I smell nothing," a deeper, husky voice answered.

"Are you sure," the lady said, beginning to cough. There was an echo of a few more coughs.

"I can hardly breathe," a shaking voice said, "I have to get out of here." I heard the overturning of a chair, the front door open loudly, and then slam shut. All at once, the building was filled with the sound of people coughing.

"Everyone out!" a man yelled. "We're being gassed!" There was a stampede to the door. "Search the outside of the building, there must be some canisters somewhere," he ordered. I heard the door clang shut, and Levi immediately lifted out the bar securing the door. We put our regulators in our mouths, snapped our goggles on, and entered. The room was empty. I glanced up at the vent in time to see two faces pull away. I took my place at a computer and began searching through files, clicking repeatedly.

"We need a gas control team here ASAP," a man yelled into his walkie-talkie from outside the window above me.

"The next team is an hour away," the radio buzzed back.

"How is that possible?" he yelled.

"They've been sent to a gas leak at one of the camps," A calm voice said back. "Is there anyone in the building anymore?"

"No," he replied.

"Is there anyone visible in the perimeter?"

"No, there's no one, sir, we've scoured the area but found nothing."

"There must be a leak somewhere in the building. Keep everyone away from the site. It could be hazardous. The team will be there in half an hour, sit tight Major."

"I think it's an attack," he stated. "It is not natural gas. It is something else!"

"If the attackers are not in the vicinity, there is nothing we can do at present. I'll put a message to all patrols to move to your area and begin sweeping for rebel activity. Stay put, Major."

"Roger that. Over and out," he said. I then heard a smashing sound as he threw down the radio in frustration. "I'm going in there," he announced.

"You heard the Colonel, stay put," another officer said.

"I can't sit here and do nothing," he growled.

"You have orders," the young man said.

Meanwhile, I clicked through hundreds of files. There was nothing. I saw orders for guns and ammunition. There was a command for more troops sent two days ago. There were detailed plans of the city, each block carefully mapped out. This must have been used to capture all the citizens at the beginning,

I thought. I moved onto the next computer. I looked at the screen and none of it made sense, but I continued searching. Grace, Levi, and Lizzie had dispersed through the building, trying to access every computer. I looked at my gauge. I only had a quarter left. I tried to shake the thought of running out of air and instead I ran to find Levi. I tapped him on the shoulder, showing him my gauge. He nodded, looking at his watch, and then went back to the computer. There was a pile of documents on the floor. I began to file through them. They were all old orders and unit reports.

> *Thursday 20 October*
> *0200 hours*
> *Area 21 Bayfair Mt Maunganui*
> *Guerilla group attempted to break out two persons from camp 102.*
> *Escaped persons were Jennifer Summers, now missing, and Evee*
> *McGrath, killed in escape.*
> *Shots fired. Two killed.*
> *One Evee McGrath, other discovered to be Leah Stripling.*
> *Both died of multiple gunshot wounds.*
> *Bodies buried separately in Tauranga Cemetery*
>
> *Lieutenant Thomas Shiel, Unit 27*
> *Report 18*
> *Next report due: Saturday 05 November*

I held the paper in my hand breathlessly. There it was. All the proof was there: Leah was gone. I folded the paper and put it in my pocket. I felt my lungs beginning to constrict. I tried to breathe, but there was hardly any air. I began gasping, feeling compelled to take out the regulator. Levi saw me, and I made the obvious signal I was out of air. He grabbed Grace's hand and tapped on Lizzie's shoulder. Then we ran out of the building. My lungs burned, and the warehouse began to spin. Black spots crept into my vision. I stepped out of the backdoor and tore off my regulator. I took a deep breath and fell to my knees. There was no time to recover. We ditched our air tanks and left them there. Hopefully, by the time they found them, we would be long gone. We sprinted down the road gasping for air. Finally, we were far enough away to slow to a walk. I wheezed.

"Are you OK?" Lizzie asked.

"My tank ran out. I haven't had time to breathe," I managed to say between gasps.

"Levi, let's rest for a moment," Grace said, overhearing our conversation. I gratefully stepped into the shelter of a doorway. I stood there, gulping air for a minute or two before we took off running once more. As the sun completely crested the hill, we sped into the bush and out of sight. Finally, we slowed to a walk and made our way to camp.

The crackling of a fire brought comfort to my ears. We were home. The shelter emerged into view between the trees, and I was smothered with a crushing hug.

"You are all OK!" Jennifer called. "When the sun came up, I panicked," she said breathlessly.

Lizzie fell laughing into Dylan's embracing hug. "We did it! I can't believe we actually did it!"

"I had my doubts," Dylan said, "but you pulled it off."

"Yeah," Lizzie said, sighing happily. "It worked, and none of us are hurt. That's all that matters." It was true. Nothing else in the whole world mattered right now. We were safe and perfectly OK. All of us had returned. We sat around the fire.

"What did you find out?" Dylan asked as he stirred a pot of hot chocolate. I clutched tightly at the piece of paper in my pocket. It didn't matter, and it wasn't important to anyone save Jennifer and me. I took it out and handed it to her, watching her eyes brim with tears.

Dylan picked it up and read it. "We're sorry." He placed a hand on Jennifer's shoulder and looked sympathetically at me as well. "I know you still had some hope despite it all."

Lizzie took the paper from Dylan, and everyone else read it as it passed from hand to hand. No one said anything.

"Did anyone else find anything," Dylan said at last.

"I found something," Lizzie said quietly. She pulled a crumpled piece of paper from her jean pocket and unfolded it. "It's a transcript of a speech Marion made on the lead up to the election."

I took the paper from Lizzie and stared at it. The words took me back in time, to when I was sitting curled on the sofa, while Mom and Dad leaned forward in their seats, listening intently to the TV. It was one of the very last speeches Marion made before the war began. He had been candid and earnest in his address; one of his endearing qualities.

"Our country is a good country, and I have done my best for you," Marion began in his refined voice. "You all know the lengths I have gone to. I lowered taxes. I gave people homes by increasing benefits and lowering interest rates. I provided for the education of the young, and the health of the elderly. You asked, and I gave you what you wanted." Here, Marion paused, allowing himself to smile in reminiscence. Mom and Dad didn't say a word as some people in the audience jeered at him. Marion raised his hands to quiet them.

"Yes, I know that not everyone remembers those glory days, which seem so long ago. But I am one man, and there are forces that are outside of my control. The pandemic has crippled our country, and rather than being understanding of the perilous state we find ourselves in, our friends have turned on us, demanding us to pay back money we no longer possess. I am being honest with you when I say that things will not, and cannot, continue the way they have over the last few years… our country is crippled with debt. That is the truth of it. No matter who you choose to govern you, the fact remains that the coming years are not going to be kind to New Zealand. I ask you to vote for me, because you know that I have New Zealand's best interests at heart. I have demonstrated that I will do everything in my power to right the wrongs that have been done, and restore New Zealand to her former beauty."

I remembered asking Mom and Dad if they were going to vote for him. They shrugged. Half of the country remembered the glory days that Marion referred to, the other half blamed him for our financial struggles. "I'm not sure which way I'll go yet," Dad said. "But it's going to be a close race."

Grace gently took the speech from my slackened grip, pulling me unwillingly back to the present.

"He really did believe he was doing right by us," Grace said as she skim-read the page.

Lizzie snorted. "Even if he did believe it, that doesn't make it right. And besides, he already knew he was losing. He was never going to give anyone a chance to vote, despite that piece of shit he spouted."

"Those riots sounded really scary, though," Jennifer said.

"People were dying—he had to do something," I added.

Dylan handed out the hot chocolates in assorted camping mugs. "So, he rounds up the civilians and throws them into prison camps. What a great solution."

"It's not a solution," Grace said, cradling the mug in her hands and savoring the heat. "What is he planning? What's the big finale? He must know he can't keep the citizens contained forever."

We all swapped looks with one another. No one had an answer.

Finally, Levi said, "Whatever it is, it can't be good."

Chapter Nineteen

Levi

Sometimes the camp felt cramped. Frustration often bubbled over, and arguments broke out. Typically, Lizzie was involved. None of us hated each other, we were just stewing in boredom and anxiety. Grace and I had snuck away from the camp after another argument between Lizzie and Jennifer. Lizzie was adamant fighting was the only way forward. Jennifer thought hiding in safety was the best option. I stayed out of it.

Lizzie was right, of course. But everyone had the right to their own opinion. We couldn't force anyone to risk their life. Even though, often we did.

I followed Grace's petite frame as she trotted along the path to the river. We liked to hang out here. It was peaceful, and far enough away from camp that our conversations were not easily overheard. She perched on her favorite rock and dangled her bare feet in the smoothly flowing water. "I'm sick of the fighting," Grace said as she gently kicked at the water.

I lounged against a tree next to her. "The war?"

"The war, and around camp, all of it," she said. "I hate it."

"It's not so bad," I said with a shrug.

Grace laughed aloud. "Not so bad? Are we even living in the same world?"

"I mean, it could be worse. We could be locked up. Or dead."

"You have a point. But that doesn't stop me wishing things were back to normal."

"What's the first thing you'd do if everything was back to normal?" I asked, trying to distract her.

She glanced over at me with a knowing look on her face. She was on to me. "Grab a cheeseburger from my favorite burger joint," she said with a giggle.

I laughed. "I know you're lying. Lizzie told me how much you actually hated them," I said as I gently squeezed her waist. "You only want to see the guy serving up those burgers."

Grace blushed a little and looked away from me. "Maybe," she said coyly. "What about you? What do you miss?"

"Hmmm." There were a lot of things I missed. "My gaming console."

"I don't believe you. I'm sure there's something you miss more."

"Music," I said instantly. I thought back to before the war. Cruising down the open country road blasting music through the stereo. I missed those days. They were carefree and safe. "I miss driving with my stereo blaring and singing as loud as I can."

"Me too," Grace said. I shuffled closer. "Though I can't imagine you singing."

"I'm actually good," I insisted. Truthfully, I was terrible.

"Sure you are."

I playfully splashed her. She shrieked, before splashing me back. The crackling of leaves behind me made me spin around. Jennifer was walking down the path toward us.

Grace looked back with a smile. "Hey, Jen."

I stared at Jennifer. We had come here to try and get a break from them. I guess our camp really was small.

"Come sit," Grace said, motioning beside her.

Should I leave? I didn't want to. She could say whatever she wanted in front of me.

"What's up?" Grace asked.

Jennifer looked uncomfortably at me.

"Just spit it out," I said. "Grace will tell me later, anyway."

Jennifer let out a long sigh. "Do you agree with Lizzie? Do we have to fight?"

Grace looked surprised at her question. I wasn't. She was trying to get people on her side. It was inevitable we would go and fight again.

Grace looked down and kicked at the water. Thinking. "Yes." Grace looked up, past Jennifer, and met my eyes with hers.

"Why?" Jennifer asked, clearly feeling trapped between us.

Grace was gentler than Lizzie, though. She didn't attack Jennifer but instead gave a measured answer. "Because no one else can. There is only us."

"Grace is right," I said, trying to sound approachable. "There is no one to fight for the dead and the imprisoned. They're our people, and we have to try."

Jennifer sat silently between us, deep in thought.

"You might be right," she said quietly. "Maybe we have to fight back."

Night had fallen, and we all sat around our small fire. "We could kill the Prime Minister," Lizzie said, breaking the comfortable silence. It was a stupid idea.

"That's ridiculous," I said. "It's too dangerous. More like a suicide mission if you ask me."

"I don't know then," Lizzie said, throwing her hands in the air in frustration. "Why do I always have to come up with the ideas?" She stared hard at all of us sitting around the fire.

"Here's one," Dylan said. "We could infiltrate the army, dress up like them, and then kill them from within."

"That's also dangerous. Even if we managed to avoid suspicion at the start, how would we get away after?" Grace dismissed.

"Also, someone might notice a bunch of teenagers dressed as soldiers," Jess pointed out.

"What do you suggest instead?" Dylan asked her.

"We should start small and do things we know we're capable of. Then, build up to bigger plans later," Grace said sensibly. I was persuaded to agree with her. "We hardly succeeded in our warehouse attack," she continued. "I think you forget Levi, Jess, and I were almost killed."

"Dylan and I had a narrow escape too," Jennifer said. "I think your idea makes sense," Jennifer said, looking over at Lizzie. "I know you think I don't want to help—that's not exactly true. I do. But I don't want to be stupid… I don't want to throw my life away."

Lizzie looked a little sheepish.

"You're right," Jess said, smiling at Jennifer.

"I wish you could see yourselves from where I am. All you've done since we got back from the warehouse is plan how to get back at the soldiers. It's an obsession. We need to slow down and think," Jennifer said passionately.

For once, Jennifer had all our attention. Dylan nodded in agreement, and Lizzie actually looked guilty.

"Sorry, Jen, you're right. I've been a little carried away," Lizzie admitted.

"A little?" Jennifer said, only half-joking.

"Fine, a lot. But I can't stand it, knowing this war is all because of a few corrupt people. We've lost our homes and families because of them. It makes me mad," Lizzie said, her lip trembling.

"We're all angry. But we can't let it cloud our judgment," Jennifer said.

"You're right," Dylan said. Had he finally accepted her into our group? "We need to take a step back and give ourselves time to think. We've been rushing into this too much."

I yawned loudly as the conversation started to die down. The fire was warm, and sleep pulled at my eyes. I leaned against Grace and let sleep overtake me.

"Levi, wake up," Grace said. I groggily opened my eyes. She was standing over me, a look of fear on her face. "Levi," she said urgently. I was awake now. Dylan was snoring loudly with Lizzie sleeping against his shoulder. Jess was trying to shake Jennifer awake.

"What's wrong?" I asked, sitting upright.

"I think the soldiers are here," she said. "I heard people walking through the bush."

I was on my feet before she had finished her sentence. I dashed into the shelter and grabbed as many guns as I could carry. "They're probably looking for us," I said, marching back to our campfire. I handed Jennifer a rifle. "Just shoot," I said. Jennifer nodded, white-faced.

"Use the trees for cover," Dylan said as he ran to me and grabbed two machine-guns. He gave me a worried look. "Shoot to kill, right?" he said with a forced smile before he took off into the forest with Lizzie close behind him.

Only Grace, Jess, and I were left by the fire. I dished out the rifles and directed them into position. Our camp was blanketed in silence as I crept toward the old kauri tree that grew in the clearing. Grace was crouched behind it, waiting for me.

"Are you all right?" I whispered as I squatted beside her.

"I'll be fine," she whispered back, holding her gun firmly. "Where are they?"

The crisp crunching of boots and the snapping of branches grew louder. I peeked around the tree, trying to peer through the blackness.

A sudden burst of gunfire blasted from the bushes to our

right. Bullets smashed into the trees around us, coming from all directions. We were surrounded. Grace crouched low to the ground. I pressed myself against the tree. It was chaos.

"Shit," I said to Grace. "We need to move… now!" I urged as gunfire sprayed the bush. Grace nodded but was too terrified to move. "Come on," I said to her. I couldn't wait for an answer. Grabbing her arm, I dragged her farther into the woods. Eventually, she regained her composure. We sprinted together until we were out of the fire.

"Cover me from behind," I said to her.

She obeyed, and we stood as quiet as we could back to back. I could feel Grace trembling up against me. A soldier emerged a few meters in front of me.

"Run," I yelled at Grace. The soldier unleashed a stream of bullets. Grace and I dove for cover behind a tree. The shooting abruptly stopped as he reloaded. I was ready. Aim. Fire. There was a scream of pain. Bullseye. I moved to go in for the kill shot.

"Levi, wait. Just wait," Grace pleaded with me. "It's suicide to go out there now."

I relented, and instead, we crouched together in the bushes. Eventually, the sound of gunfire became sporadic. Then it was quiet, except for the grunts of pain from the one I shot. Grace let my arm go, and I ran out to the injured soldier.

"How many of you were there?" I demanded, aiming the rifle at his head. This bastard was going to pay.

"Three," he managed to say between his bared teeth and grimace of pain. Dylan and Lizzie arrived.

"We've killed two," Lizzie said.

"He must be the last," Dylan muttered to me. Jennifer and Jess arrived.

"Go on… kill me," the soldier taunted. His face contorted in pain.

I stood stoic. The gun unwavering. "We need to kill him," I said to Dylan. "He knows where our camp is."

"I know," Dylan said.

Lizzie stormed forward. "Did you know we were down here?" she demanded.

The soldier was now breathing heavily. Pearls of sweat crawled along his brow. He was going to die anyway.

"Yes," the soldier replied, looking Lizzie dead in the eyes. Lizzie didn't flinch. If they knew we were here, there would be more of them. I was sure of that.

"Don't lie," I growled. I wanted to punish him. But we needed information. I let the gun fall to my side and punched him. A red mark on his cheek appeared. The soldier spat out a mouthful of blood at my feet. He grinned, revealing bloodied teeth. This bastard wasn't going to tell us anything. It didn't matter if they knew we were here or not. Our hideout was compromised. We had to leave.

"Even if you kill me, they'll know it was you. Backup is coming," he wheezed and flashed us another bloody smile. He looked at his radio. Had they radioed in? We had to assume they had. That meant we didn't have long. I had to kill him. Now. I took a deep breath to summon courage. I glanced back at the others. Grace's face was white and terrified. Dylan gave me a reassuring nod. I lifted my rifle. I didn't want to do it. I couldn't pass this off as self-defense. This time it was murder.

"We've killed a shit load of you guys. I guess another one isn't going to make a whole hell of difference," I said. My voice was hollow and dead. No emotion. I moved to cock the rifle, but I hesitated.

Lizzie snatched the gun from my grasp. "I bet you think you're doing this for the greater good," she said to the soldier. "But Marion's wrong. You must know this is wrong."

The soldier laughed at her. "And you think you're different? Face it. We're the same."

Lizzie was wired with adrenaline, her body shaking with it. "We didn't start this. We're not killing for fun. You attacked us, it's different."

"It's not. Before long, I bet you'll go out there, planning a hit. You'll kill my friends, and reason it's only right."

"We're nothing like you!" Lizzie screamed at him.

The soldier smiled at us, a knowing look in his eye. He knew he was going to die, but he made no move to save himself. I felt sick to my core, wondering if what he said was true.

"We're different!" Lizzie cried, with tears of frustration flowing down her cheeks. Then, the frustration morphed into a blind rage. "Fuck you," she yelled at him, cocked the rifle and shot him point-blank. His face exploded in a blast of blood. Grace screamed, and the rest of us stared at Lizzie in shock. Lizzie let the rifle fall to the ground and stalked off back to the shelter.

We all stood, staring at the body on the ground. Grace stood silently next to me. Just staring. She wasn't crying. She wasn't doing anything. Then all of a sudden, she turned around and threw up into the bush. I turned my face away from the horrific mangled mess of the soldier's face that was now splattered open. Dylan wisely threw a jacket over the bloody scene. I went to help Grace, who was still retching into the bushes.

"Are you all right?" I asked her, pulling her hair back.

"I will be," she said weakly. She stood upright and took a couple deep breaths. "Was he telling the truth? About the radio, I mean," Grace added, looking at all of us. Dylan and I looked at each other. I shrugged.

"No idea," I said. "But you would think a planned attack would have more soldiers."

Grace bit her lip but didn't respond. She looked as worried as I felt.

"We need to leave," Jess said, her eyes darting around in panic. "What if it wasn't a bluff?"

"There's nothing we can do now. It's dark, and we won't get far. Where would we go?" Dylan pointed out.

"Running blindly into the dark won't help us. We need to make a plan," I said, agreeing with Dylan.

"Someone can keep watch overnight, but we need to wait till morning," Dylan said. Jess and Jennifer looked terrified. Grace looked pale but composed.

"Meanwhile, we have to get rid of these guys," I said, jerking my thumb in the direction of the soldier.

"What?" Jennifer asked, her face losing color.

"We have to bury them," Dylan clarified.

"Oh," Jess said. Her face fell.

"I'll get the shovel," Dylan said, marching off toward camp.

"Help me carry him over," I said to Grace. I looked up at her. Horror passed over her face as it lost its remaining color.

"I'm going to check on Lizzie," she said and quickly walked away.

I turned to Jess. "Please," I said to her. She took a deep breath and came toward me. Dylan returned and began digging the first shallow grave. I stood over the body. Apprehensive. "We should search him," I said to Jess. She glared at me. "Someone has to do it."

"Fine." Jess began turning out his pockets and removing anything useful. I piled his spare ammunition and weapons next to me. Then, we dragged him to his grave and rolled him in. Dylan had already started on the next hole. Jess, Jennifer, and I used our hands to fill in the dirt. "The other ones are a few hundred meters that way," Dylan said, pointing. Jennifer, Jess, and I followed his direction and found them easily. We numbly searched them too, taking their army kits and weapons.

Then, Jennifer and Jess grabbed a leg each while I picked up his arms. We half carried, half dragged him to the second grave. Exhausted, we dropped him unceremoniously by the unfinished grave. Dylan was covered in sweat, and he panted loudly.

"I need a break," he said and sat heavily on the ground to catch his breath. I dutifully picked up the shovel and took over. I finished it off, and Dylan rolled the body into the hole. One more to go. Lizzie and Grace returned from the camp. Halfway into the third grave, my hands were blistering and my arms aching with effort. I handed the shovel off to Lizzie, who took it silently and jumped down into the small pit. She worked hard, refusing help when Grace offered. At last Lizzie threw down the shovel, the grave complete. Dylan and I shoved the body into the ditch and pushed the mound of dirt back into place.

"Finally," I said and sat hunched over on the ground, covered in dirt, blood, and sweat.

"I need to get this blood off me," Grace said and made her way to the stream. We all followed her, too afraid to go alone. After washing off, we dragged ourselves back to camp. It was only a few hours till daylight. "I'll keep watch," I offered. No one argued with this. Everyone retired to the shelter except Dylan.

"I'll keep you company," he said and slumped onto the log next to me.

"You look like shit," I said to him. His face was tired, and a scruffy beard was starting to grow. He was thin too. The war was starting to take a toll on us all.

"You're one to talk," he said, looking up at me with a grin. But he was the same Dylan I had known for years.

"What are we going to do?"

"Beats me," Dylan said, staring at the ground.

"I feel like we are fighting a losing battle," I said, looking deep into the forest. Hunting for a sign of the soldiers.

"That's because we are. This isn't a war we win. It's a war we survive."

He was right. We had to do what we could. And try and make it to the end.

"I suppose we have to run… find a new hideout," I said.

"It's the only option we have right now." He looked sideways at me. Something was on his mind.

"What?" I asked him, laying my rifle across my lap and

resting my elbows on my knees.

Dylan cast his eyes down and sighed. "Do you ever think about all the people we have killed?"

"I try not to."

"Me too. But sometimes... I can't help it."

"You look tired. You should sleep. I'll keep watch."

Dylan nodded sadly and made his way into the shelter. The truth was, I wanted a moment alone. A single tear crept down my cheek. I knew how Dylan felt. I tried to justify the killing too. It was war. We were fighting to save our country. It was self-defense. But what it boiled down to... was murder.

Chapter Twenty

Jennifer

A STIFF BREEZE BLEW through the forest and rustled the leaves. The slightest sound sent fear racing through my body. It was only a few hours ago that the soldiers had infiltrated the camp. I was trying to get some sleep but felt too on edge. Even the thought of Levi out there keeping watch didn't make me feel safe.

Instead, every cracking twig and whisper of the forest set my fear alight. To distract me, I thought about how stupid I had been earlier. Foolishly, I had felt there was nothing wrong with staying hidden in the forest and waiting out the war. It wasn't ideal, but I was the only one who seemed to think it was better than the alternative: risking our lives against a force much stronger than us.

"It's cowardly to stay here with everything we know," Lizzie had said to me while eating breakfast only yesterday. She was always the one to spur us to action. I was inspired by her conviction and determination, but I couldn't see what good fighting would do. It was another excuse for death to track us down. Grace, who was busily eating her porridge, looked up at us, clearly expecting a fight to break out. She glanced sideways at Levi, who began to edge away.

"It's safe to stay here," I retorted, looking over at Lizzie.

She pursed her lips and then scowled. "There's a greater good out there, and sometimes we actually have to fight for it." A hint of anger trailed into Lizzie's voice. Levi and Grace stood up and made a quick getaway in the direction of the stream.

"I'm not a fighter," I said.

Lizzie looked at me critically. "None of us are fighters, but sometimes we have to fight anyway," Lizzie continued, trying to keep her voice even as she sipped her tea. I stood up and marched away. Frankly, I was sick of arguing too.

A twig snapped and brought me back to the now, where I lay in the shelter surrounded by the others in fear for my life. Had Lizzie been right? I knew the answer to that. Yes. Even Grace had known it was cowardly to stay hidden.

"There's no one else," Grace had said to me when I asked her what she thought about fighting back. It was that simple. But it wasn't until I was hiding alone in the forest, gun in hand, and listening to the soldiers creeping up on us in the dark that it became clear. It wasn't safe. Anywhere. This was war, and war didn't discriminate.

Jess shuffled around next to me. "Are you awake?"

"Yeah." I rolled onto my side to face her.

"I'm too scared to sleep."

"Me too."

We listened to the soft rhythmic breathing of the others for a minute. I couldn't figure out how they could fall asleep.

"I can't get the mangled face of that soldier out of my head," Jess whispered.

"I keep thinking there are soldiers about to sneak up on us," I said back.

"Levi's out there."

"Yeah…" My voice trailed off. I knew Levi had some army

training from his dad, but sometimes I worried he would goof off.

"Where do you think we're going to go?" Jess said.

"Who knows, probably find another spot in the bush."

"I don't care where we go. As long as it's away from here."

"Maybe we can stay at a farmhouse," I said, feeling hopeful.

"It would be nice to stay in a bed."

"Imagine not getting soaked when it rained."

"I can't remember what sleeping in a bed is like," Jess said.

I tried to think back to before the war, but it felt like another life, so long ago. "Me neither."

"There's no way the others would let us stay in a house," Jess continued.

"It's too dangerous," I said, sighing.

Everything was too dangerous. Even hiding in the bush. I was naïve to think the war would pass by and leave us unharmed. I only had to look back on what happened to Leah and Evee to see no one was safe. The soldiers came into our homes, took us in the middle of the night, and imprisoned us. Lizzie's brother had been killed, and who knew if the rest of our families were alive. We never talked about it.

I was starting to feel anger. And, I was starting to see where Lizzie was coming from. It wasn't about being reckless and throwing away our lives. It was about fighting for all we had lost and trying to get back the life we had. I didn't want to spend the rest of my life hiding in the forest, feral and wild. Nor did I want to spend my days behind lock and key, waiting for the chance to be free. All I wished for back in the prison camp was freedom, and revenge. And now that I had it, I had to do something with it. I didn't know why it had taken me so long to see it.

"Is anyone else finding sleep impossible?" Grace said loudly, cutting through my thoughts.

"I am now," Lizzie said.

"Dylan's snoring," Jess pointed out.

"He could sleep anywhere," Grace said, sitting up.

"What time is it?" Lizzie asked.

"Almost dawn," I said, looking at my watch.

"There's no point trying to get any more sleep," Grace said. She wriggled out of her sleeping bag. "I feel bad, we left Levi out there all night on his own." She wrapped a blanket around her shoulders and left to join Levi. Those two were inseparable. Soon, their muffled chatter drowned out the silence of the forest.

"I'm going to miss this place," Lizzie said.

"I'm not," Jess said, rolling over onto her back and staring up at the tarpaulin roof.

"It was starting to feel like home," Lizzie said. "Our little haven in the woods."

"A haven full of bad memories," Jess said.

"This whole country's full of bad memories," I added.

"Jen's right," Dylan said as he tried to stifle a yawn.

"It has good ones too," Lizzie insisted, almost like she was trying to will the good times from the past to the present.

"I can't remember them anymore," Dylan said. I knew what he meant. Blocking out the past was the only way to keep moving forward.

"I look around, and all I see is death, and our suffering," I said.

"When I think back to before the war... it makes me sad. I miss what was," Jess said. "I miss my family, my house... my whole life."

"It's better not to think about it, Jess," I said.

"But what about all the good times?" Lizzie said.

"What about them? I'm doing all I can just to make it to tomorrow," I said.

"The sadder thing is... New Zealand will never be the way we remember it again," Dylan said.

"That's depressing, Dylan," Lizzie said.

"It's realistic. I hate to break it to you, Lizzie, but even if this war ends, the cleanup will take years. New Zealand won't be the same."

"Dylan's right. Think about how wrecked other countries are after civil war," Jess added.

"New Zealand's different," Lizzie said.

"It's only different because it's worse. Our entire population is imprisoned and all our cities destroyed. It will be decades before we live in anything resembling New Zealand again," Dylan said, getting up and pulling a hoodie over his head.

"Then why are we even fighting back?" Lizzie said, a challenging gleam in her eye. She wasn't about to let Dylan tell her fighting back was pointless.

"Because anything is better than this hell," Dylan said as he ducked out of the shelter and walked out into the early dawn light.

Lizzie flopped back down onto her pillow, dejected and exhausted. "I wish those soldiers never found our camp," Lizzie said eventually.

"I'm sick of running," Jess added. I felt the same way. But war was here, and like a bloodhound, it had our scent.

CHAPTER TWENTY-ONE

LIZZIE

A NEW MORNING HAD brought renewed hope. Our camp was undisturbed during the night, which had allowed everyone to calm down, and I had snuck away from the busy morning rituals to gather myself. Sitting at the foot of my favorite tree, I had a good view of the gurgling stream, and could faintly hear the chatter of the others back at camp.

Steam rose in small tendrils from the mug of tea I held warming my hands as I watched Dylan wade into the stream with only his boxers on and he began washing some of the dirt and grime off his body. His skin looked soft and lightly tanned in the fresh morning sunlight. Dylan then dunked his head under and tousled his blond hair, before standing up and stretching, staring into the distance as beads of water rolled down his toned frame.

"Dylan," I called, laughing.

He turned and faced me, a warm smile on his face. "God, have you been there the whole time? Spying on me, eh, Lizzie? I didn't even see you. Still, you weren't very lucky. I didn't strip right down," he joked.

"I wouldn't call you stripping in front of me lucky," I said. That wasn't entirely true. I wouldn't have minded, but I kept that thought to myself as I sipped at my tea.

"How would you know? You don't know what you're missing," Dylan said, shaking his head before chuckling. He waded out of the stream and sat down beside me. "I assume you came out here to think… or spy on me." Dylan grinned, his body still wet with tiny shimmering droplets.

"I thought you'd be able to guess what I'm thinking already… we have to leave here immediately," I said uneasily to Dylan, who just sighed. It was about the fifteenth time that morning I had voiced my opinion.

"We will. Everyone else is packing already, but we won't be ready for a few hours," he said, also for the fifteenth time.

I rubbed my eyes. I had tried to sleep, but there was no way to hide from what I had done. He was the first soldier who I had killed face to face… maybe even the first person I had killed, full stop. I had thought a stray bullet of mine hit the mark when we were escaping from the mall, but there had been no way to know whether it was by my hand or by someone else's. Bullets had been flying in the dark, and people yelling everywhere. This time, there was no doubt.

Grace had tried to talk to me and make me feel better. It had worked, sort of. We all knew that the soldier had to die. If it hadn't been me, Levi would have killed him. But the soldier's words burrowed deep into my bones, filling me with guilt and resentment. I shouldn't be made to feel this way, I thought. I had to believe he was wrong about us. We were on the right side, weren't we? Even if we weren't, it changed nothing. They killed my brother, and they had our families in captivity. We had to fight.

There was also no way to escape from the feeling someone was watching us, and had been watching us for some time. What if the soldiers knew we were here, trying to hide? What if a helicopter soared overhead and spotted our campsite? We didn't know what it looked like from above. We tried our best to keep the conspicuous things—like the tarpaulin—covered with leaves and branches, but what about the smoke we tried hopelessly to fan away from the fire every time we cooked? What about our loud arguments that happened frequently?

I knew I was paranoid. It had been several months since the war started, and these three soldiers were the first to actually make it into our campsite. I needed to calm down. I took a deep breath and closed my eyes, feeling the sun's warmth on my face.

But that soldier's bloodied, triumphant grin flashed before me, and I opened my eyes abruptly. "We should have made precautions for this sort of thing. Why didn't we think of this before? We were bloody lucky Jess and Grace were still awake."

"You're right about how lucky we were," Dylan agreed.

"I don't think we will be that lucky next time."

"Then what's your plan?" Dylan asked calmly.

I stood up, brushing off the flecks of dirt that had clung to my jeans. "I don't know."

"Lizzie without a plan? I'm not sure that adds up," Dylan said.

"Actually, scratch that, I do have a plan," I said, as an idea sprung into my mind. It would at least set my mind at ease if I could see our camp from above. I set my mug on a nearby log. "I'm going to climb the tree."

Dylan raised his eyebrows. "Go ahead then, I'm watching," he said, also standing up and staring at me as though I was crazy. "I'll even give you a leg up if you want." He was clearly amused. I approached the tree and grabbed the nearest branch above my head. Dylan gripped my leg and gave me a helpful boost up onto the branch.

"Thanks."

"What are you doing?" Dylan asked, curiosity obviously

getting the better of him.

"If you want to know, then come up here yourself." I smiled as I reached out to pull myself higher on another branch.

"Fine," Dylan said, rolling his eyes at me. He pulled himself onto the first branch with relative ease. I was already farther up the tree, climbing as high as I could. I stopped on a branch that seemed stable enough for both of us. Dylan soon caught me up, his height working to his advantage.

"Wow, you can see everything from here," he exclaimed. He was right. It was like we were floating on a sea of green. I was surprised at how well hidden our tarpaulin was, barely visible beneath the dense carpet of trees. If I hadn't known it was there, I wouldn't have known where to look.

Dylan immediately caught onto my plan. "You can't see our campsite at all."

"This is a much better sentry place," I noted, sitting down on one of the branches. Not that it mattered now. "We should find a tree like this to keep watch at our next hideout."

"Yes, it would be easy to spot the movement as they pass through the bushes... even if you couldn't see them well enough," Dylan agreed. "It could work. Nice thinking Lizzie."

"Thanks," I said and smiled at him, then looked away, trying not to stare at his naked chest. We sat on the branch for a while, looking out over the forest. It was truly amazing. Smaller trees blanketed the floor, with taller ones, like the Douglas-fir trees, stretching up toward the sky. Then, there were the really old trees, like the kauris that towered over everything else: nature's skyscrapers.

"Are you OK, Lizzie?" Dylan asked.

"I'm fine," I dismissed.

Dylan's forehead creased with concern. "Grace said you might want to talk."

"Grace is always meddling," I snapped back.

"I think she's looking out for you," Dylan said.

I sighed. "I feel terrible about how I killed the soldier last night."

"I'm not surprised."

"What's that supposed to mean?"

"I mean, of course you feel horrible. How could you not? We aren't killing machines—we have a conscience." It was so simple. Dylan was right.

A loud humming disrupted my thoughts. I scanned the sky, locking onto a large plane in the distance. We pressed ourselves against the trunk of the tree, terrified that the approaching plane would spot us. I was sure it would. It roared overhead, alarmingly close.

"Dylan, maybe we should get down from here," I suggested, my ears still ringing from the noise.

Dylan stared after the plane.

"Come on, it's gone, let's get down before it comes back," I said, touching his bare shoulder lightly.

"I can't believe it," Dylan said, angrily shaking his head.

"What do you mean?" I asked, staring after it.

"Oh, come on Lizzie, didn't you see what was emblazoned on the side of that plane?"

"I was more concerned about staying in the tree," I retorted. "Not to mention it flew by fast enough."

"It was a private jet, Lizzie. The Prime Minister's private jet, probably headed to the airport. I remember seeing it on TV a while ago... it's the same huge one he used to take to international conferences," Dylan said, reminiscing, a sour look on his face.

"It was Marion's jet? I can't believe it," I said, now repeating Dylan. "He's flying around on a luxury jet while our country is in the midst of war... he really is a bastard," I said angrily.

"I know. I thought there was stuff in place to prevent people like him abusing power."

"Yeah, but they don't always work. How can you tell the

Prime Minister he's wrong? He's got so many people supporting him. By the time people react, it's too late."

"We need to do something," Dylan said, urgency in his voice. "I can't sit here any longer. Fuck it. I don't care what the others say. We're leaving, and we're leaving now. I don't even care what sort of destruction we cause, but I'm getting back at him."

I had never seen Dylan this angry. He climbed halfway down the tree before jumping the rest. I had to hurry to catch up with him. "I'm going to kill him," Dylan said as he charged toward the campsite.

I jogged to catch up to him and grabbed his wrist. "Wait," I said, pulling him back.

"Wait for what, Lizzie?" Dylan snapped back.

"We can't go alone. We need the others' help."

"We both know they won't go along with it," Dylan said under his breath.

"What were you thinking of doing then?"

"I was going to give them an ultimatum. Either they join our cause or—"

"Or what, Dylan? We need their help," I said.

Dylan glared at me. "They won't agree. I know they won't."

"Levi will be on board, and Grace—"

"Grace will shut the whole thing down. Tell us to start small, take a breath. I don't want to take a fucking breath."

Deep down, I knew Dylan was right. Grace, Jess, and Jen would never go along with our plan. But that didn't mean we couldn't change their minds. An idea was starting to take shape. "There might be another way," I said slowly, meeting Dylan's eyes.

"What do you suggest?" Dylan asked. "I can't think of any way to convince them."

"All we have to do is make them see the plane," I said. "Make them follow us into town. They don't need to know our real reason for going." I don't know what made me say it. It was an evil thought, fooling our friends so they would follow us into danger.

"You mean trick them." Dylan eyed me suspiciously. "I don't know how I feel about that."

"More like mislead them. We just need them to pass by the airport. When they see the plane for themselves, they'll feel the same way."

"But still… if something happens… it's on us, Lizzie," Dylan said.

"Once we get to the plane, they'll choose to help. I know it."

Dylan studied my face for a moment as he thought it over. "We'll try it your way," he finally said.

"Even if the others don't agree, I'm coming with you," I said quietly. Action was what we needed right now. I had been pressing the others to fight back, and now, at last, Dylan seemed to be taking charge. I knew the others would get on board. They wouldn't leave us on our own. I usually felt guilty about pushing them into a decision. Not this time, not when I knew I was right, and there was nothing else we could do.

We left immediately after burying the tarpaulin near the trees, covering over our fire pit and packing up our camp. Dylan and I mentioned the plane and said our camp might have been spotted. This spurred them into immediate action. I took a final glance behind me. We didn't know how long we would be gone, but there was finality in the air. We wouldn't be returning anytime soon. We trudged over the usual track with our backpacks heavy and burdening our shoulders. I walked with Grace, Levi, and Dylan out in the front. Jennifer and Jess walked behind us.

"Ergh, the packs are so heavy," Grace complained as she readjusted the straps of her bag.

"I think I have raw rub marks already," I said.

"Where are we going to hide while we plan what we're going

to do?" Grace asked me. I shrugged. My mind was racing. All we needed to do was to get close to the airport.

"Maybe an empty house in town? We'll need to post a sentry and get some sleep," I said.

"That's dangerous," Levi said instantly. "Soldiers are everywhere around there. If you're set on a house, at least pick one out here in the country."

"I think one in town is a good idea," Dylan said, agreeing.

"Hell no," Levi said. "I want to survive this war."

"Think about it, mate, we would have eyes and ears on the soldiers. It would be easier to learn their routine and plan an attack if we were nearby," Dylan said.

"I'm not convinced," Levi said. "What's the target?"

"The port," I said instantly. It was far. We would need to go through town to get to it. And, pass by the airport. Maybe it would be enough to convince Levi.

"That's ballsy," Levi said. But I knew I had struck a nerve. After all, he had mentioned it would be an important hub of operation. "You want a place closer to the port so scouting is easier?" he said as he mulled the idea over in his mind.

"Exactly," Dylan said.

"Actually, Grace used to live near the port. Maybe we could use her place as a base?" I said. If I could get Levi or Grace on our side, the other would eventually agree.

Grace's face brightened. I knew she wouldn't be able to resist if we dangled the possibility of finding out something about her mom in front of her.

"The rumpus room upstairs would be a good lookout. Also, there might be a clue about what happened to Mom," she said, barely containing her excitement.

"Wouldn't she have been voting?" Levi said.

"She was supposed to... but I was at Lizzie's so I don't know if she ever went," Grace said.

"That rumpus room would be perfect," I said, feeling

rejuvenated as we pushed through the rough terrain of the bush, shrugging the ferns carelessly aside. Levi saw the smile on Grace's face, and I knew he wouldn't rob her of this.

"If your mom never made it to the voting booth… you might not like what you find," Levi said quietly to Grace.

Dylan caught my eye and gave me a knowing look. So far, the plan was working. "So, you're in?" Dylan said to Levi. He ran his hand through his hair and looked over at Grace. She was still beaming at the chance to go back to her home, regardless of what she might find.

Levi sighed. "For the record, your plan is shit. But… I'm in," he said as he looked back toward Grace, who was now marching onward with renewed purpose. I was a horrible friend for doing this—taking advantage of her. But now was not the time to dwell, if she ever found out she would forgive me. She always did.

"I'll tell Jen and Jess," I said as I glanced back at them. They had been silent throughout the whole debate. I was sure they would go along with us, but regardless, majority ruled. I dropped back to see where they stood. Neither of them seemed to have a problem with it, despite Jennifer's previous view of wanting to stay on the safe side. Maybe the soldiers intruding on our camp had made her realize we couldn't stay hidden forever. There was no safe place.

We were quieter as we approached the road. It was like this every time—that first step from the grass of the forest onto the tarmac had a serious effect on me. And this time, I wasn't sure we were going back. With that thought, a stream of emotion ran through me. I didn't know whether to feel scared, excited, or angry. Finally, the soldiers—and Prime Minister Marion—would face the same fear they had instilled into us.

We were forced to stop walking when we got into the open space, as it was too dangerous to travel around in broad daylight. So, we spent the rest of the day underneath some trees at a kiwifruit orchard off the main road, waiting until it was dark enough. Dylan kept watch for us, and I lay on the ground, staring up at the low and thick cover of the vines, the cold barrel of a rifle right beside me.

I WOKE WITH A jolt, and my hand reached for the gun.

"Lizzie, it's time to move again," Grace said nervously. I nodded and got to my knees. I had slept away the hours until night, and I could barely make out Grace's shape in the darkness. I pressed a button on my watch, and it lit up. Ten p.m.

"You must have been really tired," Grace said as if reading my thoughts. I merely nodded and shouldered my pack to march onward. It would be a long walk to the airport.

"I think we should take the back way to mine," Grace said. "It might take a bit longer, but we can avoid going anywhere near the mall."

Levi grunted in agreement.

Dylan looked over at me. We needed to go past the mall.

"That will take way too long," Dylan said. "It might add a couple extra hours. I don't want to be out there any longer than I have to be."

"I'd rather risk going past the mall," I added.

"It's like you two are on some sort of death mission," Levi said.

"It's a calculated risk," Dylan said. "We're going to be out on the street for an extra two hours if we go the long way."

"He's right," I said.

"We're running out of time," Jess said. "Make a decision." She crossed her arms and stared at us.

"Screw it. Lead the way, Dylan," Levi said, flicking us a look. "Just don't get us killed." It was all going according to plan. We left the cover of the kiwifruit orchard and made our way along the highway into town.

"I never realized how far it was from Omanawa to my place,"

Grace whispered several hours later.

"Hmm," I agreed. "It's far. If we don't get there soon, we're going to have to find somewhere to hole up."

Summer coming had been a bit of a detriment. Of course, it wasn't as cold, but the days were longer, and light came early. It wasn't long before we were quietly moving past the roundabout near the mall, trying to block out the memories of the last time we had been there. The airport was only ten minutes away now.

Suddenly Jennifer stopped.

"Evee," she said, a catch in her throat, staring fearfully up at the looming mall.

"Come on, it's all right," Jess comforted her. She, too, looked tearful, but managed to hold it together. "We need to keep going, Jen."

"But what if Evee's still alive, somewhere in there?" Jennifer said pleadingly.

I shook my head. "Jennifer, we watched her die. She's gone."

Jennifer broke down and cried: a loud wail.

A soldier from around the mall called out to his mate. "I think I heard someone," he said in a low voice.

Levi clamped his hand over Jennifer's mouth, and her crying became muffled.

"It was over here," the soldier said, who had managed to convince his comrade to help him investigate. I looked desperately around. We weren't in the best place. It was open and near the road with no cover for several hundred meters. A torchlight flickered somewhere in front of us.

"Shit, we're going to have to run," Dylan muttered to me. "Ditch the packs."

I threw my heavy pack to the ground and started sprinting up the main road, hearing the footsteps of the others crashing loudly behind me. A shout of discovery sounded from one of the soldiers, and the flashlight beamed across the road as the soldiers chased us.

"Where do we go?" I puffed to Dylan.

"Stick to the plan," Dylan said, his voice cold.

So, we ran. My lungs were burning, and my muscles cramping with fatigue. We'd already been walking for hours, and my body was reaching exhaustion. It felt like I couldn't breathe, and I didn't understand how my body kept working when every breath was a struggle, our panted gasps becoming shorter and shallower. But there wasn't a choice to stop either, only the endless agony of each step into the darkness.

Chapter Twenty-Two

Levi

"This way," Dylan yelled as he jumped over a low fence. We emerged into a dark empty paddock.

"Faster!" Lizzie shouted. My body wanted to give up, as I gasped for breath. But I had to keep moving. Gunfire echoed behind us. They were still giving chase. Grace tripped beside me.

I grabbed her arm and yanked her to her feet. "Come on!"

She stumbled forward, and we sprinted to catch the others. A piercing scream cut through the dark. Grace had fallen behind me. She screamed in pain as another hail of bullets sprayed us from somewhere in the darkness.

I ran back to her. "Are you hit?" I wheezed.

She managed to get to her feet and limped for a couple of steps. I wasn't going to lose Grace now.

"I think so," she said through clenched teeth. We kept running forward. If we lagged, they would kill us. "Help me, Levi," she cried. I supported her, and we ran together. I peered ahead into the seemingly unending darkness.

"Where are we going?" Jess shouted over the hail of bullets.

"Away from here," Dylan yelled. The familiar roar of a helicopter came closer.

"Oh no," Grace moaned. A beam of light exploded through the blackness.

"Shit, spotlight," I cursed. Nothing ever went our way. The paddock was illuminated. It flashed over what looked like an airplane.

"We're at the airport," Dylan yelled.

"Just our luck," Lizzie said.

"The beam is coming this way. Hide!" I sprinted in the opposite direction of the light and dove into a scrubby shrub. It wouldn't give us cover for long. Grace was not far behind me. "Ouch," I muttered as she dove on top of me.

"Help me strap my leg," she said, frantically feeling around on her leg. I reached down and felt her leg for the wound. It wasn't hard to find. Her calf was soaked in warm blood. I moved my hand up her leg and felt a long gash across her thigh.

"I think it grazed you," I said as my fingers probed carefully at her wound.

She let out a strangled squeal of pain.

I ripped the bottom of my shirt off and tied it tightly around her leg. "Better?" I asked. It was all I could do.

"Thanks," she whimpered through tears.

I peered out and finally saw the paddock clearly. It definitely wasn't an empty field. The spotlight showed an airplane waiting on the tarmac with the small airport building behind it. The light flashed over dozens of soldiers stalking the field. The others were nowhere to be seen.

"Let's head to that plane," I said as the beam of light made its way farther away from us. "We can hide under it."

"OK," Grace said nervously.

"Don't worry," I said. "You're going to be fine."

She let out a tearful sob, embraced me in a crushing hug, and cried into my shoulder. I wrapped my arms around her. She felt so vulnerable. In that moment, I couldn't imagine my life without her.

"Levi, you mean a lot to me. You have to know that, just in case," she whispered. Just in case she didn't make it. I didn't want to think it. I helped her up, and we ran through the darkness. I saw the faint outline of a soldier in front of me. Silently, I drew my gun and fired. There was a bright flash of light from the end of my gun as the soldier fell. I sprinted forward but tripped over the fallen soldier. With some difficulty, I resisted the urge to swear. Grace pulled me to my feet.

We ran onward, and I felt something wet and sticky on my face. My stomached lurched. Was I hit? I hesitantly ran my fingers down my cheeks and wiped the sticky blood onto my jeans. I couldn't feel a wound. My stomach lurched again: it wasn't my blood. The spotlight skimmed over the airplane only a hundred meters ahead of us. I prayed the light wouldn't come to us. There was nowhere to hide. And I had no energy left to dodge it. The light was thirty meters away, twenty meters, ten meters, then… it moved away.

"Thank God," Grace whispered. We used the last of our energy to sprint underneath the plane. Grace collapsed to the ground in agony. For the moment, we were safe. The light couldn't find us here.

"Levi," a voice whispered nearby.

"Grace?" I asked.

"What?" she said, confused. I felt a tap on my shoulder and jumped in fright.

"What?" I asked Grace worriedly. Grace pointed to the plane above us.

"Levi, up here," Lizzie said impatiently. I looked up and saw her. The luggage compartment was open a fraction.

"What are you doing up there?" I whispered.

"Get on the plane," she said. "I'm lowering a ladder down now." This was a stupid idea.

"But…" I tried to say. She was gone. A rope ladder was flung from above. "You go first," I whispered to Grace. She nodded and struggled up the ladder. I could tell she was in pain but would have to deal with it for the moment. When she was safely helped into the compartment, I scaled the ladder. Dylan helped me in. Lizzie pulled up the ladder and shut the door. The compartment was faintly lit with the 'door armed' sign. Lizzie, Dylan, Jess, and Jennifer were huddled among a few elegant luggage cases and large padlocked boxes. I spotted the emergency supply box in the corner and noted the open lid.

"The ladder came from there," Lizzie said before I could ask.

"I need the first aid kit," I said to them.

"Grace, you're bleeding!" Jennifer said and quickly moved over to her. Dylan looked at my torn shirt and then at the bandage wrapped tightly around her thigh.

"Nice improvisation," he said with a smirk. I ignored him. This was serious.

Lizzie carefully peeled the makeshift bandage off the large gash on Grace's thigh.

"Shit," Dylan said, hardly above a whisper. "Does it hurt?"

"Of course it bloody hurts," Grace said back, her voice strained.

"You shouldn't be running on this," Lizzie joked.

Grace glared at her. "Soldiers shouldn't have been shooting at us," Grace said. Her face contorted in pain as Lizzie poured alcohol over the wound from the first aid kit. She strangled a yelp as Lizzie tightened a proper bandage around her leg. "Thanks," Grace said in a strained voice. A deafening rumble shook the plane as the engines started up.

"We need to get off," I said urgently.

"You don't get it, do you," Lizzie said.

"Get what? We need to get the hell out of here," I whispered back.

"Maybe he's right, Lizzie," Dylan said, looking uncertainly at

Grace. Lizzie glared at him. What was going on?

"This is the Prime Minister's plane. This is our chance," Lizzie said.

"What chance?" Jennifer asked. "Grace is hurt, and we don't know where this thing is headed."

"We can kill him," Dylan said coldly.

"Dylan, are you out of your bloody mind?" I said, trying not to raise my voice. Lizzie and Dylan stared at me.

"You two planned this whole thing," Grace said through clenched teeth.

"We didn't plan anything," Lizzie said.

"I saw the plane's emblem when we were running," Dylan said quickly. Grace had her eyes shut, trying to ignore the pain. But I saw the look in Dylan's eye. He was a terrible liar.

"This isn't funny," I said. "We can't shoot him on the plane. There will be soldiers up there. We're dead if we try."

"We don't know that," Lizzie said back. "Plus, who knows where this plane is going. Maybe we'll even be free."

"Do you really think that?" Jess interrupted. "We are on an enemy plane, and I'm not an idiot. That means this plane is headed to an enemy base."

"What other option did we have?" Dylan asked, trying to sound practical. "Even you ran for the safety of the plane."

"We never planned to actually get on," Jess said defensively.

"Don't lie, Dylan," I said, interrupting. "You've been trying to get here since this morning."

"You're delusional, Levi," Lizzie said. The plane jerked forward as it sped down the runway.

"Do you think we're idiots?" I asked, outraged.

"Of course not," Dylan said. His eyes moved from Grace lying injured on the floor of the plane, to Lizzie who sat fuming next to him. They had made a mistake.

"I hope you've learned something. If what Levi says is true... this is all on you," Jess said to them.

"You better hope Grace doesn't bleed out," Jennifer said as she tried to put pressure on the wound.

"We're supposed to make these decisions as a group," Grace said, her eyes still closed. "You guys just pulled us up here. You didn't even give us a choice."

"There wasn't any time for discussion," Lizzie said.

"Bullshit," I said. "What if Grace and I hadn't made it here? Would you have left without us?"

"Of course not," Lizzie said back. My stomach lurched as the plane lifted off.

"You were already on the plane. When it began moving were you just going to jump out and hope you landed on a soft feather mattress?" I said enraged.

Grace put her hand on my leg, urging me to calm down.

"If they weren't so hell-bent on killing Marion, you wouldn't have got shot," I said to her.

"I want to be mad at them, Levi, but I don't have the energy," she said back. Always the peacekeeper, I thought.

Lizzie glared at me.

"Usually, you're the practical one, Lizzie," I said. "What happened? Now we're on an enemy plane going to God knows where. There's an army searching for us, and another one sitting right above our heads. Seriously, what were you thinking? What if someone comes down here?" I asked, pointing to the door a few meters away.

I took a few deep breaths to calm myself down and glanced at my hands. They were shaking uncontrollably. I shoved them into the pockets of my jeans and opened my mouth to launch another attack against Lizzie.

"Shhh," Grace hissed. "I can hear voices."

We all looked upward.

"I formally apologize for the incident on the airstrip before takeoff. We have been searching for that guerrilla group for a long time," a crisp female voice announced.

"All is forgiven, Dion," a man's voice said.

"Would you like anything to drink, Prime Minister?" Dion asked.

I glanced at Lizzie. Her face was carefully blank, but I knew she was worried. Maybe their stupidity was finally sinking in.

"Yes, please. I think some tea would be perfect," Prime Minister Marion said. We heard Dion's muffled footsteps moving away. A few moments later, they returned.

"Your tea, sir. And the Captain has advised me that our flight time to Orlando is fifteen hours."

Panic rose in my chest. It couldn't be. Orlando? I looked over at Lizzie, who fidgeted with her hands, concern briefly passing across her face.

"Thank you," Marion said curtly. We heard Dion begin to move away. "Dion, a moment, please."

"Yes, sir," she said as she returned.

"Did you catch the guerrillas?" he asked.

"Unfortunately, not, sir. They took off into the forest again. The men on the ground are sending the search dogs for them any minute now," Dion replied.

"Useless," Marion said with anger in his voice.

"If we could force the guerrillas to work with us, they could be of use."

"Perhaps."

"Anyway, you have a long flight ahead of you. You should get some rest," Dion said.

"I don't need any rest. Have you received an update on the rocket yet?" Marion asked.

"Absolutely. Our contacts at the American Institute for Space Discovery say that so far everything is in order and ready for immediate action upon your arrival."

My mouth was dry. I hoped they were talking about a rocket being launched into space. For some reason, I knew otherwise.

"And you thought we were heading to safety," I whispered to

Lizzie.

She looked guiltily at us.

"The coordinates for your England target were sent through to our men at AISD moments ago. Everything is going remarkably well, sir," Dion said professionally.

England? I hoped I wasn't reading into what they were saying.

"That's terrific news," Marion commented with a note of satisfaction in his voice.

What was he planning? Flying a rocket into England? Surely not. Why would he do that? We had just escaped one pot of terror. Who knew what the next one would be like. Disaster was coming. I could feel it. My stomach twisted and turned.

"Well, shit," Dylan whispered.

Shit, was right.

"What now?" Jennifer asked.

"Nothing," Grace said. "We're stuck thirty thousand feet in the air, we can't go anywhere."

"We could kill him now…" Dylan said.

"We're not killing him here. It's too dangerous," I whispered back.

"Why not?" Lizzie asked. She got to her feet and started sneaking toward the door, rifle at the ready.

"Lizzie," Grace said. "We'd get ourselves killed."

"Maybe not. There's nowhere for him to run," she said.

"Yeah, and neither can we," I retorted.

"Sit back down, Lizzie," Grace said. "You've already got me shot. Don't go getting yourself killed. This is a big plane. You don't know how many troops are up there."

Lizzie sulked back to the group.

"If killing him is out of the question, what do we do?" Dylan whispered.

"What else can we do? We have to try and stop the rocket. We're the only ones who know about it," Jess said.

"That's impossible," Jennifer said.

"Thousands of people could be killed. We're the only ones who have any idea about what's happening," Lizzie said as she perched herself on top of a large box.

Grace shuffled closer to me, scuttling away from the cold air conditioning vent. I lifted her injured leg onto my lap to try and elevate it a bit. She winced but seemed to relax. Her blood was already soaking through the bandage. I was genuinely worried. Was she losing a lot of blood? I knew nothing about first aid. Grace was petite, and her skin had already turned unnaturally pale.

"Stopping that rocket's going to involve sneaking into AISD… whatever that is. We're going to get thrown in prison," Grace said weakly. I knew what she said was true.

"Then we'll be careful," Lizzie said.

"People are going to think we're terrorists," Jennifer said.

"Let them think whatever they want. We have to stop that rocket," Lizzie said with a determined ring in her voice. Her mind was set. There was no way to make her change it. It seemed we were going to stop the rocket, whether we wanted to or not. There was silence as everyone made their decision. I knew we would all come to the same revelation. Hundreds, maybe thousands of people would die if we didn't stop it. Every instinct told me not to do it. But I couldn't do nothing.

"Lizzie's right," Dylan backed her, "and you all know it."

"I still can't believe we're going to America," Jess muttered, shaking her head in disbelief. "I thought I'd never be able to go back there."

Jess' words brought back memories from before the war. Though they had been better days, life was far from perfect. New Zealand was still on the banned travel list. We had been since the first cases of the virus emerged in some dairy cows in the Waikato. It spread to humans like wildfire. And even when the virus was wrestled under control, we were still outlawed.

"If anyone finds out about us, they'll send us right back," Dylan said, shoving his hands in his pockets.

"Surely not," Jennifer whispered. "Someone would be sympathetic to our cause."

"That's wishful thinking," Lizzie said.

There was no doubt in my mind that we would be sent on the first plane out of there. Probably escorted by a whole team of infection control specialists. Because, even after all the cattle were slaughtered and burned, and our economy crumbled, the World Health Alliance warned that our land was still contaminated. Which meant we were, too.

"Sir," another male voice said from above. Immediately our conversation ceased. "Pardon my interruption, but may I have a moment to speak to you… er… off the record?"

"I suppose, go ahead, Joshua," Marion said with a sigh.

"Firstly, I support you, and your war one hundred percent," he said.

"I'm glad I have your backing," Marion said.

"Thank you, sir," Joshua said nervously. "However, are you sure you're doing the right thing?" I could imagine the courage it took him to say that to the face of his leader. There was a tense silence.

"Of course, I'm doing the right thing. Do you doubt me and my abilities?" Marion said, only just managing to keep his tone calm.

"Definitely not. I'm only wondering how it can be beneficial to involve two other countries in this war. Our army is large now, but if the Americans and British realize what we've done, there's no way we can hold them off."

"Joshua," Marion said, chuckling. "Joshua, Joshua, Joshua."

"Um, yes, sir?" he said uneasily.

"I appreciate your concern. But I will tell you what I have told everyone else who has asked me that question… nothing will go wrong."

"What if they discover your plan?" Joshua asked.

"They won't," Marion said, annoyed. It seemed Joshua had noticed the change in his voice too because he didn't reply. "Tensions between England and America have been high for a while. They aren't friendly like they used to be. Any trigger and they will fall into battle with each other. They've been on the cusp for years, a prod is all they need."

"I still don't understand why you are doing this?"

Stiff silence answered. We strained to hear the muffled voices over the noise of the plane. I looked at Dylan, had we missed his answer?

"It's a precaution," Marion said finally.

"A precaution against what?" Joshua pressed.

I was sure this would be one question too far. But Marion didn't seem bothered.

"Have you ever played chess, Joshua?"

"Yes, sir. But I'm not very good at it."

"Why don't you sit down. Let me show you how it works."

"Sure," Joshua said. He sounded relieved that Marion had dropped the conversation.

"Black or white?"

"White."

We all slowly relaxed, thinking the best part of the conversation was finished. A game of chess was hardly interesting. But we were wrong.

"It's all about distraction," Marion said. There was a gunshot, and we all jumped. Jennifer stifled a cry, and Marion proclaimed, "Checkmate."

EVENTUALLY, LIZZIE'S HEAD DROPPED onto Dylan's shoulder as sleep overtook her. I stretched out on the floor and wadded my jersey into the shape of a pillow. Grace tried to relax with her head resting comfortably on my stomach. She was quickly asleep, exhausted. I lay there listening to the hypnotic humming of the engines and let my mind drift.

I thought about Grace and everything we had gone through together, not that we ever were 'together'. I had talked to her about taking our relationship further, but she was worried about things getting complicated. I accepted that. But it felt like we were already together. And things were already complicated.

I looked down at her small figure asleep next to me. Her mouth was slightly open, and she breathed softly. She looked beautiful and at peace. I gently rested my hand on her head and ran my fingers through her silky chestnut hair. What was I doing? Dylan looked up at me quizzically, and I quickly withdrew my hand. I glanced over at Dylan, who appeared in much discomfort. He was trying to move position without waking Lizzie. I smirked at him, and he stared back, unimpressed. I peered into the dark cavity of the luggage hold, my mind idling from one thing to the next. I must have fallen asleep at that point because what seemed like only minutes later, I was being shaken awake.

I opened my eyes drowsily. "What?"

"We're descending," Jess said, her voice tight.

"How do we get off the plane?" Lizzie said urgently. My mind went blank. We hadn't even thought of it. We couldn't wait until the baggage was unloaded, or we would be found and deported back. Or worse, the soldiers would find us. That left one option. We had to get off before the plane docked.

"We're going to have to jump," I said.

"There has to be another way," Grace said, shaking her head.

"There isn't," Dylan said.

"We jump out when the plane is taxiing, and run for it," I said. My stomach dropped as the plane completed its descent. The tires bumped along the runway, and the plane began to slow. Dylan and I disarmed the door and pushed it open. I breathed a sigh of relief when I realized it was nighttime. The humid air rushed in, soothing my nerves. The plane was moving at a crawl, but the concrete below whizzed past.

"We have to jump now," Dylan yelled above the rush of wind as he leaped out of the door.

"Go, Grace," I called at her. If she was afraid, she never showed it. She carefully dropped from the plane. "Lizzie and Jess, go next," I said ushering orders. "Go, Jennifer," I called.

"I can-can-can't," she said in a terrified voice.

"You have to," I said back.

"No, I can't," she repeated.

"Jump," I said loudly as I leaped from the plane. I knew she would follow eventually. My stomach dropped horribly, and the wind blew me strongly as the ground rushed out to meet me, I braced for impact. I crumpled to the tarmac and rolled to avoid breaking anything.

"Shit, that was high," I said after I got shakily to my feet. A few meters away, I saw Jennifer getting up with wobbly legs. I knew she would do it. I glanced around and saw the plane heading toward the airport. That was the last time I looked back. Jennifer and I ran for the fence several hundred meters away. We dived through a hole and took off into the night. The others were waiting for us a few hundred meters from the airport.

"Are you all OK?" Dylan asked.

"I'm all good," I said.

"Good," Dylan said as we took off again. When we had no energy left to run another step, we had made it to what looked like a small park. Lizzie and Grace sat on the ground puffing and wheezing.

"I can't take another step," Grace cried, exhausted. Blood was oozing down her leg again, and she sobbed uncontrollably. There was no point arguing. We all felt the same way. I sat down heavily on the ground as my legs succumbed to cramp. I rubbed them furiously trying to get rid of it.

"We made it," Jess said. For once, I let a tiny smile escape. We were, for all intents and purposes, free.

Chapter Twenty-Three

Grace

The late afternoon sun blazed through the tall American Beech trees. I sat moodily on a rotting log as Levi fussed over my leg, trying to stop the bleeding that had soaked through my bandage. The park we found was close to the major airport and was sheltered enough to prevent any prying eyes laying sight on us.

"How's that?" Levi asked as he ripped another shred off his shirt and tied it tightly around my thigh. I let out a grunt of pain but nodded. The t-shirt he wore was now so ripped it barely served any purpose at all. His disheveled hair, scruffy beard, and haggard face looked out of place in our new free world.

The adrenaline rush from all that had happened in the last twenty-four hours had subsided, and now, the pain was very real.

"I haven't finished yet," Levi said quickly as I risked a glance down at my exposed leg. My stomach squirmed at the sight of it. Blood spilled from a very deep looking gash and ran in little trails, dripping onto the dirt.

"It's pretty nasty isn't it," Levi said as he caught a glance at my expression and smiled weakly.

"Am I going to be OK?" I asked, feeling fear build. Levi glanced at Lizzie, who seemed to think there were bigger problems than my wound.

"You're going to be fine," Jess said with a comic smile. I nodded and tried to think of something other than the throbbing pain in my leg. Levi continued patching up my leg, eventually covering the horrid gash with the rest of his shirt. Noticing that Levi now looked like a homeless man, Dylan offered up his jumper.

"We should take her to a hospital," Jennifer said. Her face became pale as she stared at my leg. I purposefully looked away, not wanting to catch another glimpse of it.

Dylan shook his head. "That's not an option."

"Why not?" Jennifer asked, evidently worried.

"We have no money, and they will find out we are here illegally," Dylan said as he flicked me a half-hearted look of sympathy.

"I've heard the horror stories of the American health system," I said quietly.

"So, you know it's not an option to take you there," Dylan continued.

"Yes. I know."

A terrified shriek from Jess pierced the air, and she instantly jumped up onto the log I was sitting on.

"What?" Dylan asked.

Jess pointed shakily at the ground. A huge pitch-black snake hissed threateningly at us. It lifted its head, swaying entrancingly back and forth.

"I hate snakes," Levi muttered and jumped up onto the log beside me. Lizzie and Jennifer had backed away, clutching each other in fear.

"Is it poisonous?" I was in too much pain to move and was in striking distance of the snake's looming mouth.

"Look, it has a white chin," Levi said, trying to take my mind off the fact that the snake was staring right at me.

"I don't care about what its chin looks like," I managed to squeak. The snake rushed at me with alarming speed. Levi leaped off the log and pushed me backward. I fell painfully onto my back. Dylan yelped and hit it with a stick. I sat up, shaking the leaves from my hair. The snake stopped its charge at me but now had its gaze fixed on Dylan.

"Do something, Levi," Dylan said, his voice shaky but calm. Levi shrugged and looked around. No one had any ideas.

"Hurry up," Dylan said, hardly above a whisper. He backed up slowly as the snake advanced. Levi, not knowing what else to do, yelled at the snake and charged at it. It hesitated before slithering away into the trees.

Dylan let out a long slow breath. "Thanks."

"I want to get out of here," I said as Levi helped me back onto the log.

"I agree," Jess said, her voice shaky.

"What are we going to do?" Lizzie asked, sounding frustrated as she ventured closer to us.

I sighed and glared at her. The snake had made me forget Lizzie was the reason we were stuck here, but now the anger was back. "Don't ask me. You're the one who dragged us into this mess," I said a little more harshly than I intended.

Lizzie approached me with a murderous look on her face. Dylan stuck out his arm and prevented her reaching me in her fury.

Levi stood rather protectively in front of me. "She's hurt and bleeding. She has a right to feel on edge."

I didn't like anyone fighting my battles for me, but at the moment, I was too tired to care.

"It's only a graze," Lizzie said as if it was a small paper cut.

"Next time you get shot, tell me it's no big deal," I said, my cheeks flushing in anger. Dylan grabbed her hand and pulled her aside. Levi looked at me sympathetically.

"We have to think about this logically," Jennifer said as she tried to calm the volatile atmosphere. "We need a place to stay, and we need money."

I nodded in agreement. Their selfish plan had got us stuck here without food, money, or shelter. We couldn't raid houses or steal from shops to survive. Here in Orlando, that would be theft. If these things weren't problems in themselves... we were here illegally and hadn't escaped the war at all. It had followed us, and we had no choice but to try and stop whatever the Prime Minister was planning.

"I have an uncle that lives here," Jess said.

"Good," Lizzie said with an air of authority in her voice. "Will he let us stay with him?"

"Probably, he has a pretty big house."

Things were looking brighter.

"Then we need to call him," Lizzie said.

"But we have no phone and no money," Levi said.

"Then we need to get some," Lizzie concluded.

I felt new frustration rising in me. "You can't mean steal some?" I asked very calmly.

Levi seemed to be thinking the same thing.

"Why not? We don't really have any other choice," Lizzie continued undeterred.

"It's illegal," I said, outraged.

"That never stopped us back home," Lizzie said.

"But back home, the circumstances were different. There's no war here, Lizzie. We can't go into someone's house and take their food."

"Our circumstances are exactly the same, and I'll steal if I have to," Lizzie said defiantly.

"You can't be serious. You're the one who—"

"No one is stealing anything," Dylan said loudly with finality. Lizzie gave him a sour look. "We'll go to the airport and ask someone if we can borrow a phone. Jess will call her uncle, and he will pick us up. It's the logical solution."

"I agree with Dylan," Levi said instantly. Lizzie huffed, but she knew Dylan was right.

"Do you think you can make it back to the airport?" Dylan asked me.

To be honest, I didn't think I could, but I had no choice. Dylan seemed to read this from my face.

"We'll go slowly, we can even carry you a bit," Levi offered.

"I'll walk by myself," I insisted, though I dreaded the prospect of standing up. Levi helped me slowly to my feet, and I tried not to show any pain on my face. Dylan seemed to have accepted I was going to soldier through this. It was slow-going, and I knew I was holding everyone up. I told them to go on ahead, and I would catch up, but apparently, I was key to their plan. I looked the most innocent, and people would pity me, so I would have the most luck using a phone. At least my injury was going to be useful for something. I rested my hand lightly on Levi's shoulder for balance.

We finally made it out of the wooded park we had hidden in and arrived on the main road. I had lost sight of the others a while ago, but spotted them fifty meters or so down the road. A young couple dragging their suitcases hurried past. Their eyes caught sight of Levi and me, but they quickly looked away, avoiding all eye contact. I moved to head in their direction, but I caught sight of movement from the corner of my eye.

"Excuse me, miss, are you OK?" a middle-aged man with a kind face and square glasses said to me. He had come up from behind, but now stood facing me with a look of genuine concern over his sun-kissed face.

"I-I-I'm fine," I said. I realized how long it had been since I had spoken to anyone except our little group.

"I could call an ambulance?" he offered.

"She's fine," Levi said, protectively stepping in between us.

"Are you sure? She's limping quite badly," he insisted, reaching into his pocket.

"Really, we're fine," Levi said as he pulled me forward and away from the kind stranger.

"I think we look suspicious," I whispered to Levi as he helped me hobble away.

Levi let out a half-hearted laugh. "We look homeless," he said.

People swarmed around us, heading to the airport up ahead. I looked around, overwhelmed at seeing crowds again. Shrinking closer to Levi, I felt vulnerable and self-conscious.

"Maybe we should ask one of them if we can use their phone," I whispered to Levi.

He shook his head. "Jess needs to track down her uncle's number first. She needs a phonebook."

"Right," I muttered, keeping my head down and trying not to let the commuters around us see the tears dripping down my cheeks. People stared at me unwaveringly, judgment heavy on their faces. A few tried to approach me and asked if I needed help. I wanted to yell out to everyone that I wasn't homeless, and we had come from war. Then, maybe, they would understand.

"Ignore them," Levi said. I kept my eyes focused on the pavement and continued limping forward. Finally, the entrance to the airport was in sight. For a moment, I couldn't believe I was looking at an airport. A small river twisted and turned, flowing toward the building that looked more like a cruise ship than an airport. Fresh green tropical palm trees reached skyward, framing the river and giving the impression of a serene oasis in the middle of the city. Dylan and the others were waiting for us at the bridge that would take us to the terminal.

"I can't believe that's the airport," Dylan said.

"Where's the concrete jungle, and where are the queues of taxis and buses?" Jennifer asked, looking around. We could hear cars zooming in the distance, but from where we were standing, it seemed they had been swallowed by the exotic sanctuary in front of us.

"Let's keep going," Lizzie insisted. I managed to hobble across a bridge that took us over the river. Levi looked down over the railing.

"I think I see an alligator," he said excitedly.

I sighed and rolled my eyes, limping over to the rail to see for myself. I wasn't sure what I was looking at.

"See its head there in the water," Levi said. He pointed with a childish grin spread across his face.

"I think it's a log," I said resting gratefully against the railing.

Levi shook his head. "I don't care, in my mind, it's an alligator." Levi was insistent. We were at a safe distance from the log or whatever Levi had decided it was. Everyone else was well and truly ahead of us again. I walked as quickly as I could to catch up to them with Levi dutifully by my side. By the time we reached them, they were already at the entrance.

"Where were you two?" Dylan asked, sounding annoyed.

"I saw an alligator," Levi said.

"Really?" Dylan asked.

"It was a log," I interrupted.

Levi shook his head. "She's being pessimistic and doesn't want to admit I found the alligator, and she didn't," Levi explained.

"Who cares about the stupid alligator," Lizzie said in a huff. "We need to get in contact with Jess' uncle."

"OK, OK," Levi grumbled and stomped off through the automatic doors and into the air-conditioned airport.

The inside was equally impressive as the exterior. Fountains squirted water high into the air. Palm trees in pots maintained the illusion of an oasis. Dylan quickly eyed a row of payphones in the corner and walked over with Jess, who promptly began flicking through a phone book to find her uncle's number. Dylan wandered along the row of phones, reaching into the change slot of each one, hoping to find a quarter to make the phones work. Dylan returned with a shrug, telling us he had found nothing. Jess had written her uncle's number on her hand with a pen attached to the phone booth. Levi scanned the airport and pointed out an information booth to me.

"You and Jess should go," Lizzie explained, pointing at the both of us. Jess grabbed my arm to help me balance, and I limped over to the lady at the counter. She noticed we were coming to see her, and a look of sympathy spread over her face. She was a plump woman with short black hair and thick makeup caked onto her face.

"How can I help you, dears?" she asked in a thick American accent, followed by a professional smile.

"I don't have any quarters," I said, sounding quite distraught. "And I really need to use the phone."

"Ah, I see," the lady said simply.

"I was wondering if you had a phone I could borrow to make a quick call," I asked, trying to sound innocent and upset at the same time.

"I'm not supposed to let patrons use this phone for personal use," the lady said politely, obviously trying not to upset me. I let the tears of pain pour down my cheeks. The lady appeared conflicted over what to do. Then her face softened, coming to some conclusion.

"I can't let you use this phone, but I have a quarter you can use in one of those payphones," she said with a smile. She dug into her pockets and fished out the coin, dropping it lightly into my open palm.

"Thank you so much," I said, flicking her a smile.

"It was no trouble. You look like you need it more than I do. Have a nice day."

Jess took my hand again, and we limped away.

"I can't believe it actually worked," Jess whispered to me.

"Me neither," I replied.

"I was so sure the lady was going to turn us away," Jess said with a smile. Our luck for once seemed to be turning. Jess left me with Levi when we reached the group and took off toward the phones.

"I knew you looked innocent and desperate enough for someone to give you money," Dylan said.

"You make a great homeless person," Levi said with a smirk.

"I'm not some charity case," I said, annoyed.

"No? That woman gave you money because you looked helpless," Levi said with a pouty lip.

"Maybe I'm good at acting," I said as I turned away from Levi to talk to Jennifer.

"Now you've made her grumpy," Dylan joked with Levi. I ignored them and their childish behavior. Our conversation was abruptly interrupted by Jess, who had returned.

"He said we can stay with him!" she said excitedly, practically bouncing up and down.

"Really?" Lizzie asked as her face brightened. This annoyed me. I was angry things were working out so well. Lizzie and Dylan had got us in this mess. I wanted it to be harder so they would learn a lesson. Levi seemed to read the look on my face.

"You've been shot," he whispered to me. "You're allowed to be angry. No matter what happens."

"He says he has a few errands to run but he can pick us up after that," Jess said. "He suggested we wait for him by the park," Jess continued. She looked at me and frowned. "He didn't really give me a chance to change the meeting spot."

I sighed. "It's fine."

"Why don't we call him back and and ask if he can pick us up here?" Jennifer asked.

"And go beg for some more money?" Lizzie said, crossing her arms. "I don't think we'll get lucky again."

"You're probably right," Dylan said.

"Look. It's fine. I can make it back," I said. Levi gave a concerned look. "Really, I'll manage. How long do we have?" I asked, as I resigned myself to walking back to the park.

"He said he's going to meet us in an hour."

"I guess we better get moving then," Lizzie said as she took charge again, looking over her shoulder at me. I sighed a little louder than I had intended.

Lizzie glared at me. "There is no other way to get there but walking, so suck it up, Grace," she snapped at me. I wanted to yell at her and tell her to try and walk with a bullet wound in her leg, but I kept my mouth shut. Lizzie was tense enough as it was. Instead, I followed them without another word, holding back tears. Levi helped me along as we lagged behind the rest of the group.

"I told you we would be OK," Levi said to me.

"Do I look OK to you?" I asked.

"No," Levi said with a shrug, "but at least you are alive."

"Barely," I said. "I feel weak and useless… I'm a burden."

Levi wrapped his arm around my shoulder as I struggled onward. "I need to rest," I said, and hobbled over to a log.

Levi sat next to me. "Look at me," Levi said, lifting my chin gently with his hand. I looked up at him and met his soft gaze with mine. "You aren't a burden."

I was close to sobbing, and I cast my eyes down in embarrassment. I caught sight of the blood-soaked bandage around my leg and broke down into tears. I couldn't go on anymore. Levi looked confused, unsure of how to comfort me. He settled for just sitting quietly next to me until I calmed down.

"I'll carry you," Levi eventually said.

"I can walk." I was tired and weak, but there was an end in sight. Tonight, we would have a roof over our heads. A real roof and, hopefully, a real bed. Perhaps a good sleep and some decent food would make Lizzie and Dylan see how stupid they had been. Their little stunt had got me shot, and they didn't seem to care. It was like they were blind to everyone else. Fresh anger fueled me onward. I clenched my fists, stood up, and headed toward the others. Tomorrow we would sort all of this out. But, tonight, I needed sleep.

CHAPTER TWENTY-FOUR

DYLAN

A LARGE SUV WITH tinted windows pulled into the parking lot where we waited patiently for Jess' uncle. Its sleek black exterior winked in the sunlight as it rolled up to us smoothly, finally coming to a halt in front of me.

"Is that him?" Jennifer asked.

"It wouldn't surprise me," Jess said brightly. The drivers-side door opened, and a confident man stepped out. His shaggy black hair was streaked with gray, but youthfulness still sparked from his green eyes. He was obviously rich, but his faded blue jeans and loose-fitting striped shirt gave the impression he was just like us. A warm smile broke over his face as he caught sight of Jess.

"Jessy!" he said, his accent thick with American twang as he crushed her in a bear hug.

"Uncle Ross!" Jess muttered into his shoulder.

"I haven't seen you since you were tiny. Now you're all grown up and beautiful," he said, holding her at arm's length to get a good look at her.

"Thanks," Jess said, sounding embarrassed.

"And who are these scruffy young men?" her uncle asked, looking at Levi and me.

"Dylan," I said confidently and extended my hand.

He grasped it firmly, and I caught a whiff of his fresh but spicy cologne. "Call me Ross," he said with a huge smile that revealed perfect teeth. Ross then turned his attention to Levi, who promptly introduced himself. Moving on to Lizzie and Jennifer, he politely kissed them on their hands. They blushed a deep red. Grace, however, teetered on the verge of fainting. Her face was pale, and she was sweating profusely, leaning heavily on Levi to stay upright.

"You need a doctor," he said urgently when he noticed the blood soaking her through her makeshift-bandage. Grace shook her head vigorously.

"I can't," she replied, "we don't have insurance." Grace looked uncomfortable and unsure if she should tell him we were illegals.

Ross studied her for a moment. "We will have to do what we can."

"I don't want to bloody your car," Grace said.

"I can get it cleaned," he dismissed. "Get in, and we'll get you patched up."

"Thanks," Grace said as Levi and Ross helped her into the car.

"It might be a bit of a squeeze," Ross added.

"It will be fine," I said, taking a peek in the spacious eight-seater. Plush beige floor mats complemented tan leather seats.

"You look thin," Ross said to Jess as she took the front seat. "Have you been eating OK?" A single line drew itself across his forehead.

"We've been eating… I wouldn't call it eating well though," Jess replied.

"I've asked my chef to cook us up something. Hopefully you like steak."

The thought of steak sounded too good to be true. I craved fresh red meat more than anything else.

"Love it," Levi said eagerly. "It's been ages since we ate anything decent."

"We've had nothing but tinned spaghetti for months," Grace said.

"Don't forget about the beans," Jennifer added. There was a collective groan.

"No canned food, I swear," Ross said.

I slid onto the back seat and was instantly caressed with the sensual scent of smooth leather. Leaning back into the bucket seat, I finally relaxed as Ross fiddled with his GPS.

We were safe. I took a deep breath into the very bottom of my lungs. I hadn't felt this safe since before the war started… and even then, the constant reminders of riots on the news had caused an undercurrent of tension.

Lizzie perched beside me in the center seat. "Nice car?" she asked me with a soft smile and a sideways glance.

"Sure is," I answered, looking over at her. For once, Lizzie's face was calm, and her blond hair was pulled up in a messy ponytail. Tiny butterflies tumbled in my stomach. I had been pushing these feelings down for a while now.

"This car is pretty sweet," Levi said.

Ross chuckled and slid a pair of aviators on. "I got it a week ago. Custom built," he added as he pushed a button to start the car. It purred into life.

"So, what do you do for work?" Lizzie queried.

"I'm retired now. But I was the CEO of an oil company. Have you heard of NOFY Oil?" he asked as he pulled away from the curb.

"Yeah," I said. "Didn't they have some controversial oil deal go down a few months ago?"

"It seems they've fallen apart without me. That's part of why I quit though, if I'm honest." He turned on the radio by touching a couple buttons on the steering wheel.

"You seem too young to have retired," Lizzie pushed. I caught her eye to warn her about prying questions. But Ross didn't seem offended.

"It was an enticed retirement. I wasn't on board with the direction the company was going in. They basically paid me out to leave," he said with a shrug.

"I'm sorry, Uncle Ross," Jess said.

"It's not so bad, Jessy. I get double my salary 'til I'm seventy, so there really isn't anything to complain about. Besides, I don't miss making the hard decisions," he added as an afterthought. "We were the ones buying farmers out of their properties. I knew the prices we offered were only a fraction of what we'd earn off their land. Working in oil... it's... controversial," he tried to explain. After a few minutes of driving in silence, Ross cleared his throat loudly. "You kids have a story of your own to tell... I'm not an idiot. You came here illegally," he said bluntly, looking suspiciously at us in the rear-view mirror.

"About that—" Jess said slowly.

"How did you ever get out of there?" he interrupted. "There's been no contact with New Zealand for months—full communication blackout. At first they said it was because of the virus, but now they're saying it's war. A couple wealthy businessmen made it out to Australia in private planes," Ross said. "It's been all over the news. They say it's a military coup?"

"To be honest, we were lucky," Lizzie said carefully. "We were in the right place at the right time."

"Are your parents OK?" Ross asked Jess with a wave of concern passing over his face. I could tell he'd been watching for news about his family for months, and it saddened me that we had nothing to offer him.

"I don't know," Jess said, her voice shaking with emotion. "I think they were taken."

"Taken where?" he asked, attempting to hide the worry

edging into his voice.

"Prison camps. That's where everyone is. Unless they're dead," Jess said as she began to tear up.

"Shhh Jessy," he said as he cautiously took one hand off the wheel and gripped her hand.

"I'm sure my big sister will be fine. She's always lucky," he said as a smile warmed his face. "At least you're OK." By now, we had turned off the interstate and were cruising through the suburbs. As we twisted our way through the web of streets, the cookie-cutter homes gave way to gated mansions.

"Jess never mentioned her uncle was loaded," Levi whispered in my ear as we turned down Ross' driveway. The gates were open wide, inviting us into an expansive cobbled courtyard. Ross carefully drove around the splashing fountain and pulled up outside the front door. I stepped out of the car and stared in awe. Two polished white pillars guarded the double oak front doors and held up a picturesque balcony. My mind wandered, and I imagined Lizzie and I standing together on that balcony, our lips locked in a passionate kiss. I smiled at the thought. One day when this war ended, we would be safe, and we could be together. I pulled my eyes and thoughts away from the balcony to the rest of the house that spread out expansively in both directions.

"Welcome," Ross said, waving his hand at his home.

"It's huge," Grace said.

Ross laughed. "Thank you. Come in, come in," he said and beckoned us forward. He unlocked the front door and turned off the alarm. I followed Jess into the house, slipped my shoes off, and felt the smooth cedar floor beneath my feet. In front of me, a sweeping marble staircase was chased by an intricately carved handrail to the next story. A crystal chandelier hung from the high beamed ceiling, sparkling sunlight around the room while low plush settees lazed around the outside of the circular foyer.

"I need to sit," Grace said. She looked exhausted with her hair half secured in an unraveling bun, and she stood shakily supporting herself with one hand on Levi's shoulder and the other on the wall. Ross' forehead creased in concern.

"Of course, come to the dining room," Ross said. We followed him, and he directed us to sit around a crystal-clear sheet of glass that hung from the ceiling by steel cables. I sat down cautiously, not wanting to break or dirty anything with my filthy war clothes.

Lizzie caught my eye, "This is too fancy," she mouthed.

"Make yourselves at home. There is nothing here you can break that I can't replace," he said and smiled knowingly. Ross left the room, but Grace hesitated and stood supporting herself with the chair.

"I don't want to bleed everywhere," she whispered to us. Already, small drips of blood trailed from the doorway to the table.

"Looks like you already have," Levi said, pointing.

"I'm so embarrassed," Grace said with a shake of her head.

"Don't be," Levi said to her quietly, with a look of genuine concern passing over his face. When he thought we weren't looking, he put his hand over hers. I had never seen Levi like this with anyone. Levi caught onto my glance, and I quickly looked interestedly around the room.

"That's a strange picture," Lizzie said into my ear as she pointed at an abstract painting.

"Are they naked?" Levi asked as he, too, stared at it in confusion. His hand was now innocently by his side.

"Maybe, but I can't tell. Are they even people?" Grace asked as she twisted to see it.

"They're definitely people," Jess said with surety. "But I can't tell if they are wearing clothes or not."

I stared at the mass of swirling colors, trying to make some sense of them.

"I see you're admiring my art," Ross said as he returned,

followed by a woman.

"It's… interesting," Lizzie said. Ross chuckled before bringing his attention to Grace. "Let's have a look at your leg, first of all," Ross said and beckoned for Grace to roll up her pant leg. Grace did as asked, and with a deep breath to prepare herself, she removed the scraps of material to reveal her wound.

"Shit, that looks deep. How did you say it happened?" Ross asked as he called the woman forward.

"I got shot," Grace said matter–of–factly.

Ross paled for a moment but then steadied himself. "You're the first gunshot victim I've ever had in my house," he said, trying to crack a joke. He managed a strained smile as he ran his hand through his hair.

"I need to clean it properly, and maybe get a new bandage," Grace said quickly. "It's just a graze."

"It needs stitches," Ross said, shaking his head. "But I suppose in the meantime, we'll have to settle for a more secure bandage."

Ross addressed the woman with him, who was called Abbi, and explained Grace's situation. Abbi looked not much older than us. She nodded as Ross gave her some instructions, tucking her chocolate brown bob behind one ear. She motioned for Grace to follow her. Grace stood up, and Abbi helped her from the room. Levi's eyes lingered protectively on Grace as the door closed behind her.

"What's that painting?" Jess asked.

"It's called 'persone nude ad una festa'," Ross said in a butchered Italian accent.

"And what does that mean?" Levi asked.

"Naked people at a feast," Ross said as another maid walked in with a tray of glasses, which were set in front of us.

"I knew they were naked," Levi said, pumping his fist in triumph. Ross laughed heartily. The maid began pouring fresh orange juice.

"It's an interesting painting choice for your dining room," Lizzie said.

"That is why it's here. Why would I want to be normal? Why not throw in a bit of chaos at a meal? Inappropriateness begets hilarity," Ross said as he sipped at a glass of wine. The maid reappeared, this time carrying trays with juicy slabs of steak and heapings of mashed potato dripping in gravy. I felt my mouth water at the sheer sight of it.

"Dig in," Ross said as he began to cut into his tender fillet. I greedily dug into mine and dipped the meat into the creamy gravy and mashed potatoes. The smell wafted enticingly, tingling my senses.

"This food is amazing," I said with my mouth full. Lizzie scorned me as she meticulously cut her meat into tiny squares.

"I forgot food could taste this good," Levi said as he gulped his mashed potato with a spoon.

Ross smiled. "I'm glad you're enjoying it."

We ate the rest of the meal in silence. When the maid had cleared our dishes, Ross finally spoke, "I hope the meal was OK."

"It was perfect, Uncle," Jess said with a huge grin. "Thank you so much."

Ross waved his hand in dismissal. "It's the least I can do for my favorite niece," he said as he wiped his mouth on the corner of his napkin. Jess smiled.

"I had one of my assistants purchase some new clothes for you. How about I show you to your rooms, you can have a shower, get freshened up, and then come back for dessert?" Ross said. He chuckled to himself. "I've done this all backward. I should have let you get cleaned up first."

"Trust me, we don't mind. The food was great," Levi said reassuringly with a dorky smile over his face. Still laughing, Ross stood up from the table, and we followed him up the marble staircase we had seen earlier. At the top of the stairs, my feet sunk into the thick warm carpet that covered a spacious lounge area. Framed baseball cards and posters of athletes ran in a continuous line around the room. One half of the room was taken up by two comfy leather couches, while the other half housed a foosball table and a dartboard. I caught sight of a minibar tucked away at the back of the room before we walked through into a hallway that branched left and right. Grace met us with Abbi, coming through a door at the far end of the hall.

"There's an elevator," Grace said as she approached us. "For a second, I thought I was going to have to climb that staircase."

"You missed an amazing meal, Grace," Levi said, looking pleased and relieved to see her. She did look a lot happier, and her injured leg was wrapped tightly with a fresh bandage.

"I ate with Abbi," Grace said.

"I'm glad you're doing better now," Ross said. "I was about to show everyone their rooms. Boys, your room is to the right, and girls, there are two rooms for you down that way." Ross pointed toward the rooms. Levi and I wandered toward our room. All the doors along the hall were closed except one, which we assumed was ours. Levi slowly pushed it open.

"I can't believe we get a bed," he commented as he ran and belly-flopped on the closest one.

"What did you expect? Hammocks?" I asked as I peeked into the en suite.

"I mean, we get to sleep in beds. Finally," he said, stretching out onto his back with a groan.

I chuckled. "Do you mind if I take the first shower?"

Levi shook his head.

I stepped into the bathroom and closed the door. I lay the fluffy-navy mat on the floor before quickly stripping off and stepping into the shower. I turned on the water. A steaming rush of hot water rained down on me, and I sighed slightly louder than I had intended.

"Don't get too excited," Levi called from the bedroom.

"Shut up," I said. "I'm going to get as excited as I want." I lathered shampoo through my hair and stood under the hot water for a few minutes. I turned off the tap and wrapped a towel around my waist. Wiping the condensation off the mirror, I looked at my reflection. The person looking back at me was not the one I remembered. I stepped back in shock. My face was thinner than I remembered, and scruffy with an unkempt beard beginning to show. Looking down at my exposed torso, I could tell I had definitely lost weight. And the beard had to go. I rummaged through some drawers till I found a razor and then set to work quickly getting rid of it. When I was done, I rinsed my face and admired the new and refreshed me. To my relief, it looked more like the old me.

Levi banged on the door. "Are you done yet?"

"Yeah," I called back and opened the door.

"That looks more like the Dylan I remember, though it looks like you've lost some weight," he said as he walked past me and tapped my stomach, before closing the door behind him.

"Clothes are in the wardrobe," Levi yelled from the bathroom. I ambled over and opened the closet doors. A light blue polo shirt and black jeans suited me fine. I tousled my hair before laying back on one of the beds and closing my eyes. The shower hissed in the background, accompanied by Levi's horrible singing. Ten minutes later, Levi reappeared, looking clean and freshly shaven with his cheeks flushed from the hot water.

"I kind of liked the beard you had going," I teased.

"Yeah, right. I looked like I had a scraggly hamster growing off my face," Levi said as he stood in front of the wardrobe before picking a plaid shirt and some faded blue jeans. I sniggered.

There was a quiet knock at the door.

"Come in," Levi called.

The door opened slowly, and Grace and Lizzie walked in. Levi and I stared at them.

"Why are you guys looking at us weird?" Grace asked hesitantly.

"Yeah, Dylan, why are you looking at them weird?" Levi mocked.

"You're wearing a dress," I said to Lizzie. She looked stunning.

Grace pulled uncomfortably at her soft blue, tight-fitting dress she was wearing. She stood cumbersomely on one leg.

"For some reason the only clothes Jess' uncle thought to get for us were dresses," Lizzie said with a small look of annoyance passing over her face as she glanced down at her own flowery dress that puffed out slightly from the waist. She hitched up her stockings unglamorously. "You clean up good. And no more facial hair," Lizzie said, looking at me.

"You never mentioned how hideous it looked," I said as I stroked my smooth face.

"There was nothing you could've done. So, there wasn't really a point," Lizzie said.

"You know, we have never seen you in anything except dirty war clothes," Levi said. "You guys look… amazing."

Grace blushed.

"Anyway, dessert's ready," Lizzie said. Levi's face lit up at the sound of dessert, and he raced out of the room before doubling back to help Grace, who had started a slow hobble.

"Are you coming?" Lizzie asked, looking at me.

"You know you look really nice," I said. Lizzie's face softened into a smile. "Your hair even smells good," I said before realizing how creepy it sounded.

"Um… thanks," Lizzie said. Her gray eyes sparkled in the dim lighting, and I could have sworn she was wearing lip-gloss. "Now come on, they're waiting for us," Lizzie said as she grabbed my hand with her own and pulled me gently out the door. She let go as we caught up with the others. We took the elevator with Grace and Levi, and the doors opened on a landing just off the main living areas. Grace seemed to know where to go, and we followed along after her. My heart was pounding, and all I could think about was me and Lizzie standing on the balcony after the war. She would be wearing her flower dress, and I would take her hand, and we would kiss.

"Something on your mind, Dylan?" Levi asked me with a knowing wink, jolting me out of my imagination. I realized I had been standing in front of the dining room table, staring.

"I'm just tired," I said vaguely as I looked at the spread of cakes on offer.

"That's better," Ross said, as he looked us all over. "Cake?" he offered. Levi greedily grabbed the nearest slice. Grace whispered something into his ear before giving him a disapproving look. Levi stared at her for a moment before reaching for a dessert plate. Then he sheepishly took a fork.

"I can't thank you enough, Ross," Grace said. "It's amazing to be clean… and not bleeding everywhere."

It was strange to see everyone like this. Normally, they were dirty and didn't give a toss about how they looked. Now, I saw a glimpse of what they were like before the war. And I liked what I saw. Lizzie delicately combed her fingers through her glossy blond hair. She caught me looking at her and smiled. Her face still retained a little of the warmth from her shower, and her fair skin had a healthy glow. I winked at her, and she grinned, delicately raising some cake to her soft lips. Once we were relaxed and enjoying dessert, Ross cleared his throat.

"You need to tell me your story," he said gently. We looked at each other uncomfortably, each of us hoping someone else would start.

"Well…" I said, not sure where to begin.

"What was it like there?" Ross pressed.

"Awful," Jess said. "Most of the time we tried to stay away from the main centers. It was safer out in the bush."

"Like camping?" Ross said a little bit too cheerfully.

"Yeah, like camping. But this type of camping drags on for months, with barely any supplies, and with men hunting you down," Levi said as he glanced down and moved some of the cake pointlessly around his plate, before he moodily pushed it away. There was no hiding the horror we had been through.

Ross sipped his wine and set it down. "Clearly, you've been through a lot. There's no way I can even begin to understand how you feel. But if I know what you went through, maybe I can help."

"I don't know what you can do to help," Lizzie said with a shrug.

"Neither do I. But I can't try unless you tell me what happened," Ross encouraged. "I need to know the truth."

Jess looked around at us. I could tell she wanted to tell her uncle everything. The entire truth. And, considering he had taken us in, it seemed rude not to share our story.

"Let's start at the beginning. How did the war start?" Ross said. He waited patiently for us to speak with a warm smile spread across his face.

Jess took a deep, slow breath. "The first I knew of the war was when Leah and I heard the trucks stop at Leah's neighbors. They wouldn't leave their house, and we heard gunshots... so we rushed into the safe room Leah's parents made when they built the house. Later, when we came out, everyone had gone. And then these four showed up," she gestured to Levi, Grace, Lizzie, and me. "If it weren't for them, I don't know what Leah and I would have done."

"Thank you," Ross said to us with sincerity. "Thank you for saving my niece. You're heroes."

We didn't know what to say. Heroes were people who acted on courage. It didn't take much courage to follow your gut instincts during a war. I had often thought about how we had saved Grace and Lizzie, but it had never occurred to me what would have happened to Leah and Jess if we hadn't run into them.

"Where is Leah?" Ross asked.

Grace's eyes quickly filled with tears, and she reached across to squeeze Jess' arm as Jess looked away in sadness.

Ross realized he had crossed a line. "What happened?" he asked softly.

Jennifer was the one who spoke up as Jess started crying. "She was shot when they rescued me from the prison camp. There was nothing we could do. The soldiers came in the dark. We thought we had killed them, but one was still alive and shot Leah. We had to leave her there."

Ross brought his hand to his mouth in shock before gently resting a hand on Jess' shoulder. "She was such a sweet girl," Ross said with sorrow creasing his face. "I remember when you two would play here as toddlers." His eyes brimmed with tears at the memory. "But how did you get here? And why here?"

"Soldiers had been chasing us, and they had cornered us in what we had thought was an open field but turned out to be the airstrip. We snuck onto a plane to hide, but it took off, and now we're here," Lizzie said in one breath. She conveniently left out the part where we stupidly tricked the others into going there.

Grace stared at me with contempt. Clearly, she hadn't forgiven us.

"They were armed?" Ross asked.

"Of course they were armed," I said with annoyance creeping into my voice.

"They shot me," Grace said, pointing to her leg.

"Well, you should stay here," Ross said. "I couldn't live with myself if I let you all get sent back there."

"I don't know," I said slowly. "I want to. But our families are still in New Zealand. And if we don't stop the rocket, thousands of people will die."

Alarm spread over Ross' face. "What do you mean by that?" Ross asked as he downed the rest of his drink.

"Have you ever heard of AISD?" Levi asked.

"Yes. It's a government space program. They're in the public eye, but their missions are usually top-secret," Ross said. That made sense why I had never heard of it.

"Apparently, they are launching a rocket," I said.

"Of course," Ross said, "it's been on the news."

"Well, it's being hijacked," Levi said as he too drained his drink.

"What do you mean?" Ross asked as he gripped his wine glass tightly.

"I mean, it's a weapon," I said bluntly.

"A weapon? That's absurd!" Ross dismissed.

"Not so much," Levi said, shrugging. "The Prime Minister was on our flight. He's here for the rocket launch."

Ross looked at Levi cautiously as he slowly began to work out what we were saying. "So, you're saying your Prime Minister came here with his entourage, and they are going to hijack the rocket for use as a weapon?"

"Yes," I said.

"That's ridiculous!" Ross said angrily. "How do you know this?"

"We overheard it," Jennifer said simply.

"Is this true, Jessy?" Ross asked, looking at his niece for confirmation.

"Unfortunately, yes," Jess muttered.

"This can't be happening," Ross said with a trace of frustration in his voice. He abruptly stood up from the table and returned a moment later with his laptop. He opened it and began typing furiously. Levi and I exchanged concerned glances.

"You're sure he's here for the rocket launching? I can't find any information that mentions him. They did struggle to find funding for it though," Ross commented. He skim read from the computer, "It says: *After funding for AISD's new rocket 'The Architect' was denied by the US Government, AISD sent out a plea for assistance to help create their revolutionary space-explorer. A wealthy investor donated all the funds required for completion of the project and provided additional scientists to allow for rapid completion. The rocket has been finished ahead of schedule, and testing is currently underway."*

"That's got to be him," Lizzie said.

"I don't know..." Ross said as he scratched his head. "But even if you're right—which is a big if—you can't seriously be planning on stopping the launching of this rocket. I mean, why would you? You're free."

"For one, we're the only ones who know about this," I said. "And two, if we can expose our Prime Minister, it might stop the war. What if this is our one chance? No one in New Zealand has the power to take him out... but here? If he was caught and convicted as a terrorist? Our families would finally have a chance at freedom."

"That might be true," Ross said. "God, I'd like to see my sister safe. I would do anything for her, but I don't think it can be done. This launch has had too much publicity. No one will believe your story. Heck, I'm not sure I believe it," Ross said with frustration.

"If AISD won't stop it, we will have to do it with force," Levi said, as he resumed eating his cake. Lizzie and Jennifer sat in silence, swapping worried glances with one another. The launch date was closer than we had thought.

"What are you saying, exactly?" Ross asked.

"We are going to head over to the launch site, and stop the rocket," Levi said. "Simple as that."

"That's impossible," Ross said.

"We have to try," I said.

"No, you don't understand... these things are classified. The lab is at a secret location, and the launch time and date won't be made public."

"No way," I said.

"You can search if you want," Ross offered. I grabbed his laptop and began furiously searching for details about AISD. Levi hovered over my shoulder. But, Ross was right. Apart from some publicity articles giving generic information about the rocket, there was nothing. After finding nothing on the rocket launch, I did a quick search on Prime Minister Marion. I opened a few biography articles. But they contained nothing of interest. He was born and raised in New Zealand, before entering the political scene in his early twenties. Nothing out of the ordinary was mentioned. I was disappointed. I didn't know what I expected to find, but I had hoped for something useful.

"There has to be another way," I said as frustration boiled inside me. I slammed the laptop shut.

"We'll do whatever it takes," Levi said.

"You're talking of doing things illegally. It's dangerous, and you could go to prison," Ross said angrily.

"I honestly don't care," Levi said. "If it stops people dying, then I really don't give a shit."

Ross simmered with anger. He knew there was nothing he could do to stop us, but Jess was another story. "I will not let you do this, Jessy." Ross turned to his niece.

"I'm doing this, Uncle," Jess said softly. "It is something I have to do."

"No. I forbid it," Ross said as he clenched his fist. "You're only sixteen for God's sake!"

"I'm going to help, Uncle," Jess said with finality. "Either you help us, or we will do this alone. And honestly, I don't care what you choose to do. I hope you realize how many lives are at stake here… it's not only ours." She stood up from the table.

Ross looked up at her and sighed.

"Goodnight, and thank you for the wonderful meal," Jess said pleasantly as she gave her uncle a brief hug, and then she left. We sat in awkward silence. Levi tried to hold in a sneeze, but it escaped. Loudly.

"Look," Ross finally said. "I know I can't stop you but… you have to look after Jessy for me."

"Of course," I said instantly.

Ross grimaced. "I can tell you're good kids, reckless kids, but good kids. When I met you earlier, I thought you needed a parent figure, but obviously that is not what you need right now. You need an ally," Ross said with surprising awareness. We sat patiently listening to him speak. "I'm glad Jess met you rather than the soldiers."

"So are we," Lizzie said finally as Jennifer yawned beside her.

"Get some sleep," Ross said as he glanced at the time. "You've been through so much. Rest, and we can talk more in the morning when our heads have cooled."

"Thanks," I said and got up from the table. The others followed. Levi and I departed from the girls and wandered into our room, closing the door behind us.

Levi collapsed onto a bed and yawned loudly. "I'm knackered."

"I'm not," I said. The jetlag must have been kicking in, because I felt wide-awake despite the eventful day.

"There was a TV in that games room," Levi said.

I shook my head. I didn't feel like watching some stupid show, not when the world was about to fall apart, and we were the only ones who knew it. And then I remembered what else was in that games room.

"Be back in a minute," I said to Levi.

I strode down the hall and into the games room. The lights were off, and it was shrouded in shadow. I walked past the foosball table and straight over to the minibar.

"Jackpot," I whispered as I pulled out a bottle of tequila. I hurried back to our room with my secret score, and nearly crashed into Lizzie and Grace in the darkened hall.

"What are you doing, Dylan?" Lizzie whispered.

"Nothing," I said.

"Is that…? It totally is," Lizzie said with a knowing smirk as she caught a glimpse of the tequila I was trying to hide behind my back.

"What?" Grace said.

"Shhh, get inside before Ross comes," I muttered. I opened the door and shepherded them in.

"You can't drink that," Grace said as soon as she saw the bottle.

I made sure the door was completely closed. "Why not? We deserve a break," I said.

Levi grinned when he saw what all the fuss was about, and Lizzie flopped onto my bed.

"For one, it belongs to Ross and I don't think he'd be happy. For two, we're underage in America," Grace said.

"Ross won't notice it's gone," I said.

"And we're all drinking age in New Zealand," Levi added. "All of us except Lizzie, anyway."

"Actually, I turned eighteen a couple weeks back," Lizzie corrected him.

"Well, there you go," I said, winking at Lizzie. "A belated birthday bash. What better reason is there than that?"

But Lizzie was looking at Grace. She bit her lip in concern. "We don't have to…"

"Oh, come on. What's going to happen? It's safe here," I said. "We get to be teens. Just for one night. We can go back to saving the world tomorrow."

Grace was wavering.

"Please?" I asked.

"OK," Grace relented.

"Birthday girl first then," I said as I sat next to Lizzie and passed over the spoils.

She cracked the bottle open and took a healthy swig. "Phew that's strong," she said with a cough before handing it back.

I took a drink and felt the alcohol burn down my throat. We

handed it around the room. It didn't take much for the alcohol to hit. My head was buzzing, and the familiar wooziness was making it hard to think straight. But as far as I was concerned, that was exactly what the night called for.

"You never told me it was your birthday," I said to Lizzie. She was still wearing her flower dress, and I wondered whether I should make a move.

"I didn't know what day it was. Not until today," Lizzie said with a careless shrug. "And it wouldn't have been much of a celebration."

"If I'd known, I would have…"

"You would have what?" Lizzie asked. I didn't know what I would have done, except I knew she deserved a better eighteenth birthday than the one she had. I leaned closer, trying to convince myself to make a move. Kiss her. Put my hand on her knee. Just anything. But I was still unsure—what if she was still in love with that other guy she had been dating before the war started?

"I don't think Grace is doing so well," Levi said, interrupting us.

We looked over to Grace who was now sitting at the foot of Levi's bed, sobbing.

"What did you do?" I said to Levi.

"Nothing, I swear," Levi insisted. "She got really drunk, and then she started talking about how her dad would be ashamed of her."

"Oh no," Lizzie said, grimacing. "I think I better get her back to our room." Lizzie got up and walked over to the bathroom, grabbing a wad of tissues for Grace.

"Can I help?" Levi asked Grace, trying to calm her.

"N-n-no you c-c-can't," Grace said. Levi looked crestfallen.

"It's OK, she just needs to sleep this off," Lizzie said, swatting Levi away and handing Grace the tissues.

"I'm s-s-sorry," Grace wailed, burying her face in her hands.

"You haven't done anything wrong, Grace," Lizzie said gently. She helped Grace to her feet and Grace staggered to the door with Lizzie supporting her.

I was disappointed. "Will you come back?" I asked when she opened the door.

Lizzie looked back at me and smiled. "Thanks, but I think we'd better call it a night." She closed the door behind her with a loud click, and it was back to being just me and Levi.

I capped off the half-empty bottle of tequila and shoved it out of sight in a cupboard before crossing to the bathroom. I was sort of pissed at Grace for ruining it all—our party was finished before it had really started.

"What was that about?" I asked Levi through a mouthful of toothpaste.

Levi stripped down to his boxers and climbed into his bed. "I have no idea. Grace's dad died, and she doesn't talk about it."

"Yeah, I remember you saying not long after we first met her. Has she ever told you how?"

"I think some sort of accident. Like I said, she doesn't talk about it." Levi flicked the light off, the conversation over. I fumbled through the dark to my bed, and lay there silently.

The way Levi said it, I wasn't sure if it was Grace who didn't talk about it or if Levi didn't want to betray her trust. But it was a shame the night had to end that way. My skin prickled intensely as I thought about how I had nearly kissed Lizzie. But there was still tomorrow. So long as we were free, there would be a billion chances to let her know how I felt. There was no gun under my pillow and no rain dripping on my face. For once, we were safe.

CHAPTER TWENTY-FIVE

JESS

It was strange sleeping in a bed again. The funny thing was, I couldn't get comfortable. It was like the bed was too soft, swallowing me whole. Eventually, after rolling around until the sheets twisted around my body, I gave up and yanked the pillows and blankets down to the floor. I was still like that when Grace woke me up halfway through the next day.

"Ergh... Grace go away," I complained, burying my head into the pillow and snatching the blankets back as she tried, unsuccessfully, to take them away.

"Jess, come on. You've been asleep for ages... and what's with sleeping on the floor?" she asked, sounding bemused.

"The bed was too soft," I grumbled.

"Right," Grace said. "Anyhow, hurry up and get dressed. I suggest togs. The rest of us are at the pool."

"It's winter," I said, my mind still fogged with sleep.

"Yeah, winter in Orlando. It's like mid-twenties out there, and the sun is so warm," Grace said, smiling. She seemed a lot happier than she had been last night, and I wondered if she had forgiven Lizzie and Dylan for tricking us into getting onto the plane. I wasn't sure if I had, but I couldn't stay mad at them. We were free. For a moment, that knowledge made my heart soar. And then I remembered the rocket, and what Dylan had mentioned about exposing Marion. If we managed to stop this rocket, everything would change. If we exposed Marion, maybe we could even resume our lives in New Zealand. For a word that was only two letters long, 'if' sure was weighty.

"Fine, I'll be out in a minute," I said.

"Here," Grace reached in a drawer and threw a swimsuit at me. It hit me squarely in the face.

"OK, I get it. I'll come," I said as I grabbed the swimsuit from my face and stared at Grace. She laughed and left the room. I was about to cross to the bathroom when there was a knock on the door.

"I said I'm coming, Grace!" I yelled. "Oh," I said as Uncle Ross opened the door.

"Jessy. I'd been waiting for you to wake up," he said brightly. "I wanted to ask you if there was anything wrong with this bed?" he asked, gesturing to it as he sat and tested the springs. "I can replace it…" he offered awkwardly.

"The bed's fine. It's me who's not." I smiled sheepishly at him. "We're used to sleeping on the ground. It's nothing to do with the bed. I think I need some time to get back to normal life," I explained to him.

"That makes sense," he said, some of the worry leaving his voice. "Also, I wanted to let you know I have some things to do in the study, and later in the afternoon I have a meeting to attend, so you'll all be on your own for a bit. I hope that's OK."

"I thought you retired?"

"It's not work," he said, shaking his head, "I managed to secure a meeting with someone who might be able to help stop the rocket, or at least hear us out."

"Really?" I asked with hope blaring in my voice. Maybe this

would be less of a fight than we thought.

"Yes, but don't get too excited. It may all come to nothing," Uncle Ross warned me. "Also, breakfast is downstairs whenever you want it. Abbi went to the store and bought some fresh croissants and pastries, they're on the table. Your friends are by the pool out back," Uncle Ross added as he stood.

I nodded. "Thanks. And I really mean that," I said softly. My uncle raised his hand in a gesture of 'it's nothing.' But it wasn't nothing, and we both knew it.

I crossed to the small en suite bathroom and changed into the swimsuit. It was a pretty shade of green, and I noted the price as I ripped the tag from it. I shouldn't have been shocked. I knew too well what my uncle was like. He always had a lot of money, and he wasn't afraid to spend it. Back in New Zealand, my family was fairly well off, but it wasn't every day I wore a swimsuit that cost several hundred dollars. I put the tag down and grabbed a towel from the cupboard.

For a brief second, I caught sight of myself in the mirror. I had been trying not to look too hard at my reflection since coming here. I was almost a little scared to face myself, unsure what I would find if I looked too deeply into my own eyes. Oddly, I didn't look as different as I expected. Surely if I had changed so much on the inside, it must have altered my appearance too? My face stared back at me with mistrustful green eyes. After a moment of close examination, I decided there was something different, after all, though I wasn't certain what it was. Was it the way I held myself more carefully and warily, or the way I stepped so lightly across the floorboards barely even realizing it? Maybe it was the tiny crease that had appeared in between my eyebrows from stress and worry. Perhaps it was the seriousness present on my face? Whatever it was, I couldn't place my finger on it. There's something about a person you can't see, but you can sense it in the way they move and speak. It was this part of me that had matured and changed. I tucked one of my copper locks behind my ear.

Sighing and turning away from the mirror, I wrapped my towel around my waist. I walked barefoot out to the hallway and down the stairs. A good deal of laughing and splashing echoed from the patio outside. I grabbed a croissant from the table and opened the sliding door that led out to the courtyard at the back of the house. Taking a bite of the buttery croissant, I tossed my towel onto one of the recliners and sat back in the sun.

Grace was laughing at Levi, who was trying to splash her while she lay sunning on a recliner. Ross had given her strict instructions not to swim until her wound healed.

The Florida sun beamed down brightly in the sky, and I lay back, soaking up the warmth. For a brief moment, I wondered what it would have been like if my parents had never moved to New Zealand. This would be my life, and I wouldn't be worried about any war.

"The croissants are good, right?" Jennifer said, grinning at me. "I can't believe it took you so long to wake up."

"I guess I was tired," I said with a smile. The others swam to the edge of the pool after a little while and sat on the underwater seating that ran along one wall.

"This is really nice," Grace said, smiling from her lounger.

"Thanks to Jess, we're living it up," Lizzie agreed. She stretched her arms out behind her, smiling as the sun's rays caught on the drips of water in her dark blond hair.

Dylan and Levi glanced at each other, trading stressed looks.

"We should be thinking of how to stop the rocket," Dylan said. "Not living it up. There can't be much time until the launch. Levi and I were talking to Ross about it this morning. He tried making a few calls. But it's hard to talk to someone important over the phone... even for someone like Ross."

"He said he had a meeting with someone this afternoon," I said hopefully.

Almost on cue, Uncle Ross' voice came through the door,

shouting into his phone.

"You better listen to me, God damn it… if someone doesn't do something about it, thousands are going to die," he yelled. I stared through the glass panel in the door. Uncle Ross was right behind it, his face scarlet with rage. "I think I need to talk to your supervisor," he said acidly. I finished eating my croissant and walked over to the sliding door.

"Everything OK?" I mouthed worriedly at him.

"Not now, Jessy," he said, shaking his head and walking away a bit. I stood there in the doorway watching him. His forehead was lined with wrinkles, and he looked ten years older than last night when he had first welcomed us to his house. Looking at him, I felt unbearably guilty. I had brought all this worry and stress to him. It was my fault he was caught up in this huge mess.

"You think this is funny? I'll give you funny. By the end of this week, hundreds of people are going to be either dead or injured. Maybe thousands. It would be an international disaster if something like that were to happen. Do you want that on your hands?"

He threw the phone down and ran his hands through his hair, collapsing onto one of the leather couches "Fuck. They hung up on me," he said. He looked up at me. "Your dad would kill me if he knew I was swearing around you," he said apologetically.

I laughed. "You think I don't hear it everywhere else?" I looked over my shoulder at the others. "This war brings out the worst in us."

"You've grown up so much, Jessy," he said, looking at me wearily. "I don't know if I've seen any kid as mature as you at your age. You should be out there having fun, partying, doing what you love. Not messed up in all of this. I want to get the rest of your friends US citizenship. I think I can do it if I pull a few strings."

"But what about the rocket? What about the meeting?"

"They canceled the meeting," he said. "Face it, Jessy, no one is going to believe you. Why don't you forget all about this… it's time for you to be a teenager again. Your parents would have wanted me to look after you."

"And you have," I said, sitting down beside him, "but I meant what I said last night. We will see this through no matter what, Uncle Ross."

He looked at me helplessly.

"We can't just give up. My parents—"

"Your parents would expect me to protect you," Uncle Ross said.

I shook my head. "You don't get it. You weren't in New Zealand. I have to do this… I will do this with or without your help."

Ross studied me critically but he still didn't look convinced.

"And," I added, "what about Mom and Dad? I can't abandon them."

"You wouldn't be abandoning them," Ross said, shaking his head.

"You don't understand what it's like over there! Yes, they want me safe, but what about their safety? Don't you care about Mom at all?" I said, upset.

"Of course, I do, Jessy. But—"

"You said last night you would do anything for her," I said accusingly. I knew I was being childish and selfish, but I didn't care. "Prove it." Standing up from the couch, I left him.

BACK AT THE POOL, the others had shifted onto recliners in the sun, but despite this peaceful setting, none of them looked like they fitted in. I was used to seeing them holding guns in the dead of night, and seeing their faces streaked with mud like mine, lying next to them in a roughly built shelter. We weren't used to this life anymore. It was too easy, too comfortable, and too insignificant. It was time for me to stop following the lead and become the leader. And, for once, I had an idea.

"We should go to the Pentagon."

"What? Jess, that's crazy," Jennifer said.

I shrugged. "What else are we going to do? We can't stop it by ourselves. We need to talk to someone with power."

"Why the Pentagon?" Levi asked skeptically.

"That's where their home security is based," I explained. "If no one on the phone will listen, we'll have to make them listen. They can't hang up on us if we're standing right in front of them."

"I'm not convinced," Lizzie said, shaking her head. "How would we get in? And once we manage to get inside, what's stopping security shooting us dead on the spot? This isn't New Zealand anymore."

"I'm sure there's a way," Grace said.

"Also, we would have to ask Ross to help us get there... that's if we could even convince him," Lizzie said. She was fiercely independent and clearly felt uncomfortable accepting the generosity from my uncle.

"What, so you want to stay here and do nothing?" Levi said to Lizzie. She glared at him. "You're the one who got us into this mess. Surely, you, of all people, don't want to sit on your ass and wait for other people to fix it."

Lizzie's face exploded in anger. "I never said that. Stop putting words in my mouth."

"I think everyone needs to take a breath," Grace said. "Clearly, we can't sit around and do nothing. We've all decided that much, right?" she said, looking steadily at us all.

"Yes... we need to do something. Does anyone have any better ideas?" Lizzie asked. We were silent. Everything that could be done right now had already been done. This was the only avenue left open to us.

"If Ross can somehow help us get there, I'm sure we can find a way in... or at least confront someone when they leave and make them listen to us," Dylan said.

"Whatever we decide to do, it better be legal," Jennifer added. "There are real consequences here."

"There were real consequences back home too, they just involved being shot at," Levi pointed out.

"I'm sure it will be above board," Lizzie said uncertainly.

"So, we're in then?" I asked. I knew there was no way they would let such destruction come upon a city if they could help it. We were the only ones who knew, and now it was our job to do something to stop it. And, at the back of our minds was the idea that continued to fuel us all, every step of the way: the end of the war.

"We're all in," Lizzie said.

THE REST OF THE day dragged on slowly. Levi and Dylan said they'd talk to Uncle Ross. If he wasn't willing to lend us some money for the trip, we had no other choice but to give up. Without some sort of help, we weren't going to be able to go anywhere. Grace outright refused to be involved in stealing a car, and flying was out of the question. We all lounged nervously around the house, moving from room to room. Despite being here in Florida, the same tension that plagued us in the bush buzzed through the air.

"I'm kind of worried about telling Uncle Ross about it," I said to Grace. "There's no way he's going to be comfortable with us going all the way to Virginia alone. Besides… I kind of went off at him earlier," I said guiltily. We sat in one of the lounges with the TV on, but we weren't watching it.

"Let Levi and Dylan talk to him. Maybe it'll be easier for them to discuss it more objectively since they're not related," Grace said consolingly. "Ross only wants to protect you."

"I know." I rearranged the cushion behind my lower back.

"You are young, Jess," Grace said. The comment sounded condescending, but I knew she didn't mean it that way. "We all are. And though we might think we know best, to people with no connection to our situation, it comes across a bit insane. Give him time to think on it and wrap his head around everything. It's a lot."

I didn't say anything and instead moodily turned my gaze to the TV. There was some comedy show on, and the audience roared with laughter as the comedian said something particularly witty.

"Do you think we should even be going?" I asked.

Grace stared at me critically with her brown eyes. "If you've changed your mind, that's OK, Jess. We'd understand if you wanted to stay here, with Ross. He's your family."

"That's not what I said. I want to do this. I just want to make sure everyone else does too. Our situation has changed massively, and I don't think it has entirely sunk in for all of us."

In truth, there were two warring sides in my head. Selfishly, I did want to stay. I wanted to remain here, where it was peaceful, and go to school. Live a normal life again. But our parents and our families were back home, waiting for the war to end. And there were plenty of other people who were calmly living their lives, not knowing their end was so close at hand.

"We're the only ones who know anything about what's going to happen. What if we didn't do anything? Would we be able to live with ourselves?" Grace asked. She was clearly thinking along the same lines.

"I suppose not," I agreed.

Lizzie walked into the room and sat down beside Grace on the couch. "TV's so boring. I can't believe we used to watch it so much before the war started."

"Oh, come on, Lizzie. If something good was on, you would be glued to it," Grace said, rolling her eyes.

"Maybe, but I don't know." Lizzie flicked a couple of channels before turning the TV off. She turned around to face us. "I just saw Ross. Levi and Dylan have told him our idea."

"What did he say?" I asked her.

"He was actually really nice about it," Lizzie said, surprise in her voice. "He's getting everything organized and finding us a hotel. He said we could take one of the cars."

"Really?" Grace asked.

"Yes, really. To be honest, I didn't think he'd let us go."

"I said something to him earlier… it may have guilted him into helping us," I said awkwardly. "He misses my mom—his sister—and I accused him of not wanting to help her." The guilt that was eating me lessened slightly as I voiced it aloud.

"I'm sure he can make his own choices," Grace said, gently touching my shoulder. "You didn't guilt him into anything."

We were silent for a moment, thinking of the momentous journey ahead of us. I hoped it would work.

"Levi will be ecstatic," I finally said with a smile as I thought about the road trip. Lizzie and Grace laughed.

"You can say that again. Did he say what type of car it was?" Grace asked, standing up.

"A Chevy, one of those old Impalas from the fifties," Lizzie said.

Grace shrugged. "I really don't understand the fascination with cars. I would have thought the newer, the better, but apparently not," she said, raising her eyebrows. It was obvious she wouldn't have a clue what an Impala looked like if it was right in front of her.

"It's a muscle car, Grace," I said. "You can't tell me you've never heard of muscle cars."

"Of course, I have. I just don't know why they get all excited about it," Grace replied.

"Oh, Grace, let them have their fun," Lizzie said playfully. "You already have Levi wrapped around your finger, don't take this from him."

"I do not have him wrapped around my finger," Grace said, crossing her arms. Lizzie and I giggled.

"He would do anything for you… anything," I added. Grace blushed, muttered something about needing a shower, and limped out of the room. Lizzie and I sat in companionable silence.

"I'm sorry for not going along with your idea at the start," Lizzie said eventually.

"It's OK, I hadn't thought it out."

"No, you were right. I was the one who got us in this mess, and I am the one always forcing you into battle with plans much more dangerous than yours."

I smiled softly at Lizzie. "That's all in the past. All that matters now is saving lives."

CHAPTER TWENTY-SIX

DYLAN

LEVI AND I SAT around Ross' dining table, putting the final touches to our plan, while next door in the office, Ross made some last phone calls.

"I hope this works," I said when we were finally done. Levi tipped back in his seat, stretching his arms out.

"Me too," he yawned.

Ross charged into the room, carrying a manila envelope. "Everything's sorted," he said as he handed it to me, along with a cell phone. I moved to grab it. "Be careful," he warned, moving it out of my reach. "And… look after Jessy."

"We will," I said. He handed the envelope over, and I tucked it under one arm. The elevator dinged, and I looked up to see the girls lugging some heavy duffel bags into the room. I marched over to help Lizzie as she struggled with hers, and we made our way to the garage. Ross tossed Levi the keys.

"The Impala's two cars down," he said, pointing. Levi and I looked at each other eagerly.

"Bags driving first," Levi said quickly, as he jogged to the car. I followed, disappointed. Levi sat idly in the driver's seat as I hauled the bags into the trunk. We piled into the car and waved to Ross as Levi reversed and pulled out onto the road. Then Levi gave a final toot of the horn, and we took off up the I-95. I sat between Levi and Grace on the roomy front bench seat, watching Levi jealously as he sped onward. Grace opened the glove box and started rummaging, eventually pulling out a well-worn map of the States.

"First up is Georgia by the looks of it," she said, tracing the interstate with her finger. "Then up through South Carolina and North Carolina. Finally, Virginia before getting to Washington DC."

"Ross said it should be about thirteen hours driving," Levi added.

"I thought the Pentagon was in Virginia? Why are we driving all the way to Washington, DC?" Lizzie asked. I looked in the rear-view to see Lizzie looking unimpressed about having to spend so much time cooped up in the car. She caught my eye and forced a smile.

"It's right on the border. Our hotel's in Washington DC," Jess said.

"You can drive through Georgia, then we can switch," I said to Levi.

"Sure."

"Should we play a game?" Grace suggested. Silence. "Eye spy with my—"

"No," the rest of us said in unison.

"Fine," Grace said, dejected. "I was only trying to make it fun."

"How about music?" I suggested and fiddled with the nobs on the old-style radio. Finally, a classic rock station crackled through the retro stereo-system. How fitting, I thought. Levi wound his window down.

"It feels like years since I drove with the music blaring," he said as the wind buffeted his face. Grace wound her window down and hung her arm out, as Levi began to headbang.

"This is a good one," I called over the wind. Levi grinned, and we both began to sing, badly. Grace tapped her hand against the car to the beat and occasionally joined in. Taking a peek in the rearview mirror again, the girls in the back were sound asleep. For the next few hours Levi, Grace, and I sang along with every song that came on. It had been a while since I felt like this—myself. There was no worrying about soldiers, and I could let loose.

When we passed the sign welcoming us to South Carolina, Levi pulled into the first gas station we came across. He ran in to grab us some food, and I slid across into the driver's seat. He returned with an armful of sandwiches and cans of root beer. We dug in while I pulled out onto the interstate. The crisp blue sky eventually darkened into the chilly night. By the time we reached North Carolina, the temperature outside had plummeted to below zero. The girls in the back continued sleeping the hours away, leaving only Grace and Levi to chat with.

"So, what's the deal with you and Lizzie?" Grace asked with a small smirk once Levi had also drifted off to sleep. I felt my cheeks flush a bit.

"What do you mean?" I replied innocently.

"Oh Dylan, you know exactly what I mean," she said softly with a small laugh.

I remained focused dead ahead on the road.

"Fine, be like that," she said.

We sat in silence for a few minutes before I finally gave in. "I don't know," I said.

"How can you not know? It seems pretty obvious to me. She likes you."

"But what about that guy?"

"What guy?" Grace asked, confused for a moment. "Oh, you

mean Ryan?"

"Yeah, whatever his name is."

"They were never going to work out. He was a massive jerk."

"She's never said if she's over him," I said awkwardly.

"Why don't you ask her," Grace encouraged.

"Isn't that too obvious?"

"Yes, but Lizzie is so oblivious. She won't know you like her unless you hold up a sign. Even then…" Grace said.

"Can you ask her?"

Grace studied me for a moment. "OK, fine."

"Lizzie," Levi said loudly. He opened one eye and winked at me.

"Were you listening the whole time?" I said under my breath.

"Yup. I heard the whole thing," he said, sitting up and stretching.

Lizzie stirred in the back, opening her eyes. "Did someone say my name?" she asked groggily.

"Sorry, we didn't mean to wake you," I apologized.

"It's fine," she said, eyeing the clock. "I've been asleep for long enough."

"What are your thoughts about Ryan?" Grace asked Lizzie.

"Wow, subtle," I whispered to Grace. She smiled cheekily back. Levi sat smugly between Grace and me, clearly enjoying the situation.

"Great, you guys have been talking about me," Lizzie said sourly.

"Well," Grace probed, "you can't possibly think you guys are still together. It's been months. Plus, you were on rocky ground before the war broke out."

Lizzie hesitated for a moment. I looked into the rearview in time to see Lizzie blush a deep red.

"Fine, if you must know," she said, glaring at Grace, "I think I am over him now. It sounds horrible to say since he could be imprisoned or… dead."

"I knew it," Grace said, giving me a wink.

"You two are impossible," Lizzie said.

"When do you think you were over him?" Grace continued.

"I don't know. It happened slowly. Then, one day I realized I hadn't thought about him in weeks."

"What about you, Jennifer?" Lizzie asked, changing the subject when she noticed Jennifer was awake. "Did you leave a boyfriend behind when the war started?"

"No," Jennifer said defensively.

"What about you, Grace?" Jennifer asked, throwing the question back in a full circle.

Lizzie grimaced. Clearly, this had crossed into bad territory.

"No," Grace said, her tone sharp.

"Sorry for asking," Jennifer said.

I glanced behind me at Lizzie, who indicated I shouldn't press it any further.

"At least you have Levi now," Jennifer added.

I laughed loudly while Grace and Levi blushed a deep red, cowering in the front seat.

"I don't think Levi and Grace are a thing… yet," Lizzie said, speaking for them, as she tried to quell her laughter.

"How far away are we?" Grace said, trying to change the subject.

"Probably a couple hours," I said.

Levi and I switched driving one more time once I felt tiredness pricking the back of my eyes. Finally, we pulled up to the Twin Acorn Hotel. Ross had picked it for its proximity to the Pentagon. Jess flipped Ross' credit card out from her purse, and she and Jennifer walked briskly inside to check us in. I stepped out of the car into the crisp winter air to stretch my legs. Through the reception window, I watched Jennifer and Jess chatting to the lady at the front desk.

"It's bloody freezing," Levi commented as he pulled his jacket around him. Grace leaned casually against the car, while Lizzie sat on the hood. Finally, Jess and Jennifer returned. "We've got three rooms," Jess said.

"I guess Lizzie and I will take one room," Grace said, giving a sideways glance at Levi. I couldn't tell if he was disappointed or not. She grabbed one of the keys from Jess' hand, and Lizzie took their bags from the car before they walked off toward the elevators together.

"Let's meet at nine a.m. in the lobby," Lizzie called back to us. I zipped my jacket up tight, and rubbed my hands together for warmth. Although it wasn't snowing, it was freezing.

"It would be weird if Levi and I stayed in the same room, right?" Jess said.

Levi looked surprised and glanced at me for support. What was she on about?

"Grace would probably murder you," I said uncertainly.

Jess laughed. "I was joking. Obviously, I will share with Jen," she said and tossed me a key. "Come on, let's go," she said to Jennifer. They left Levi and I staring after them in confusion.

"What the hell was that about?" I asked Levi.

"Damned if I know," he said with a shrug. "I don't know what the heck she's playing at."

"Maybe she likes you," I commented as I grabbed our bags from the trunk.

"She can back right off," he said, locking the car. "She's trying to cause trouble." Levi shoved his hands deep into his pockets and trudged toward the hotel. I followed him, carrying both our bags. "We have a good thing going in our group, why would she try and mess with that," Levi continued, clearly annoyed.

"She said she was joking."

"It didn't need to be said," Levi said, storming toward the elevators.

"Mate, you're overreacting," I said with a laugh. Levi looked at me seriously.

"I'm not. Grace is going to flip out," he said, running his hand through his scruffy hair. I followed him into the elevator.

"So, what do we do about it?"

"Jess isn't coming with us tomorrow," Levi said, as we reached our floor.

"She's not going to be happy."

"I don't care. We can make up some bullshit about Ross not wanting her to be in danger." Levi shoved the key aggressively into the lock and threw open the door to our room.

I tossed the bags on the floor. "Grace should stay back, too," I said with a grimace.

Levi sighed and sat on one of the beds. He kicked off his shoes and lay back. "I know," he said, with his tone softening.

"Her leg is a massive giveaway. She can hardly walk."

"She's going to be pissed," Levi said, staring at the ceiling. We drifted into silence and then to sleep.

I WOKE EARLY THE next morning. Bleary-eyed, I looked over at Levi, who was already up. "Coffee?" he asked as he stood in his boxers and waited for the jug to boil.

"Please," I said.

"I couldn't sleep," he said as he stirred the steaming mugs before carrying one over to me. He took a sip of his before disappearing to the shower. Thirty minutes later, he reappeared, dressed in a pinstriped suit with his hair gelled.

"I think I look pretty damn good," he said with a smile.

"You look old," I said with a laugh.

"Great. That's the plan, right?" he said. "You're up. We better not be late. Lizzie will have our heads."

"Too right," I said. I quickly showered and dressed in a navy suit. Ross had got me a pair of thick-rimmed glasses, which completed my geeky intern look.

Levi burst into laughter when he saw me. "Since when do you wear glasses?"

"I don't," I said. "How are we for time?"

"Crap, we're late," Levi said, checking the clock. He grabbed the manila envelope from the desk, and we raced to the elevators where we found the others waiting for us impatiently.

When I saw Lizzie, I had to stop myself from commenting aloud. She was in a clinging black dress with a gray woolen overcoat. Her legs were attractively slimmed with a pair of black heels. Levi nudged me in the ribs.

"Stop staring," he whispered.

"Are we ready?" Jess asked eagerly.

"We are changing the plan a bit," Levi said carefully, looking at me for support.

"It seems dumb for all of us to go. What happens if something goes wrong?" I said, trying to soften the blow.

"What are you saying?" Jess snapped back.

"I am saying you and Grace need to stay behind," I said.

Grace looked furious as she rounded on Levi. "I'm not staying behind!"

"You have to," Levi said, attempting to calm her down. "You're obviously limping and will draw attention to us."

"Plus, your bandage has leaked through again." I pointed unhelpfully at the red blood patch spreading under her sheer stockings. Grace gave me a murderous look.

Jess crossed her arms. "Why me?"

"We couldn't make Grace stay on her own," Levi said. "It wouldn't be fair."

"You drew the short straw," I said with a shrug. "Sorry. Here's the phone. If anything happens, we'll call." Grace snatched it from my hand and stormed off to her room, with Jess not far behind.

Lizzie pushed the button for the elevator. "You are going to get an earful from Grace later," she said to Levi.

"Dylan and I were talking last night, and we thought it was the best idea," Levi said.

"She isn't going to see it that way."

"Why did you make Jess stay?" Jennifer asked, as the elevator door opened and we stepped inside.

"She pissed me off last night," Levi said. "I don't know what she was playing at. It was like she wanted to cause trouble."

"What did she do?" Lizzie asked. Levi blushed a little.

"She basically said she wanted to share a room with Levi," I explained.

"What?" Lizzie said. "She was joking, right?"

"Who knows."

"But she was stirring trouble," Levi grumbled.

"You need to calm down, Levi," Lizzie warned. "We can deal with this after."

"Lizzie's right," I said.

Levi ran a hand through his hair. "I know."

We stepped out into the crisp morning air, and Levi hailed a taxi. "Pentagon, please," he said to the driver who nodded and pulled away. We drove in silence for a few minutes as the Pentagon loomed ahead of us. All I could think about was what we were about to do. It was crazy… it was never going to work. They would arrest us and send us to prison. We weren't in New Zealand anymore. There would be consequences. The anxiety was back. I pulled at my collar, eventually loosening my tie and undoing a few buttons on my shirt. My pulse was pounding in my ears, and I rolled the window down, letting the crisp air surge into the car. I breathed deeply.

"What are you doing, Dylan? It's freezing," Lizzie said next to me, as she pulled her coat around her.

"Sorry," I muttered, winding it back up. She glanced over at me, clearly noticing something was wrong. "It's just nerves," I said.

"What entrance?" the driver asked.

"The Metro," Levi replied monotonously. The cab driver gave him an inquisitive look but asked no further questions. He turned a corner and then stopped behind a large line up of cars dropping people off.

"You walk up that path," he said, pointing. Levi thanked him and gave a generous tip before we walked confidently away. My stomach squirmed uncomfortably as we drew nearer. I looked up and felt very small. Levi stopped us before we got closer and handed us each two cards and a piece of paper.

"What are these?" Lizzie asked.

"Ross did us a favor," Levi explained quietly. "These are alien registration and social security cards," he said.

"How did he get those?" Lizzie asked.

"He knows people," I said quietly, out of earshot of a passing worker.

"What's this piece of paper?" Jennifer asked.

"Permission to be unescorted visitors for the day," Levi said as we continued walking to the doors.

"How did we get those?" Jennifer asked, sounding worried.

"Ross," Levi repeated.

Lizzie frowned. "When he asked to take our photos, I didn't think… I don't know what I thought," she finally said.

"Don't worry," I said to Lizzie and placed a hand on her shoulder. "They're good fakes and the letter's authentic." It was more to reassure myself than anyone else.

"If you say so," Lizzie said, before taking a deep breath and resuming her professional appearance. I looked down at the terrible photo of me and quickly shoved the cards and paper into my pockets. Once we got closer, we dispersed from each other as we entered the crowds of people queuing for security. Lizzie moved away from me and out of sight. I was alone. I re-buttoned the top of my shirt, fixed my tie, and walked right up to a burly security guard who glared down at me. I tried to keep a neutral expression.

"I'm on the visitor roster," I said calmly and looked confidently up at the guard.

"Name?" he requested.

"Dylan Saville," I said plainly. He began typing into the computer beside him.

"ID," he ordered. I handed him my alien card and the social security card. He took them and typed a few numbers into the computer before staring at me critically. Everything was going to be fine. The guard paused for a second. He typed the numbers for a second time.

"Is something wrong?" I asked as evenly as I could. The computer bleeped in response.

"May I see your letter of approval?" he asked, sounding bored now. I handed it to him.

"NOFY Oil?" he asked as he considered me for a moment. "You seem a bit young to be working for them."

"I'm in the last year of my internship."

He shrugged. "You must be here regarding the NOFY Parfan oil deal?"

"Yes."

"Your paperwork is in order. Proceed through the metal detectors and have a nice day," he said as he handed me back my papers and I moved off. I let out a sigh of relief and walked briskly to the metal detectors. I pushed through throngs of people toward Levi, Jennifer, and Lizzie, who were waiting by a large map.

"We need to go to the north side of the building, in the D ring near corridor eight," Levi said as he contemplated a map on the wall. We were looking for room 2D817.

"That way," I said, pointing to one of the signs. We walked with purpose around the outer ring until we reached corridor eight.

"Almost there," Levi said as he turned down the corridor. Reaching ring D, we passed the offices of the Army and Airforce that had been redone after 9/11. I walked past office doors; 2D820, 2D819, 2D818 with the others following behind me. Levi and I stopped outside a plain-looking door. 2D817.

"This is it," I said. *Secretary of Defense* was written in gold on a black plaque fixed to the door. Here we go, I thought. I took a calming breath and knocked hard on the door.

"Come in," a gruff voice said loudly. I turned the handle and eased the door open. A stout oak desk stood in the center of a spacious office. An American flag hung behind the desk framing an equally impressive table covered in piles of documents. A middle-aged man reclined behind the desk in a comfortable leather chair. His face was weathered, but his dark eyes were alert. Gray-black hair was combed back neatly with gel, and his black suit was pristine. He looked up at us with suspicious eyes.

"How can I help you? I don't have an appointment scheduled," he said in a deep voice.

"My name is Dylan Saville," I said, trying to sound professional and put my hand out for the secretary to shake.

"And who are you, Mr. Saville? Why are you in my office?" the secretary asked, ignoring my hand.

"I work for NOFY Oil, and there is a matter of national security you need to be made aware of," I said. The secretary looked up at us skeptically.

"And I assume the rest of you are all from NOFY oil?" he asked as he scratched his head. We nodded in unison. We were definitely suspicious. "I see. And you say there is a matter of national security I don't know about?"

"Yes," I said. "Do you know about the rocket being launched shortly?"

"Of course," the secretary said.

"It's been hijacked," I continued. "It sounds absurd, but it's true." I cringed at the words coming out of my mouth. They sounded weak. We should have rehearsed something earlier.

The secretary started rifling through some pages on his desk, apparently losing interest. "Trust me, that launching is secure. There is no one attending of concern."

"The New Zealand Prime Minister, and his team," Levi said.

With that, we finally had the secretary's attention. Concern lined his face. "Really?"

"Yes," I said, and felt relief flow through me. Maybe this wasn't doomed, and maybe he would help us after all.

"They're responsible for the war in New Zealand, and they're going to fly that rocket into England," Levi explained.

But a smile was growing on the secretary's face. He didn't believe us at all. "That's one of the most original jokes I've heard in a long time. Now, let's be serious. Why the hell are you in my office?"

"We just told you," Lizzie said, her face white with fury.

"Fine. What is your source?" the secretary asked, trying to catch us out.

"Us," I said. "We had reports from our New Zealand branch. They heard about the attack and managed to contact us using some radio equipment. Trust us, sir, you need to stop that rocket launch."

"I'm sorry, but without concrete evidence, there is nothing I can do about it," he said with a wave of his hand.

"Are you kidding me?" Levi asked, barely suppressing his anger.

"No, I am not kidding. You have no grounds for me to believe you," the secretary said with a shrug. "Please leave my office."

I refused to move.

"I said, leave my office," he ordered, standing up. "How did you even get in here?" He picked up his phone, obviously about to call security. In a moment of stupidity, I reached over his desk and hung his phone up. He grabbed my wrist and pushed me up against the wall, knocking off some picture frames in the process.

"I know more about the security of this country than you can imagine," he seethed in my ear. "I do not appreciate a bunch of kids mocking the integrity of our operation. Now, get out before

I call security and have you arrested." He released me and pushed me toward the door.

"You are going to be sorry," Lizzie said, her eyes flashing dangerously. "We risked our lives to warn you, and all you do is shrug it off. I thought this country had improved its defenses, but clearly not."

I grabbed Lizzie's arm and pulled her to the door. "Thank you for your time," I said to the secretary as we left the office. Levi and I dragged Lizzie out the door and closed it behind us.

"Get off me," she said, shrugging us off her. Walking down the hall, I felt a fierce rage building up inside me.

"Are you OK?" Jennifer asked me.

I wasn't. I was furious. "Let's get out of this place before I hurt someone," I said through clenched teeth while we walked briskly toward the exit. Lizzie's face was contorted with anger. I led us back the way we came. Without a glance at anyone, we burst out the front doors. I hailed a taxi, and we rode back to the hotel in gritty silence. We all wanted to fume about the absurdity of the US government, but I knew the taxi was not the place to do it. It pulled up to the hotel, and we quickly got out of the car. I thrust a handful of bills into the driver's hands and slammed the door as we stormed inside the lobby. As we approached the elevators, the doors slid open, and two guests began to slowly get out.

"Can you hurry it up," I berated them. They threw me a dirty look and rushed out. Finally, with the elevator to ourselves, I couldn't hold the anger in any longer. "What the hell was wrong with that guy? Secretary of Defense my ass." I was shaking with anger.

"I wouldn't believe us," Jennifer said. "It's a ridiculous story."

"But it's true. Every word of it's the bloody truth," Levi said as the doors opened on our floor. We rushed out of the elevator, and Lizzie knocked on her and Grace's door.

"What happened?" Grace asked as she pulled the door open.

Jess was hovering behind her shoulder.

"He's not going to do a bloody thing! He laughed in our face. The stupid fucking American government!" I said, pushing past Grace and punching one of the pillows on the bed. "Fuck!" I said again. I was angry and had every right to be. We risked our lives and freedom to warn him.

"Maybe he'll reconsider it?" Grace said, trying to inject some sort of hope.

"Doubt the bastard will give it a second thought," Levi said as he flopped onto the bed, dejected.

"What do we do now?" Jennifer asked, "give up?"

"I suppose," Jess said.

I didn't want to give up, but what other choice did we have? There was nothing left to do. Grace sat down lightly beside Levi.

"No one is giving up," Levi said loudly. We all stared at him. "Dad always told me I take the easy way out of everything. Not anymore. I'm not quitting this time. People are going to die, and just because we failed once doesn't mean we should stop trying. So what if the government is a bunch of assholes? We will find another way." Deep down, I knew he was right.

"But we've tried. We could stay here in safety like my uncle suggested. We can be safe until the war is over," Jess said hopefully.

Lizzie scowled at her. "Could you really do that? Stay here and do nothing while hundreds of people die. To be honest, I could never breathe again with that on my conscience… maybe you're different."

Jess stood up to get a drink of water. "I've tried and tried to do the right thing. But sometimes you have to look out for yourself and not be the hero."

"Sometimes the world needs heroes," Lizzie retorted.

"So, you see yourself as a hero?" Jess said.

Lizzie stared her down. "No. But right now, there is no one else, and we have nothing."

"I don't know about you, but I've lost everything," Grace commented. "I have no home here and no home in New Zealand. I have no family. So... I agree with Levi and Lizzie. We'll try again."

"It isn't our job to save the world," Jennifer retorted. "We've done our bit. Now it's time to let everyone else do theirs."

"No, it's our job to save the world, because no one else will," I said, backing up Grace. We had come this far; there had to be another way.

"Dylan's right," Levi said, "and you both know it." He loosened his tie and threw it to the floor. "I am going to keep trying. You can do whatever the hell you want."

"Screw you, Levi," Jess said furiously, grabbing her coat and heading toward the door. She turned back to look at us, "You know if they catch us, they'll send us back to New Zealand. I sure as hell don't want to go back there."

Jennifer followed after Jess and slammed the door on her way out.

"That was harsh, Levi," Grace said.

"There's something up with her, she's not herself," Lizzie commented.

"I need air," I said. "It's suffocating in here." I stood up and walked out of the room, heading to the elevators. I needed some space to think.

"Wait," Lizzie called from behind me. I hesitated, letting her catch up. We waited together for the elevator to arrive.

"What do we do, Dylan?" she asked, looking up at me. Afraid.

I shook my head. "I don't know," I admitted, defeated. The elevator doors opened in front of us, and we got in.

"I feel like I have the whole world on my back," she said softly, swiping a wayward strand of blond hair behind her ear.

"I know the feeling." We walked through the lobby in silence and into the bitter Washington winter. I pulled the stupid glasses from my face and tossed them on the sidewalk, smashing them.

"Bloody waste of time," I murmured.

Lizzie laughed half-heartedly. I spotted a bench up ahead and made for it.

"I feel like every time we get close to a win, something kicks us in the face," I said, sitting on the frozen seat. "And I'm sick of it."

"We're due for a win, right?" Lizzie asked, sitting next to me.

"You're freezing," I said, noticing she didn't have her coat. I quickly removed mine and put it around her petite shoulders.

"Thanks," she said.

I tried to ignore the chill biting through my thin suit. "I don't know if I can take another setback. Ever since this bloody war started, I feel like it's been blow after blow."

Lizzie shuffled closer to me. I was keenly aware of her light floral perfume, and her hand millimeters from mine. "We have to keep trying," Lizzie said simply. She always had so much fight in her, even when it seemed like there was nothing left to fight for.

CHAPTER TWENTY-SEVEN

JENNIFER

WHY HAD WE THOUGHT we could make a difference in this war? We had failed to get the Secretary of Defense to believe us. But, to be honest, it wasn't surprising. I knew from the moment we heard about the plan on Marion's plane that we were doomed to fail. We were in over our heads, and frankly, we never had a chance despite what the others thought. Jess and I had left the others in Lizzie and Grace's room and stormed off to ours. Jess thrust the door open and burst into the room.

"I can't stand them," Jess said as she began throwing her scattered clothes into a bag.

"You don't mean that," I said as I began to gather my stuff. "It's only because Levi made you stay behind."

"I mean it," she said, looking over at me. "I don't care about being left behind."

"You're upset because we failed. We all are."

"No. They think they are god-sent to save everyone."

"I'm sure they don't think that." Sometimes their plans were reckless, but I knew they only wanted to help. It was painfully obvious to everyone that we were human. Enough people from our group had died for them to know that. Jess was saying rash things. Something was wrong.

I thought back to last night when Jess started stirring trouble by suggesting she wanted to share a room with Levi. It was uncharacteristic, and I had confronted her about it. We had tossed our bags into the room. Jess flopped backward onto one of the twin beds and sighed. I had been uncomfortable with what she had said to Levi. Eventually, I couldn't take it anymore.

"Why did you say you wanted to share a room with Levi?" I said, cutting straight to the point.

Jess looked up at me sheepishly. "I didn't mean it."

"You definitely caused a stir, Levi looked mortified."

"I'm not into him or anything like that. I thought it would be funny to change things up."

I looked at her critically. She sat up and stared back at me.

"You can't cause havoc like that. Grace is our friend. She's definitely going to hear about this."

"You won't tell her," Jess said confidently.

"I won't, but you can't stop Dylan telling Lizzie… and Lizzie can't keep her mouth shut."

"I don't really care."

"You aren't yourself."

"It's nothing, Jen," Jess dismissed.

"Something's wrong, we should talk about it."

Jess sighed and fell back onto her bed. After a minute or two of silence, Jess finally spoke again.

"I feel alone. The others are so close, and they all have each other. I am sick of being the odd one out."

"You have me," I said. "We're the loners together." It was true. The others were nice and tried to include us. Unfortunately, the truth of it was we were outsiders.

"I know I have you, and I know they have my back. But it's not the same. I don't have my person."

I was confused by what she meant by this. "Do you mean you want a boyfriend? Because given our circumstances, we can't really change that."

"A boyfriend, or a real friend, either really."

I was offended she thought that, and judging by the way she looked up at me, she realized it too.

"I didn't mean to upset you, but it's the truth."

"Well, I'm sorry you feel that way. Maybe if you let people get close to you and allowed us to be your friends, you would feel better," I snapped.

Jess glared at me.

"Causing strife like you did before isn't going to win you any friends. The best you can hope for is that Grace lets it slide." I flicked my light off and went to sleep.

The whole conversation from that night was playing again through my mind as I watched Jess packing up to leave back to Ross'. I was still hurt by what she had said. In my mind, we had been bonding and actually developing a friendship. Clearly, she didn't feel the same way. I didn't know what she thought was going to change. Unless, by some miracle, we got to stay here, we would be sent back to New Zealand at some point. I prayed that wasn't going to happen. Ever.

"Do you think we should try again with the rocket?" I asked Jess. She sighed with a look of confusion passing over her face.

"I honestly don't know. We have a chance to be free again, and I would do anything to have that. I know my parents would want me to be safe," Jess said with a sigh as I struggled to zip up my bag. I finally got it shut and sat down heavily on the bed.

"Is it bad that I don't care about it anymore?" I asked. "The rocket, I mean."

Jess smiled weakly at me. "It's not bad. I don't really either. We broke into the Pentagon for God's sake."

"Not many people can say that," I said, agreeing. "But the others won't rest until we stop it."

"I know," Jess said. "They're going to end up getting us imprisoned… or killed."

"That's what I'm afraid of."

Even though the war had followed us, the US wasn't at war. We couldn't run around guns blazing like back home. There were rules to follow and consequences if we broke them. It felt like the others had forgotten about this. I sure hadn't. I wasn't about to risk my freedom again for an impossible mission. Once was enough.

Plus, we all knew we were headed home if we got caught. The world wasn't the same as it was a decade ago. With all the political tension, and the economic instability, no one accepted refugees anymore. Especially not people from New Zealand. Even before the war, the virus had made international travel and immigration almost impossible.

The virus started by spreading through our cattle. A resurgence of mad cow disease, but this time, the virus had evolved. It jumped person to person, and the death rate was staggeringly high. Within weeks, New Zealand was segregated from the rest of the world in an attempt to stop its spread. All flights in and out were cancelled, leaving us stranded in a country on the verge of collapse. But now, unbelievably, we had made it out. And I wasn't about to give that up.

"I don't want to go back to war," I said quickly. "I can't do it." I had been thinking about this for a while but hadn't been able to voice it. The others were so passionate, and already thought I was a coward. Dylan had said so on multiple occasions. Levi was nice, but the way he looked at me sometimes made me think he felt the same way as Dylan. Lizzie and Dylan seemed like they shared a conscience. Whatever one of them thought, the other agreed. Grace was the nicest one. She would never say it to my face, but given all she had been through, she was strong. Much stronger than me.

"Yes, you can," Jess muttered. "We all can. You and I… we're just afraid to go home."

"I'm not afraid," I said defensively. Jess looked over at me.

"The both of us are," she said solemnly. "Look at how Levi and Dylan would jump into battle if it meant they could save someone's life."

"It's because they are stupid."

"It's because they are selfless."

Jess' comment made me feel guilty, but I wasn't sure if I cared or not. Sometimes you have to be selfish. Should I feel bad about wanting to survive this war? Any logical person would say no. My parents would want me to stay here. It was safe. But willingly going back to the war? That was stupid. I wasn't sure how I was going to tell them I wanted to stay here. But, I had a thirteen-hour car ride to think about it.

We grabbed our bags and carried them into the hallway. The others were waiting by the elevator. We took a silent trip down to the ground floor where even the sight of the Impala wasn't enough to put a smile the boys' faces. Dylan got in sourly behind the wheel and started the engine. I closed my eyes and listened to the engine purring. The engine noise was steady, rhythmic, and reassuring. All I wanted was to feel safe and comfortable. I had tried to save people's lives. Was that not enough? Why wasn't everything we had already done enough? It frustrated me to no end. We tried so hard and failed, which only meant we would have to risk our lives again. I was sick of risking my life. I wanted normal. I wanted peace. I wanted freedom.

Chapter Twenty-Eight

Lizzie

"This is bullshit," Levi said forcefully, banging his hand onto the dashboard. None of us said anything in reply. We were too wrapped up in our own thoughts. I sat in the front in between Levi and Dylan on the leather bench seat. Out the window, cars rushed by either side of us on a major freeway. The roads in America seemed like they ran on and on forever—you could drive endlessly for days on end and still be no nearer to your destination. I fiddled with the stereo knob to find the classic rock station.

Dylan grinned. "Highway to Hell, huh?"

"Pretty much," I agreed, laughing.

"I didn't take you for the type to like classic rock," he said, looking briefly at me before returning his gaze to the road.

"Are you kidding, Grace and I love it," I said, remembering all the times spent at each other's houses.

"We knew Grace was a fan, we had a good singalong for a few hours on the way here when you were passed out on the back seat," Dylan said.

I glanced in the rearview mirror at Grace, who was sound asleep. "She can play the guitar, you know, and she has always wanted to get an electric one. She used to say she would buy herself one once she graduated. Looks like that's not happening anytime soon, though," I said.

Levi shook his head in disbelief. "Every time I think I know Grace, she comes out with a completely different side to her." A small smile grew on his face.

"I know," I agreed. "I used to think that too. She's kind of mysterious, you never know which side is going to come out next, but nothing surprises me about her anymore."

"She's amazing," Levi said. I turned my head toward Dylan to look out the window on his side, hiding my smile. Since Grace and had met Levi, I had seen a complete change in her. This was another side of her I hadn't seen in a long time. It was a good change.

Dylan caught my eye and winked at me. "Oh, Levi... you're amazing too," Dylan crooned. I erupted into a fit of giggles.

"Shut up, Dylan," Levi muttered before awkwardly looking out the window.

We had already been on the road for six hours, wanting to reach Ross as soon as we could to discuss our next move. It sounded stupid, but for some reason, I couldn't give up. What did it matter? I asked myself for the billionth time. It wasn't like it would affect us directly if the rocket crashed into England or not. There was no logic in the way I was feeling. But there were principles, and I did have a conscience.

Ever since the start of this war, my moral compass had switched itself on. And, the fact there was a chance we could help, meant my mind wouldn't rest until we had done something, anything at all. I sighed and returned my gaze to the window. I tried to tell myself that my conscience had always been like this. But I knew better. The truth was, deep down, I knew why I cared so much. My soul was crushed when Jaden was shot in front of me. He was dead, and I had to flee, leaving him there to rot alone. He deserved a funeral and a proper goodbye—he deserved better. I didn't want to see them destroy anyone else's lives if I could help it. And if there was a chance it would bring Marion down in the process, then I would do anything.

"What are we going to do next," I asked, my voice mechanical. I knew we had to keep trying. If something fails, then we try another path. It was that simple.

"I'm not sure we can do anything to stop it launching," Dylan said, gazing steadily at the road. His comment sounded offhand but left me feeling completely betrayed. Dylan had been in my corner only hours ago. His sudden turn-around made me livid, but I kept quiet. Maybe Grace or Levi would speak up.

"I mean, we don't know where it's launching from, or when it's launching," he continued.

I couldn't swallow my anger any longer. "Dylan, are you being serious? We are not giving up. No way in hell are we giving up!" I yelled at him. I was so angry that I wanted to punch, kick, and fight him even though none of this was his fault.

"Lizzie, calm down," Levi said, touching my arm.

"Don't touch me, Levi!" I shouted, rounding on him instead.

"What's going on?" Jess asked from the backseat as the others woke up with the shouting. We ignored them.

"Lizzie…" Levi tried to say.

Dylan pulled over to the side of the road. "Lizzie stop being such a bitch," Dylan said, glaring at me.

"So, I'm a bitch for wanting to keep all those people alive?" I shouted.

"Lizzie, shut up," Dylan said, turning to me and grabbing me roughly by my shoulders. I wrenched myself out of his grip and slapped him hard across the face.

"Screw you, Lizzie," Dylan said angrily, grabbing hold of my wrist forcefully and pinning me to the seat. Suddenly all the anger went out of me, and instead, tears began to stream down my face.

"I don't want it to happen," I said thickly through my tears. "Dylan, I don't want to see it happen."

"I know that Lizzie," Dylan said, relinquishing me from his deadlock grasp and hugging me instead. "I don't either. All I said was that there's nothing we can do about the launch. You didn't give me a chance to say that maybe we can still help." I buried my face into his shoulder.

"I think we all need to calm down. There's no point trying to make a decision now... we're still angry and not thinking straight. Let's discuss this with Ross," Grace said calmly. She was right. I took a few breaths to calm myself.

"We'll talk about this later," Dylan said. "For now, we need to get back to Ross, and then we can make a solid decision about what we do," he said quietly to me.

"Do you want me to drive, Dylan?" Levi asked. Dylan nodded and untangled himself from my arms. Dylan and Levi both got out of the car to change sides.

"I'm sorry about hitting you," I said to Dylan. His cheek was tinged pink from where I had slapped him. I didn't realize the force of my own anger. In some ways it scared me, but I always knew, since the start of this war, I needed my anger for strength. Without it, I would've been lost a long time ago.

"It's OK," he said gruffly. Then he chuckled. "I probably needed it to wake me up anyway. Driving makes me so tired."

I looked up at Dylan. His face was lined with worry, and his blue eyes looked out to the distance. He looked down at me and smiled wearily. I hesitated and then took Dylan's hand in mine. Dylan gave my hand a reassuring squeeze. Levi's head was buried in the map, and after consulting it for a few minutes, he pulled back onto the road.

"It's not much farther," he said.

"That's if you like to drive like a lunatic," Jennifer said from the back.

Levi glanced in the rear vision mirror and smiled back. "Maybe I do. Hold tight guys."

"Levi, don't!" Grace whined as we picked up speed. I didn't really mind. The faster we went, the sooner we could do something about the rocket. A few moments later, Dylan was asleep, leaning against the window. I too felt drained and exhausted. We had been driving nonstop, only stopping for fuel, food, and toilet stops. I leaned back against the seating and tried to get comfortable, but kept slipping sideways toward Dylan. It seemed like everyone except for me and Levi were asleep. I closed my eyes and started drifting off, but slipped sideways again.

"Don't worry about it, Lizzie," Dylan murmured, putting an arm around me. I leaned into him awkwardly. Even when I was being an absolutely awful person, Dylan didn't seem to care. He never took it personally. I finally had someone who understood me.

DYLAN AND I WOKE to tapping on the window. It was Ross, we had made it to Orlando once again. I suddenly realized I was still leaning against Dylan and sat bolt upright.

"Where are we?" Jennifer asked, yawning and not even bothering to open her eyes.

"You're back," Ross said, as Levi wound down the window.

"That garage over there?" Levi questioned, pointing to it.

"Yeah, that one's empty. I'll open the door for you, and you can drive right in." Ross disappeared for a minute, and the garage door began opening. Levi slowly drove forward and parked the car in the empty space.

Ross walked over and closed the garage behind us. "No luck?" Ross said as he looked at our glum faces.

We shook our heads sadly.

"Don't rush off," Ross instructed us as we began to file out the car, "I want to talk to you."

We waited obediently and followed Ross into the house where he gestured at us all to sit down around the table.

"I've been calling around while you've been away," he said carefully, looking at each of us. "And I've managed to pull a few strings here and there. You all have a visa if you want to stay here," Ross said.

"You can do that?" Jennifer asked.

"I know people in the immigration department. So, what do you say? I know you must be disappointed, but you've done all you can now," Ross said, eyeing Jess in particular.

"We haven't," I said bluntly. Dylan quickly put a hand on my arm, afraid I might explode into another fit of rage. "Ross, we can't give up until it's over."

Jennifer glared at me. "Well, I feel we've done enough."

"I don't," I argued.

"Maybe Jen's right, Lizzie," Grace said. "We've tried all we can here... what more can we do? Go to England and try to prevent it from hurting people over there? That would be impossible," she said, looking at me with her soft eyes. "I know you never give up, but sometimes we have to pick our battles and admit this is too big for us."

"What you said makes sense, Grace," I said, some hope returning.

"Well... good... then we're taking Ross' offer?" Jennifer said, glancing from me to Ross.

"Not about that. About going to England. We should go explain the situation to them, and have the main centers evacuated," I said.

"Evacuate? Lizzie, you're crazy," Levi said. "They'd never believe us, and even if they did, how would they evacuate millions of people in such a short space of time?"

"This could be our last shot. If we don't do something now,

it's on us. We're the only ones who can help." I knew I had touched a nerve when I said that. Levi had been the one determined to keep fighting back in Washington. Their eyes clouded with guilt; they knew thousands could die. And we were running out of time.

"God knows how we're going to get you out of the country and into London, but if this is what you want..." Ross said at last.

"You're actually letting us go?" Jess said surprised.

I felt a rush of gratitude to Ross for supporting what I knew was the right thing to do.

"I'm not letting you go by yourself," Ross muttered, looking sharply at his niece. "That would be irresponsible. Going on a road trip is one thing, but leaving the country on fake identification is a completely different thing altogether," he said resignedly.

Everyone began getting up and moving off in different directions. I stayed where I was. My hand gripped the heavy cable suspending the dining room table. It was going to happen. And we were, stupidly but determinedly, putting ourselves in the line of fire to try to minimize the damage to others. I felt like I wanted to be sick. It was all because of me, because I couldn't give in.

"Lizzie," Dylan said. I glanced up to see him standing at the doorway. "Come on, we should rest up. It's been a long couple of days."

I nodded and rose from the table without saying anything, feeling nausea swirl in my stomach.

"You were right, you know," Dylan said, as if reading my mind.

"I hope so." Some people might have thought what we were doing was brave. But when it comes down to it, brave and stupid are pretty much the same thing.

CHAPTER TWENTY-NINE

LEVI

I WAS DREAMING. THE sound of the sea crashed pleasantly in my ears, waves rolling and breaking on the shore. Dylan and I lounged lazily about the bach my mom took us to in our holidays. It was a typical kiwi holiday home with hodgepodge rooms filled with dated sixties décor and modern appliances. It overlooked a rolling surf beach that was basically our own. There were some kites and other sports equipment propped up in the corner of the room, and stacks of board games under the TV that barely ever got used. I turned to Dylan.

"Hey Levi," he said.

"Yeah?" I mumbled back automatically.

"Levi," Dylan said again, and I opened my eyes to Dylan in real life, grinning in the seat beside me. I had fallen asleep on the plane, the roaring sound of the engines bringing back nostalgic childhood memories of the beach. Dylan nodded toward the air hostesses who were coming around with a food trolley.

"Great," I said, sitting up, "I'm absolutely starving."

"You're always starving," Grace said.

"Beef or chicken?" asked the air hostess.

"Beef, please," I replied.

"And I'll have the chicken," Grace answered.

"Me too," Dylan said.

"So, Dylan," I said as I dug into my meal.

"Mmmm," he responded through a mouthful of mashed potato.

"Do you remember the bach we used to go to?"

Dylan laughed. "Yeah. Good times."

"I miss it," I said, thinking back to my dream.

"You and me both," Dylan agreed.

"Where was it?" Grace asked as she cut up her chicken into little morsels.

"A couple of hours south of Napier. On the coast, in the middle of nowhere. No cell reception, and no internet," I said with a grin.

"Sounds idyllic."

"You'll have to come next time… after the war, I mean," I offered without thinking. Dylan raised his eyebrows. Grace looked at me a bit perplexed.

"I mean, everyone can come next time," I said.

"I'd love to come," Grace said with a smile. "What do you guys do there?"

"You mean apart from drink?" Dylan said with a cheeky smile plastered on his face. I chuckled. Grace looked at us, uncertainly.

"Chill on the beach and surf on the nice days, and play cards on the rainy ones," I said.

"Sounds like my ideal holiday," Grace said.

"You can surf?" Dylan asked with a hint of surprise.

"Yeah," Grace said. "I'm not very good, though," she added quickly.

"Honestly, you're full of surprises," I said.

Grace smiled, clearly a little embarrassed. "I hope we survive this war. I really want to see this bach. It would be fun hanging out with you… under better circumstances."

"Me too," I said.

"It's good to finally talk about the future," Grace said. "All we've been doing is living one day to the next."

"Yeah, it's weird to think about us in the normal world."

"Would we all have been friends if we hadn't met during the war?" Grace asked.

"I'd like to think so. You were practically stalking me anyway," I said, thinking back to working at the fast-food joint. It felt like a lifetime ago. In reality, only a few months had gone by. Grace blushed. I felt my heart skip a little in my chest. She often had that effect on me.

"I think we would," Dylan said. "Even though we drive each other mad, I think we make a good team."

"We do make a good team," Grace said as she looked up and met my eyes. If Dylan wasn't here, I thought, I would kiss her right now.

"I'm going to try and get some sleep," Grace said, tearing her eyes away from mine. "Wake me when we are going to land." She pulled her headphones over her ears and shut her eyes.

"The connection between you two is intense," Dylan whispered in my ear.

"I know," I replied, feeling a little embarrassed.

"At least she's hot," he said back.

I elbowed him in gentle warning.

"What I mean is, you should go for it. It's obvious she's into you."

"I'm not taking any advice from you," I said. "You haven't made a move on Lizzie. Have you?"

"No," Dylan replied sheepishly. With that, we fell into a comfortable silence. I turned a movie on but wasn't really paying it any attention. My mind was racing. I hadn't thought about life after the war, and now I was realizing I wanted Grace to be there. That was why I had invited her to the bach. I could see a future with her, and it scared me.

THE PLANE LANDED SMOOTHLY on the runway at London Heathrow Airport. Ross led the way as we stepped off the plane and into the tunnel that joined to the terminal. We all traipsed toward International arrivals. We lined up to go through customs. Ross and I were the first to make it through.

"Why are you letting us do this?" I asked as we waited for the others to pass the checkpoint. Ross nervously watched Jess as the immigration officer inspected her fake passport.

"Jess' mom and I... we've had a rocky relationship, but she's my sister. Over the years, I've come to regret the things I've done in my past. I drove her away, and one of the consequences was I rarely got to see her or Jess. I haven't always been the best brother... or the best uncle. To be perfectly honest, I wasn't a good person," Ross said. "I've been trying to change that recently." His voice was laden with guilt. I wanted to ask him more, but then Jess joined us. We waited in silence for several more minutes until everyone was back together, and then we continued toward bag drop.

"So, do we have a plan?" Lizzie said immediately to Ross.

"Yes, Lizzie, we're going to visit Big Ben and then do some shopping," I said. "I thought you were meant to be the one with the plan. After all, you're the one who had the insane idea of coming here."

"Actually, Levi, you're not far off when you say Big Ben," Ross said, the corners of his mouth twitching upward. "We have three options as far as I see it. We can go to the Houses of Parliament and see if we can contact anyone that way. We could head to the police station, or there's Whitehall, and the Ministry of Defense. The Houses of Parliament would be easiest since they allow visitor access and even have tours. The police probably won't help us, and you never know who to trust with them. The Ministry of Defense would be the best option, but I don't think they'd let us walk in off the street," Ross said, outlining our choices for us.

"Could we get into the Ministry of Defense?" Lizzie asked, sounding doubtful. Ross shrugged, and then let out a sudden bellow of laughter. Grace jumped in surprise.

"What?" Jess asked him.

"Sorry," Ross apologized, looking at our serious faces before bursting into laughter again.

"What?" Jess repeated, annoyance creeping into her voice.

"Jessy…" he said, shaking his head. "It's surprising you kids would even consider the difficulties involved in getting into the Ministry of Defense after getting into the Pentagon."

"If we can't get in, maybe we should give up," Jennifer said bluntly. She was still against doing anything that would compromise our freedom.

"There's that old saying for you… where there's a will there's a way. We just have to find it."

OUR CHOSEN WAY, IN the end, was nothing too glamorous—Ross insisted on a less intrusive approach. And frankly, when we got to Whitehall, I was relieved about that. The taxis from the airport dropped us at the main building. It was stately. Imposing. It's massive size alone made me give up any idea of breaking through their security to find the Minister of Defense himself. Even if we had been able to break in without getting caught, we wouldn't have made it any farther. With several dozen floors to a building that spanned nearly a whole street block, it would have taken hours to find anything. We stepped out of the taxis, and Ross asked the drivers to wait.

"Levi, Dylan, you're coming with me," Ross said, adjusting his tie.

"What? We're not coming?" Lizzie said, immediately glaring at Ross. "We need to do this all together. You're going to need all the support you can get," Lizzie said, her cheeks coloring with anger.

"No, you're not coming. I need people who can think clearly and remain calm, Lizzie. And right now, that's not you. You would do anything to stop this, I know. But this situation requires a great deal of sensitivity," Ross said carefully.

"So, you bring Levi," she said with a cruel laugh. I ignored her baiting, knowing if I said anything it would only prove her point. Dylan pulled her aside, and I saw him whisper something to her before squeezing her hand.

"Why Levi and Dylan?" Grace asked.

"Because they look the oldest," he said apologetically. "And, as much as I wish things were different, the world still takes men more seriously than women."

"So, this is a guy thing now?" Jennifer asked.

"Look," Ross said ruthlessly, "every second we stand here debating this is a second wasted. We need to go. Here"—he flicked a platinum card to Jess—"take our bags and find us a hotel out of central London. Make it a nice one," he added.

Jess hadn't said anything about not being able to come. She looked at Ross, livid. "Fine. But I don't even know why we're here. Jen and I didn't want to come, but you dragged us here, and now we have to wait like obedient children in the hotel room," she said. "They better believe you." She opened the passenger door of the taxi and slammed it. Lizzie, Grace, and Jennifer reluctantly joined her in the taxi.

"Let's go," Ross said, abruptly turning on his heel as their cab disappeared around the corner.

"That was because you didn't want them to get hurt, right?" I asked Ross.

"If… if anything happens, at least Jessy will be out the way. And the girls will be able to live safely in London for a bit on that card," Ross admitted.

"They're a lot stronger than you give them credit for," Dylan said with a grin.

"I know. I trust Grace and Lizzie to manage any situation and to keep Jessy and Jennifer safe. God, those two kids... they're only what... sixteen? They deserve a normal life," he said, shaking his head.

We stopped talking as we got closer to the entrance, and Ross' face changed from concern for his niece to diplomacy. His persona was smooth and confident. I took a deep breath and forced myself to assume a similar expression.

"Ross Logan, NOFY Oil," Ross said, extending his hand to the security guard at the main entrance. The guard hesitated warily before shaking his hand.

"What's your business here today, Mr. Logan," he said, eyeing us.

"We need to speak to the Minister for International Security and Strategy," Ross said.

"Wait a minute," the security guard said. He stepped out of hearing range. His eyes were still fixed on us, watching our movements as he consulted someone through his headpiece.

"Your meeting isn't on our approved schedule," the security guard relayed to us.

"We know. With respect, sir, this is a matter of utmost urgency. We've only just got off the plane from the United States, and it is imperative we speak with him, or someone connected to this country's defense," Ross said. The guard looked him up and down, obviously confused as to what a billionaire from a US oil company had to do with England's national security. He consulted through his headset. Then, he waved us through.

"Wait there for more security to arrive. You need to be checked before you go through," he said.

We stepped through the doorway. I let out a breath. We were soon dragged through into a room and asked to strip down. They searched our pockets thoroughly, and the lining of our suit jackets. Then we were cleared to continue. The guards led us to a reception area to take our names and details. Again, we were told to sit and wait for someone to see us.

I was getting nervous. My hands broke out in a cold sweat as I tried to maintain the confident face that had allowed us to get this far. We were the only ones waiting in the room. I glanced at Dylan, who shrugged back at me, not saying anything. He looked nervous too. Like me. The countdown to impending disaster weighed on me. Any minute the rocket could impact. Every second we waited was one second closer to the end. Would we be in the impact zone? What a way to go, I mused. Survive the war, but die here, free.

A man marched confidently toward us. He wasn't tall but had an aura of self-assurance that seemed to fill the room. His brown hair drifted above intelligent blue eyes.

"Welcome to the Ministry of Defense, gentlemen," he said, his voice layered with a strong English accent. "Please, follow me."

We followed him through into yet another room. This one had been set up for conferencing, complete with a board table and chairs. He gestured us to sit.

"I am Theodore Marshall, the Secretary to the Minister of State for the Armed Forces. The man himself is rather busy, as I'm sure you'll understand, so I'm here in his place. I've been told you had an urgent matter to discuss?" He looked expectantly at us.

I didn't know what to say, my mouth sucked suddenly dry. Why did we come? Because there was a slim chance they might believe us. Sitting across the board table, I thought we were totally naïve. Why should they listen to us without any credentials to back our story? We should have been searching for tangible proof to use against Prime Minister Marion. Instead, we were here, trying to do the impossible.

"You must understand Mr. Marshall," Ross said, clearing his throat, "that what I'm about to tell you may not make much sense to you at all, but you will listen. Because if you don't, thousands of people may die." Ross stared Theodore down.

"Is that a threat?" Theodore said, his gaze narrowing.

"Because I assure you, sir, if you are in any way involved with terrorism—"

"This isn't a threat. We're turning in some information," Dylan said, cutting Theodore off mid-sentence. "We want to warn you."

Theodore stared at him, his mask of confidence dropping with surprise.

"Levi and I, and a few more of us, came from New Zealand—recently," Dylan explained.

"That's impossible, New Zealand has been in the midst of a civil war for some time now. How did you escape?" Theodore asked.

"We were trying to survive. The soldiers were hunting us down. And the plane was the only place to hide. Once we were aboard it was easy enough to hide unseen until we reached our destination," Dylan continued.

"You landed here, in England?" Theodore asked.

"No, in Florida, which is where we met up with Ross. I'm not sure whether you've heard of a rocket launching...'*The Architect*'?"

"Yes, that launching has been in the headlines for weeks," Theodore said uneasily, "but what does that have to do with England?"

"We believe New Zealand's Prime Minister funded the rocket. And he is personally attending the launch on American soil. A bit strange, don't you think? Considering New Zealand is currently at war?"

"That is interesting, to say the least." Theodore agreed. "But you still haven't explained how England is involved."

"The plane we snuck aboard was his plane. We overheard a ton of conversations. The rocket has been hijacked by New Zealand to be used as a weapon," I said.

"A weapon against England?" Theodore said disbelievingly. "And you're sure about this?"

We nodded in unison.

"Since the war broke out, we lost all communications. It wasn't unexpected, considering the state of things," Theodore said. "But we know very little. Our government isn't willing to send our troops into a war we know nothing about in a country that's still a bio-risk. Aside from that, what am I supposed to do?"

"Warn people. They need to know," I said.

"England is a big place. How are we meant to know where exactly the rocket is to hit? Do you have co-ordinates?" he asked interrogatively.

"No," Dylan admitted uneasily.

Theodore took a deep breath. "We're going to have to get the police involved with this. It needs to be treated like any other terrorist threat. Which means it will probably hit a crowded area, almost definitely in London. Maybe Trafalgar Square… somewhere busy. Mr. Logan and I will carry this information further. You two"—he jerked his head toward me and Dylan—"need to get to somewhere safe. Under usual circumstances, I would have to send you back to New Zealand. The risk of infection… since the pandemic, you understand," Theodore said uncomfortably. "But if what you say is true about the rocket, that's a risk I'm going to take."

"The virus was basically stamped out before the war started," Levi said.

"We haven't been sick," I added.

Theodore's face was serious. "That's what I'm counting on. But you have to see it from our perspective. We've been trying to get intelligence from New Zealand for months. For all we know, a fresh outbreak could have occurred during that time. All I'm asking, is that you keep a low profile while you're here. You and your friends."

"They should be at a hotel, somewhere safe," Ross said.

"Go there, and for now, stay put. Ask for my limo driver,

Albert, at the front desk. He'll take you. We'll be in touch as soon as we can," Theodore said, getting up. I stood too, feeling the fear roll off my shoulders in waves of relief. We had done it. We had convinced at least one person. And they had the power to do something about it.

"Levi," Ross said, grabbing my shoulder before Dylan and I could leave, "ring them on the cell I gave you. And when you get there, tell Jessy I love her, in case anything happens. I'll make sure we do everything we can." Then he turned and walked away.

CHAPTER THIRTY

GRACE

"AND IN FLORIDA TODAY, the much anticipated NOFY oil deal has finally been approved. This means the government will inject another two billion dollars into probing for new oil by NOFY in potential oil sites all over the globe. This highly controversial deal has opponents outraged over the destruction of habitats, the increasing risk of oil spills, and the diversion of key funds away from pioneering research. The government acknowledges these risks and assures us precautionary measures will be taken. However, the dwindling oil supply is already costing thousands of jobs worldwide due to the closure of hundreds of factories that still depend largely on fossil fuels. This is Malinda Hodges reporting for Global News."

This was the sixth time this story had run, but I was avidly watching and praying that no breaking news headline would pop up.

"There must be something else we can do," Lizzie muttered in frustration.

The waiting was excruciating. Ross and Theodore were doing all they could to evacuate, and to figure out where the rocket was going to crash. But that wasn't enough to stop the fear that we might still fail.

"We've done everything we can," Jess insisted. Now, the weather was back.

"London's weather is looking fairly grim over the next few days. A deep low-pressure system is moving across England this evening, and a cold front will bring rain with possible thunderstorms tomorrow. And, there appears to be no break from the rain over the rest of the week," the weather girl said.

"There's always something else that can be done," Lizzie said, shaking her head in denial.

"Like what?" Dylan asked. "I'm all for doing more, but what else is there?"

Lizzie shrugged and flopped hopelessly on the bed.

"Theodore and Ross will succeed... I can feel it," Jennifer muttered from the chair in the corner of the hotel room. I glanced out the window of our fifteenth story hotel room and peered out into the gloomy but bustling streets of London. I sighed loudly and rested my head on a pillow.

"Everything's going to work out fine," Levi said confidently as he appeared through the hotel door carrying food.

"You look cheery," Lizzie said sarcastically.

Levi glared at her and began handing out lunch. "Nothing has happened yet, so we have nothing to moan about," he explained as he opened the wrapping of his hamburger. "Come on, we're in London, at least watch a movie," Levi said with a huge grin on his face. I couldn't help but smile. Levi marched over to the

TV and changed the channel.

"Oh, it's a chick flick," Dylan pointed out immediately.

"I want to watch it," Jess said instantly.

"I don't," Levi said as he threatened to change the channel.

"There are more girls, so I automatically win," Jess said triumphantly. Levi looked at her sourly but silently accepted defeat. As Jess and Jennifer became enthralled in the movie, I found my mind wandering. What if we failed? How many people would die? What would happen to us? Although I tried to be fearless, I was terrified about being sent back to New Zealand. But I knew that was our fate, I could feel it in my gut.

"Are you going to eat?" Levi whispered in my ear.

I looked down at my untouched meal and shook my head.

"I went out and got that for you, the least you can do is eat it."

"I'm not hungry," I whispered back.

Levi studied me carefully. "None of us are, but you need to eat something," he insisted. I glared at him and moodily took a bite of my burger.

"Happy now?" I asked, flicking him a scowl.

"Very," Levi said as he stole one of my French fries and popped it in his mouth with a wink. I chuckled and turned my attention to the movie. Jess and Lizzie were in a fit of giggles on the bed.

"What's happening?" I asked Levi quietly.

"Sarah was locked out of her car because the popular girls hate her and stole her keys. But Dean, the mysterious yet handsome guy who no one knows anything about, gives her a ride home. Sarah falls hopelessly in love with him but feels he doesn't notice her. Unknown to her, he feels the same way and is the culprit behind the anonymous love notes she has been receiving," Levi said, with his attention turned back to the TV.

I stared at him.

"What?" he asked. "It's a good movie, I've seen it before," he answered with a shrug.

Dylan laughed loudly. "It's a shit movie, but Levi's always had a soft side."

Levi ignored him.

Suddenly the power flickered and went out. My breath caught in my throat, bringing back memories of when the war started.

"What's happening?" Lizzie asked, glancing around. A few moments later, the backup generators kicked in, and power was restored. I grabbed the remote and flicked the channel to the news. The woman was talking about the Tottenham Hot Spurs again.

"I don't think anything happened," Jennifer said as we watched the news intently.

"Paranoia, right?" I asked nervously. The woman moved onto the next story about the tennis.

"Oh no!" Lizzie shrieked as the breaking news banner flew along the bottom of the screen.

"Maybe there is some other breaking news," Jess said. We all knew what had happened. The replay flicked to a live screen showing a somber-looking Malinda Hodges.

"We have breaking news," she said. *"Reports are coming through regarding a terrorist attack on parliament."*

I stared at the TV, horrified.

"Well fuck," Dylan said in disbelief. "We failed."

The parliament buildings were reduced to rubble. I watched the TV in a daze as it showed a rolling reel of burning buildings, billowing with smoke. Civilians screamed, covered in blood, dirt, and ash. Hundreds of ambulances and fire trucks made a symphony of sirens while police and firefighters dragged the dead and injured from the destruction. Tears streamed down my cheeks.

"Firefighters are at the scene trying to put out the blazes, and rescue workers are already sifting through the rubble, searching for survivors."

Lizzie had tears welling up.

Levi put his arm around my shoulders. The TV flicked back to the live video feed of the horror not too far from where we were sitting.

"Early reports and eyewitness accounts suggest the weapon in question was a rocket. It is believed the attack originated from the US, but US intelligence and counterterrorism claim their rocket was tampered with during construction, and modified into a weapon. This theory has already been discredited by a number of sources, who explain the heightened tensions between the two countries may be to blame."

"We told them," Levi said. "We warned them," he muttered angrily. I could feel the tears wetting my cheeks. They were tears of pain, tears of frustration, and tears of hopelessness. International relationships had been broken, alliances discredited, and trust lost. Whatever was holding the governments of the world together was quickly unraveling. We were on the brink of another world war. I could feel it in the air now, the same feeling we all had in New Zealand during the riots all those months ago. But this time, I knew it for what it was: a last breath of freedom.

We watched the TV for hours, not knowing what to do. It was pointless to go over to the scene now. They had already explained there was no access permitted. We were transfixed and too depressed to move or speak. I had my head against Levi's shoulder while his arm was wrapped tightly around me, watching the horror unfold minute by minute. Jess sat beside me with her knees pulled up to her chest.

*"The bodies of two men have been identified so far, but
the death toll is expected to soar into the hundreds."*

Two pictures came up on the screen. There was a shriek from
Jess before any of us realized who we were looking at.

"It's Ross," Jennifer said quietly. I felt the tears flow.

"No!" Jess yelled at the TV. "No, no, no!" she wept. "He was
all I had left! We should've stayed in America!"

Lizzie hugged her while Levi's mouth hung open in shock.

"That's Theodore, too," Levi said sadly as he noticed the other
victim on the screen. It was unfair. All they did was try and help.
The worst part was they were the only ones who knew the truth.
Now it would never get out. Then the phone rang. Dylan glared
at it, daring it to ring again. It did, and he reluctantly picked it
up.

"Hello," he said disheartened. He nodded before hanging up
the phone without saying goodbye. "Albert's here," Dylan said
simply.

"Who's Albert?" Lizzie asked.

"Theodore's driver," Levi said.

"Why?" Jess said through her sobs.

"I guess we'll have to find out," Levi answered. We all stood
up gloomily and moved down to the lobby. There was nothing to
say. It was the failure that hurt the most, and now, everything
seemed futile. With Ross and Theodore dead, there was no hope
for us either. We were going back home. I knew it, we all knew it.
We entered the lobby and found Albert waiting anxiously for us.

"Hurry!" he said and motioned us to follow him. We trailed
after him and got grudgingly into the limo. "Theodore told me
everything. He ordered me to come get you if the rocket hit...
why the glum faces?" Albert asked, looking into the rearview
mirror.

"You know why," Dylan muttered as Lizzie stopped him trying to open a bottle of whiskey he found in the fridge. Albert started the limo.

"You did everything you could," Albert said.

"But it wasn't enough," Lizzie said sadly. "And now Theodore and Ross are dead," she continued.

"Theodore's dead?" Albert said as tears filled his eyes.

Jennifer nodded shakily.

"His picture was on the news," Levi said in explanation.

Albert shook his head. "He was a good man. And a good friend," Albert said with his face fallen. I looked out the window at the distraught people running through the streets. In the distance, I could see the smoke and haze of disaster.

"Where are we going?" Jess asked quietly.

"To get the truth out there," Albert said with determination. "Theodore wanted me to keep you safe, but I have a feeling that's the last thing you want to do right now."

"Too right, Albert," Levi said and attempted a smile. Albert floored the accelerator, and we sped closer to the devastation that we hadn't been able to stop. The acrid smell of smoke hung like a dampening smog, clinging to the wet air. It encircled us all in a ring of sorrow. Not too far away, people were dying, reminding us of our failure. Up ahead, there was a roadblock. Crowds of people stood around as the police held them back. They gaped at the scene in front of them, and already reporters from different countries were setting up around the perimeter.

"No one is allowed past here, sir," a policeman said sternly to Albert. I looked ahead, and through the dust and smoke, I could just make out the tattered shell of what had been the home of British politics for over a century. I imagined it as its former self, sitting grandly beside the river Thames. The gothic-style clock tower watched over the presiding of parliament. Smaller towers stood like soldiers over worn limestone walls. It was an impressive place, but now a monster had crumbled it down to its foundations.

"I have a pass," Albert explained as he held up a card that he used to get Theodore restricted access. The policeman sighed and studied the pass. Finding nothing wrong with it, he grudgingly waved us through. Albert crawled the car toward the damage. Levi put the window down, not caring about the dust and debris swirling in the air. The dust was bad, but the screams were worse. The forms of injured people screaming, trying to get out of the destruction were shadows in the smoke. A rescue worker dragged a woman from the rubble, heaving her over his shoulder and running to the nearest ambulance. Her face was burned, while her exposed arms were caked with blood. Her screams echoed around the site.

"Oh God," Lizzie said. "What have we done?"

"We haven't done anything," Dylan commented. "It's what we failed to do."

"There," Levi pointed ahead at the mobile police headquarters.

"I see it," Albert said, and he accelerated toward it, braking near the front of the door. Levi flung the limo open and jumped out. Dylan wasn't far behind. "Good luck," Albert called after us. And luck was what we needed.

All around me, people caked in dust and covered with burns and cuts walked dizzily around, not sure what to do. Hectic paramedics worked intensely trying to revive a man bloodied and crushed.

"Charging... clear!" a paramedic yelled, wiping sweat from his brow. The electric paddles were charged, and the power released into his chest. He was jerked upward before falling limply back down on the stretcher. The paramedics looked anxiously up at the screen showing the heart rate.

"He's still in defib," a doctor said.

"Try again," the head doctor ordered.

"Clear!" Once again, the paddles were charged and put firmly to the patient's chest. Again, they attempted to revive him. The rapid spikes on the screen narrowed into a flat line.

"It's no use, he's dead," the head doctor announced. They limply held the paddles at their sides, but there was no time for them to dwell on the lost life. Another man was quickly on their stretcher requiring assistance. Levi grabbed my hand and pulled me away. Dylan charged up the steps to the police unit and rapped furiously on the door. It opened quickly, and a huge security guard took up the entire doorway, barring our entrance.

"Show me your ID," he said gruffly.

"We have no ID," Levi said honestly. We may as well be truthful with these men.

"Then you cannot enter," the guard said with a shrug. "This area is restricted."

"We aren't going anywhere. We have information," Dylan explained calmly.

The guard pulled out his gun and drew it level with Dylan's face.

"I asked you to leave," he said politely as his eye twitched, fixed on Dylan.

"We have information," I said loudly so the men inside could hear. "You have to listen."

Gratifyingly, there was movement behind the security guard. "What is going on out here," an agent asked as he pushed past his guard to look at us.

"They say they have information," the guard explained, with his gun still pointing at Dylan, who hadn't lost any of his composure. The agent had cropped honey-blond hair that was messy about his face. A scar zigzagged down his otherwise clean-shaven cheek. The agent surveyed us carefully through his royal blue eyes. He drew up to his full height that brought himself level with Dylan and placed his hand on the guard's gun, forcing him to lower it.

"Why are you here?" he asked directly.

"We have information about the rocket," Dylan answered as he looked confidently at the agent. They stayed like that for a moment. After deciding we weren't terrorists, the agent swung the door open. We followed him into a cramped room where an older man was sitting at the round desk, holding a large mug of steaming coffee and sifting through a large stack of papers.

"Miller, have you called intelligence again? We need the information on the rocket launch to come through," he said gruffly. The man's dark brown hair was graying and fell loosely about his round face. He lifted his ivy green eyes. "What's this, Miller?" he asked the agent with us.

"They say they have information, Hayes," Miller explained calmly.

Hayes sighed as the worry lines etched deeper into his brow. "They lie," Hayes muttered with a wave of dismissal.

Dylan's face became livid. He was furious now. "I'm sick of people saying we're liars!" Dylan pushed past Miller, placing his hands firmly on the table. "If people had listened to us in the first place, none of this would have happened, but big-headed people like you are too caught up in their own egos to take us seriously. Now hundreds are dead," Dylan lectured as he looked challengingly at Hayes.

Hayes studied us carefully. "Sit," he said softly.

We sat. I knew they had no information, and they had to follow every lead.

"Start from the beginning. I want nothing left out."

Dylan took a deep breath and began, "Before being here, we were in New Zealand."

A look of surprise spread over Miller and Hayes' faces.

"That's impossible," Hayes dismissed quickly with a wave of his hand. "No one has had any word from them for months. They're at war and refuse to disclose what's happening," Hayes said as he plunked his coffee cup down with a loud thud.

"We managed to escape," Dylan continued, ignoring Hayes

and instead making eye contact with Miller.

"Tell me how," Hayes said, almost laughing at us.

Dylan glared at him. "We snuck onto the Prime Minister's plane. We were being chased by soldiers who were shooting at us, and that was the only place to hide."

"You can't prove it," Miller said plainly.

Dylan looked defeated. We sat there, awkwardly, in silence for a moment. I shifted uncomfortably in my seat and winced as another wave of pain rippled through my leg.

"Yes, we can," I said suddenly as Dylan looked at me confused. I stood up and began to roll up my pant leg. Hayes looked at the bandage curiously. I winced as I began undoing the wrappings. The injury had been worse than we had originally thought, but I had refused to let Ross take me to a hospital. They would know it was a gunshot wound, there would have been an inquiry, and we would have been sent home. I let the bandages fall to the floor.

"It can't be," Hayes muttered as he got up from his chair and crouched to examine my leg. "That's a gunshot wound," Hayes said. "Large caliber, too, by the looks of it."

Miller stood up and came to look for himself.

Hayes looked up at me sympathetically. "What happened?" he asked me.

"We were running from the soldiers, and I was shot as we were trying to get away. This is your proof. I knew getting shot might have some benefit," I said with a laugh, trying to make light of the situation. The stone faces looking back at me told me my attempt at humor wasn't welcome. Hayes seemed more convinced of our story, but we had told him nothing of value yet. Hayes got up and jotted something on a pad of paper.

"Even if you did escape New Zealand as stowaways on the Prime Minister's plane, how does that have anything to do with the terrorist attack?" Hayes asked. "All you've told me so far is a very amusing story."

The phone rang. Hayes stared at it for a moment but then decided to ignore it. He had his only potential lead sitting in front of him.

"You told us to start from the beginning," Levi said, sounding annoyed.

"I did," Hayes replied. The phone started ringing again. "I think you should get that," Hayes said to Miller. "They obviously want to talk to us." He returned his gaze back to us.

"We heard the Prime Minister talking about the rocket launching," Dylan explained. "But more importantly, he was talking about coordinates for a target in England."

"So, you definitely heard the words 'England target'?" Hayes said, getting clarification and jotting down a few more notes in his notebook. Dylan nodded. Miller returned.

"So that's a negative on any information from SIS, they are still running with the US story, in other words, the rocket decided to crash itself or changed its own coordinates," Miller said with a wave of his hand. "Those agencies are never any use. They demand you answer them even when they don't have any information for you. They think they're so important with their fancy badges and codes," Miller continued to vent.

"Now is not the time for whingeing," Hayes said irritably to Miller.

"When is?" Miller asked. "Tell me, what is so special about the SIS?"

"Their headquarters," Hayes answered with a noticeable trace of frustration creeping into his voice.

"What is SIS?" Jennifer asked dumbly.

"MI6," Miller answered. "One and the same."

"Then who are you?" Levi asked, confused now.

"MI5," Hayes answered quickly. "So, you believe that your Prime Minister hijacked the rocket launching, changed the coordinates, had a bomb loaded on the rocket, and then caused the rocket to crash into our parliament for no particular reason,"

Hayes said summing up Dylan's story.

"When you say it like that, it sounds ridiculous," Dylan muttered.

"If it weren't for the fact that all of you are spouting the same story, I'd get you to undergo psych assessments," Hayes said.

"But?"

Hayes sighed. "But, I don't know what to think," he finally admitted. "The current theory is almost as wild as yours but involves an attack by the US, which makes less sense. It would be political suicide for the States to consider even mentioning an attack of that sort."

"I can't say I believe you, but your story is compelling," Miller said, sounding interested.

"That's it?" Levi asked, shaking his head. "You can't believe us, but you will consider it? In case you haven't noticed, people are dying out there."

"I need your names for witness statements," Hayes explained. We gave him our names in turn, and he began entering them in his system. "You're New Zealand residents. Can I see your passports please," Hayes asked politely.

"We don't have them," Lizzie said sadly as she looked over at me.

"You don't have them?" Hayes asked again. "You mean you are here illegally?"

"Yes," Lizzie muttered.

Hayes rolled his eyes. "Perfect. Refugees. And when did you cross the border," he asked, his hands poised at the keyboard.

"Into England? Earlier today," Dylan said.

Hayes snapped his head up. "Today?"

"Yes... like we said, we escaped—" Dylan began again.

"Fuck," Hayes said, sudden alarm lighting his features. He pushed his chair back from us. "You should have told me this earlier. I assumed you'd been here for a few weeks, at least. New Zealand still hasn't been cleared from quarantine. You could be infected. Christ, this whole office needs to be decontaminated."

We just stared at him.

"You have to go back," Hayes said.

"You wouldn't send us back," I said outraged as I redid my bandages.

"The risk is too great," Hayes said, shaking his head. "All this shit to deal with and now I'm going to have to quarantine myself for god-knows how long."

"We're fine, we're healthy," Jennifer insisted, with tears in her eyes. "Please, don't send us back."

"We gave you information," I said, feeling fear rise in my chest. I had to sit down.

"That doesn't matter now," Hayes said blankly.

"You're sending us back to face our deaths," Levi said as he stood up, forcefully knocking his chair over in the process.

"Hayes," Miller said, trying to calm things down. "Must we send them back?"

"Organize a plane for them with the military," Hayes directed Miller. Miller stared at him and then turned to us. Lizzie had quiet tears streaming down her cheeks. Dylan was restraining Levi from attacking the MI5 agent. I looked away from everyone and stared intently at the ground. I knew there was no hope. There was none to begin with.

"But Hayes," Miller interjected. "I'm sure we can come to some agreement. They are basically refugees!"

"Refugees that could cripple our country with disease. Let's hope the damage isn't already done. We are sending them home, and I want no record of them being here."

"There must be something we can do," Miller said.

"If you value your job, you will do as I say," Hayes said as he made a phone call.

Miller sighed and motioned for us to follow him. He led us out the backdoor and into two waiting police cars. Miller walked with an air of authority as he kept a close eye on us. I thought about running, but common sense told me better. Running was a death sentence. Miller jerked one of the doors open and directed us into it. I followed Levi into the police car. Levi's face was screwed up into a hideous scowl. Jennifer sat down on the other side of me, with anger rippling across her face. She sat in determined silence. Miller got into the passenger seat after making sure Lizzie, Jess, and Dylan were securely in the other car.

"Why are you doing this?" I pleaded with him. He sighed and turned around.

"Because I have to," Miller said as he ran his fingers through his hair like Levi and Dylan did when they were stressed.

"You don't have to do anything," I explained with tears coming to my eyes. "I don't want to go back. We are going to be killed—"

"There's nothing I can do about it," Miller said as he directed the policeman driving the car where to go.

"Why not quarantine us? It's better than sending us back," I pleaded as I rubbed my tears away.

"If it was up to me, maybe I would help you. But it's more complicated than that."

"Why? Surely, it's more trouble to send us back."

Miller shook his head. "No. You don't get it. If it gets out that you were here… the public will panic. We're in the middle of a catastrophe already. We don't need the threat of the pandemic looming over us, too."

"Oh," I replied. I dropped my gaze. Miller was trapped. His conscience was telling him to help us, but he knew the consequences that could go with it.

"It's going to be OK," Levi whispered into my ear.

I glared at him. We both knew that was a lie.

CHAPTER THIRTY-ONE

DYLAN

"WE WON'T GO BACK," Lizzie said through gritted teeth. "You can't make us go back."

The police officer yanked her out the car and to her feet.

"Actually," he said, "I think you'll find we can."

Miller had dropped us at a small police station manned by a group of burly police officers who didn't offer us their names. They were dressed in black hazmat suits and were far less sympathetic than Miller. As soon as he left, they handcuffed us and drove us miles out of London to an army base where a plane was waiting for us. Lizzie, Jess, and I were forced to stand in a line. The second car arrived, and Levi was pulled from the vehicle. Another police officer roughly forced Grace out of the car.

"Don't touch her," Levi said with warning in his voice.

"Or what?" The police officer laughed. Levi launched himself at the policeman and tackled him to the ground. There was the sudden cocking of a gun, and instinctively everyone froze. Levi had managed to rip the mask off the man, and he was bleeding from his head. The man looked at Levi in horror, and Levi grinned with satisfaction like he couldn't care less. Two soldiers restrained Levi and pulled him to his feet.

"So, these are the kids then?" an English soldier asked behind his loaded gun. His military hazmat was a camouflage green. A band that circled the man's arm identified him as Major J. Murchison. With the facemask obscuring everything but his eyes, I couldn't tell what he was thinking.

"These are them. Is the plane ready?" one policeman asked.

"Captain Reid!" Murchison yelled. A soldier appeared at his side from the background where a plane was being prepared for takeoff.

"Major," he said, raising a hand in a brief salute.

"Is the plane prepared?" Murchison repeated the policeman's question to the young captain.

"Yes, sir. It's all ready for takeoff. All operations are checked and cleared for flight."

"Good. Get your Section over here Reid, these kids need to be escorted to the plane."

"Yes sir," Reid repeated again, waving his Section over. With guns pointed at us, we were marched onto the plane and forced to sit. The police officers got back into their cars, and we watched them drive away. The country we tried to save was turning its back on us and sending us to our graves.

"Captain Reid and his Section will be accompanying you on your flight back," Murchison said, not looking at us directly. I thought I saw a flicker of sympathy in his eyes, but I couldn't be sure.

He turned to Reid and clapped the man briefly on the shoulder. "Be careful. You know the orders. Do the drop and turn around immediately. There's no room for error."

Reid nodded, and Murchison left the plane. I watched Murchison through the window. He paused at the wall of one of the buildings and leaned against it heavily. He stripped his mask off and stared up at the sky, breathing deeply. The sun glistened off his face, and I realized he was crying. He knew he was sending us to our deaths, but he couldn't do a thing about it. Murchison followed orders like every good soldier.

The plane engines started, thundering in our ears, and we unwillingly strapped ourselves into the seats. Reid came around with the keys and let us out of our handcuffs now that we were leaving. The rest of his Section, made up of eight soldiers, found their own seats and positioned themselves, so they still had us covered in case we tried anything.

There wasn't exactly anything we could try, short of hijacking the plane and turning it around and then landing in a country where we were unwelcome. It didn't matter what we did. In every scenario, we were screwed.

An army medic went over to Grace. He cleaned her leg wound, numbed it, and stitched it closed in silence. "It's all I can do for you," he said sympathetically. "The stitches will dissolve on their own in a few weeks."

"If they make it that long," one of the soldiers remarked.

Lizzie was sitting silently next to me. Her face was unnaturally still, her gaze fixed on the fraying edge of the chair in front of her.

"Lizzie, are you OK?" I asked her quietly.

She closed her eyes and took in a breath, her shoulders shaking and breathed out again, slowly but calmly. "I'm not OK, Dylan. I never will be, so there's no point even asking that question," she said. She opened her eyes again, brimming with unshed tears.

"Lizzie, you know you don't need to bottle everything up all the time. You have me to lean on," I said, touching her shoulder.

"Don't you understand, Dylan? This is my way of coping. I bury things deep down to move on because at the moment... it's the only way to survive," she said, almost pleading with me to understand her.

"It's not the only way, and you know it," I said with frustration edging into my voice. I was trying to offer her support, and she shut me down, again. "Why don't you ever realize you're not alone?"

"Maybe I want to be alone," she retorted, cutting me even deeper.

"I won't let you." I was on the verge of tears myself. I forced the seat-divider up and wrapped my arms around Lizzie in an unsolicited crushing hug.

"Dylan, get off," she said, trying to pull away from me.

"No," I muttered stubbornly. She tried to squirm away again, but then, she burst into tears.

"We couldn't stop it, Dylan... now... so many people are dead," she sobbed. "We tried so hard and couldn't change a single thing. It was stupid. We should have stayed in America. Ross died because of us."

There was nothing I could say to make her feel any better, so I held her while she cried herself out. Eventually, she fell asleep against me, her face streaked with tears.

After a while of watching her sleep, I lifted a shaking finger and stroked the side of her cheek. Lizzie murmured and then stretched slightly, pressing her body against mine. She opened her eyes and looked at me sleepily. She had rolled over against me in her sleep, and I could feel the curves of her body beneath the layers of clothing between us. Awareness slowly lit her face, and I waited for the imminent blush and apology before she pulled away, but it didn't come. And I wasn't sure I wanted a knee-jerk apology. What I wanted was to forget these last few hours. Lizzie leaned in, her hair tickling my neck, her face inches from mine. I reached out and put a hand on her cheek before closing my eyes and kissing her tentatively. Her lips responded with a forceful passion.

The plane jerked with turbulence, and I was thrown awake, bolt upright in my chair where I had dozed off, feeling electrified. The dream had seemed so real.

"Bad dream?" Lizzie asked as she rubbed her eyes. "Jesus, you gave me such a fright."

"Not bad exactly," I said, feeling embarrassment flood my cheeks. I ignored her curious stare and instead glanced across the aisle to where Jennifer was seated. "What's happening?" I asked as the plane nose began to dip downward.

"We're landing," Jennifer muttered, "in Hong Kong for a refuel."

"Can't you let us off there," Grace pleaded to Captain Reid.

"You could turn the plane around and go back to England. No one would ever know what happened to us. They would think we were in New Zealand, and you wouldn't have to risk your lives by coming that far with us," Levi argued desperately.

"I have my orders. I can't do that. And they would know; every plane has a tracking system."

"Then turn it off," Jennifer begged.

"That would be stupid... I would lose more than my job. I'd go to prison," Reid replied. He turned away guiltily from our fallen faces.

"We should never have left America. It was idiotic," Jennifer said, frustration in her eyes. "Lizzie, I hate to say I told you so."

"Jennifer, that's enough," I said, but Lizzie was competent in dealing with the situation herself.

"At least I don't have any regrets. We did all we could, Jennifer. So, stop acting like a child and deal with the situation," she replied with a fiery flash of her eyes. "And if you suggest it was my fault Ross died again... let's just say you don't want me as an enemy."

"I never said that," Jennifer argued.

"If you say it was my fault we went to England, then you're saying the same thing," Lizzie replied shortly.

"OK, Lizzie, calm down," Jennifer said. Lizzie looked, if possible, even more furious but held her tongue as the plane sharply hit the ground and came in from landing.

The soldiers stood on Reid's command. Six of them covered each of us with a gun while the remaining crew disarmed the doors and went out to refuel. We stayed in our seats in silence.

"I need the bathroom," Levi announced to the soldier that was covering him.

"You can wait forty minutes until we're in the air again," the soldier replied, not budging, his gun still pointed at Levi.

"What, you want me to piss on the seat or something? Dude, I need to go," he said. The soldier mentioned something to one of his comrades.

"Get up. Don't make any sudden moves unless you want a bullet in your head," the soldier said resignedly. Levi got up from his seat, his hands raised, and they walked down the aisle to the toilet. I felt a sense of unease prick the back of my neck as I watched him slowly proceed down the aisle. There was no way Levi needed to go, and the soldier knew it. Levi was up to something. He stepped into the tiny cubicle and shut the door. For a little while, I was convinced I was wrong about Levi's intentions. The toilet flushed. Water ran. I relaxed, and then suddenly Levi flung the door open. The door hit the soldier in the face, and the gun fell to the floor with a clatter. In record time, Levi picked up the rifle and was aiming it at the soldier. The soldier dropped instinctively to the floor, lunging at Levi's feet. Levi let out an involuntary shout as he tripped and fell, the gun flung out of his reach. The soldier kicked it away from him. He dragged Levi up, wrenched his arms back behind his back, and grabbed the gun, pointing it at Levi.

"Try anything like that again, and I swear I won't hesitate," the soldier said, breathing heavily through his facemask. "Get back in your seat, now!" he yelled before pushing him forward with his rifle. Levi stumbled back to his seat without another word. He looked broken. The reality was setting in; we weren't escaping.

Thirty minutes later, the plane was ready to leave again. The engines started up with a roar. I wished for some technical difficulty to delay the plane, but nothing like that happened. The pilot ran through the final checks before sending the plane down the runway. Any hopes of escaping in Hong Kong were long gone as the plane's nose tilted up toward the sky.

Grace got up and looked over to where I was sitting. The soldiers tensed, though they didn't stop her as she made her way over to me.

"Could I swap with you, Dylan? I mean, I'm not interrupting anything am I?" she asked, looking at Lizzie and me. I blushed deeply, remembering the dream.

"Ah, no. No, you're fine. Um, yeah, I guess we could swap," I said. Grace looked suspiciously at me as I stood and exchanged places with her.

"What was all that about?" Grace asked Lizzie as I began to walk toward the empty seat next to Jess.

"I don't know… he's been acting weird ever since he woke up," Lizzie said.

"I don't understand how it's possible," Jess said to me out of the blue.

"How what's possible?" I asked, confused.

"Surviving," she said. "I don't know how to keep going now Uncle Ross is gone. Obviously, it must be possible because I survived when Leah died. It's like everyone I've ever known in my whole life makes up a little piece of me, you know? And every time I lose somebody that piece of me is torn away. How much can a person handle until they've been torn down to nothing?"

"You're tougher than that, Jess. Think of everything you've been through already. You have coped, and you will do it again," I said.

"Maybe. But how? How can I continue?"

"Take it one day at a time. Keep breathing, and after a while, you can start to live again. Somehow, you'll find a way to carry on with it," I answered.

Jess didn't say anything in response. I hoped that I had helped her in some way. The fear that she would try to kill herself again was still very real. Her small angular face was still. There were no tears this time.

Jess looked at me. "It's OK, Dylan. I can see what you're thinking. It's as plain as day. I won't try to commit suicide again. To be honest, I don't know if I would have ever done it. Besides, imagine what Uncle Ross would say to me when I saw him in heaven. He'd send me straight down to hell," she said and laughed bitterly. I relaxed a little at her morbid attempt at humor. But I wasn't completely convinced. I leaned my head against the headrest and closed my eyes, waiting for a wave of sleep to take me away.

"Dylan, wake up," Jess said from the edges of my sub-consciousness. I opened my eyes, hoping that somehow a miracle had happened and we couldn't land in New Zealand.

"We're not landing in New Zealand," Jess said. But my flame of hope was doused as quickly as it had come with her next sentence. "We're skydiving."

"We're what?" I said, still trying to push away the heaviness of sleep.

"Skydiving. Out the plane," Jess repeated. "It's too dangerous for them to land."

"But we don't know how," I said, terrified.

"Dylan, we are in a war zone. Do you really think they care?" she asked, jerking her head toward the soldiers. "But we're going two at a time if it makes you feel any better," she said, patting me sarcastically on the shoulder.

"Great. So, if one of us mucks up, two of us die. That makes it so much better," I said, stunned. A fine target we would make for the enemy soldiers.

"Get over here," Reid ordered us. We unwillingly obeyed and listened as he ran through the basics of skydiving. I tried to remember every little thing he mentioned in my head. We were thrown the gear. Lizzie picked up the harness and looked at it, confused. One of the soldiers helped us strap ourselves tightly together with the pack on my back and Lizzie in front of me. Grace was with Levi and seemed to be nervous but keen to get off the plane. Levi, on the other hand, appeared excited.

"I'm not doing it," Jennifer said in frank denial. "I won't."

"Jennifer, let me put the stupid thing on," Jess said in frustration. The soldier that had helped us went over and assisted Jennifer and Jess.

"I'm not going, I can't," Jennifer said, looking panicked.

"For saying that you're going first," Reid said. He had obviously dealt with people like Jennifer before.

"What?" she shrieked, "there's no way we're going first!"

"Are we ready?" Reid called to the pilot, ignoring Jennifer completely. The co-pilot gave him the thumbs up, and Reid disarmed the door. Jennifer was nearly green and tried to back away from the whizzing scenery below. Jess dug in her heels to no avail as Jennifer dragged them both away. The soldiers grabbed Jennifer by the arms and forcefully pulled her toward the open door.

"You ready?" one of them asked Jess. She nodded uneasily, and the soldiers forced them out the door. We heard a slight shriek before Jennifer's panicked scream was lost in the wind.

"Who's next?" Reid asked. We had to make a quick jump before the plane had flown miles away from Jess and Jennifer.

"We will," Levi volunteered. He and Grace approached the door. Grace was white with fear, and Levi gave her hand a comforting squeeze. Levi turned back to me, a scared smile on his face, before they stepped out into thin air. One minute they were there, and the next they were gone. But I had no time to worry about them. It was only Lizzie and me left now. Together, we walked toward the door. I could feel Lizzie shaking against me. "We'll be fine," I whispered in her ear. She nodded silently. "On the count of three," I said. "One, two, three."

We jumped. The air whizzed past so fast it made me dizzy. The constant rushing of wind in my ears and the surge of adrenaline as we hurtled toward the ground that was getting ever closer was disorientating.

"Dylan, pull the chute!" Lizzie yelled at me.

"Not yet," I shouted back.

"Now, Dylan!" Lizzie screamed. I could tell we weren't quite close enough. Just another second…

"Now!" Lizzie screamed again. I pulled it. It was abrupt. One minute we were falling, the next we were floating. The green pastures of New Zealand stretched out before us. It was beautiful, but it was different. I stared out into the wild.

I wasn't prepared for the landing. We hit the ground hard and rolled, the breath knocked out of me. I wrapped my arms around Lizzie, who was breathing fast. We lay there, staring up at the sky as the plane flew away. For now, we were alive.

ACKNOWLEDGMENTS

This book wouldn't have been possible without the help and support of a number of people. Firstly and fore-mostly, we'd both like to thank Ashley's sister, Dr. Melodie Lindsay, who kindly offered the services of her company, Doclins, to copy-edit and proof this book. She has been an incredible help, and Mel, we are hugely indebted to you for all your hard work.

We'd also like to thank our cover designer Lance Buckley, who did a spectacular job of designing an eye-catching front cover.

Personally, I'd like to firstly thank my husband, Dan, for always being supportive of my creative endeavors. Your help in everything technological has been a huge blessing to me, but also your constant and willing ear as I talk non-stop about the characters that roam around in my head.

Secondly, my family, friends and teachers who all inspire my writing. Superficially, this is a story about a war, but underneath, it's really a story of fighting for family and a home we deserve. I couldn't have asked for a more beautiful group of people to call my tribe. The home you gave me growing up, and the quality of our relationships shine through in my writing and my understanding of what makes family and home so important.

And last but not least, thank you, Ashley. What a journey we've been over through the years to bring this story to the world. We've done it! It was an awfully long time ago when we sat down on that fateful day and started writing together. Sixteen years later, we've created not only this book, but a business, and I'm beyond lucky to have you—not only as a writing and business partner, but as a lifelong friend.

~ Sarah

First, I would like to thank my husband, James. You have always encouraged my writing, and provided unwavering support. Thank you for reading these books (sometimes more than once) and believing in them, and us.

I must specifically thank Mrs Price, my high-school English teacher. You might not remember me, but I will always be grateful for the passion for writing, structure, and stories that you passed on to me.

To my family and friends. Thank you for your support. Writing comes from a life time of experience and inspiration. Without you, I would have neither of these.

Finally, I have to thank Sarah. Obviously, this book would not have been possible without you. It's so strange looking back at what this book used to be, and where we are now. We have accomplished so much together, and I know I would not be the writer, or person I am today without your friendship. This book started as a social studies project, and has turned into something magical.

~ Ashley

ABOUT THE AUTHOR

Sasha A. Linderson is the joint pen name for collaborative authors Ashley Lindsay and Sarah Anderson. Ashley and Sarah grew up together in the small city of Tauranga, New Zealand, and in high-school they began co-authoring the first draft of the Black Skies series.

Soon, their lives took some major plot twists—Sarah moved halfway across the world and is now an operating room nurse in Canada, and Ashley completed a PhD in Chemistry and became a researcher for the University of Auckland. But despite the distance, after a hiatus of several years they returned to the Black Skies series with fresh eyes and new determination. Their passion for writing and co-authoring has remained strong, and along with the Black Skies series, they have a number of other writing-related pursuits in progress.

For writing tips from Ashley and Sarah, visit the blog at www.lindersoncreations.com, or tune into their podcast by the name of *Dear Writer,* available on your podcatcher of choice. Or, join the tribe and sign up for new blog posts, and be the first to learn when the next installment of Black Skies is expected.

COMING SOON:

BLACK SKIES: BOOK TWO

THE PRICE OF PANDEMONIUM

They never expected a home-coming party. When the teens land back in New Zealand, they're greeted by a ghost-town. The houses, empty. Farms, untended. And their families remain imprisoned. The Prime Minister's soldiers control the nation, patrolling the streets and eliminating any resistance. Alone again, the teens fight to survive. But this time, it's different—they won't let the enemy gain the upper hand. As they plan their biggest attack yet, the teens must rely on each other for strength. Victory is theirs for the taking. But even victory comes at a cost.